Lightning Source UK Ltd.
Milton Keynes UK
UKOW03f1253090914

238278UK00004B/96/P

The Perpetual Astonishment Of Jonathon Fairfax

Christopher Shevlin

ALBATROSS

Published by Albatross Publishing, London

Copyright © Christopher Shevlin 2011

ISBN 978-0-9569656-0-8

Version 3. Full release edition, August 2012.

Cover illustration and design, and typesetting in Minion Pro and Baskerville Old Face, by Christopher Shevlin.

Visit **www.christophershevlin.com** to find out more about the author and to read his blog, or **www.albatrosspublishing.com** for information about the publisher.

ACKNOWLEDGEMENTS

Thanks to Andrew Nelson and Laura Morris, who were the first people to like this. Thanks to Neil Ferguson for teaching me. Thanks to Paul Tyrrell for his encouragement and help. Thanks to my cousin Robert for contributing roughly 80% of the title. And thanks to Melissa Pimentel at Curtis Brown for her time and good advice.

The Perpetual Astonishment of Jonathon Fairfax

SUNDAY

CHAPTER ONE

Being murdered is a surprisingly effective way of losing weight.

The thought would never have occurred to Sarah Morecambe if she had not recently been stabbed to death in her own kitchen. Blood, for example, is remarkably heavy. A good, deep stab wound can take half a stone off you in a couple of minutes. And then there's the famous 21 grammes that the soul weighs. It's not much, but every little helps.

Sarah was trying hard to look on the bright side, to find what her mother called 'the rainbow in the storm'. But nothing – not even dramatic weight loss – makes up for being killed over a late-afternoon cup of tea in your own newly decorated kitchen. To make it worse, she had left the cat's Sunday fish frying on top of the cooker. There was almost no chance that the murderer would think to turn off the hob, and then her house would burn down before she had even finished decorating it. And how would anyone be able to solve her murder then?

Some of her hair was trailing in the cat's bowl and the body was lying in an awkward position, with its left arm behind its back and its right leg bent double. She saw now that the leggings had been a mistake, but the knitted-silk top was good. Burgundy suited her, though it didn't go at all well with the bright red blood that was pooling out all around her, spreading so fast that the murderer was having to take little steps back to avoid staining his white trainers. She realised, as she watched him bend to leave the knife on her stomach, that the murderer's balaclava was exactly the same colour as her top.

He muttered 'Sorry, love' – as though he had just accidentally pulled out in front of her at a junction, rather than deliberately stabbed her to death. Then he backed out of the kitchen. She didn't hear his footsteps in the hall. Neither did she hear the front door close. Had he gone? And how could she hear anything when her ears were lying dead on her beautiful new slate floor?

There was no doubt that she *could* hear. The click of the cat-flap was, if anything, sharper and louder than usual as Purrdey nosed it open from the outside. Sarah now bitterly regretted having saddled the cat with a joke name. She had meant it to be a joke on joke cat names, but now there would be no one around to explain those two incriminating Rs on Purrdey's bowl. There would also, she suddenly realised, be no one around to fill the bowl.

Purrdey saw Sarah's body and froze. Both ears swivelled to their 'alarm' position. After a long time Purrdey blinked, then padded very slowly closer to the body. The cat sniffed at the blood, gave it a tiny lick and then sat down and let out a thin miaow. Sarah had always hoped that Purrdey loved her, but it's difficult to tell with cats. The real test of their loyalty and affection is whether, left alone with your dead body, they refuse to eat you.

CHAPTER TWO

Earlier that same Sunday…

Jonathon Fairfax was astonished. This was nothing new. His first memory of being astonished dated from the age of three, when his mother had quite casually suggested that, instead of wearing a pair of comfy watertight pants, he should spend the rest of his life holding in his wee and poo. Now, seventeen years later, he was astonished because a huge, terrifying man in a smart dark-red balaclava was asking him directions.

'Sorry?' said Jonathon, putting down his laundry bag and taking a firmer hold on his box of washing powder.

The street, a canyon of old red-brick terraces, was deserted. It was wide but thickly lined with cars. Nearby a cluster of houses had been infected by that feared North London disease that turns any unwary building into a chicken shop.

The day was cold, and the March sky overhead was a perfectly neutral grey: the sort of sky that can happily sit above any kind of weather.

'I said, do you know where Acacia Road is?' The man spoke slowly and emphasised the words by shrugging his shoulders into his suede bomber jacket. They were large shoulders, as though when it came to building the man's upper body, God had decided simply to use a whole cow.

'Acacia Road?' asked Jonathon, goggling.

'Yes,' said the man. He really was enormous. Some might have said that he had no neck, but this was an illusion caused by the fact that he had so much neck. It started at the edges of his huge shoulders and tapered only slightly to meet his muscular head. *Did the man somehow do a head workout?* Jonathon wondered. Though it was dwarfed by his neck and covered by his balaclava, the man's beefy head looked as though it could bench-press two hundred pounds on its own.

'We, um, we're on … This is Acacia Road,' said Jonathon. He stood on one leg: a gesture he had done for comic effect as a child, but which had now become instinctive when he was in awkward situations.

'Is it? It don't say so. Where's the signs?' The man stared hard at Jonathon, as though he suspected him of having stolen all the signs.

Jonathon was easily intimidated. In fact, left alone for long enough, Jonathon could probably have contrived to intimidate himself. But, now that he was being stared at aggressively by a giant in a balaclava, he was more astonished and confused than afraid. The man seemed to be waiting for an answer. Had he asked a question? Jonathon couldn't remember.

'Um. Sorry?' he said.

The man sighed impatiently and pinched the bridge of his nose. He stopped, then put his hand to his cheek as though to confirm what his fingers had told him, which was presumably that he was wearing a balaclava. This seemed to surprise him.

'I get a cold face,' said the man.

'Yes,' said Jonathon, stupidly.

'Right,' said the man. He slapped his big cauldron of a belly, shouldered his way across the empty road, pulled himself into an old grey Jaguar and drove off.

Jonathon stood for some seconds in the grey empty street, paralysed by astonishment, before carrying on down the road and into the launderette.

Jonathon stuffed his washing into the machine and sat down. Like much in London's Holloway Road area, the launderette had apparently been transported directly from Soviet Russia. It was a large, pocked, windowless cell full of fluorescent light, 1960s washing machines and instructions fixed in place with yellowing Sellotape.

Looking in his laundry bag, Jonathon remembered that he had, the previous Sunday, inadvertently laundered the book he was reading. He looked around for distractions, but the other people in the launderette were silently watching their clothes rotate, intent on avoiding eye contact. He got up and collected a selection of the leaflets and flyers that lay on the windowsill, some so old that the writing on them had faded almost to invisibility.

Jonathon sat back down. 'Missing cat', announced the first leaflet, displaying a photo of a cat with one ear. He realised that he couldn't possibly face looking at the next leaflet, and so settled back, like the others, to watch his clothes go round and round.

Jonathon was in London waiting for his life to begin – waiting to be recognised, though he had no idea for what. Balladeer, advocate, swordsman? He should start learning to do something. More urgently, he needed friends. He felt that if he didn't make friends soon he would die. Actually, it was unlikely he would die. Instead he would have to take the more effortful and dispiriting alternative of going to live in Humberside – the latest stop on his dad's quest for perfect bleakness.

'You're going to London?' his dad had said, in much the same incredulous tone he would have used if Jonathon had announced that he planned to have his head laminated.

'Is there any more marmalade?' Jonathon had replied.

'London chews people up and spits them out like pancakes.'

'Like pancakes?' Jonathon asked.

'Yes, I think there's some left. Why?'

'Are we talking about marmalade or pancakes?'

'We're talking about life. London is a mistake. The most unfriendly city on Earth.'

Now the point at which Jonathon would have to concede that it was impossible to make friends in London was fast approaching. How, he wondered, did anyone in London come to know anyone else? There seemed to be no situations at all in which it was remotely permissible to talk to people you don't know: public transport, launderettes, pubs, cafes, swimming pools, shops, pavements, libraries – all were strictly off-limits. You could ask directions and buy things. Nothing else was allowed.

Even at work he had no friends. He had stupidly chosen to get a job at Harrods, because it was famous, but the rigid and inflexible caste system that operated among its employees meant that he would have to be there for at least another ten years before anyone might, for example, ask him if he'd had a nice weekend. By then the prospect of ever actually having a nice weekend would have irretrievably vanished.

As a result, although he had been in London for only three months, he was already living too much in his own head. He had constructed an extraordinarily detailed fantasy life in which he divided his time between his studio in Paris and his apartment in Constantinople, visiting London tanned and full of mystery, hailed as Europe's foremost poet and stockbroker, or something. His clothes were elegant and simple, hand-tailored by the finest hands. His shirts made beautiful women weep.

The fantasy bore no relation to any element of his current or past life. He lived in a tiny room in a gigantic house shared by strangers. And the clothes that the washing machine was currently hurling around inside itself were boring threadbare jeans and jumpers. How, he wondered, had he acquired such childish, sensible and unsexy clothes? They were perfect for a camping trip in 1950s Norway, but utterly unsuited to the roiling fleshpot of London in the mid-1990s.

Eventually, over the course of the cycle, he forgave his clothes. When they were clean and only slightly damp he put them in his laundry bag and made his way over to the door, where he was escorted from the premises by the implacable stare of the flint-eyed attendant who sat in an orange plastic chair. The bell beside the door gonged his exit.

No sooner had Jonathon set foot on the street than he saw the huge terrifying man – this time without his balaclava – pull up in his old Jaguar. Jonathon thought briefly of turning around and going back into the launderette, but the awkwardness of doing so scared him even more than the huge terrifying man did. He would pretend not to see the man.

He squinted his eyes as though blinded by the dim grey sun and walked on.

CHAPTER THREE

The murderer was furious and deeply frustrated. For fifteen minutes he had been hunting with no sign of his prey. Then, just as he was on the verge of giving up, he spotted it. *The parking space hasn't been born that can outsmart me*, he thought. It had done its best, sandwiching itself between a rotting yellow Volvo and a dirty white Bedford van.

But he had sniffed it out, and now he was going to fill it.

He glanced in his mirror, stopped, put his arm around the passenger seat and reversed into the gap with a single, liquid move. Satisfaction surged up from his belly and put the first smile of the afternoon on his face. He had never tried heroin, but he doubted that it beat a really good bit of reverse parking.

Having to go away and come back had cost him a lot of time, but it's stupid to go and kill someone when you've just been seen in the victim's street wearing a balaclava. You have to leave time for the memories to fade. The murderer had taken a spin up to Highgate, had a half, watched a bit of a match and come back. Not unpleasant, but still a waste of time.

It was all that kid's fault. Some people can take a balaclava in their stride, but that kid had stared at him like he was astonished or something. The army, thought the murderer, isn't the answer to everything, but it would knock the astonishment out of a kid like that in a second. Selective conscription, that's what they needed.

He checked his face again: no balaclava. Good. The balaclava was a present from his niece. It was fantastic – cashmere and extremely comfortable. The problem was that it was so comfortable he couldn't tell whether or not he was wearing it. This was quite a big problem, because people tend to look askance at other people wearing balaclavas. This was, he felt, a national disgrace: men wearing balaclavas had fought and died for Britain.

Anyway, this time he would make sure that he didn't put it on until the last minute. He patted his inside pocket to make sure the kitchen knife was there. Then he unlocked the glove compartment, opened the box and took out a fresh pair of surgical gloves. He could put those on now.

Just as he was about to open the car door he looked up. *Not again*, he groaned to himself. There, coming out of a launderette, was the kid he'd asked for directions. The kid was squinting, carrying a laundry bag over his shoulder and a box of Persil under his arm, spilling a fine line of powder behind him. Had the kid seen him?

CHAPTER FOUR

A huge terrifying man wearing a balaclava asks you for directions. You tell him that the street he's looking for is the one he's currently in. He gets in his car and drives off. Later, you see him again in the same street, this time without his balaclava, just about to get out of his car. He sees you and drives off again.

This would be a confusing sequence of events for anyone. For Jonathon, who hovered perpetually on the brink of confusion, it only confirmed his decision to have a nerve-steadying coffee. He gripped his box of washing powder more firmly, settled his laundry bag more comfortably over his shoulder and rounded the corner.

The Brown Cafe was not its real name. But since Jonathon knew no one, and particularly no one who knew the Brown Cafe, it made no difference what he called it in the privacy of his own head. The outside of the cafe was the colour of toffee, the windows sepia-tinted and today smeared with a sticky-looking substance that appeared to be – but surely could not be – semen. Its fawn sign glinted in the late afternoon sun, and upon it, written in large beige letters, were the words 'Caffe Acropolis'.

Inside there was nothing relating to the Acropolis, to Greece or even to southern Europe. Everything, however, was brown. Many things were also sticky. Jonathon took his place at one of a pair of umber tables in an alcove. On either side of the alcove were waist-high structures made of hazel brick, containing leafy synthetic plants that had faded to a dull khaki. In the main part of the cafe, two rusty metal columns held the roof up, or the floor down. The ceiling was painted the colour of nicotine and the walls gradually faded from caramel to buff as they approached the sticky sienna floor.

Jonathon put down his laundry bag and his washing powder, settled his leaflets in front of him, and then went to the counter where there was a weathered woman apparently made of mahogany. She scowled but permitted him to order a coffee.

'You wait,' she told him. 'Sit down.' She motioned him away with a flick of her hand.

Taking his seat again, Jonathon looked around. From his table he could see the whole of the cafe, including the door. He was afraid that at any moment the bell next to it would tinkle and in would walk the terrifying man in the balaclava – or, as the case might be, not in the balaclava.

To take his mind off the prospect of seeing the terrifying man again, Jonathon carefully prised one of the leaflets from the sticky tabletop and pretended to study it carefully. It was the one about the missing one-eared cat. He couldn't focus on it. He raised his eyes and looked at the other customers.

Two tables away an elderly couple sat side by side wearing matching quilted coats and watching their table as intently as if it were showing repeats of The Dukes of Hazzard. Near them, but not too near, sat a small man wearing an old tan suit. Jonathon thought that the cafe probably gave the man an ease he didn't feel elsewhere. He was eating a plate of chips, half covered with a glutinous brown mass which could well have been a pie. The man looked up, Jonathon reflexively smiled and the man looked away.

He was the only man Jonathon had ever seen who was halfway through growing a comb-over. This intrigued and astonished Jonathon, sending his mind spinning into new avenues of distracted speculation. The strands of hair, teased over from the right-hand side of his head, stopped in an abrupt ridge just before the apex of his cranium, leaving the left-hand side of his shiny scalp entirely exposed.

Jonathon had always assumed that the comb-over happened gradually, as the hair slowly fled. But this man was deliberately growing a brand-new comb-over on an already bald head. What was the explanation? Had he woken up one morning to find that all the hair had fallen out of the top of his head? Was he a former monk who, on leaving the order, had found that his tonsure was now permanent? Jonathon did not know.

He couldn't stop thinking about it. After the agonising decision to grow a comb-over, there must have been the question of what to do with the flap of hair as it grew. Should he allow it to fall naturally over one ear? Tie it in a small bunch? Tuck it away coquettishly? This man had decided to paste it over his head as far as it would go. The decision was reasonable: seen from the right, he already looked like a man with almost a full comb-over.

A coffee-cup crashed down in front of Jonathon, making him jump. He realised that once again he had been living in his own head, imagining the half-bald man's plight rather than, for example, working out how to sort out his own life.

At that moment the bell beside the door tinkled. Jonathon looked up.

The man who walked in was not the terrifying one who had asked him for directions, but someone who looked almost equally out of place in the Brown Cafe. He was tall and annoyingly dashing, in his late twenties, and wearing a jacket that fit perfectly – in a way that normal people's clothes just don't. His shirt, Jonathon suspected, might well have already made a beautiful woman weep that day. Possibly more than one woman. Possibly more than once. *He's probably called something cool like Lance or Ivan*, thought Jonathon, resentfully.

The man was followed by a striking and dignified lady in her late fifties. Jonathon didn't usually use the word 'lady', even in his thoughts, but there was really no other word for the lady who had walked in after the dashing man. She wore a kindly but imperious air and an expensive trouser-suit, and there was something about her that suggested that she might once have been famous, possibly for being Lauren Bacall, if Lauren Bacall had been English and in colour.

They strode magnificently over and sat at the table next to Jonathon's in the leafy alcove, where the light was a little less overpoweringly brown and there was some protection from the stickiness of the kitchen at the back. Jonathon immediately took up his leaflets again and began to study them furiously. *So*, he thought, *a cat has gone missing. There's a missing cat. A cat is missing. Cat.*

'Whoa!' said Lance. 'Hold it right there!'

Jonathon sneaked a look at them. Lance had put out a hand as though to shield Lauren Bacall from some horror. With the other hand he pointed to something on the menu.

'I dare you,' he said, 'to have the seafood platter.'

Lauren Bacall looked at the menu and giggled. All her imperiousness dropped away and she seemed like a little girl.

Jonathon realised that he had been staring at them, so he quickly occupied himself in removing the sticky film from the surface of his coffee. It struck him that the sight of him spooning the skin from his coffee and draping it on the table might offend them just as much as being stared at, but he had to continue. After all, how could he drink it when it had more skin than he did?

'Then I *shall* have the seafood platter,' said Lauren Bacall. 'But only if you have the meat soup, ducky-lamb. And if it's edible I'm sending it straight back. I already suspect that this isn't the worst cafe in London.'

'It is. I swear.'

'Let's ask this young man what he thinks – he looks discerning. If he says it's nice we're leaving immediately.'

Jonathon tensed. He was going to have to talk to people.

'You wear the trousers, lady,' said Lance.

Lauren Bacall turned to Jonathon.

'Excuse me,' she said, 'what's the coffee like here?'

He would not, he decided, become confused. He would certainly not run away. Hadn't he already survived both the launderette and the man with the balaclava and the muscular face?

'Um'. What was it like? *Just say anything that comes into your head – it doesn't matter.* 'Brown,' he said.

He thought again and added, 'and quite sticky.' He cocked his head on one side in another of those once-comic gestures.

Was that weird? he wondered. But Lance and Lauren Bacall seemed perfectly happy with his answer. They looked at each other and exchanged a nod.

'And the food?' Lance asked.

'I, er, I didn't dare try the food.'

Lauren Bacall turned to Lance. 'We shall stay.'

Lance looked around. 'Do they have waitresses here?' he asked.

'Sort of, but I don't think they take orders. I think you might have to go to the desk over there,' answered Jonathon, pointing.

'Good sign,' said Lance. He unfolded himself from his seat and made his way over to the counter.

'Do you come here often?' asked Lauren Bacall. She was very English. And also very much not black-and-white. She definitely wasn't Lauren Bacall.

'This is my second, no third – uh, fourth – time. Is this your first?'

'Yes. We take it in turns to take each other to lunch, every couple of weeks. He takes me to the worst places he can possibly find and I show him the nicest ones. It's a very amicable arrangement.'

Jonathon laughed and this made the lady who wasn't Lauren Bacall smile.

'So ducky,' she asked, 'are you here because you like horrible cafes?'

'No. Um,' he said and considered. He couldn't tell her that he was here because he had seen a man in a balaclava and then the same man not in a balaclava, or that he couldn't stand the idea of sitting in his little bedsit any more. He couldn't tell her that he had decided to come here rather than going to the area's nicer cafe because he was afraid the staff in the nicer cafe might ask him why he spent so much time alone in cafes. In fact, there wasn't anything he could tell her that would put him in a good light.

'I'm here through religious conviction,' he heard himself say.

At that moment Lance returned and draped himself over the chair again, exhaling slowly upwards through his mouth, blowing his long fringe about.

'You sit in terrible cafes as a form of worship?' he asked, smiling and apparently intrigued.

Jonathon nodded sagely.

'Still, you'd have to be pretty devout to come to this one,' said Lance.

'I'm an archbishop.'

And so the conversation began. Jonathon was drawn into the talk of these two pleasantly odd people as they improvised the details of his cafe religion and the hierarchy of its priestly order. They seemed to feel that discussing actual *things* was beneath them. Their conversation was an odd, semi-surreal mixture of deliberate banalities, light ironies and playful banter. Jonathon felt at home with this. In a world that obstinately refused to make any sense at all, Jonathon had always felt it was presumptuous to talk as though it did.

This belief was confirmed when they introduced themselves. The dashing man really was called Lance, Lance Ferman (his name, like James Bond's, lent itself to being delivered in two instalments). Disappointingly, Lauren Bacall's name turned out to be Jane Archer-Hollis, and Jonathon decided that she probably hadn't once been famous after all.

'So what's your name?' asked Lance, after they had invited him to their table.

'Um, Jonathon Fairfax.'

'Oh. Any relation?'

Jane looked at Lance quizzically.

'There's an author called Richard Fairfax – writes airport novels,' Lance explained.

'He's my dad,' said Jonathon. 'Sorry.'

'No! He's really your dad?'

'Mm-hmm,' Jonathon replied, nodding like Stan Laurel – another of those gestures.

Lance laughed loudly, though whether at the gesture or the information was impossible to say.

'I read most of *The Carousel Code* when I flew over to Holland a couple of weeks ago. It's pretty good – better than *Orly Riser* or *Excess Baggage*.'

The conversation was interrupted by Lance's mobile phone – the first Jonathon had ever seen at close quarters – making a distressed peeping noise. Everyone in the cafe looked over at him. Even the old couple tore their eyes away from the fascinating table.

'Sorry,' said Lance. 'I'll leave that.'

The peeping continued.

'I've never seen anyone answer a mobile phone before,' said Jonathon.

'But I'm not answering it,' said Lance.

'Oh.'

'OK, just to please you.' Lance picked up the large black brick, pulled out its aerial and pressed a button.

'Lance Ferman,' he said.

'Yes. Yes, I am.'

'No, fine.'

'Really?'

Jonathon wished Lance would repeat the question in his answer, as in Australian soaps and English exams.

'Cool.'

'No, I'm glad you called me–'

'Yes. I'll be right over.'

'No problem. I–'

'Yes, great. No, it'll probably take me a bit longer than that.'

'No, I don't think so.' He craned his neck, looking around.

'Oh, sorry – someone at *your* door. Right. OK then, bye.'

Jane looked at him sidelong. 'Was that a *young lady*?' she asked.

Lance put the phone down, but carried on looking at it. 'No.'

He continued to stare at the phone for a couple of seconds and then shook his head, as though breaking a reverie.

'All right. Granted, it was a young lady, but not a *young lady*. Not the way you mean it. She's a civil servant. Her name's Sarah Morecambe.'

CHAPTER FIVE

Just as the door was opening, the murderer remembered that he hadn't put his balaclava back on. *Fudge*, he thought. A slightly overweight woman opened the door, speaking into a cordless phone.

'Of course *my* door. See you later. Bye!'

She gave a slight jump when she saw the murderer.

'Sorry,' she said, smiling and pointing at the phone. 'Trying to do two things at once. I'm having one of those days. Now – what can I do for you?'

The murderer wished that he had put his balaclava on. It would have made it much easier. Now she was being nice to him.

'Can I come in?' he asked. His voice sounded, to him, serious and businesslike. That was the way to do this.

She looked surprised, but opened the door and stepped back.

'Yes, of course,' she said. 'Is this about the Neighbourhood Watch?'

He moved into the hallway, the shoulders of his suede bomber jacket touching both sides of the doorframe. She bustled along in front of him, fidgeting with a bracelet. Her house, he noticed, was a right mess.

'Cup of tea?' she asked.

'Go on then,' he said.

She filled the kettle from a water purifier beside the sink. He looked around the room.

Click. The cat-flap half opened and a black nose appeared, sniffed and then withdrew.

'You must think I'm terrible – all this mess. I only moved in a bit ago.'

There was a pause, a silence.

'Go smooth, did it?' the murderer asked, not really knowing why.

She raised her eyebrows at him.

'The move,' he explained. 'Did it go smooth?'

She laughed. 'I'm sorry, I'm miles away today, you must think I'm terrible. I'm not usually as bad as this.'

She laughed again, shaking her head. '*Miles* away,' she repeated. 'The move was absolute bloody murder I'm afraid to say. The lorry – carrying all my worldly goods – got lost on the way here. It didn't arrive till the next day. *What* a cock-up! Thought I'd never get it back. And it's taken me ages just to get the kitchen done. You'd think I'd learn after last time. Have you moved often?'

'Just once, a couple of years ago. Nightmare. Broke all our plates.'

He was still looking around. The kitchen units were new, but the walls were unpapered and the floor had traces of plaster on it. There were lots of little strip-lights under the units to illuminate the work-surfaces, but the main light in the centre of the ceiling had no tube in it. Behind him the gas flame hissed under a pan of fish on the hob. The cooker controls glowed blue and were reflected in a half-drunk sherry.

He met her eyes: she'd seen him looking at the sherry.

'I know,' she said, 'you must think I'm terrible, hitting the bottle when it's – my *God*, it's not even five.' She reached down two mugs from a cupboard. 'I'm not really an alky – honest m'lud!'

She laughed and he smiled politely. His hand slipped into the pocket of his jacket.

'Biscuits?' she asked.

'What? No – cheers.'

His leg was jigging compulsively up and down, the breakfast-bar stool on which he sat was becoming desperately uncomfortable. Sarah was slowly taking the tea bag out of his mug. As she poured in the milk, she looked up and met his eyes.

'Now. How can I help?' she asked.

CHAPTER SIX

'I met her at that conference in Holland a couple of weeks ago,' said Lance. 'She's a secretary, works at Defence, so I gave her my card and she just called to say she's got something she'd like to discuss with me, off the record.'

'I suppose you lied and told her you're a journalist,' said Jane.

'Yes, yeah I did. Well, I mean no one would tell me anything if I said I was a spy.'

'Lance likes to think he's a spy.'

Lance laughed but looked a little bit hurt.

'I work for a leading investigative solutions consultancy,' he explained. 'I can't tell you its name – *careless talk costs lives.*'

'Lance can't remember the name of the company he works for,' said Jane. 'And he's more a loss-adjustor than a spy. Don't ever listen to anything he says.'

The waitress arrived with coffees for them all, and the conversation stopped while they extracted the skin. All three of them silently piled their skin in a single heap in the middle of the table, and this soon became a game.

'It's a sculpture.'

'But of what, Lance my darling, of what?'

'It's abstract,' said Lance.

'Oh, wait,' said Jonathon. He gave the pile of skin a couple of deft pats with his teaspoon.

'It's Michael Winner's nose,' he said.

'Golly,' said Jane.

'I have to admit,' said Lance, 'that really does look like Michael Winner's nose.'

Jonathon smiled, disproportionately pleased with his creation.

'So anyway,' said Lance, 'Sarah works for Andrew Thompson. She's his secretary.'

Jane made a face to express her distaste. Jonathon also tried to show his disapproval.

Lance laughed. 'Are you trying to do an impression of Princess Anne?' he asked Jonathon.

'I was trying to scowl.'

'Your scowl needs work. Your Princess Anne impression, however, is excellent.'

'Thompson really is a nasty piece of work,' said Jane, seriously. 'He's such a horrid little man.'

'He's my boss,' said Lance.

Jonathon and Jane both stared at him.

'Well, indirectly,' Lance conceded.

'What do you mean, "indirectly"?' asked Jonathon.

'Jonathon, do you have any contacts in the world of politics, big business or intelligence?'

Jonathon had no contacts. Not even electrical ones. He had nothing.

'Not contacts as such, no.'

'Then I'll tell you this in confidence…'

Jonathon had noticed that when people feel safe and aren't being forced to compete they often reveal the most intimate information.

In fact, being almost the embodiment of non-threatening, Jonathon had found – before moving to London – that they often chose him to reveal it to. Previously, the people he had affected in this way had mostly been strangers on buses, and often drunk. Now, for the first time in his life, it seemed he was about to be told something interesting.

'I work for an investigative agency which is trying to break into the political scene. We've been doing surveillance work for news agencies and insurance firms for years, but … Anyway, we were taken on by Andrew Thompson to get some background info on one of his enemies – Graeme Hutton.'

'He's the big pink one, isn't he?' asked Jane. 'Pensions or something?'

'Yes, that's him. Pink or purple – he can do either. So I was in Holland at some EU thing, posing as a journalist, but actually watching this guy, Thompson's enemy. He's got to be hiding something–'

'*The best place to hide something,*' said Jonathon, '*is in the home of a man who thinks he is hiding something else.*'

'That's deep,' said Lance. 'What are you talking about?'

'Sorry, it was in a children's programme I watched. *Professor Albino's Circus Factory.* Have you ever seen it?' Jonathon looked at them both, suddenly feeling that saying anything that came into his head wasn't such a good idea after all.

'I haven't,' said Jane, 'but Lance and I are a little bit older than you. When I was growing up we didn't really have children's programmes – or indeed television. Lance?'

'Drawing a blank. Sorry.'

'It's all right. Even people who are exactly the same age as me haven't seen it. No one has – I don't know why.'

'Perhaps it was broadcast just for you, ducky.'

'Maybe. I thought you might have seen it, for some reason. It was good: Professor Albino would draw the curtains at the end, after the adventure, and give a piece of odd advice. The one about the best place to hide something is the only one I remember now. But anyway, sorry, you were watching Hutton at an EU thing. I'll shut up now.'

Lance looked at him, frowning, as though checking that he really would shut up. Then he smiled and continued.

'Yes, Holland. A lot of politicians really let their hair down at European stuff – the tabloids don't bother sending journalists over there, and the local papers don't care what British politicians do, so they're not on their guard–'

'Did you get anything?' asked Jonathon.

'Not there, no. I've got a little bit on him – finished the file last week. I hope it's enough. If not I'll be back to investigating insurance fraud faster than you can say knife.'

'Knife?' asked Jonathon. He'd never heard the expression before.

'Much faster than that. You say knife slower than anyone I've ever met.'

'Sorry.'

'Hey. Don't sweat it.'

'You were telling us about Sarah, darling,' said Jane.

'Yes, that's why I was talking about Holland. That's where I met Sarah, Thompson's secretary. We got talking and I think she was putting out feelers about leaking stuff to me.'

'How do you know?'

'Call it instinct. Anyway, I gave her my card and now she's called–'

Jane said, 'But if you're working for Thompson why would you want her to leak anything to you? Surely it would embarrass him.'

'Is it so that she wouldn't leak it to anyone else?' asked Jonathon.

'Oh, clever,' said Lance. 'No, its more just idle curiosity – or professional curiosity, I forget which. Maybe we would tell Thompson, it depends. But I won't know unless I go and see her.'

'Perhaps this Sarah just wants to lure you to her house?' suggested Jane.

'Why do you think I carry this around?' said Lance, pretending to use his hefty phone as a club.

'What I can't understand,' said Jane, 'is everybody saying how attractive Thompson is. I mean – he's my husband's age. I just don't see it, I really don't.'

'He's got that twinkle in his eye that women just can't resist. And his own castle.'

'But he *is* a repellent man. He always wears that nasty little smirk on his face, as though…' But she couldn't think what it was as though. Instead she said, 'I don't know, I really don't.'

'Have either of you heard of Nicholas Emir Brunsengett?' asked Jonathon.

They both shook their heads.

'He has this um theory…'

'Go on,' said Lance.

'Well, he thinks that women like tall, strong, handsome men for evolutionary reasons. But he also has this research that says that – as well as the tall, strong, handsome thing – every woman also has a Non-Evolutionary Predilection–'

'An NEP,' said Lance.

'You have read his book!' said Jonathon.

'No. Just a wild guess. What's his book?'

'*Men Are From Mars, Women Are Also From Mars.*'

'Ah. What's an NEP?'

'It's um an attraction for a certain type of man that can't be explained on evolutionary grounds. Each woman's is unique, and Brunsengett thinks that they are randomly determined.'

'Huh,' said Lance. 'Give me an example.'

'There's loads of examples in the book. I've forgotten most of them. No wait, I remember: Brigitte Bardot was driven wild by men with pot bellies and spindly arms, and Garbo liked short bald men with buck teeth. There are others.'

'Do you know, that would explain a lot,' said Jane. 'It would explain nearly all my friends' husbands.'

'Well, I just hope it doesn't catch on,' said Lance, getting up. 'I don't need competition from ugly guys too.'

He looked at his watch. 'And I better make a move. Don't like to keep a lady waiting.'

Jonathon stood up, followed by Jane, who said, 'You really must come to lunch tomorrow, Jonathon.'

Lance nodded.

Jonathon was surprised. 'I'm working tomorrow,' he said, and quickly added, 'I think my lunch break's at one though.'

'Well then, we shall meet at ten past. Where do you work?'

'Um, Harrods. Part-time.'

'Goodness. Which department?'

'Men's Ready-To-Wear.'

'Well then, I know a wonderful little place near the Natural History Museum. About ten past one?'

'Um, yes. I'll see you then, then. Then.'

'Shall I tell you the name of the place and where it is?' She smiled.

'Oh, um yes, that might be useful.'

They arranged it, and Jonathon remained at the table for a couple of minutes after Lance and Jane had left, gathering up his laundry bag and washing powder. He decided to leave the leaflets, which by now had probably formed an indissoluble adhesive bond with the table. He felt slightly embarrassed to be left there alone, but he didn't want to leave too soon in case he bumped into Lance and Jane again outside and had to say goodbye all over again. He had managed it fairly well the first time, he thought. He didn't want to mess it up – not before he'd even had a chance to mess up meeting them a second time.

CHAPTER SEVEN

'Where to, mate?'

'Do you know the Wilmington Arms?'

'Just next to Acacia Road?'

'That's it.'

Lance didn't know why he hadn't asked the taxi driver to take him to Sarah's door. Perhaps he would look back one day and say that this was the moment that his detective's instinct was born. Or perhaps his impulse to lie was just so strong that he couldn't even tell a taxi driver the truth about where he wanted to go.

They arrived. He got out, cleverly avoiding a puddle, and paid the driver. It was half past five, still Sunday, still just about light.

He looked wistfully at the pub, then rounded the corner onto Acacia Road. It lay in that vast, worryingly ugly area that seems to surround Finsbury Park in all directions, as though anti-style gas is leaking out from a vent beneath the station. It had rained while he'd been in the cafe, and the buildings, like the dogs, now looked either bedraggled or aggressive in their dampness.

There was only a dribble of daylight left, not enough for him to see the house numbers, so he walked up the path of the first house he saw. The number turned out not to be a number, just a fancy brass knocker with 'Victory' written on it. The next house did have a number on it, but as he was peering at it he noticed that an old lady was peering at him through the window, holding a small worried-looking dog in her arms.

He waved cheerily at them, and tried to signal that he was just looking at the number on the door. Finding that there is no signal capable of conveying that message – or at least that what signals there are look very like those for 'I'm coming in to kill you and take all that money you've got under the bed' – Lance moved on.

Finally, he found the right house, number forty-two. Pushing open the painted wooden gate, he made his way up the path, past a small, wet garden, half overgrown and half newly-dug, and up to the door. An ornamental wagon wheel leant against the front wall of the house, which disturbed and disappointed Lance. It seemed unlikely to him that someone who had an ornamental wagon-wheel would also have anything interesting to tell him. He rang the bell and waited for a while.

There was no answer and no sound from inside, though a light was on in the hall. He tried knocking – pointlessly, since his knock was much quieter than the bell. There was still no answer. He checked the number on the door, then rang the bell again. He looked at his watch. It wasn't much more than half an hour since he had talked to her. Had she popped out for milk? Fallen downstairs and knocked herself out? Been hideously murdered? He just didn't know. Perhaps she was waiting for him on the couch in a silken negligee. If so he would tell her that he was already in a committed relationship, but probably not that the committed relationship was with his self-respect and every attractive woman he could find.

He gently turned the handle and even more gently tried pushing the door. It moved easily, soundlessly. He didn't open it properly, just a crack, just enough to know that it was unlocked. If he heard footsteps he could close it again without anyone noticing that it had been opened. He waited. He did not hear footsteps. He glanced around quickly and casually, as though to see if it looked like raining again. He opened the door, stepped inside and closed it after him.

In a large number of films that he had seen, doing exactly what he had just done proves to be a very unwise move. Was there a little girl with red eyes, rotting green skin and razor-sharp teeth standing perfectly still by the door? He checked. No, there wasn't. He retrospectively changed his motivation for checking. *It pays to know where you are*, he thought. *Take in all available information.*

'Miss Morecambe?' he called.

His voice was a little bit higher than usual, and there was something about calling 'Miss Morecambe' in a slightly high, wavering voice that made him feel ridiculous. He felt, all at once, as if he were Terry Scott.

'Sarah?' he tried, in a deeper voice.

There was no answer. The house was completely silent.

Take in all available information, he repeated to himself. He knew there was no rotting, demonic, possessed little girl standing by the door, but he realised he had not really absorbed anything beyond that. Besides, he shouldn't be thinking about horror films; he should be thinking about more realistic dangers, like teenagers with guns and poorly developed senses of right and wrong.

Lance surveyed the hallway: someone was moving in or out. By the stairs stood a stack of packing crates. In one corner lurked a colony of curtain poles. On his right sat a pile of blankets. Beside them huddled a family of battered suitcases. Nearby, a box of empty jam jars awaited, he imagined, a long and fruitless storage under the stairs. All around were other domestic refugees in this camp for displaced decor, made harsh and pale by the naked light bulb that hung in the centre of the ceiling, amplifying the angles of the artex.

Lance moved slowly forward, his feet scrunching on the once-deep pile of the carpet. As he drew parallel with the stairs, his foot caught on something. The handle of a paint roller skittered away, demolishing a neighbouring pile of coat-hangers. Lance winced as they clattered to the floor, and then jumped as he heard a sudden, terrifying noise from upstairs. It came in a burst, then stopped. He waited, not breathing.

Seconds passed, then the noise sounded again. It seemed to be coming from one of the upstairs rooms. Lance prided himself on being one of the most self-possessed people who has ever lived, but that noise spooked him. When it sounded a third time, he broke out in a brief, localised sweat. The noise was like nothing he had ever heard before. If someone invented a small motorised device for destroying carpets at great speed, that was the noise it would make.

Lance took stock of himself. He found he had adopted an absurd crouching position and that he actually was holding his phone like a club. His head was sweating and his pulse was racing. What had happened to him? He was supposed to be *cool*, for God's sake. He straightened himself up, mopped his face on his sleeve and decided that the cool thing to do would be to just wander upstairs and see if anything interesting was going on around there, maybe hang out and shoot the breeze if there happened to be an armed intruder about. This, of course, was also the stupid thing to do, but that was less important.

He sashayed up the stairs, looking casually about him, trying to ignore the idea of a murderer shredding carpets in one of the bedrooms. The house was very nearly as vile as anything Lance could imagine. The carpet on the stairs was the sort of swirling orange, green and black nightmare that had been popular in the Seventies. The wallpaper was such extreme flock that the pattern seemed to stand a good two inches off the wall, and the stalactites of artex on the ceiling threatened at any moment to snap and impale him.

Even under such extreme conditions, even with his heart pounding, his stomach pumping, and his head sweating, Lance still noticed all details of interior decoration. On the landing was a frieze, starting to become unglued, depicting a satyr cavorting with half a goddess. He was so distracted by it that when a dark mass came hurtling towards him from one of the rooms he fell downstairs.

CHAPTER EIGHT

At almost precisely the same time that Lance was falling down Sarah's stairs, Andrew Thompson – 'an indiscreet delight' according to the *Telegraph*'s society columnist – was descending the four stone steps leading away from the main lawn at Blythesides, his country estate in Oxfordshire.

'Andrew darling, it's the telephone,' said his wife, Margaret, meeting him on the path.

'I know, Gargy darling. You have already shouted it twice across the lawn. People will think you're drunk.'

'Will they be going soon? You know I can't stand the Brendans.'

'What's wrong with whispering it quietly in my ear? *Telephone, darling.* Or telling a waiter? White gloves, a discreet murmur. The soft smile. "Would you excuse me, I have a rather important call to attend to?" Much better.'

'I adore Tristan and Claudine, but why always the Brendans? No one reads the *Telegraph* any more.'

'Is it the one in the drawing room or the study?'

'The study. I think it's going to rain this evening. The tablecloths will be ruined.'

'Oh, hang the tablecloths.'

'I love you Andrew.'

In his study he closed the door, sat down on the Thomas Hope chair and took up the receiver.

'Yes?'

He stared intently at the dial.

'It's done? Good. Thank you, Jenkins.'

He leaned back in the chair, his favourite.

'I shouldn't worry about that. Your services will not go unrewarded.'

He replaced the receiver in its cradle and looked out of the window. It had been a beautiful afternoon but now it was clouding over. The dark was falling and his guests would be getting ready to go. The weekend was over. Tomorrow he would return to the Commons, return to the fray.

Part of what he enjoyed about these weekends was imagining that he was glad to be away from London. In fact, nothing could be further from the truth. During the long recesses he pined for the Commons.

As a boy, he had once heard his father say to a friend, 'Home's all right for a visit, but I wouldn't want to live there.' Now he felt the same way. It was the way an Englishman of the best sort, the old sort, *should* feel. After all, hadn't the Empire itself been simply one enormous excuse to pop out for a bit, get away from wives, children and mothers-in-law, stretch the old legs, kill people and indulge in dangerous and exotic sexual practices?

The only time he had resided permanently at Blythesides was that awful period eleven years ago. He had seemed to be finished, washed up, as the Americans say. Washed up and left in the cold on the rack to slowly drip dry. Then the letter had come, the offer, and again the steady upward tick of his fortunes. He would not allow anything to interrupt that. Was he still, he sometimes wondered, bound by the terms of the agreement he had made?

He came down to see them off, those last few who had not already left. They were hanging about on the blue carpet in the entrance hall, assembling coats, checking keys, waiting to say goodbye. The door was open, admitting cold fading light into the hallway, softly illuminating the great oak beams and the stonework of the outside wall.

These last few, like all today's guests, were largely people he disliked but hoped would be useful. Thompson reached the foot of the stairs.

'Goodbye Andrew – thanks for a wonderful party,' said Peter Hampden, a Treasury minister who looked like a sackful of ghosts.

'Goodbye Peter,' said Thompson, shaking the man's baggy white hand.

'Goodbye Margaret,' said Peter.

'Yes. Goodbye.'

The next to shake his hand was Michael Apotolomito, who looked like a handsome man who had unexpectedly had a mixed grill attached to his face and who always said 'serviette' instead of 'napkin'. After him came Brian Brendan, who was something at the *Telegraph*, and then Tracy Bannister, deputy chairman of the party. Each of them had a spouse (to be kissed or back-slapped) whose name Thompson could not quite remember.

Finally, there were the only guests for whom he had any real affection: Tristan and Claudine Mangiafuoco.

'Bye, Tris,' said Thompson.

'Splendid party, Andrew.'

There were just the four of them now, standing on the front steps, watching the cars pull away. Tristan Mangiafuoco was short, with a flat bald head which would have made an ideal place to rest a drink, had he not been so obviously one of his party's great hopes for the future.

Mangiafuoco pulled his wife's fur coat more snugly about her neck and stroked it down over her shoulders. Mangiafuoco was easily the calmest and least Italian person Thompson had ever met. His surname, Italian for 'fire-eater', didn't suit him at all. In almost fifteen years, Thompson had never known him to lose his temper. He was Italian only in looks, with his light olive skin, the sheen to his long black moustache and collar-length hair, and the fact that all his jackets – even the tweed thorn-proof he favoured for country wear – were double-breasted and shiny. Claudine, his wife, was taller and her personality was as quintessentially French as Mangiafuoco's was not Italian. She had made Hampden bring her drinks all afternoon rather than using the hired waiter, and she disdained entirely to speak to Michael Apotolomito.

'So lovely to see you again, Claudine – you're looking wonderful,' Thompson told her.

'Yes. You are looking old but still a little bit handsome.'

Mangiafuoco, who out of habit was standing two steps higher up than her, took her hand and kissed it.

'Come along, my love. Stop flirting with Andrew. Goodbye Margaret. It was a fine party. You must come to us next. Andrew, I will see you in committee tomorrow.'

'I *am* coming along,' said Claudine, a little drunk.

'Till tomorrow Tris. If Brendan does his part then Apotolomito won't know what's hit him in committee. He'll be finished. And if all this will not do we'll drown him in the Malmsey butt within.'

'Shakespeare, *Richard III*.'

Mangiafuoco was constantly attributing Thompson's literary allusions. It was the one thing that irritated Thompson about his friend. However, there was a great deal to set against that single annoying habit. He knew everybody, was colossally rich – in a way that put Thompson's inherited castle to shame – and everything always went exactly the way he wanted it to.

'Quite so,' said Thompson. 'I do wish you wouldn't do that though, Tris.'

'Oh you know me – if I know something I can't resist showing off about it. I was a modest man until I met you.' His eyes slid to his brand-new Rolls-Royce where it sparkled in the driveway.

They had been friends even before they went into politics. Thompson had been in the House longest, followed five years ago by Mangiafuoco, who had waited until he was indisputably and unassailably rich.

'Showing off is the fool's idea of glory,' said Thompson.

'Is that a quotation?' asked Mangiafuoco.

Uniquely in politics, their friendship had endured. They complemented each other: the extraordinarily wealthy businessman and the raffish semi-aristocrat, and their areas of interest did not conflict. In politics, everyone is alone, possibly because it's difficult to make friends when everyone around you is detestable. It is an immense advantage to know that there is one person in the House who will not betray you, even if they know that – for example – you are a serial adulterer with a truly gigantic collection of Hitler memorabilia. That was why Thompson and Mangiafuoco were the rising stars in the firmament of the Commons. They had few secrets from each other.

'It is a quotation, yes. Bruce Lee, the noted martial artisan,' said Thompson

'There you have me. I know nothing about that world. About everything else, on the other hand, I know everything. As I said, I was a modest man until I met you.'

Claudine tutted theatrically, flashed her eyes at Thompson, and said to her husband, 'He is really a bad influence on you.'

It took Lance a couple of minutes to work out where he was and what was happening. Then he remembered he was lying at the bottom of a flight of stairs in someone else's house with a folding garden chair digging painfully into his shoulder. He looked up from his supine position and into the biggest, greenest pair of eyes he had ever seen.

The cat and he remained frozen, watching each other warily, silently, for a good two or three minutes, until eventually the cat broke off eye contact to lick its bottom. It had clearly been the cause of the carpet-destroying noise upstairs. A wave of relief swept through Lance, closely followed by a wave of embarrassment. He hated anyone to see him when there was a folding garden chair digging into his shoulder.

With some difficulty and reluctance Lance arranged his body once more in a vertical position and began again the slow climb upstairs. He was shaken by his fall, and his initial relief was ebbing away. True, the terrifying noise had turned out to be only a cat. But there was no reason why there couldn't be both a cat and a homicidal sociopath in the house.

The cat sat perfectly still until Lance got halfway up the stairs and then barrelled away again at top speed, into the bathroom. It almost seemed as though the cat was deliberately trying to unnerve him. The bathroom was the closest to the top of the stairs, so Lance decided to begin there. He stood against the wall and pushed at the door. It swung slowly inwards until its handle clunked quietly against the wall. This gave him a view of the whole of the darkened room: the sink, the toilet, the bath and some flat-pack boxes containing a self-assembly shower unit. The cat sat beside the toilet, looking aggrieved that he had followed it. There was definitely no one in the bathroom. He summoned his nerve and peered into the bath. There was definitely no one in the bathroom. This seemed to him uncannily like the sort of thought someone would have shortly before being killed or demonically possessed by something lurking unseen in the bathroom. Ridiculously, he looked up to make sure that there was no one clinging to the ceiling, poised to drop, and then checked behind the door. This time he was certain of it. There was definitely no one in the bathroom.

Meanwhile, the cat had grown tired of his intrusion and padded off into the room next door. When Lance entered this room the cat looked at him with undisguised impatience. *You again!* its eyes seemed to say as it trotted away.

This was obviously the main bedroom. There was a large double bed in the middle of the room, a dressing table, a huge pile of discarded clothes, some packing cases, a rolled-up carpet and a wardrobe. Lance checked over his shoulder, then lowered himself slowly to the ground. There was nothing under the bed except shoes. He forced himself to move over to the wardrobe, slowly, quietly. He grasped the handle and flung it wide, leaping back at the same time. An Indian-style dress fell to the ground, the coat hanger hitting the floorboards with a clunk. The wardrobe patently contained only clothes.

The next room contained packing cases, a pile of curtains and a rowing machine. A dismantled bed leant against one wall. There was nowhere to hide, but Lance checked. He even looked behind the headboard of the bed, where he found the cat again. It looked at him with frank incredulity, its eyes flashing *Oh, for fuck's sake* before it dashed away.

The final room was much smaller. Lance was getting a bit careless now. He walked straight in without checking behind the door. Then, suddenly realising this, he whirled around and came face to face with the cat, which had climbed onto the top of a bookcase. *Will I never be free of this poltroon?* said its grave green eyes. There was no one under the empty desk or hiding in the pile of dust sheets in the corner.

Sarah was obviously not in.

He was being stupid. She had clearly just gone out and left the door unlocked, and Lance wanted to get out of the house before she returned and found him there. He stumped downstairs, feeling a bit embarrassed. The best thing to do would be to go now. He would just look in the kitchen and living room first.

The living room was empty, but in the kitchen he found a large dead woman. It was Sarah Morecambe. Her hair was lying in the cat's bowl. His first reaction to the sight of a dead woman in a kitchen was relief that she hadn't heard him wandering around the house and falling downstairs. The relief was followed by guilt at feeling relief when a woman was dead. The guilt was followed by apprehension that he would be blamed for her death. Confused, he gave up on feeling and went back to being cool.

Perhaps he should make sure she really was dead before he jumped to any rash conclusions. *Oh yes,* said a voice in his head, *maybe she's just resting on the kitchen floor with a knife-wound in her abdomen.*

Perhaps that's how she relaxes.

He had to pull himself together. He couldn't stand around making sardonic comments to himself in his head while a woman lay possibly dead in her own kitchen. He crouched down, careful not to get blood on his shoes, and gingerly felt her neck. It occurred to him that he had no idea how to interpret the results of a neck-feeling. Her neck felt quite dead, but how could he be sure? After a while he decided that if a person not only owned a neck that felt like the one he was currently feeling, but also lay motionless in a pool of blood and bore an obvious and horrific wound, that person could not possibly be alive. Back on his feet, he decided to look around for exactly three more minutes before contacting the police.

The kitchen was the most completely decorated room in the house. It had fitted pine cupboards and expensive-looking worktops. On the new cooker, a very black piece of fish continued to fry. Nearby, on one of the expensive-looking worktops, were a woven bag, two cold cups of tea, a small sherry, a Post-It note and a Manila file stamped 'HM GOVERNMENT'. Written on the Post-It note in big, looped writing underneath the words 'To do', were the following items:

1) Journalist

2) Grouting

3) Get rid of wagon wheel

4) Cat food

Lance very nearly added *5) Get stabbed to death*, but the tiny part of his mind which dealt with morality and ethics asked him not to. The brain is a very adaptive organ, and Lance's was no exception. It had long ago noticed the lack of moral judgements it was required to make and had begun to store information about suit fashions in that area. His moral centre had been moved to the much smaller part of the brain which normally deals with Prunella Scales. An image of her came to his mind as this part of his brain kicked in again, telling him to call the police, before shutting down, exhausted.

At that moment the fish pan caught fire. Looking around, Lance saw a tea-towel lying on the draining board. He quickly ran it under the tap, threw it over the pan, and turned the gas off. There was a very loud hiss, as though an evil spirit were leaving the pan, and a great cloud of steam went up. Just as he was beginning to calm down again, the smoke alarm went off.

NURP-NURP-NURP-NURP-NURP-NURP-NURP!

Shit. *NURP-NURP-NURP-NURP-NURP-NURP-NURP!* The sound

was painfully loud – surely the neighbours would come round to protest and he'd be seen. *NURP-NURP-NURP-NURP-NURP-NURP-NURP!* He frantically grabbed the folding garden chair from the hall, wrestled it open and upright – *NURP-NURP-NURP-NURP-NURP-NURP-NURP!* – clambered on it and pulled the cover off the smoke alarm – *NURP-NURP-NURP-NURP-NURP-NURP-NURP!* – then feverishly ripped out the battery. The noise stopped instantly.

Lance sat down. His ears were ringing. He felt now as though he was somehow implicated in the murder. He'd had a good snoop around, felt her neck, put out the pan fire. If he hadn't been there the pan would have continued to burn and the house could have caught fire. Was there such a thing as inverse arson?

He needed to get a hold on himself. His mind was all over the place, and he wasn't thinking clearly. Where was his cool, now that he needed it? He ought to call the police right now, he thought. No. What he needed to do was relax and get his head together before thinking about anything else. He took a deep breath, checked his reflection in a metal tray leaning against the fridge, and then sat down on one of the stools. He took a sip of sherry, made a face because he didn't like sherry, and opened the Manila file.

CHAPTER TEN

Jonathon emptied the laundry bag onto his bed, carefully filed the washing powder on his bookshelf between *Valhalla Rising* and *Xenocide*, and looked down at his table. On it was an untidy sprawl of papers, spattered with an untidy sprawl of writing. There was an article-writing competition in a local newspaper, and Jonathon had decided to enter it and make his name in journalism.

He sighed. He had two weeks to write three hundred words on 'My Holloway'. The article was trying to come into being, but Jonathon hampered it at every turn by watching television, doing his laundry, despairing, romantically obsessing over women he had never met, going off to work, making plans to learn the violin, finding out how to become a bus conductor, and a thousand other things. He counted the words again. There were still thirty-six.

Jonathon sighed again and sat down. During those times when he was actually sitting at the table, he mostly attempted to write the article by staring either out of the window or at the wall. Today he chose the wall. Its bareness made him anxious and confused, but he found that any poster or picture – no matter how much he started off liking it – became embarrassing within hours. As a result there was a small bundle of rolled-up posters under the bed and all that remained on the wall was the fugitive corner of an embarrassingly old-fashioned and pretentious painting of either Homer or Aristotle contemplating the bust of either Aristotle or Homer. That wasn't the kind of person he was at all. But then neither was he the kind of person who has a Blur poster (now under the bed), or a Salvador Dali poster (wrapped around the Blur poster), or any of a dozen other posters (wrapped around the Salvador Dali poster). He certainly wasn't the sort of person who owns any ridiculous soft-core pornographic magazines, and yet there were three of those under the bed as well.

Most rooms have a certain feel to them, perhaps reflecting the constellation of emotions experienced there over the years, or perhaps – equally plausibly – not. For Jonathon the room had a desperate feel, accentuated alternately by its posters and by its lack of posters. He had just had his first apparently successful social encounter in London and already his excitement about it was beginning to falter, as though it was being set upon and beaten by his walls.

Every other aspect of the room reinforced this psychological assault. It was small, with a sloping ceiling which made Jonathon stoop and a rudimentary sink that made him sick. A large wardrobe slouched near the door, the grubby orange carpet shrinking away from it as if in fear.

Jonathon wrote his thirty-seventh word ('sometimes') then turned for inspiration to a copy of the *Sun* that he had found in the kitchen on Friday. He lay down on top of his laundry and flipped through the pages. It reminded him uncomfortably of the wanton debauchery and deranged, promiscuous lust which he knew people his age ought to be engaging in instead of lying on laundry and looking at old newspapers.

He decided to cook a fish. He would feel better once he had eaten.

Having retrieved the fish from the windowsill (which was where he stored food that he wanted to keep fairly cold and relatively safe from being plundered by one of the other inmates of the house), Jonathon made his way down to the shared kitchen. In the corridor he passed the shared bathroom, which was so awful that he had begun to have nightmares about it even before he had first seen it – it had somehow projected its horror backwards in time. The threadbare staircase, with its distinctive shared-staircase smell, led down to the ground floor's scruffy hallway, payphone and kitchen.

He pushed open the kitchen door. An empty egg-box with 'Avi' written on it in several places lay on the tatty marble-effect counter. Avi persisted in writing his name on everything he bought, though by now he must surely have learned that the very most this would do was to satisfy the scholarly curiosity of those who would, inevitably, steal and eat his food.

Jonathon knew two methods of cooking things. He put the fish in a frying pan and some green beans in a small saucepan of water, turned on the hobs and waited. Looking at what he was making, he began to doubt his earlier conviction that he would feel better once he had eaten. It struck him that he'd never liked fish. He had bought it yesterday in an effort to break free of habit and compulsion. Now he realised the value of habit and compulsion.

As he waited he caught sight of his reflection in the window, the tuft of hair that he could never prevent from sticking up. It added an extra layer of absurdity to the already ridiculous business of having fibrous matter emanating from one's head. From its pan the fish regarded him with a baleful eye, uncanny and impassive like Andrew Lloyd-Webber. Were you meant to cut the head off before cooking it?

He curtailed his awkward eye-contact with the fish by putting it on his plate with the green beans and taking them upstairs to watch television. He had only three channels, and the choice was snooker, news or a drama about polio. He opted for the news. The fish continued to stare at him as he cut a chunk out of it and brought it towards his mouth.

Nearly five minutes later Jonathon was still sitting, shuddering, a piece of fish poised halfway between his mouth and the plate, when there was a knock at the door. He lowered his fork. The fish seemed to look slightly affronted.

Jonathon put his plate aside and stepped up to the door. Suddenly, he pictured the terrifying man standing there, balaclava stretched taut over the rippling muscles of his face. Oh God. Perhaps his time had come. Jonathon couldn't console himself with much. He couldn't honestly tell himself he'd had a good innings. In fact, he was still waiting to bat, having spent most of his life as an out-fielder. At least, he reflected, he hadn't eaten the fish.

He took a deep breath and opened the door.

Standing there in the doorway was a girl. To be more accurate, standing in the doorway was the most deeply and woundingly beautiful girl Jonathon had ever seen. The first word which leapt into his mind when he saw her was 'svelte'. He almost said it. He had only to see an attractive woman and unhelpful adjectives would climb into his head, followed by random mental noise. His next thought was 'butterfly', then, less explicably, 'Hovis'. Then, sense giving out altogether, 'grefetionuytuuuu'.

Jonathon was aware that he was reeling slightly. He tried to get his thoughts in order.

The girl said, 'Hi, I'm Rachel. Does a guy called Mark live here?'

She had a very slight Scottish accent and her voice had that over-smooth quality that appears when people are nervous and trying not to show it. Jonathon immediately realised why the Holloway Road and Finsbury Park area was so ugly: all the available supplies of beauty had been channelled into Rachel's face. Her eyes were huge, and her hair was a lustrous shade of perfectly medium brown. It fell over her brow and Jonathon wanted to stroke it aside. He would have been quite happy to dedicate the rest of his life to keeping her hair from inconveniencing her.

With an effort that utterly eclipsed all that he had put into trying to make himself eat the fish, he collected himself.

'Um, no. Sorry,' he said.

He felt he needed something to follow this up with.

'What's it about?'

What's it about? He screamed at himself in his head. *What sort of question's that? What's what about? Idiot.*

'About the cat,' she said. 'I think I've seen him.'

She handed him a leaflet. 'Missing cat', it said in large letters on the top. Beneath it was a photo of a cat with one ear. At the bottom the leaflet suggested contacting Mark, and then gave the address of Jonathon's bedsit.

'Oh,' he said. 'Thanks.' *Thanks? What for? Idiot.*

'Is it your cat?'

'Um, yes. I mean, no. I've seen the leaflet. I'm Jonathon. I didn't see the address before.'

'Is this the wrong address?'

'No, it's the right address' – he checked again – 'but he doesn't live here. He must have lived here before me. I've only been here two or three months.'

He said this with an airy wave at the room, as though not having been there for more than a quarter of a year excused everything about it.

'I picked it up today,' she said, 'in a cafe.'

'Um,' said Jonathon.

'But this is the address, right? And he definitely doesn't live here?'

'Yes. It is. He don'tsn't. Doesn't.'

'Oh well. Sorry to disturb you' – she looked briefly into the room – 'from your fish.'

'Um, no. Sorry. That's all right. I, er, wasn't eating it anyway. Er, would you like to leave a message?'

'A message?'

Shit, what had he said that for? He didn't know anyone called Mark. *Idiot. Salvage it! Salvage it!* Also, stop staring at her.

'Um, I'll um ask the landlord what's the last person's living here's names was and if, if he's callened Mark I'll sends the message to him.' *Way to speak, idiot.* Why had he put so many extra Ss in that? What was wrong with him?

'Oh no, that's all right,' she said. 'I'll probably see you around because I live round here anyway. So if you find out you can always tell me.'

'Um, right. OK.'

'OK, thanks a lot. Bye!'

'Yes, sorry. Bye!'

He closed the door.

'Fuck!' he said. And then he was quiet, suddenly worried that she could still hear him.

There were many terrible difficulties associated with being Jonathon, not least the utter unpredictability of all his major attributes. If he had really been universally bad at everything then life would in some respects have been easier. He could have taken a menial job, developed appalling body odour, not cleaned his teeth, worn an amusingly mis-shapen white hat and spent his time shouting at pigeons.

Unfortunately, he was sometimes good at things. He could even, sometimes, be charming. He was almost certain that he had been charming in his Harrods interview. Slightly charming anyway. Not charming like charming people are, obviously, but not uncharming either.

The problem was that his charm, like all his other attributes, fluctuated wildly and unpredictably. He had no control over what he would be good at or when. The high point of his charm *could* come while he was in a job interview or meeting the most deeply and woundingly beautiful girl he had ever seen, but it was more likely that he would be charming when he couldn't take advantage of it, while he was asleep perhaps, or on the toilet.

Which of his skills had been at its height while talking to Rachel? *Probably miniature golf,* he thought forlornly. What an idiot he'd been. Shit. How many times had he said 'um' and 'sorry' in that conversation? What an idiot. How could he have forgotten so thoroughly how conversations – and sentences and words – worked? She had even noticed his fish. How embarrassing.

But perhaps she had seen through all of that. 'I'll see you around,' she had said. And she had looked at him steadily, made eye contact, smiled. But then again most people do those things when they talk – they are more a sign that a person has talked to other people before than that they have fallen in love with you at first sight. Had she winked as she turned? No, that really was just a fantasy.

Shit, shit, shit. He should have claimed to be Mark and invited her in. Or claimed to be Mark and invited her out. Or claimed to be her and invited himself out.

Shit.

How could he see her again?

CHAPTER ELEVEN

Just as Jonathon's skill at miniature golf reached its zenith, Lance's nonchalance finally gave out. Luckily, by that point he was back in Hammersmith, outside the building where he lived. He paid the taxi driver with trembling hands, stood in a puddle and then ran inside, up the stairs and along the landing, wrenched open the door of his flat, leapt inside and slammed it shut behind him.

He was so short of nonchalance that he locked the door.

He stood there, eyes closed, leaning against the door and panting, the beads of sweat dripping from his brow onto the file tucked under his arm. When he opened his eyes, the first thing he saw was the kitchen. It was not the ideal sight for someone who has recently touched his first dead neck and stolen his first stolen documents. The kitchen was disgusting.

The flat was of an unusual and quite possibly illegal design, its front door letting straight in to the kitchen. This was one of many features that contributed to the relatively low rent, which allowed Lance to dress better than any other man in his income bracket. He knew that he should be spending less money on shirts and cocktails and more money on increasing the number shown next to the word 'BALANCE' on his bank statements. But he also knew that he should not smoke, not take advantage of impressionable women and not use short men's hats as ashtrays. He bundled all these things up together, labelled them 'things I will fix one day' and left them in a quiet corner of his mind.

Languishing in the same corner was his intention to sort out his kitchen. In the other rooms Lance tried to maintain that state of tasteful and carefree disarray that befits a single man's home – he confined his efforts to restraining the filth and picking things up off the floor. In the kitchen he had failed even to do this. It was disgusting.

The first thing everyone noticed about Lance's kitchen was the mountain of washing up. He hated the washing up. Whether he did it or not, there always seemed to be the same amount. That was why he didn't do it. Even if he were to do it all one night, he knew that when he woke the next day and came to the kitchen he would find the sink once more full of washing up, like the Gnomes of Cologne but in reverse. And who could stand up to gnomes? Wiser simply not to do the washing up.

The second thing everyone noticed was the washing up again: there was so much of it, and it seemed to have colonised every available space.

The sight of the washing up, coming so soon after his first glimpse of a corpse, proved too much for Lance. Temporarily disavowing nonchalance altogether, Lance ran to the sink and threw up vigorously over the dirty dishes. The nasty cafe food which had sat silently inside him now dashed noisily back up, making for the dirty plates and uneaten food in the sink like a lover rushing to his betrothed. It was like that except instead of catching the betrothed in its arms and falling, laughing, upon the grass, the lover spattered all over the betrothed in foul greasy lumps. Then another lover came and did exactly the same, as did the next lover, and the next. In fact, wave after wave of lovers came spilling out of Lance's bucking stomach, exploded over their betrothed and lay dead and dismembered in the Somme of his sink. He spewed them out until no more would come.

He was feeling feverish and his head was spinning. Where had all that stuff about lovers and betrotheds come from? That was weird.

After rinsing his mouth, he slumped back against the door, exhausted and wondering why he felt so bad. The obvious explanation was that he had recently seen a dead woman lying in a cat's bowl. It was, he decided, very uncool to be reacting this way. It must have been something he ate.

Incredibly, his nonchalance was not entirely exhausted. It would return if he forced it. He frowned, a vein throbbed in his neck, and he flicked the file nonchalantly on to the kitchen table where the corner, stamped 'HM GOVERNMENT', landed in some butter.

Lance forced himself to saunter a few steps and then took out his cigarettes, knowing that he looked great when he smoked. Despite there being no one around to see him, he needed the security that looking good brings, as well as the calming effect of the tobacco. He lit a cigarette and got a beer out of the fridge.

Lance looked around the kitchen again. He ought to move soon: the place didn't really fit his image. Both he and his landlord refused, on principle, to decorate it – each feeling that to do so would be to do the other a favour. They detested each other.

The landlord was a fat man who sweated too much and wore a greasy bandit's moustache. He had political (and, because of a childhood illness, physical) leanings to the right, and believed that providing services or maintenance of any kind was a betrayal of the free market.

The kitchen was the principal battle-ground in the war between the two men: a sort of domestic Middle East, fuelled by conflicts in all the other rooms of the flat. Neither side could compel the other to clean or decorate it, so they vied with each other to despoil it, hoping it would become so unbearable that the other side would have to give in.

The kitchen's one redeeming feature was that it did not have a large dead woman lying in the middle of the floor. Lance looked again at the Manila file lying on the table with its corner in some butter. He still hadn't seen what was in it, beyond glancing at the thick paper branded 'Girard Leviticus', the word 'CONTRACT' and Andrew Thompson's name printed in thrilling black at the bottom of one of the pages. Together, these things had tripped the hair-trigger which controlled

Lance's compulsion to steal, lie and cheat.

The most important factor in his decision was that any documents left at the scene of a murder must be interesting. Besides, these were unquestionably documents that Sarah Morecambe had meant to leak to him. The documents he had stolen from her house were almost certainly documents that she had stolen herself. Did the two thefts cancel each other out? Was he simply carrying out Sarah Morecambe's wishes even in death? There was a moral issue here, Lance was clear about that. But what that moral issue might be he desperately didn't want to discover.

Then there was the question of who had killed her, and why. If the murderer had left the file behind then the killing must have been personal, but there was something about that which didn't seem right.

Suddenly, Lance was up and making for the door. He ran down the stairs, across the street, down the road, around the corner, along three more streets and into a telephone box which was convincingly far from his house. He called 999, putting on a bizarre Scottish accent which sounded much like the real thing, telling them simply, 'Murder, forty-two Acacia Road. Dead.' Then he hung up and ran half the way back.

Since he was too cool to exercise and way too cool not to smoke, Lance was close to haemorrhaging by the time he arrived back at his kitchen. His veins were bulging, throbbing and pounding, as though someone had pumped too much blood into them and they might burst at any moment. He rested his head in his hands. His brow was drenched in sweat. 'Fuck' he said, breathing hard as the sweat poured off him and made a real mess of his Valentino shirt. He opened a beer, drank it, and then drank another. After a third beer and quite a lot of cigarettes he was breathing normally and had stopped sweating. He stumped off to the shower.

Lance's was of the old school of showers, a traditionalist. It staunchly believed a real shower was one so cold that it would be mid-afternoon before any feeling returned to one's extremities. Lance had tried everything: he'd reasoned with it, repaired it, made his landlord repair it (in happier times), and started going out only with women who had better showers. None had been satisfactory. Now, resigned, he simply blow-dried his genitals as part of his post-shower routine.

Lately, he had come almost to appreciate the shower. He went to the shower feeling dirty, guilty and sinful, and came away feeling really cold. It was a device for turning moral problems into purely thermal ones.

Within three minutes the shower had worked its magic. No longer even remotely interested in the dead woman he'd discovered or the political miasma he could be wading into, he was occupied only with restoring the circulation to his armpits. He towelled himself vigorously and then went to sit by the fire in his kimono.

While he warmed himself he stared at the file. When he opened it a wave of nausea came crashing over him. He tried to make himself read it but his mind refused.

Lance saw then with a blinding clarity that he had to go to the pub, have several beers, and get laid. He flicked the file onto the kitchen table again, with a less effortful nonchalance this time, and went to get dressed.

The pub Lance had in mind was about fifteen minutes away. It was a bar really, rather than a pub – an overdesigned place where one wall was red and another powder-blue, where the floor was wooden and the chairs were fiendish metal skeletons. It would be infested with marketing men, advertising women and computer persons. But there would be people inside, people Lance knew and didn't particularly like, and that was all that mattered. He could be loved there for what, not who, he was: a cool, good-looking man with a mysterious job.

Once inside he scanned the crowd for a familiar face. If he couldn't find one, he decided just to speak to someone who resembled one of his friends: it wouldn't make much difference. But there in an alcove by the bar he saw a group of about a dozen people he knew, clustered around Loud Phil.

Loud Phil caught sight of Lance as he approached. He was in sales and marketing, or S&M as he frequently joked – often as many as twenty times in a single day. He stood up and shouted 'Lance!', exaggeratedly throwing his arms wide, baring his teeth in a white oblong and shaking his head so his completely straight hair waggled crazily.

'Loud Phil,' said Lance.

'Lance, sit down man! Good to see you! What can I get you!'

'Hey it's OK, I'll get these,' said Lance.

'No, come on! What do you want!'

'OK, I can see this means a lot to you. I'll have a Sambucca and a Grolsch.'

'Anyone else!'

There wasn't. They moved round so that Lance could sit down and he sat down.

'Awright there Lance mate?' asked the man on Lance's left, with a sniff.

His name was Roger, and Lance was always surprised to find that he quite liked him. Roger was ludicrously tall and had such a strong East London accent that it sometimes seemed a real struggle for him to speak. He was in his twenties and worked in TV but habitually pretended to be an elderly jellied-eel merchant, a shtick that had stuck.

Lance sniffed back. 'Yeah, I'm awright. You awright?'

'Yeah, not so bad. Well, apart from the old … you know, the old trouble.'

'Playing up again is it?'

'Something chronic, my son.'

Loud Phil was approaching, shouting something to them from the other side of the bar. Roger shuffled to his aid and the two came back loudly carrying drinks. Phil sat noisily down and began to open a packet of strident peanuts.

'Nuts anyone!' he shouted.

The packet of nuts was offered first to Duncan, who was a DJ, then to Natalie, who worked in advertising, then to Jake, who wore a pink shirt, then to Paul, who could touch his nose with his tongue, then to Anne, who wore her hair sprayed into the shape of a crash helmet, and on and on around the whole table.

Lance and Roger talked most, interrupted frequently by the assorted others. Lance took up absent-mindedly seducing a girl whose name he hadn't quite caught, like a great painter idly doodling on a beer-mat. She vaguely knew Roger but was here with two other friends who had come to sit down with the larger group because it was larger. They had the kind of conversation that both parties know is mainly to justify the sex which will follow, but Lance enjoyed talking to her. She was pretty, with long, straight, red-brown hair falling round a tanned, apple-cheeked face. After more drinks Lance talked almost solely to her, and Roger laughed with a guy called Nick instead.

'Ssshhhhhh!' said Lance, tripping over another stair.

Behind him another flood of stifled giggles burst out. He turned and shushed at the girl from the pub again, even more theatrically this time, and she collapsed, laughing too hard to breathe. They trod more stairs. Lance waved the key near the lock, then fumbled and dropped it. This was so hilarious that both he and the girl whose name he hadn't quite caught staggered helplessly around for some minutes, incapacitated by the dense clouds of laughter being pumped into the corridor. Finally she leaned on the door handle to steady herself, the door opened and she flopped into the kitchen.

She lay on the floor, completely disabled by silent laughter, until she recovered enough to say, 'You forgot to lock the door!'

Lance thought this was the funniest thing anyone had ever said to him. He sank to his knees and gripped his sides. Then he found the key lying on the floor, and he discovered that *this* was the funniest thing that had ever happened to him.

He closed the door and they collapsed again.

Eventually Lance managed to say, 'Can I get you something to drink?'

The girl, who had quietened down, began giggling again at the hilarious offer of a drink.

They sat together on the settee with their drinks and some mindlessly happy music.

'I'm sorry to distorb you there miss, so I am,' said Lance in the worst Irish accent ever heard, 'but you have something down your dress, so you do.'

She giggled. 'It's your hand, isn't it?'

'Ah, to be sure, to be sure, so it is.'

He had completely forgotten about the file of stolen documents, his call to the police and Sarah Morecambe's body lying dead in her kitchen.

MONDAY

CHAPTER TWELVE

'Aaaah,' said Thompson, stretching his feet out in front of him and making several other commuters almost imperceptibly look up from their papers.

Monday, often such a travail, was glorious. The clouds stacked themselves on top of one another like nebulous building-blocks, the azure of the sky behind contrasting delightfully. Andrew Thompson, MP, minister, *myth*, rode the train back from his country estate with an unusually light heart. After a weekend at Blythesides he was refreshed and rejuvenated, made young again by sleep, sex, exercise, his cars, his dogs and his wife.

He straightened the seams on his blue trousers and returned to his crossword for a second before thinking, 'Damn it, why should I look at the paper when there's so much outside, and so much pleasure to be had simply from sitting.' He leaned back and enjoyed the rocking of the train, the repetitive noise of the carriage-springs and the friction between the rolling stock and the tracks.

At the next stop, his mood improved still further when a young lovely came and sat opposite him. She had light, honey-coloured skin, satin lips, slightly parted, and eyes the colour of which he couldn't quite discern.

He adjusted his tie and inspected the high gloss on his beautiful shoes. The woman flicked her eyes up at him, and quickly lowered them when he caught her glance. He leaned forward, assuming his most charming and debonair smile.

'I'm about to go to the buffet car,' he drawled. 'I wonder if I might get you something. A coffee perhaps?'

She looked up at him.

'No thank you,' she replied. 'I'm hoping to remain untainted by evil.'

He was shocked, but managed to salvage his smile and retain it as he walked, straight-backed, to the buffet car. Of course she hated him – he had seen, too late, the copy of the *Guardian* on her lap. People like that hate anyone connected with the Defence Operations and Ordnance Ministry, even ordinary soldiers, never mind the minister responsible for the Defence Exports (Armaments Technology) Headquarters. If people like her had their way Britain would probably be defended by a gigantic raffiawork shield handcrafted by African villagers. It made him so angry that he bought a packet of biscuits.

When he returned she had gone, and the other passengers all seemed to be reading their papers with almost imperceptible smiles on their faces. People, he reflected, are scum. When you become too successful they can't wait to see you fail.

CHAPTER THIRTEEN

The girl from the pub had left a soft hollow on one side of the mattress. She had got up earlier than Lance, and he had refused to wake. He hadn't wanted to deal with her. Not only did he not want to stand about in his kimono making her tea and exchanging awkward bits of conversation, but he especially did not want to be reminded of the events which had made him go out to that bar with those people in search of casual sex. Specifically, he did not want to be reminded of the dead woman, or of the collection of documents that now lay on his table. Luckily, with the girl from the pub gone, he managed fairly effectively to suppress these thoughts.

Unfortunately, he managed to suppress not only these thoughts but all others too, with the result that he fell back to sleep. He woke with a start, realising instantly that he was once again going to be late for the Mmm, or Monday Morning Meeting. The thought of Sarah and the file hit him once more, so he had a shower, even more cruelly cold than usual, and this made him think only of how to make his penis the right size again.

He threw on his Zegna suit and checked his reflection in the mirror, feeling relieved to see that being tired and hungover had made him look more dashing, rather than simply shit, as he had noticed it tended to with other people. His strong jaw rose proudly from the open neck of his fresh shirt, the contrast of clean white cotton and golden stubbled flesh heightening the effect of both. His hair fell in strands across his brow, hanging just in his eyes. The suit clung and hung as if it had been sketched on him by an expensive designer.

The mirror gave him the strength he needed to get out and endure the Tube, where handsome and ugly alike are crushed into an indistinguishable human pulp. He went to Tottenham Court Road and then walked the couple of minutes from there to Number 12 Soho Square and the offices of Lenin & Plover Associates. He nodded to the security guards in their moustaches and oversized blazers and stepped into the lift, where a polite woman's voice said, '*Doors* closing. Lift … going *up*'.

As he entered the meeting eighteen people turned to look at him. Mr Lenin glanced up from his agenda. He was as slim as an exclamation mark, with an immaculate coiled quiff balanced on top of his razor-thin head. His intense eyes moved across Lance from left to right, as though speed-reading him.

'I'm going to b-buy buy you an alarm-clock, Lance Ferman.'

Lance took his place, apologised to someone whose coffee he had just spilled, and returned an absent 'thank you very much' to Mr Lenin. People laughed, and even Lenin allowed himself a wry smile, equivalent to hysteria in any other man.

Bob Plover, the other partner in Lenin & Plover Associates, clapped his hands.

'Right, let's get on with this Mmm, shall we?' he said. He was one of those people who have mastered looking tiredly cheerful, which is the secret of creating rapport. Plover's ability to do this was increased by his face: he looked like Walter Matthau wearing a latex Walter Matthau mask.

He sighed, smiled and rubbed his pouched and rumpled face, then returned to the piece of paper before him, ticking items off: 'Minutes: done. Apologies for absence: yes. All that other shite: check.'

Lenin interrupted him: 'Ah, items fall-falling under the rub-rubric of "other shite", Mr Plover: one, the cars; and two–'

Mr Lenin, Barry Lenin, liked to speak in numbered lists or bullet-points wherever possible. When he wasn't around, Lance liked to do impressions of him talking dirty to his wife: 'I f-firmly intend t-to: one, t-touch one or both of your breasts, um, bitch; two, h-have full sex with you; three:…'

'Yes?' interrupted Plover

'Two, your CCTV "feeds". In the year since you j-joined us, they have produced little–'

'They will,' interrupted Plover with a smile.

'W-will will they though?'

'Yes.'

Plover grinned tiredly at Lenin until Lenin looked away.

'Forty buildings, two hundred cameras, a few bribes and one under-employed editor: it'll work, mate, trust me. Talk about it at lunch?'

Barry Lenin tipped his head in a nod and looked down again at his agenda.

Plover continued, 'So now it's – This Week's Work. Sally, your team – where you at?'

Sally was a capable woman in her late thirties who liked to wear yellow.

'Well Bob,' she said, 'me and Hedda and Nigel are still doing the insurance work for Possum Holidays – that should take another two, two and a half weeks – and Lance finished the file on Hutton on Friday, so he'll be helping us out on Possum now, which I know he's looking forward to.'

She looked over at Lance, who shook his fist at her in burlesque rage.

Plover interjected, 'Actually, Lance'll be doing another political job. That side of the business is coming on now – Andrew Thompson, a few others. We've done some research on Graeme Hutton…'

'Hutton?' someone asked.

'The big pink one,' explained Plover.

Everyone nodded. Lenin stepped in, 'It's co-comm, it's comm, it's comm, oh fuckit, it's common knowledge that Hutton's not going to be in government for much longer, so I assume that the Hutt-Hutton job was by way of being a test. Wh-wha-what we have now is far bigger. If-if we can secure an ongoing contract, it will be: one, a sig-significant c-coup for us; and t-two, it should begin to take us in the di-direction in which, as an agency, we want to go in.'

'It's in your hands, Lance,' said Plover, 'like a blow-up doll. *Don't* take that as a signal to fuck it.'

'What's in my hands?' asked Lance.

'I got a call this morning from Thompson,' said Plover. 'The body of Sarah Morecambe was found dead at her house in the Holloway Road area late last night. She was Thompson's diary secretary. The journalists are round there now. And the police.'

Lance felt as though he had just changed down a gear and put his foot on the accelerator. His whole body seemed to over-rev. He continued to sprawl casually in his chair, trying to suppress the feeling that everyone in the room – particularly Plover – was watching him intently. With a great effort he managed to confine his movement to one eyebrow.

Lenin jumped in. 'We have been asked to, one: shad-shadow the police investigation and try to find out who they think killed Ms. Morecambe and whether it was politically motivated – that is, whether it was directed at Thomp, erm at Mr Thomp-Thompson. He wants advance warning of anything that could be embarrassing for him.'

The meeting continued, but Lance was no longer in it. Mentally he was back at Sarah's house, picking up all the hairs and flakes of skin he might have deposited there, and wiping his genetic code off the kitchen worktops.

CHAPTER FOURTEEN

The murderer put on his suede bomber jacket again and sighed deeply. He looked at the clock: half nine. This was taking frigging ages. He stumped over to the bottom of the stairs.

'You ready, love?' he called.

There was a sound of squealing laughter from upstairs, and the patter of tiny feet, followed by his wife's tired voice.

'I can't find her shoes!'

The words were slightly muffled, but the note of frustration was very clear. It sounded dangerously close to tearfulness.

He sighed again and ran upstairs. Lisa was sitting in the middle of the bedroom with Gemma on her knee, doing up the buckle on her tiny red shoe.

'I thought you said you couldn't find her shoes?' he said.

'I've only got one, haven't I!' she shouted at him.

'All right, sorry love. Didn't mean to snap.'

He knelt down on the floor, on the edge of the Postman Pat rug. His eyes were level with his daughter's. Gemma was playing with a cardboard box. It had contained a family of toy cows which had caught the murderer's eye, but Gemma was only interested in the box.

'Gemma?' he said in a soft, cajoling voice, as he waggled his finger towards her. She pretended not to hear him, but could not stop herself from smiling as she continued to play with the box.

His finger wormed closer towards her.

'Ge-mem-ma?' he sang.

She tried to suppress her giggles, but it was too late. His tickling finger reached her and began to do its work.

'Aaaaaa-wigglewigglewigglewigglewiggle,' he said.

She dissolved into laughter, wriggling around on Lisa's knee.

'Aaaa – wigglewigglewigglewigglewigglewigglewiggle,' he continued, tickling her under her arms this time.

She grabbed his finger.

'Where's your other shoe, Gemma?' he asked in a funny, high-pitched voice. Like many men, he assumed his daughter would prefer it if he sounded like Paul Daniels when he spoke to her.

She laughed again and tried to bite his finger.

'Oy. No. Gemma – where's your shoe?'

'Where's your shoe?' Lisa repeated.

'Guck gok it?' Gemma said, pushing the murderer's finger away.

'Guckgokit? What's that? Where's your shoe?'

Lisa looked down over the top of Gemma's head, and the child craned back to look at her.

'Duck got it?' asked Lisa. 'Has your duck got the shoe?'

Gemma nodded solemnly and turned her attention back to the box.

'Oh, *duck*. Course. I'll get it, love,' said the murderer, getting up.

He went into the bathroom and looked around. After a while he found the plastic bath duck behind the toilet, next to Gemma's shoe. Catching sight of his reflection, he paused for a second to look at himself in the full-length bathroom mirror. He straightened his jacket and squared his shoulders, sucking his belly in. Powerful build, no doubt about that, but lately his chin had started to get on his wick. The belly didn't worry him too much, but a double chin was bad news. He stuck his jaw out, clenched his neck muscles and moved his head about, trying to make the chin disappear. Turning so he was profile on, he looked at his new, lean jaw out of the corner of his eye.

'Gemma, what's Daddy doing?'

Lisa was standing in the doorway, smiling, holding Gemma in her arms. Gemma continued to play with her box, oblivious. Lisa whispered in Gemma's ear, still grinning at the murderer.

'Does your daddy think he's a hard man? Does he? Yes he does.'

The murderer roared and beat his chest, pretending to be a gorilla. Then holding up his hands like paws he bounded over and grabbed his wife and daughter in a great bear hug.

Lisa and he shared a few kisses before she said, 'Come on you, or we'll never get her to playschool.'

'Right. Back to business.'

He felt his pockets for his car keys as they went downstairs.

'Is her seat in the car?' he asked.

'Yes. Don't you remember putting it in last night?'

'Did I?'

'Course you did.'

'Oh yeah. Course I did. I put it in last night.'

They bundled Gemma out to the car, the murderer carrying her wellies and coat.

'Is the phone fixed yet?'

'Give them chance. We only told them yesterday.'

'Maybe I should get one of them new mobiles coming in.'

'Then who'd take messages for you?'

'Take my own.'

'What, and leave me out of a job?'

CHAPTER FIFTEEN

Afterwards, Lance sat in his office with a dull rawness at the bottom of his gut, contemplating the picture on his wall and waiting for a file of background information on Thompson. Lance had his own office, which distinguished him from the rest of Sally's team, and from Sally herself. He had never done anything particularly to deserve this honour; he was simply the sort of person who should have his own office, so he had one.

This was typical of the way Lenin & Plover worked. Generally in commercial concerns, where money does not have to be spent, it is not spent. Lenin & Plover worked differently. Here, the things that had engaged someone's imagination were sumptuous, and everything else was left to rot. Lance's room was typical: he sat in a large chair made of black leather and surgical steel (which could be adjusted in seventeen different ways), at a school-surplus table, with old, pitifully worn slabs of nylon carpet tile beneath his feet.

The room was lit by a long cylinder of delicately curved metal, almost as tall as himself, which stood by the desk. The light strip, housed snugly in the metal, emitted a light so clean and white it was almost daylight, but it fell on smudged walls still painted that shade of bile common to all walls in the Seventies and Eighties. Where other companies all had beige computers, the one that sat on Lance's desk was a shard of breathtakingly elegant sleek blackness that lacked both a keyboard and any identifiable on switch. The whole company had the air of a school project knocked up by some bright but easily distracted fifth-formers with a great deal of money.

The company had always been like that, but since Bob Plover's arrival it had become more so. One day he had walked into Lance's office and said, 'We need some cars. What do you reckon?'

'Black,' Lance had said immediately. 'And German.'

'BMW?'

'Five series.'

'Good call.'

'And make one of them a turbo.'

'Why?'

'They go faster. You could have that one.'

A week later, three black BMWs had turned up, one a turbo.

Disconcertingly, just as Lance was remembering Plover walking into his office, there was a light rap on the door and Plover walked into his office.

'All right, Lance mate?' he asked, apparently genuinely solicitous. Plover, with his soft voice, easy grin and rumpled face, possessed an infinite capacity for setting people at their ease. His beautiful and expensive clothes were crumpled and ill-fitting. Whoever you were, he made you feel that he was like you, that you were better than him, and that he was somehow worth trying to please.

'Bob baby,' said Lance, grinning.

Plover handed him a sheaf of papers and began to pace about the room, distractedly kicking at loose edges of carpet tiles and looking at Lance's stuff. Lance riffled through the papers. There was the case brief, on company headed paper, and some photocopies of old newspaper articles about Thompson, as well as a short biography culled from some official source. In short, there was nothing much. Lance looked up and saw that Plover was still kicking at the carpet, but was now also watching Lance.

'Oh sorry mate,' Plover said. 'There's this on the secretary as well.'

Plover handed Lance a couple of sheets photocopied from a personnel file. The sheets, crumpled from their short internment in Plover's pocket, also contained very little. Sarah's address was there – out of date – along with her next of kin, blood type and allergies. There was also a form she had filled in at the time of her transfer to Defence.

'You said you knew her?' said Plover. There was only the faintest hint of a question mark at the end of the sentence.

Lance thought quickly: he was sure he hadn't told Plover that he had met her.

'No,' he said, not looking up. 'Why?'

'Just thought I saw something when her name was read out in the Mmm, that's all. My mistake.'

Lance continued to skim through the sheets. When he looked up Plover was pretending to be lost in contemplation of the picture on Lance's wall. It was the only painting Lance owned. At first sight it appeared to be a jolly, wholesome depiction of a market day in rural France: a fresh loaf was prominent on the right-hand side, a brawny-armed butcher with a goatee had almost sold out of sausages in the foreground, two young bald men with rosy noses conversed behind him, and all around were geese, ornamental drapes, platters of fresh salmon, and more in that vein. Looked at in a very slightly different state of mind, it became clear that it was a picture of a nubile woman at an orgy engaging simultaneously in several explicitly depicted and deeply unwholesome acts.

'So, what do you see?' asked Lance.

'I went to a market like that once, in Marseilles. Got shut down by the vice squad.'

'But which picture do you see first?'

'What do you mean?'

'Do you see the pornographic picture or the market scene?'

'Still don't get you. I just see what's there: penis bread, some drunken tits, a tray of–'

'But… It's one of those pictures that sort of flips between looking like one thing and another. Salvador Dali did tons of them – like those two faces looking at each other in profile? And you look closer and it's a chess piece?'

Plover looked blank.

'You know?' said Lance. 'You see them all the time when you're a kid. Like those rabbits which also look like ducks.'

'Yeah, we used to have a rabbit like that when I was a kid.'

'But Bob, they … I'll show you.'

Lance took a piece of paper and a pen and began to doodle a duck with its ears drawn in such a way as to make the whole thing look like a rabbit's beak. He pushed it over to Plover.

'Like this.'

'Yeah, that's the one,' said Plover. 'Same breed.'

'Or, OK, how about this…'

He drew again and pushed the result over to Plover, who gave him a small encouraging smile. 'Yeah, beautiful crone, mate. Well done. Regular artist.'

Lance shrugged, sat back in his chair and took a pull on his coffee.

There still seemed to be something Plover wanted to say, or to find out. Lance suspected that, with his wandering around and taking time over the picture, Plover was trying to stay in the room for as long as possible, as though hoping to obtain information by osmosis, or to push Lance into saying something.

It was working. Lance was possessed by the desire to tell Plover everything, to let out the secret. To keep himself from doing so, he stood and returned to the picture.

'This might sound a bit stupid, but I've always thought that this picture's a bit like our job. You know, everything looks one way, but then you look again or change your perspective a bit and suddenly it's completely different. Do you know what I mean?'

'All this art talk goes way over my head. Things always look the same to me. You've just got to use your eyes.'

Lance picked up the sheaf of papers and put them in his pocket. 'Better go to Acacia Road and do that now – use my eyes.'

'Exactly mate. Exactly. Don't forget to use your eyes.'

CHAPTER SIXTEEN

Time drags when you have to stand about being obsequious to people all day, and today the sheer Monday of it all seemed to lend the hours extra weight. Jonathon checked his watch yet again. It was old and cheap and all tuckered out: it told the time like he felt.

The watch's poor shrivelled hands had dragged themselves to the one o'clock position. From this Jonathon deduced that it was probably actually somewhere between seven and fourteen minutes before or after one o'clock: time to meet Lance and Jane.

This vagueness was the result of Jonathon's attempts to make himself punctual. While still at school, he had set his watch to show seven minutes before the real time. Because seven is an awkward number to subtract, he hoped that he would simply accept the time his watch told him and thus be slightly less late.

But the mind is infinitely adaptable, and Jonathon's more or less instantaneously learned that it had an extra seven minutes. It did not unlearn this when he set his watch back to the right time. But when he set the watch seven minutes forward again his mind began to subtract another seven minutes. In trying to compensate for this he had grown hopelessly confused. He was now at least twice as unpunctual as he'd ever been and had developed a morbid fear of time itself.

He went to see Mr Reiss, who was stalking the aisles with his ramrod back and his tape measure draped about his shoulders like a badge of office.

'I um think it's time for my lunch?' said Jonathon.

Mr Reiss turned his sharp face towards Jonathon and raised his eyebrows. This was his preferred means of communication, despite the fact that the eyebrow code for 'Yes it is: go off and have yourself a great lunch – you've earned it, hotshot!' was in every important respect identical to the one that signified 'It's nowhere near time for your lunch. Stay here! Don't you realise how close you are to being sacked?' It could equally have meant 'I think I love you' or 'The weather in Paris is most clement at this time of year', so Jonathon decided just to go and have lunch.

All morning he had been thinking of Rachel and of his lunch with Jane and Lance. He kept replaying his conversation with Rachel in his mind, rewriting his dialogue. When he tried to bring her face to mind he couldn't – the image had already been worn away by over-use. But then at odd times it would flash perfectly formed in front of his eyes. This made it very difficult to concentrate, and he found himself excitedly recommending items of clothing at random – particularly, for some reason, trench coats. This resulted in an unusually large number of sales, resulting in turn in an unusually large number of rich people looking very slightly more stupid than they had done previously.

And through all this was threaded the thought of seeing Lance and Jane again. Suppose they didn't like him this time? Perhaps it was a cruel joke? Maybe he'd misheard them and they had actually invited him not to come to lunch. 'Don't meet us tomorrow, we won't have lunch,' they had probably said.

This ran through his mind again and again as he walked down Brompton Road, edging around clumps of tourists and avoiding the furled umbrellas that elderly upper-class men sought to whack into the shins of those tourists. He ran past a shop selling coffee-making equipment, and another dedicated to making wealthy women's hair look nicer.

He was also worried about the cost of the coming lunch, hoping desperately that it wouldn't be expensive but knowing that it must be. Jane probably hadn't even considered the cost when she had invited him, and he had been too polite to ask. As he saw it there were three possibilities:

1) He could claim not to be hungry, and just have a coffee. Although in reality he was starving and might well collapse without food. Besides, not eating might lead to the second possibility.

2) They might realise how poor he was and insist on buying him an enormous meal, which would make him feel desperately uncomfortable.

3) He could admit that he was starving and simply pay lots of money, which he could in no way afford.

Consequently, it was with some trepidation that he entered the small but incredibly well-appointed cafe to which Jane had directed him. As he entered, a fourth possibility struck him:

4) They might not be there.

This would mean that he had been stood up by another man and someone's grandmother. Standing in the doorway, he looked around, unable to see them. What had they looked like? Perhaps they were wearing completely different clothes, or had changed their hair.

Luckily possibility 4 was soon discounted: he spotted Jane at a table near the back, smiling and waving at him. Feeling slightly awkward, Jonathon made his way over to her.

'Sorry I'm between seven and fourteen minutes late,' he said. 'It's the watch.'

'You're exactly on time, ducky,' said Jane. 'And you look very smart too – most young people have freakishly large tie knots, but yours is perfect.'

The table was already laid with freshly-baked bread and a selection of cheeses, and Jonathon quickly remembered how hungry he was.

They began to eat and talk and minutes later possibilities 1 and 3 had been decisively discarded, and a modified version of possibility 2 was in operation. Jane knew the proprietor of the cafe and had some sort of complex arrangement whereby instead of paying for anything she simply dropped round at intervals for a chat.

'Oh, I'm afraid I forgot to mention, ducky, that Lance called about an hour ago to say that he won't be able to come. He's been put on a new case, apparently, and he has to go somewhere. I hope you don't mind having lunch with just me.'

This was one of those things that made social contact so difficult for Jonathon. He knew he had to react to the news – which he didn't at all mind – *as though* he didn't at all mind. Unfortunately, everything anyone said to him was processed through his brain, which also checked and sifted his replies before he could use them. Now that he had thought about it, his reaction couldn't be spontaneous, which meant that he would have to pretend to feel the way he actually did feel. He knew instantly that he would sound wrong – either hugely disappointed, as though he hated Jane and had come along only to see Lance, or immensely relieved, as though he hated Lance and was secretly in love with Jane. When it came to being genuine, Jonathon was a terrible actor.

He inadvertently resolved the dilemma by dropping a piece of brie on the floor, and then hitting his head quite hard on the table as he bent to retrieve it. Jane winced, Jonathon sat up again, clutching his head. A number of people at nearby tables turned to witness Jonathon's pain and embarrassment and were gratified to see that when he removed his hand the piece of brie it had been holding remained fixed to his forehead.

'Oooh, darling-heart, are you hurt?' Jane asked.

Jonathon, always easily astonished, was sent reeling into confusion by her use of the term 'darling-heart', an endearment he had never heard before. He looked up at her, wide-eyed with confusion. She smiled, gently pulled the cheese from his head, and poured him some more coffee.

He took a sip, then knocked the cup over.

'That was quite a bump, it really was,' she soothed, helping him to mop the table.

'I'm sorry,' he said, dabbing at the coffee stain.

'Whatever for, darling? Don't be silly. Whatever for?'

'Um, spilling the coffee and sticking cheese to my head. I'm afraid

I'm not very good at eating lunch, it's my worst meal. You should see me at breakfast though, I'm fantastic.' He was babbling.

'Sorry,' he concluded.

This was the other thing that made social contact so difficult for Jonathon. Sometimes the rigorous checks on everything he said were bypassed. His brain decided that it was an emergency, that there must be words, and so anything that came into his head also came out of his mouth.

Jane seemed to take the apology very seriously. She told him a hundred times that he had nothing to apologise for, explained that he must have had a difficult morning at work, noted that accidents come in threes, and even called him a ducky-lambkin, a freshly-coined phrase never before made tender. Finally, she suggested that the ideal thing would be a pair of red wines to soothe away the morning's cares.

A few minutes later Jane was telling him about her family.

'...Tabitha's the younger of the two – she's thirty-four – and she seems to be happy, although I find it very difficult to tell as she lives in France.'

'So what does your husband do now? You married him when he was in the RAF, and...'

'Geoffrey doesn't do much of anything, ducky, at the moment. He was a big cheese at Smith's, but he was "let go" two or three months ago. And of course he's annoyed because we lost an awful lot of money in some shares. But he has a club, a golfing habit and a directorship – nothing you could call work though.'

Some of Jonathon's cares had been soothed away, or if not altogether away then at least to a comfortable distance from the part of his mind that controlled having lunch. He found the way Jane spoke comforting. She talked to Jonathon rather as though he were a favourite houseplant or pet; people often tell their rosebushes things which they would never tell their human intimates.

'I sometimes think, ducky, that my husband and I live just as we would if we weren't married. It's as though we just happen to be living in the same house. I sometimes think he's forgotten who I am, that all these years it's been only good manners that prevented him asking what I was doing sleeping in his bed, bringing up his children and walking his dog – the name of which, I'm sure, escapes him.'

'My parents used to be like that,' said Jonathon, '– like they'd moved in together by mistake and found a kid there to bring up. They were both really keen on a divorce, but it wasn't until afterwards that they found how happy they had been, repressing their um ... mutual hatred. Both of them agree that the divorce was a bad move, but they can't get married again because it seems stupid to marry someone you don't like.'

'Do you know, I never thought of it that way. Of course neither of us wants to get divorced. Maybe it's just because we're old. We're together, but we don't really have any contact with each other.'

'Like a pair of testicles,' Jonathon suggested, and cursed his brain again. He should be telling her that she wasn't old – his sister, for example, seemed far older than her – instead of comparing her to components of the male reproductive system.

Jane laughed, and sipped at her wine. 'You mentioned yesterday that your father writes books, didn't you?'

'Well, Lance mentioned it when I told him my surname. But yes, my dad's an airport novelist – *the* airport novelist – Richard Fairfax. I hope you haven't read any of his books.'

'I'm afraid I hadn't heard of him until yesterday, ducky. Is he famous?'

'Well, no one mobs him in the street, but most shops sell his books. In fact shops which aren't book shops – places like newsagents and convenience stores – are most likely to sell them.'

'Do you know, I hardly ever go to those sorts of shops.'

'I seem to spend my whole life in them, getting my dad's books shoved in my face.'

'Oh ducky, you poor thing.'

They sat there for a second, Jane resting her hand on Jonathon's forearm, comfortingly. Then she said, 'Oh I say, here's Lance'.

As she watched his approach, Jonathon could almost physically feel her affection for Lance. Her eyes became very warm, and her voice, soft already, seemed to open out further.

There are people loving each other in full view all the time – couples snogging in nightclubs, old people holding hands – but generally it's the most muted, watery versions of their love for each other that are seen. It's as rare actually to see the love well up in a person's eyes as it is to see a bus driver set fire to his own beard. Jonathon, who tended to see things oddly or not at all, saw quite clearly that Jane had never got used to her children having grown up and left, and that she wanted to keep finding new ones. This uncharacteristic thought swiftly passed, leaving Jonathon with his usual palette of emotions. He felt deeply envious of Lance.

CHAPTER SEVENTEEN

Lance had been late for lunch because Bob Plover had suggested he go to the scene of the crime and see what he could find out. Lance, not wanting to tell him that he'd been there already, could do nothing but oblige. He ordered a taxi and sat in it while it whisked him back to Acacia Road.

All expressions of speed are relative. One man's whisk is another man's crawl. His plummet is her gentle descent. In London, the non-absolute nature of these terms is stretched to the limit: being whisked through the capital by taxi largely consists of remaining perfectly still.

So, barely forty-five minutes into his whisk, Lance leapt from the back seat and into a passing phone box to tell Jane that he would either be late or absent. She made disappointed noises but said that it was quite all right ducky, nothing could be done about it, never mind, she was sure she'd see him soon and so many other things on the theme of 'it's quite all right' that Lance began to wonder whether she wanted him there.

He had remained in the box for a while, thinking, lost in contemplation of the solitary prostitute's card tacked to the glass. The girl in the black-and-white photo seemed to have brunette hair and be Cindy Crawford, whereas the caption proclaimed the photo to be a genuine picture of a nineteen-year-old Swedish blonde who would participate in watersports if you asked. Was nothing as it seemed?

Sarah's house looked completely different. For one thing it was now day, and Lance had noticed that things always look lighter in the daytime. There were other, more subtle, differences too, such as the three police cars and the ambulance parked in the middle of the street. He couldn't see any reason for bringing an ambulance to the scene of a murder. Murder victims are, after all, dead.

The police had perversely stuck their sticky tape across the front door in a large cross, forcing everyone to use the back door. And there was a lot of everyone around, especially police. Lance wished the police would learn how to dress properly. They all stood around in their ludicrous nineteenth-century helmets, teamed with either an outsize fluorescent green anorak or a tight v-neck jumper like the ones school kids wore in the Seventies. Some of them were walking with that odd, slow, swinging walk the police are trained to do, absently ushering people away from the cordons and speaking strings of nonsense into their walkie-talkies. Others were earnestly debating something with the ambulance drivers.

There were also large numbers of men in suits hanging about, an absurd proportion of whom had moustaches. These men looked less earnest than the uniformed police. Some of them were even laughing. Their casual attitude gave the impression that this was what they did every day, that they probably thought on the way to work on Monday, 'Hey-ho, another week of standing laughing at murder scenes. Still, at least it pays the bills.'

In fact, almost all of the people standing around looked as though they were there in some sort of professional capacity. The other main body, apart from the police and ambulance people, were the journalists and photographers, some of whom had just hailed Lance's cab and were piling into it, gripping microphones and very large cameras. These people tended to be large, shabby men with unruly hair. There was a noticeable lack of women.

Lance felt oddly calm for a man who has just returned to a place from which he has stolen some stolen documents and at which he has discovered a woman whose deadness is now a matter of public record. This, he supposed, must be what being cool is all about. He moved casually over to a group of workmen in hard hats and big trousers who were watching the display.

'Any idea what's going on, mate?' he asked one of them.

'Been a murder, mate,' the man replied. He was a small man with a colossal pot belly and protruding teeth – just the kind that Bardot or Garbo would have gone for. 'Bird's been stabbed to death.'

'Fuck,' said Lance.

'You can say that again, mate.'

'Fuck,' said Lance.

The men all laughed uproariously, as though it were the first time they had ever heard this joke. One of them turned around and looked Lance up and down.

'You with the press?' he asked.

'Yeah. Are you?' Lance replied. He meant it as a joke, but the man seemed to take it seriously.

'You're having a laugh, encha?'

They all laughed, to illustrate what Lance was having.

'Naw, we're working down on the road down there, as it goes. Came up to see what all the fuss is about.'

'What's the ambulance for? Is the body still there?'

'Yeah. Doing f'rensic examinations. And one of the neighbours went hysterical. You're late mate – most of your boys are gone now. It's gone quiet. You should have been here when we turned up. It was all going off then.'

'Does anyone know who killed her?' asked Lance.

'Who do you fink I am? The police spokesman or summing?'

'You mean you're not?'

The man laughed, 'You're awright, mate. I tell you summing, the number of journalists would find out more from talking to people like us, out on the streets all day, keeping our eyes open, 'stead of talking to police spokesmen.'

Lance gave the man a fag, and the two stood silently smoking for a while.

'I'm Lance,' said Lance.

'I'm Arthur,' said the man.

'All right Arthur.'

'Awright Lance.'

'So who killed her then, Arthur?'

'Well Lance, since you ask nicely, it was her fiancé – ex-fiancé.'

'How do you know?'

'I talk to the cops who look bored mate. So, she lets the murderer in, no struggle, makes him a nice cup of tea, gets so carried away nattering that she forgets she got a fish on the hob – it's obviously someone she knows, right? – then it's "Why did you leave me, Sarah?" "I don't love you no more, Brian." Out comes the knife. Bang.'

'The knife went bang?'

'You know what I mean. Little bit of dramatic licence towards the end there, but all the facts come straight from the filth. And nothing in the house was touched. Passport, cash, TV: it's all there.'

'You ought to be the BBC's crime correspondent.'

'No money in it, mate.'

Lance made his way over to a small knot of police to see if they could confirm Arthur's story. The police wouldn't tell him anything about the murder, so he asked them the time, just to annoy them. They had to tell you the time.

There was clearly no reason for him to hang around, and even less reason once the police outriders turned up, sirens whooping, to clear a path for two visiting ministers. So Lance said goodbye to Arthur, gave a policewoman his card, regretted it instantly as he was obviously in grave danger of arrest, and began to wander away, looking for a main road where he could hail a cab. He sauntered down Acacia Road, thinking about all the reasons why he shouldn't be arrested. He hadn't committed a crime, he'd reported the murder, prevented the house burning down and had only taken a file of documents which would have been given to him anyway. His conscience, such as it was, was clear. He began to feel hungry, and – looking at his watch – realised he might be able to make it for lunch with Jane and Jonathon after all.

He put out his hand and within minutes was once more being whisked across London. Would he make it there before they left?

CHAPTER EIGHTEEN

'Do you know, I rather thought you said you wouldn't be able to make it today?' said Jane as Lance pulled up a chair and sat down heavily, his hair – as ever – falling dashingly across his brow.

He grinned. 'Do you know, I rather thought so myself, paper-shaker.'

'Paper-shaker?'

'I heard it in a film. Sounds cool, no?'

'I really couldn't say, Lance ducky. Do you know, your use of Fifties American slang is beginning to reach worrying proportions?'

'And your use of the word "ducky" is beginning to tickle my tush.'

Jane laughed, but looked a tiny bit hurt.

'Where does it come from anyway?' he asked, suddenly looking tired and irritable.

'It's an affectation, lambkin,' said Jane. 'My mother used to call everyone ducky and I always said that I would too when I became a mother. So I did.'

A sleek blonde waitress arrived at their table and Lance shifted instantly from irritable to darkly brooding. He looked at her from under his eyebrows, but she stared back without a trace of interest. Her beauty was precision-engineered, as though she had been designed by a committee of experts to meet all the criteria of attractiveness. She had no effect on Jonathon at all: he had fallen so completely for the girl who'd told him about the one-eared cat that he had no reserves of awkward yearning left for anyone else. His mind refused even to store the waitress in his memory.

Lance gave up being darkly brooding and slapped his thighs. 'Right, that's the preliminary abuse over with. Now for something to eat. How you doing Jonathon?'

'Er, very groovy, thank you,' said Jonathon.

'*Tickle your tush* – I don't know. Have the scones, darling-heart, they're lovely.'

'Cool.'

Lance ordered, poured himself some coffee and watched the waitress as she walked away to get him his scones.

'I'm dying to hear about yesterday,' said Jane. 'What happened?'

'Haven't you heard the news?'

'I've heard *some* news. Which news do you mean, lambkin?'

Lance sighed. 'Sarah Morecambe was murdered yesterday.'

'You can't mean it!' said Jane.

Jonathon goggled across the table.

'But why?' asked Jane. 'And who? Do they know who did it?'

'No idea. She let him in and made him a cup of tea, and nothing was taken, so the police think it must have been someone she knew.'

'An ex-boyfriend?'

'Something like that.'

'Well I never did. Did you go to her house yesterday?'

He paused only a fraction of a second. 'Yes.'

'Oh, darling-heart. Before or after?'

'It must have been after. I rang the bell and there was no answer.'

'So you went home.'

Lance said nothing.

'Could it have something to do with wanting to leak documents?' asked Jonathon.

Lance stared at him. 'How do you know about that?'

'You told me yesterday.'

Lance suddenly grinned, reached across the table and punched Jonathon playfully on the arm. 'Just testing, daddy-o.'

'Ow. Could it?'

Lance sat back. 'Listen,' he said, picking up a teaspoon to emphasise his words, 'this is a terrible country, full of injustice and … and that other bad thing–'

'Iniquity?' suggested Jonathon.

'Unfairness?' suggested Jane.

Lance pointed at Jane and touched his nose. 'Unfairness. That's the one–'

'Um. But, but that's the same as iniquity, isn't it?' put in Jonathon.

'Yes. I'm accepting Jane's answer anyway though, because that's what kind of a country we're living in. The point is that injust and unfair as Britain is, people don't get murdered for leaking documents here. Besides, Sarah didn't even leak anything, and whoever murdered her didn't take anything.'

'Oh,' said Jonathon. 'How do they know?'

'What?'

'How can they tell the murderer didn't take anything? I mean, they could see if he'd taken a TV or a table or something, but what if he just took some documents? How would the police know?'

Lance was temporarily silenced. 'They…' he began. 'They just know, all right?'

'But how?'

'Maybe there were some important documents left in full view. The kind of documents you would take if you were taking documents.' Lance picked up his teaspoon again to emphasise his point. 'The police would be able to tell that the murderer hadn't taken those.'

'Yes but–' Jonathon paused for thought. 'What if, um, the murderer planted the documents that were left behind? Or what if he was meant to take them but forgot? People forget to take their shopping all the time at Harrods. They come in, buy a suit, and then just leave the bag by the till.'

At that moment the waitress arrived with Lance's scones. Lance, who had frozen with his teaspoon in mid-point, suddenly became aware of his pose and smiled mock-bashfully at her. Not a flicker of expression crossed her face. As she left, Lance checked his reflection in the teaspoon.

'I look tired,' he said. 'And convex.'

Then as though agreeing between them that they had talked for too long about real things, their conversation slipped away into the clouds.

'So,' said Lance through a mouthful of his second helping of scones, 'You think Hamlet is all about dieting, but what evidence have you got, other than the bit where Hamlet wants to melt his too, too solid flesh?'

'Not dieting, not just dieting. I was saying it's about all kinds of weight-loss...' said Jonathon.

'As in *To be or not to be / fat is the question*?'

'*To diet, to slim / to slim, perchance to preen*,' suggested Jane.

'Well frankly Jane, I consider that to be taking too many liberties with the text,' said Lance, miming a large English professor's moustache with his napkin.

She stuck her tongue out at him, girlishly. It was odd to see a stately lady in late middle age and a young man mucking about together like children. Their intimacy and his own newness made Jonathon suddenly confused. He glanced at his watch and noticed that he was probably between seven and fourteen minutes late for work.

'Oh,' he said. 'I'm going to have to go back.'

Jane looked at her watch. 'Goodness, is that the time?'

'It'd be a hell of a weird coincidence if it wasn't,' said Lance.

They all stood up and Jonathon turned to Jane.

'Thank you very much for lunch,' he said. 'It was really nice. Thank you. Thanks'

'I think you ought to thank her again,' said Lance. 'That was only three times.'

Jane said, 'You're very welcome, Jonathon.' She kissed him on the cheek. 'Now I must go and have a word with André.'

The waitress appeared again, ready to clear the table. She pointed out André, and Jane went off to chat to him.

Lance turned to Jonathon. 'Listen, we ought to get together for a drink soon. There's something I'd like to talk to you about.'

'Um, oh. Yes, definitely.'

'What are you doing after work tomorrow?'

'Nothing really.'

'When do you get off?'

'Half six, tomorrow.'

'Cool. Name a place.'

Jonathon's mind contained the names of no pubs. Why would it? They were no fun on your own. However, he desperately didn't want to admit this to Lance. Suddenly the name of a pub fell from the subconscious realms of his mind and out of his mouth.

'The Barnaby Rudge,' he heard himself say.

Lance thought for a second. 'Charlotte Street, right?'

Jonathon nodded. He had no idea. He would have to check the phonebook. There couldn't be two Barnaby Rudges, could there?

'Never been there,' said Lance. 'What's cool about it?'

'It, um.' His brain was in the swing of this now, and instantly lobbed out a reason. 'It contains the embalmed body of Barnaby Rudge.'

'Whoa.'

'Yes. It's in a glass cabinet built into the bar.'

'Far out and remarkable. OK, see you there tomorrow, hip cat, seven o'clock, for drinks.'

CHAPTER NINETEEN

'I must say that you don't seem very upset by the fact that your secretary has been murdered,' said Mangiafuoco.

He and Thompson were standing in Sarah's spare room, looking down on the crowd in the street below. It was drizzling on the police in their helmets and fluorescent anoraks, on the photographers and journalists standing in a knot in front of the taped-off cordon, on the medical people in their white clothes and on the scene-of-crime officers in their own competing white clothes. It drizzled also on the ordinary people – the neighbours and the curious – who derived some entertainment from looking at the front of an ordinary house that they had heard contained a dead woman.

'In fact,' said Mangiafuoco, 'you don't seem upset at all.'

'I'm not,' said Thompson. 'Couldn't stand the woman. Worst secretary I've ever had. She could have been put to better use within government as solid fuel – my office is ridiculously cold in the winter.'

'You can't heat your office with dead secretaries, Andrew. I hope you're not going to say that to the press.'

'Of course not. I'm going to tell them that my grief, as that of all who knew her, is unquenchable.'

'Unquenchable?'

'Yes. Like a thirst that cannot be slaked.'

'You're going to tell the press and the electorate that your grief is like being thirsty?'

Thompson gave Mangiafuoco one of his looks.

Mangiafuoco persisted. 'I'm not sure they'll understand.'

'Well what are you going to say?'

'That I deeply regret her tragic death and sympathise with her family at this time of tragic loss.'

'That's two tragics.'

'It's a tragic thing, death.'

'Well I happen to think that the public expects a little more from me – they want a little colour, an elevated distinction of expression.'

'And you'll do that by comparing your sorrow to the need for a drink?'

Thompson patted Mangiafuoco's shoulder. 'I have an instinct for these things. Just you wait and see.'

He turned and seemed on the point of picking his way to the door through the packing cases and stacks of bathmats.

'Wait,' said Mangiafuoco. 'What I really wanted to talk to you about is what the police have told me. Slater says that the murderer was known to the victim: she let him in and made him a cup of tea – and, apparently, cooked him a fish, which he didn't eat.'

'She cooked him a fish?'

'Yes.'

'Evidently I'm out of touch with the ways of the suburban petit-bourgeoisie. Someone popped round on a Sunday afternoon for a cup of tea and a fish?'

'Yes. Or at least that's what she made him. Perhaps he didn't like it. Maybe that's why he stabbed her in the ribs.'

'They know it was a man?'

'I don't know. It always is though.'

'Do they know why?'

'Something to do with hormones, I expect.'

'I mean why he killed her.'

'No. Though that's the other thing I wanted to tell you. There was some indication that she intended to call a journalist.'

'And did she?' asked Thompson, reaching for the knot of his tie.

'We don't know. Do you know why she might have been talking to a journalist?'

'I have no idea.'

'I shan't beat around the olive tree. If you disliked her she must have known about it. That in itself gives her a reason to want to damage you. What's the worst thing she could have revealed about you?'

'Nothing.'

Mangiafuoco stared hard at him.

'I've known you a long time, Andrew.'

Thompson sat down on a crate of spoons.

'I know. But really, I can't think what she might have on me. All the obvious stuff is already out: my anonymous bid for Hitler's teeth, the Anti-Welsh Society, that researcher who I … Well, the point is that I can't think of anything.'

'No documents that could have damaged you?'

'Not that I can think of. She didn't have access to much anyway – just the routine day-to-day paperwork.'

'So there's no way the murder might compromise you?'

'I shouldn't like to be categorical, but none springs to mind.'

Mangiafuoco looked hard at Thompson, then patted him on the shoulder.

'Then it's a mystery.'

'A mystery.'

'Who would have deliberately killed your secretary?'

'Who indeed?'

'Come along, let's talk to the gentlemen of the press.'

TUESDAY

'Car?' enquired Gemma, pointing out of the window from her baby seat in the back of the Jag.

'That's right, Gemma,' answered Lisa. 'And what's that?' she asked, pointing to a house.

'Sky?'

'No, in front of the sky.'

'House?'

'Yes, it's a house.'

Gemma clapped her hands and laughed.

'She's so bright,' Lisa cooed. She turned round and began to sing to Gemma in a squeaky voice, 'She's so clever, she's so clever, well I never, she's so clever.'

The murderer changed down a gear and brought the car to a slow stop for some traffic lights. While they waited, he turned to Gemma and made a face. She laughed and clapped her hands again, delighted.

'That phone been fixed yet?'

'Not yet, love. They said they'd come this after.'

'They said they'd come yesterday.'

'I know, love.'

He pulled off, overtaking a brown Vauxhall.

'Car,' observed Gemma.

'Yes, it is a car,' confirmed Lisa.

'House?'

'Yes.'

They drove on for a while, the traffic moving fairly freely, until they arrived at a low, square building from the Sixties. The murderer eased the old girl to a halt and cranked the handbrake.

'Car?' asked Gemma.

'No Gemma, this is your playschool isn't it?'

'Yes,' Gemma agreed seriously.

They freed Gemma from the complicated sequence of straps which held her in the child seat and lifted her gently out.

'Car?' wondered Gemma.

'Yes, that's Daddy's car isn't it?'

'Yes.'

The murderer carried her up to the door of the building. Lisa followed with Gemma's coat and wellies.

When they returned to the car Lisa stretched herself out against the seat's cracked leather.

'She hasn't cried like that for ages, being left at playschool,' she said.

'I know, love,' answered the murderer.

'I wonder if there's something wrong – maybe that tummy bug's coming back, or her teeth are hurting again.'

'Maybe.'

'You all right, love?' she asked. 'You're miles away.'

'Sorry love. I was just thinking about the new kitchen.'

She gasped. 'We're having one?' she asked, her mouth open with delight, just like Gemma's.

'Course we are. You wanted one didn't you?'

'Oh, you know I do. Can we afford it though?'

'Well. I been thinking, all that work you do for me – sending letters and making up them files whenever I do a job – that's a real big help and I never give you nothing for it. And putting up with me. I reckon you deserve a medal, never mind a kitchen.'

'Oh!' she cried, reaching over and putting her arms round him as they drove. She rested her cheek on his shoulder and he grinned.

'You know that job I done at forty-two Acacia?'

'Yes,' she snuggled.

'Has Bob … ?'

'He can't, can he? With the phone. Unless he comes round, I spose.'

'Anyway, I saw in the kitchen there – new kitchen – they had all these little lights under all the cupboards – lit up the whatjercallits underneath – table things, um…'

'Work surfaces?'

'Work surfaces, that's right – lit them right up so you could see what you was doing. It looked magic, and you'd be able to see what you was doing no problem at all.'

'I don't deserve you.'

'Too right you don't,' he replied with a broad grin. They laughed, and then he added hoarsely, 'I don't deserve you.'

He pulled the car over by the side of the road.

CHAPTER TWENTY-ONE

The first Lance saw of Thompson was an unbelievably highly polished brogue the colour of ox blood emerging into the office through the window. It was followed by a leg, and it was immediately obvious that the trouser which encased the leg was the product of a skill many years in the nurturing. In fact, it might have been easier to shape the leg to the trouser for all the labour and skill that was involved. So it was that Lance was struck down by suit envy even before Thompson's second leg arrived in the room, closely followed by his jacket. The head balanced on top was less impressive.

'Just feeding the birds, Mr Femur. They become ravenous at about this time of day.'

He brushed some crumbs from the lapel of his suit.

'The balcony, though small, affords a panorama of some distinction. I like to look down on Horse Guards and across St James's Park.'

He ceased his brushing and aimed a smile at Lance.

The secretary who had accompanied Lance into the office said, 'It's not in the book, you know, this appointment.'

'Appointments, I believe, begin with a knock at the door. Without a knock, it is not an appointment, and thus not in the book.'

'I'm just saying it should be in the book.'

'And I'm conveying that one ought to knock before entering.'

She seemed on the point of replying, but he silenced her with an eyebrow.

'Thank you Janet,' he said, brushing her out of the door as though she were a large crumb that had somehow got onto the carpet.

He closed the door behind her and indicated a seat to Lance, who gave him a card and sat down.

'*Ferman*, I do apologise. Mr Ferman.' Thompson sat down and leaned back in his chair.

'I admired your speech yesterday,' said Lance.

'Thank you very much. You agree then more with the *Telegraph* than with our friends at the *Sun*, which I'm flattered to note has featured me on its front page?'

He reached over to a pile of newspapers and held up the *Sun*. Above a picture of Thompson wearing the smile of a delighted alligator was the headline 'Quench my grief!'

Lance smiled in spite of himself but turned it into the distracted frown of a man trying to remember something.

'What was it the *Telegraph* said? *An orator...*'

'*An orator of rare depth and sensibility,* or something along those lines.'

Lance nodded. 'Ah yes.'

'Now, you have with you a contract, I believe.'

Lance took a document from his briefcase and set it on the leather desktop between them.

'I hope it's everything you expected it would be,' said Lance.

Thompson weighed the document experimentally in his hands. 'Paper, varicoloured, twelve sheets: it's everything I expected and more.'

'The top sheet is the headline contract, specifying the job and the price. The second is the small print, the terms and conditions, our commitment to confidentiality and the statutory limitations on that commitment. And if you fold it right it becomes a boat.'

'You supply instructions for doing so?'

'That's extra, I'm afraid.'

Thompson laughed courteously and set the contract on the desk.

'You're curious as to why I want you to shadow the police investigation into my former secretary's murder when – you presume – I have good contacts at the Office of the Interior.'

'Yes.'

'Well, I shall say this: I have my reasons. Clear?'

'Perfectly.'

'Then we shall get along together very well. Will you be working on the case? Or do you simply do the liaison work?'

'No, it'll mainly be me working on the case.'

'And what are your credentials, Mr Ferman? Why should I trust this sensitive matter to your care?'

Lance had expected a question along these lines and had a speech all worked out. In truth there was no reason for Thompson to suppose he would do a good job. Lance had worked on the Hutton case, one of Lenin & Plover's first political assignments, but before that had – like everyone else – mostly worked on insurance fraud and industrial espionage. If Sarah Morecambe had been a new curtain-opening mechanism Lance would have been on much surer ground. As it was, he realised suddenly that the speech he had worked out was all wrong. What was called for was front, and fortunately Lance had laid in a great stock of the stuff.

He looked Thompson dead in the eye and said, 'Because I am very, very good indeed.'

Thompson raised his eyebrows and smiled approvingly.

'Splendid. Then I shall liaise directly with you, rather than communicating at one remove, as it were, through Mr Plover.'

'Cool,' said Lance. 'By which I mean splendid.'

Thompson reached across the desk and shook Lance's hand.

'And what have you discovered so far, Mr Ferman?' he asked, reaching for a cigar.

There was something in what Jonathon had said the day before that had bothered him. It rang true, the idea that the documents and the murder were linked. Something odd was going on. He decided to fish.

'Well, I know that the police still seem to think it was personal,' he said in a casual tone.

Thompson stopped midway through cutting the end off his cigar. His expression suddenly changed.

'And you know otherwise, do you?'

'I only know what the police know. Maybe a little more.'

'Or are you testing me, perhaps?' *Snick.* The end of the cigar came off.

Lance had found that the best policy in tricky situations is to say nothing. He had the sort of face that made people imagine more was going on in his head than was really the case. He would just wait and see what Thompson said next.

Thompson stared at him levelly for several seconds and then said, 'I see that you are a clever man, Mr Ferman, and also an imaginative one. Don't let yourself be carried away by your imagination.'

Thompson pulled a box of matches from his pocket with a little flourish, as though he were a conjuror, rather than simply a man who kept matches in his jacket pocket.

Lance had no idea how to respond to this, so he repeated the last thing that had seemed to produce a good effect.

'I only know what the police know. Maybe a little more.'

'What do you know about a journalist?'

How much should he let on? The journalist was, of course, himself. And the police must have seen Sarah's to-do list. Why hadn't he taken that as well?

'The deceased left a memo to herself to call an unnamed journalist.'

He hoped Thompson hadn't been told any more than that by his contacts at Oi.

'Well, I can see you're the man for the job,' said Thompson, lighting his cigar.

Lance raised his eyebrows but said nothing.

'However,' said Thompson, 'there's a problem with this contract. It's more than Mr Plover mentioned in our telephone conversation – around five percent more. I'm not a fool, Mr Ferman.'

Thompson passed the contract back to Lance. Was this some sort of test? Lance felt he had enough to think about.

'Let me see what's happened. I'll bring you a fresh one tomorrow.'

CHAPTER TWENTY-TWO

That Tuesday Jonathon was in a good mood, heightened by its contrast with his more usual state of astonishment and unhappiness. His lunch with Lance and Jane had helped to restore his spirits. For the first time he felt that he belonged in London. There were signs that London was accepting him. In fact, just that morning as he had walked from the Tube station to work, enjoying the sunny and slightly sharp day, a pretty girl had smiled at him. She almost certainly had a rare muscular disorder of the face that made her smile at random; but still, a smile is a smile.

The day didn't drag by too painfully. He managed to leave on time and arrive early at the Barnaby Rudge. Now, sitting on his own, waiting for Lance and watching the clientele, he hardly felt insecure at all. He had a book open in front of him but it was mainly for security. Whenever he tried to concentrate on it his eyes seemed to slide off the page and back to the pub.

The book was Nicholas Emir Brunsengett's latest, *Lean: The Impact of the Nonvertical*. Jonathon was excited by the prospect of adopting the revolutionary 'lean' technique, though he couldn't yet for the life of him understand what it was. The current chapter seemed to be telling him the story of a Colombian fisherman, while the previous one had extrapolated some remarkable conclusions from the life of a pioneering Russian bee-farmer. Jonathon's failure to grasp the point made him suspect that his mindset was hopelessly vertical, or else (which was equally bad) completely horizontal. While he wasn't sure what this meant, he was very clear that both ways of thinking were old-fashioned and the cause of all sorts of wars, inefficiencies and – and there, incredibly, was Rachel.

She had just walked in. Under normal circumstances Jonathon would have pretended not to see her, hoping desperately that she would see him and come over. Instead, he was surprised to find himself waving casually to her and smiling. She saw him and smiled back, then looked around and walked over.

She stood leaning on the back of the chair opposite him, her head cocked. She was wearing glasses, which she hadn't been before, and she looked adorable. Jonathon had never, ever, needed to use the word 'adorable' to describe anyone or anything before.

'Hello. What are you doing here?' she asked. Beneath her black coat she was wearing a waistcoat, which seemed unbelievably sexy and sophisticated to Jonathon, and through a gap in her scarf he could see a trickle of her skin.

'Oh, I'm just waiting for er – a friend.'

He smiled. She really was incredible. Her hair was wavier today, even slightly unmanageable. 'I'll manage your hair anytime you want darlin', he thought in a chirpy cockney sort of voice, and wished he could have said it.

She sat down with him and he felt compelled to explain his last answer.

'I don't mean that I'm just sitting here, waiting to get a friend. The friend has already been made – by me – and now I'm waiting for that friend to arrive.'

Rachel laughed. 'Oh, I'm sure,' she said, mock-sarcastically.

There he was. He was having a conversation with her – right there in the pub, on a Tuesday. For Jonathon this was an almost religious experience. She didn't seem to hate him at all.

'So what are you doing here?' he asked.

'I'm meant to be meeting Sam here.'

'Your boyfriend?' He winced slightly, because this seemed to him to be almost a confession of his love for her.

'No.' Rachel looked away and smiled, then looked up at him. 'My girlfriend.'

Jonathon was broad-minded – or at least his mind was broader than his body. He tended not to disapprove of the things people do, merely to wish that he could be doing them too. There was a curious sense of relief, in this case, that he had no male competition. Women, in his experience, tend hardly ever to punch people really hard in the face, and he felt himself to be on more of a level playing-field with them. On the other hand, he was slightly torn apart by rage and jealousy that she should be seeing someone. His good mood pulled him through.

'Oh … um … um … Good.' He smiled, trying to indicate that he was interested, impressed, prepared to accept humanity in all its varied aspects, and would also be perfectly happy if she were to stop being a lesbian and allow him to love her.

He didn't know whether the smile effectively communicated this, so he followed it up with a very small Mexican wave.

She laughed – adorably. He laughed too, delighted at her laughter.

'What are we laughing at?' she said.

'I don't know.'

She was grinning gorgeously, and had taken her glasses off. Maybe they were badly adjusted. He would gladly have held them just in front of her face all day to save her any mild discomfort they might possibly cause.

'Why did you say "good"?' she asked.

'What?'

'When I told you Sam's my girlfriend you said "good". I just wondered why… I mean thanks, and it's totally fine and everything. It's just an unusual thing to say.'

'Is it?'

'Yes.'

'What do most people say?'

She blushed and looked around the pub.

'I don't know. They … they change the conversation.'

'Oh.'

She said nothing. *Damn*, he thought. *I can't keep a conversation going with a beautiful woman even when she's neither single nor heterosexual.*

'What um what…' he began, and then groped for a good second half of the sentence. 'What do they change the conversation to?'

'Football,' she said, still blushing but now looking him dead in the eye.

'Really? Why?'

'Who knows? Maybe they think that if you … *like girls* you must like football too.'

'Do you?'

'No. And I can't honestly believe that anyone else does either. Why would you? I think they're all just pretending. After all, it's just some men moving a ball into a net across some grass. They could get a machine to do that for them.'

'Or just keep the balls in the net – no need to move them then.'

'Totally. That's totally right.'

They smiled at each other, and simultaneously turned around to check that no one had overheard them being silly.

'Do you like football?' she asked.

'No,' he admitted, 'but I pretend to.'

She laughed. 'How do you pretend to like football?'

'It's quite easy really. Say, for example, that someone says to me, "Do you like football?" Well then I say, "Yes, I do." They fall for it every time.'

'That's not what you said when I asked you.'

'I know. I forgot.'

'Do you pretend to have a favourite team?' she asked.

He nodded. 'Plymouth Argyle.'

'Why them?'

'Because when I tell people they just sort of nod and then lose interest, which is perfect. I've never met anyone who supports them. I used to pretend to like Manchester United, but people always wanted to know what I thought of them. I don't even have to know any of the players' names for Plymouth Argyle.'

'But people must still ask what you think of football teams. You can't just say, "I like football. My favourite team is Plymouth Argyle." And leave it at that.'

'You'd be surprised. Most people just want to give you their three current football observations and some statistics.'

'But they must want you to contribute *something* to the conversation.'

'Oh yes, definitely,' he said, nodding his head vigorously. 'They want me to say either "that was always going to happen" or "that was never going to happen". If they want more I give them one of my football facts.'

'Your football facts?'

'Yes. I've got three. What number do you want?'

'Number two.'

'In 1878, Charles Wollaston became the first player to win five FA cups.'

'Wow. That's boring.'

Jonathon smiled and waved his hand modestly.

'Why don't you just tell people the truth?' she asked.

'I moved schools a lot as a kid. I found by trial and error that saying you don't like football means that you're gay and want to be punched in the stomach. The three things go together like a … like a horse and um two carriages.'

'I've always been fond of that saying,' she said.

Jonathon took another sip of his pint and realised that she didn't have one.

'Sorry, can I get you a drink?'

He hoped this sounded like the offer of a polite and generous man, rather than of a man who has decided to remain hopelessly in love despite learning that his beloved is a lesbian. This latter was the truth. After all, he reasoned, there had been no realistic prospect of success before, so he hadn't lost anything, and he might get to spend more time with her this way.

'Oh – are you sure?' She did the thing whereby she cocked her head on one side again. It was a cartoonish gesture, like one of his own, and Jonathon predictably found it adorable.

'Um. Yes. What would you like?'

He went to the bar, feeling like a little boy going to the sweet-shop. What an honour. He was buying her a drink. And they were talking, and laughing – and she had told him personal things. Incredible. The odd thing – and also the rather pathetic thing – was that he was getting more of a thrill from sitting at a table in this slightly tatty pub just talking to Rachel than he imagined Lance would get from being fully serviced by two highly qualified call girls. It would be just his luck if the pub were to explode in a devastating bomb-blast while he was talking to her.

CHAPTER TWENTY-THREE

Andrew Thompson, sitting in his newly redecorated London flat with a cup of tea, had the opposite view of the way his luck worked. He was thinking that everything was going so well for him recently that he wouldn't be surprised if all his political enemies were to perish in one enormous destructive blast and he were made Prime Minister, or possibly King of the World.

His growing standing within the party was marked by the number of people who had sought him out to express their sympathy at the death of his secretary. This was so gratifying that pretending to be concerned and upset had grown more and more irksome. The pretence was especially difficult because he was delighted that so many of them had complimented him on his speech at the site of the murder. True, there was the idiotic headline in the *Sun*. And as he had climbed out of his taxi that morning a man had leaned out of a white van, shouted 'Quench my grief!' and then roared with laughter. But the people who mattered were impressed.

Nor was it going too far to include the PM's name among those who were impressed. The PM was on top form at the moment, relaxed for Questions and in total command of the Government benches. Thompson couldn't help noticing that those periods when he was in favour seemed to coincide with the PM's own periods of greatest strength. When the PM was most in control, most sparkling, most potent – then Thompson was liked. Well, he was certainly in favour at the moment. The PM had sat next to him in the chamber, had voted with him, and had even stayed to chat a while in the lobby afterwards. The old sparkle was back in the prime-ministerial eyes.

Thompson felt unstoppable. Promotion had again been hinted at. The PM had been leaving for a cabinet session, but on the point of departure had added, 'I may *see* you *soon*, Andrew'. The peculiar emphasis on 'see' and 'soon' meant, Thompson believed, that he might soon be seen in cabinet. He was almost certain he would be made a Privy Councillor in the next birthday honours. Not that he particularly *wanted* to counsel privies, as he had joked at lunch. *Everyone* had laughed.

The only smut on an otherwise pristine day had been his visit from the police. Two detectives had arrived at two o'clock and taken up a good hour. Though they were at least dressed for the present century, they were as pointlessly and inarticulately verbose as ever policemen are. They didn't actually use the phrase 'I was proceeding in a northerly direction when my attention was drawn to the sound of an altercation, whereupon I blew three short blasts upon my whistle and proceeded to give chase,' but he knew they had wanted to.

They began by confirming everything Lance had told him, or perhaps a little less. Then they asked him about his relationship with Sarah and whether she might have been privy to any embarrassing or confidential documents. These questions, they assured him, were routine, and they didn't press him on any of them – they even seemed to raise the matter with some awkwardness. This all gave him some concern, but the rest of the day had been so wonderful that he decided not to dwell on it. Besides, he had both Mangiafuoco and Lenin & Plover to keep him abreast of the police investigation.

He decided to call Mangiafuoco. He dialled the number on his old rotary phone and waited as it rang.

'Tristan? Hello, it's … Yes, it's me.'

'Oh fine. How's Claudine?'

He picked at a loose thread on a cushion as Mangiafuoco answered.

'Glad to hear it. Good day?'

'Well, that's because you have to spend so much time with policemen: witlessly sarcastic imbeciles to a man.'

'That's why they're making you do this spastic "relaunching" of the Met. Still going round putting up "under new management" signs in every police station?'

He lit a cigar.

'Quite. I've always said so.'

He picked up the phone and took it over to the window.

'I quite agree. What people don't understand is that the Flying Squad has to be disbanded and renamed every decade or so. At least since the War. Corruption thrives in it like rude people in France.'

'No, you're right. They are. And assigning new officers is like putting good fruit on a compost heap and hoping that the freshness will spread.'

He laughed and then groaned.

'Bloody fools. Listen, about this Sarah Morecambe investigation, do you get regular reports?'

'Oh. Do you have it to hand?'

His smile soured.

'Well what good is it there?'

'No, it's just that you're always leaving things in your car.'

'Of course I don't think you're trying to keep me in the dark.'

'I understand that, of course.'

He smiled again, waving the cigar to dispel his doubts.

'Yes, yes.'

'Any plans for this evening?'

'Oh.'

'Then I shall say no, I'll have an early night instead.'

'Well if my "mania" for early nights will be my downfall then you know what yours will be.'

'Exactly. No good has ever come of going to the opera. Look at Lincoln.'

'And I shall see *you* tomorrow.'

Thompson laughed and replaced the receiver.

Tristan had sounded tired on the phone. It was probably as well that he hadn't told him of his encounter with the PM that day – it would have sickened him, and made him even more desperate to be done with his relaunching of the Met.

Thompson's elation returned. He stood and soon found himself dancing about the flat, occasionally singing phrases from the newspapers. 'Firmly in the ascendant', he boomed, and then, in light Gilbert and Sullivan style, trilled, 'Mr Thompson, the subject of much favourable press recently…'

He came to a stop behind the leather sofa which dominated the room, and began an address to an imagined audience.

'In my time as your leader, I have done and experienced many remarkable things – and women. As I stand here, I often find myself nostalgicising about the past – and my thoughts turn to the period during which I served as a junior minister. Even then…'

He soon tired of this and sat down on the sofa. He wanted to make himself get down to some work – his ministerial boxes glared accusingly at him from the other side of the room – but there was a sort of prowling restlessness inside him. He roamed the flat, picking up statuettes, souvenirs, looking idly at some of his paintings. The drinks cabinet sat on the sideboard, waiting. He stalked over and decanted himself a large brandy. As he drank it, he casually pushed a newly-born hint of self-doubt beneath the clear surface of his mind and held it there until it had stopped kicking. There was no need to worry about Sarah Morecambe, the police or Mangiafuoco.

Of course, he knew that the restless hunger stemmed substantially from lust. He was, he reflected, like a panther: sleek and hungry. The mirror beckoned. It showed him in good aspect. Still that boyish look, shoulders a bit rounder of course, and hair a tiny bit thinner, but nothing really to worry about. The jowls were the thing that preyed most on his mind; the skin around his neck was becoming brown, wrinkled and saggy – rather as if Mother Theresa were clinging on beneath his jawline.

A woman was the answer. Jessica, his regular mistress of the moment, was away, but he felt like someone younger anyway, someone to reassure him. He leafed through his address book, idly scanning the pages. When he reached Mangiafuoco's address he paused. 'Tristan, Claudine and Ginia Mangiafuoco,' the entry read. Tristan would be gone by now. *Ginia Mangiafuoco*. He put the thought from his mind. Ginia was an eighteen-year-old whom he'd known for years. She had always had a girlish crush on him. He put the thought from his mind. He reached for the telephone. He laughed: what a ridiculous idea. He would just call and see if, by some chance, Tristan had not yet left after all. He dialled.

'Hello, I don't suppose Tristan's still there, is he?'

He leaned back in his chair.

'Ah. Has he? It's Andrew here.'

He found he was winding the cord around his finger and made himself stop it.

'Is that Ginia?'

He smiled.

'You just sounded so grown-up.'

'Of course you are. Listen, I just remembered something I wanted to talk over with your father. Do you know what time he'll be back?'

'They've gone to the opera?' he asked and winced. Damn, he didn't have to pretend not to know that.

'And they haven't taken you along?'

'Ginia, no one can stand opera. It's just a colossal snobbish conspiracy.'

'Yes, really. It's just like ballet and hunting.'

'Anyway, how are you?'

'Glad to hear it.'

'I'm wonderful. But of course you already knew that, didn't you?'

He chuckled.

'I rather think I am. Terrible bore though, being on one's own in London…'

CHAPTER TWENTY-FOUR

The pub had not exploded, and Rachel was still in it. Both these things surprised Jonathon as he returned from the bar with their drinks and some extra beer that he had managed to absorb into the elbows of his jacket.

Rachel took her drink, sipped, and then looked quizzically at him as he sat down.

'You ain't from round here are you?' she asked in a Southern drawl.

'Um. No – no I, I ain't,' he replied, quickly adding, 'Sorry, that was Cornish. I always get that mixed up with my American accent. Why do you ask?'

'I was just wondering where you're from.'

'Lots of places. We moved around a lot when I was a kid. My dad was always looking for exactly the right kind of dull rural nightmare and he never quite found it.'

'What does your dad do?'

Jonathon sighed. 'He's Richard Fairfax – the novelist.'

'No! You mean *the* Richard Fairfax, bestselling author of *The Carousel Code* and *Orly Riser*?'

'You ought to write his book jackets.'

'Fucking hell! Richard Fairfax – no way!'

'You really like his books?' Jonathon asked sceptically, alarmed that he might soon have to find admiration for his dad's books adorable as well.

She caught the note in his voice. 'Sorry, I bet you totally get sick of talking about your dad, don't you?'

'A bit,' he admitted.

'I haven't really read any of them. Sam's got *JFK*. I think I read a couple of pages. It's just totally bizarre meeting someone…'

'…Whose dad's a famous airport novelist?'

'Yeah.' She paused. 'Do you really not like his books?'

'Um. I suppose I can't really tell. They've always been around. It's weird, he's never encouraged me to read them, or told me not to or anything like that. They're just there. It's just – I suppose it's more just embarrassing.'

'Embarrassing?'

'Yes. I kept going to different schools and at each one they would say, "Here's a new boy, I'd like you all to nick his packed lunch and flush his head down the toilet, because he's the son of Richard Fairfax, the famous airport novelist. By the way, he doesn't like football – which means he's gay and wants punching in the stomach."'

'You poor thing.'

'The toilet bit only happened once, which isn't a bad average for your whole school life I suppose. But it just meant that everything was so much more awkward – it created a sort of barrier.'

Rachel looked at him sympathetically, and seemed unable to think of anything to say, so Jonathon continued.

'I moved to London because my dad hates it so much. We've always lived in really obscure places like Peebles or Llangollen. He uses the names of the Home Counties as swearwords.'

'What?'

'You know some people say "sugar" instead of shit, or they'll say "flip" or "fudge" instead of fuck? If my dad hits himself with a hammer – he does DIY all the time – he'll shout "Oh Kent!" I once heard him call a self-assembly shower unit a "complete Hampshire" when it fell on his foot.'

'No.'

'It's true. That's another thing that I've never really thought was odd, but seems like it now I come to tell someone else. Everyone's parents are weird though.'

'That's true, my dad's totally obsessed with radiators – he calls himself a "Heating Engineer" which is just a plumber really, but he's – he was – always going round checking our radiators at home, listening to them, letting the air out of them. He even taps them with a spoon to check their resonance or something.'

Jonathon laughed.

'Doesn't he do it anymore?' he asked.

'What?'

'You said he *was* always going round…'

'Oh, yes. Him and my mum split up, and I don't really see him anymore. He doesn't have much time for me. He's French, and he moved back there when they split up. My dad's French and my mum's Cockney and I was mostly brought up in Scotland.'

'What are you doing in London?'

'I'm a student: philosophy at UCL. My aunt and uncle live here though, so that helps a bit – laundry and … Oh, there's Sam!'

She waved in that minute way that women often signal to each other. It ought to have been imperceptible across a crowded pub, but Sam saw her straight away and made her way over.

Sam was almost the exact opposite of Jonathon, and quite unlike Rachel. She was a sleek blonde whose beauty was precision-engineered, as though she had been designed by a committee of experts to meet all the criteria of attractiveness. She wore a tight pink T-shirt under her denim jacket, and stood beside their table with her hands on her hips. Taller than both Rachel and Jonathon – though not when combined – she carried herself with a sort of assured sexiness. Seeing the two of them together, Jonathon realised that it wasn't that Rachel was perfect, but that she was imperfect in all the right ways.

Sam gave Rachel a light, quick kiss on the cheek, after which Rachel blushed, stood up and collected her bag.

'Sam – this is Jonathon,' she said.

Jonathon had been thrown into confusion by the arrival of Sam. All at once he became aware of how relaxed he had been. Now, suddenly finding himself in a crowded pub in London with two attractive women, he snapped back into his habitual awkwardness.

'Um. Um. Hello,' he ventured.

'Hi Jonathon!' said Sam brightly. And then equally brightly to Rachel, 'Are you ready?'

Rachel frowned as she messed around with her bag. As she got up to leave, Jonathon's will to live began to desert him. He had thought that they had got on too well for her just to say 'bye' in an over-bright voice and then walk off. There was no way he could ask her if he could see her again. Not in front of Sam – Sam who was so clearly superior to him in every way that it made him feel embarrassed to be seen with himself.

'What are you looking for?' Rachel asked Sam, who was frowning and looking about distractedly.

'Nothing. I heard they've got the mummified body of Barnaby Rudge here, that's all. That's why I suggested it.'

'But…' Rachel began, then seemed to change her mind. 'Maybe he's being cleaned.'

Jonathon realised he could never ask to see Rachel anyway, even if Sam didn't exist. Any woman worth her salt would shoot him down like a mangy cur before he'd even got past his first 'um'. The bright light of real life was beginning to dim again, to be replaced by the half-dark blur of his own private world.

Then Rachel scribbled her phone number on a beermat and gave it to him.

CHAPTER TWENTY-FIVE

Should he change his shirt? A white one would probably be better. It would make him look slightly less old and help accentuate the colour in his cheeks. He knew that it really didn't matter, after all this wasn't a *date*. Preposterous. It would be nice to see Ginia again, though. He changed his shirt anyway, then had some more brandy and watched the news as he waited.

Finally the bell rang. He walked slowly to the door and pressed the intercom. It was her, asking to come up. He buzzed her in. When her knock came he stood and walked languidly to the door, brandy still in hand. She stood, bending slightly forward with anticipation, the smile on her full lips revealing her large teeth as she returned his greeting. Her eyes were wide open.

She came in more slowly than she should have, overcompensating for her nervousness. They kissed, a chaste, formal greeting, and he stood for a second, waiting. Then, since she hadn't volunteered it, he asked for her coat. It was surrendered, revealing young flesh made brown by a combination of foreign holidays and upmarket sun beds. Her coat was an expensive suede imitation of cheap student chic. Under it she wore a tight grey top, a short skirt and a small bow around her neck. Thompson registered her imperfect teeth and gangliness, judging these failings with an avuncular indulgence which fought hard against the natural fussiness of a lecherous old man. He pressed a drink into her waiting hands.

The lights were rather too bright, which made him uncomfortable. But to turn them down now would feel too obvious. He gestured to the leather sofa then sat in the chair opposite her, watching her throat.

'I like your flat,' she said.

'Thank you. You're the first to see it redecorated. The work of Jenkins Nicholson – have you heard of him?'

'I don't think so. Is he an interior designer?'

'Precisely.'

'It's very, um … sensual?' He noticed with disapproval that she had the young person's habit of turning her statements into questions.

'It's intended to evoke the languor and brutality of 1930s Berlin.'

'Oh.'

'This sofa,' he said, moving to sit beside her, 'once belonged to Ernst Röhm.'

'Really?'

It occurred to him that interior design wasn't quite the right subject. She must have been thinking the same because she said, 'Are you still at Defence?'

'Yes.' He hissed the sibilant slightly.

She swallowed and looked down briefly. 'A lot must rest on your decisions.' She had the brandy glass between her knees.

'I find the weighty decisions easier to make.'

'And if you make the wrong decision?'

'I never make the wrong decision. In politics victory always goes to the most ruthless and decisive man.'

'Or woman,' she corrected automatically, then winced at her mistake. 'Are you ruthless?' she quickly added.

She'd only just arrived, but already they were sitting shamelessly close.

'Oh yes,' he replied, again with the trace of a hiss.

She recoiled, as if the sound had alarmed her. Then, regaining her self-control, she leaned closer in to him. It was the movement of someone undergoing an initiation ceremony, instinctively drawing back at the first lick of pain, then summoning the courage to continue.

She took a sip of her drink, obviously searching for something to say.

'Daddy always says that politics is the art of the inevitable.'

She winced again and blushed, but Thompson found the mention of her father almost unbearably exciting. He decided to take control of the situation, to show her exactly what this was, and what was going to happen.

'Would you like some more brandy?' His hand brushed against her breast as it moved for the bottle.

She accepted the brandy and drank some immediately, while he adjusted the shoulder strap on her top. He could see her beginning to get frightened, so he lighted on a neutral topic to calm her down.

'Have you decided which university to go to?' he asked.

They passed back and forth questions and answers about her degree. After a while he saw that, lulled by the banal, automatic conversation, her confidence had returned.

'So, Biology at Caius. Are you ambitious? Do you want to be a famous biologist?'

'I don't know. I haven't really thought too much about my future.' She paused as though she were thinking something over, and then, having come to a decision, took a big gulp of brandy, coughed, and asked, 'Were you always ambitious?'

'Always.'

'Politically? – or other ways too?'

'In all ways.'

'Absolutely all ways?'

'Yes,' he replied, slipping one hand under the shoulder-strap farthest from him. 'But especially this way.'

The brandy was taking effect. She squirmed closer to him and asked, 'Would you do anything for power?'

'Absolutely anything.'

'Absolutely anything?' She looked up at him.

He put his glass down, and moved his hand, still slightly cold from the glass, to her throat. He stroked the black choker she wore.

'Would you kill?' she asked, lips moist and parted.

'Without hesitation or remorse,' he breathed.

'Have you ever killed anyone?'

He kissed her and their teeth collided. She lay back, while he checked his dental work.

'You remind me of James Bond.'

He was immensely pleased. 'And you would be the perfect Bond girl.'

They kissed again, his hand supporting her neck, his thumb still caressing her collar.

'Or maybe a Bond villain.'

She must have seen his displeasure at this because she quickly added, 'A handsome Bond villain though. Not one of those fat ones with scars.'

His hand lingered around her throat still and she began to unbutton his shirt. It suddenly occurred to him that he could kill her and no one would suspect him. The thought increased his excitement, already stoked by how very, very wicked it was to seduce his best friend's daughter. His hands gently moved her shoulder straps down. They kissed again, this time cleverly manoeuvring their teeth out of each other's way.

CHAPTER TWENTY-SIX

Then Lance was there, striding through the pub. He walked past Rachel and Sam as they left, making eyes at Sam.

'Jonathon,' he said, dropping a Manila file on the table and putting his phone on top of it. 'Hey daddy-o, what's up?'

'Lance, hi. I mean hi – uh – amundo?' Jonathon was grinning, and his leg was jiggling up and down.

'Hi-amundo. I never thought of that one. That's good.'

'Thanks.'

'Beer?'

'Oh, yes. Great, thanks.'

While Lance was at the bar, Jonathon ripped a beermat to pieces in a distracted yet methodical way. When Lance returned the table-top was a mess of paper, and Jonathon was starting on another. Lance put the beers down carefully and draped himself over a chair.

'Are you in *lurve*?' he breathed.

Jonathon looked up with a jolt. 'Sorry?' he said.

'Nothing. Just thought you might be head over heels in love with the little lady you were talking to when I came in.'

'Wh … Um, why?'

Lance cast a silent glance across the wrecked beermats, then let it fall on Jonathon's still-jiggling knee.

'And you only said "thank you" once for the beer.'

Jonathon's face broke out in a grin, and then a blush. He started fiddling with a loose thread on his jacket. 'Maybe. I er … I might be a bit.'

'Guess you'll be pretty upset about having just ripped her phone number into about…' Lance pretended to do a quick count, 'four hundred different pieces.'

Jonathon jerked upright, looked around the table in panic and slammed his hand down on the beermat with Rachel's number written on it. He relaxed again, another grin breaking across his face.

'Jesus!' he said. He checked her number was still written on the beermat. It was.

'Have you just met her?' asked Lance.

'Sunday.'

'So what's your next move, big guy?'

'Don't call me big guy.'

'OK.'

There was a pause while Lance waited for Jonathon to answer. When it became obvious he wasn't going to, Lance asked again.

'What's your next move?'

'Do I need a next move?'

'Yes you need a next move.'

'Well, I've got tomorrow morning off, so I thought I might spend that thinking about her. Basically, my plan is to maybe just romantically obsess over her but not really do anything about it.'

'You're playing it cool?'

'I'm playing it scared.'

They both sipped their beers.

'Was that her girlfriend with her?'

'How did you know?'

'There are ways. Besides, she didn't look at *me*,' Lance laughed, but Jonathon thought he meant it.

'You know, I never met one of her type who couldn't be turned – with a little effort,' said Lance. 'You could have her if you really wanted her.'

Jonathon looked away and began choking on his beer.

'You could,' Lance insisted.

'But I do want her.'

'So then you have nothing to worry about.'

'Then why am I so worried?'

'Because you have no faith in yourself.'

'Oh.'

'You know – and I know I shouldn't say this – women are actually very simple. Seriously. All you have to do is remember one or two easy rules…'

'If you're even considering telling me to treat em mean to keep em keen then I will glass you,' warned Jonathon.

'But you do. Straight up. Chicks dig nothing more than a man who isn't responding. It makes it a challenge.'

'Believe me, when it comes to not responding, I'm a master – I could not respond professionally. But I've always found that women are drawn to the tanned hunk nearby who can somehow manage to not respond in a more interesting way than me. I think women are intrigued by a man who isn't responding only when they really want to go to bed with that man anyway. When a man who they don't want to go to bed with isn't responding they tend to put that down to surliness, and either ignore him or get their boyfriend to punch him in the face as hard as he can.'

Jonathon stopped and looked off furiously at the far wall. He finished his pint.

'Wow,' said Lance. 'I guess that blows my whole "not responding" theory out of the water. That was the most I've heard you speak.'

'Well … you know.'

'I suppose I do. Now.'

'Sorry. It's just that every friend I've ever made has at some point sat me down and set me straight about women. And it always boils down "treat em mean" or "just be yourself"–'

'That was the other thing I was going to say.'

'– neither of which works unless you're fundamentally an attractive, confident guy – in other words someone who women already want to sleep with. Plus, which of my selves should I be? There are loads of us in here.'

'I've really touched a nerve, haven't I?'

'You have no idea.'

Jonathon went to the bar for more drinks.

The drinks clanked down on the table and Jonathon folded himself back into his seat. His face was flushed, his eyes were flashing, and his hair stuck up even more wildly at the back.

'So,' he asked Lance. 'Are *you* in love with anyone?'

Lance laughed and took a pull at his beer. Jonathon continued to look at him.

'I'm sorry,' said Lance. 'I didn't realise it was a serious question.'

'It is.'

'No.'

'Not at all?'

'To be honest, the only thing on my mind at the moment is Sarah.'

Jonathon raised his eyebrows, as if to say 'Huh?'

'Sarah Morecambe, who I was speaking to on Sunday, in the cafe – on the phone.' He tapped his phone, which lay on the table, as if to illustrate his point. 'The one who was murdered.'

'Oh, right.'

There was a pause.

'You're in love with *her*?'

Lance sighed. 'No. Have you seen pictures of her? I'd have to be wearing not just my beer goggles but my entire beer wetsuit, with beer flippers, a beer snorkel and close support from a beer submarine.'

'Right. You're not in love with her.'

'Plus she's dead of course. I draw the line at dead.'

Jonathon struggled to switch gear from love to death. How did he feel? He had never met Sarah, or even heard of her until two days before, so he couldn't expect himself to be sad about her death. Even so, he had expected more of himself than this vague excitement at knowing someone who knows someone who is dead. Death, like celebrity, can make anyone interesting.

'Did you know her well?' he asked.

'I met her three times. Four if you count the time she just lay there bleeding.'

'Bleeding?'

Lance nodded very slowly, revelling in the revelation.

'What … But … What happened?'

'You want the whole story?'

'Yes please.'

'OK, but do not tell a soul about this. You understand?' Lance seemed suddenly very earnest, almost worried. But, obviously noticing it himself, he added, 'Or I'm going to have to kick you right in the watutsi.'

'That's OK. I can probably live with a damaged watutsi, but I won't tell anyone.'

'You promise?'

'Yes.'

'Because this is probably the biggest secret you'll ever be told.'

'Right.'

'OK?'

'Yes.'

Lance looked suspiciously about him, and was visibly disturbed to see that two men near them had trench coats hanging over the backs of their chairs.

Jonathon followed his eyes. 'It's the look,' he said. 'Everyone's wearing them.'

Lance shook his head in despair at other people's clothes, looked down at his own impeccable suit as though to reassure himself, and then began.

'You were with me when Sarah called me in the cafe. I told you that she was Andrew Thompson's secretary, and that she asked me to come to her house that evening, and that she thought I was a journalist.'

Jonathon nodded encouragingly.

'So I arrived at her house about five-thirty...'

CHAPTER TWENTY-SEVEN

Sarah was disappointed to find that she was still, two days after her murder, hanging around in her own kitchen.

The body was gone now and the blood had been removed, but she was angry that the police had left paper coffee cups on the work surface. It was only a little thing, but when that's all you have to look at it starts to niggle, especially if you're still shaken from having been murdered recently. They should have a bit more consideration, she thought. No, *respect*. Once you're dead it's respect that people are meant to give you.

She imagined that sooner or later someone would come to conduct her to the next world. Consciousness does persist after death, she had found, so there must be some sort of afterlife. To be honest, she was a bit annoyed about the lack of information. Every other major change in her life had been pretty well marked: periods starting, A-level results, graduation, her first pay-cheque, the keys to her first flat. At each stage there had been advice, people taking her aside and having a few words with her, self-help books, even videos for some things. Now, at this most important change of all, there was nothing. No one had even presented her with a death certificate.

Purrdey hadn't put in an appearance since Monday. She hoped that someone was looking after her. They'd left her bowl though, so perhaps it would be all right about the name. No one needed to know about the extra R.

Apart from Purrdey and trying to figure out why she had been murdered, Sarah spent most of her time wondering about the afterlife. She hoped that she would get a body again. It would be very annoying – not to mention boring – to spend eternity as a disembodied consciousness. It was like permanently being stuck in the middle of the night with insomnia, and not even being able to masturbate.

What sort of body would she get? It seemed unfair to get back the one she'd had just before dying, at the age of thirty-four. She'd got out of the habit of going to the gym in the past six months or so. Call it a year. But that shouldn't count against her for eternity, should it? If you kept the body you died with then the next world (she didn't like to think Heaven or Hell, or any of that) would be full of very old people doddering about and forgetting things, people lying in comas, and people bleeding profusely and shrieking with pain.

What she really hoped was that she would be given the body of her ideal self – the way she'd have been if she'd done everything right: diet, exercise, sleep, everything. Failing that, she hoped she would be as she had been at her best time in life. For Sarah, that meant thirty-two.

At thirty-two she had been engaged to George, who could make her laugh just by scratching his nose, and she was at Youth, Education and Lifelong Learning, her favourite posting. After she and George split up, she tried to fill the gap by concentrating on her career. A higher-grade post came up at DOOM, and she transferred just as Thompson arrived.

She and Thompson disliked each other from the start. She was from Yorkshire, and he pretended to wince whenever she dropped an H. On the second morning she mentioned having a headache and he suggested taking a couple of aspirants and did the little smirk that she wanted to remove from his face with a sand-blaster. He seemed to think she was his servant, and kept asking her to take his dry-cleaning or buy presents for his wife. When she refused he said 'silly girl'. He appeared at the most awkward times, which always seemed to confirm his prejudices about her: she'd always be eating a cake or having a conversation about whippets, or something.

She started to hate work. She dreaded going in. She slept badly. She broke her diet. And she was moving house at the same time.

One day Thompson came back from a long lunch, leant against the door frame and, looking at her through half-closed eyes, drawled, 'My God but it's fat.' She stood, her face red, trembling, and he held up a postcard of an obese cat. 'Isn't it fat?' he asked, and laughed.

After that she began to look through his files in search of anything she could use against him. She copied the keys to his office and his private filing cabinets, and when she knew he was away she ploughed her way through them, holding her breath, terrified he would come back unexpectedly and find her. Once he had come back early – a day early – from a visit to Germany, but Kathy had stopped him and asked a question. She heard his voice in time, covered her traces and locked everything up. She thought that Kathy knew what she was doing.

There had been a few choices of secrets to leak, but she wanted something that would cause no damage to the department or the government – only to him. And she wanted to be sure it would be fatal. When she found the RSG documents, she felt like laughing all day and when she arrived home she skipped around the house singing.

She thought she understood them, but there was a lot to explain to any journalist, and she didn't know any journalists. And then she had met the one with the sad, soulful eyes, and she had known he was exactly right.

CHAPTER TWENTY-EIGHT

When Lance had finished telling his story and Jonathon had finished being astonished, shaking his head and repeating the last word Lance had said in an incredulous voice, both were a bit more sober than they had been. Jonathon was almost shaking with excitement. Firstly, he knew someone who had been at the scene of a murder, who had seen a dead person close-up. Secondly, he was being asked his opinion about a file full of secret information: a file which now lay before him on the table.

'Um. Wow,' he said.

'Yes,' agreed Lance.

'I thought things like this only happened in films. You know, the sort that would be on TV on a Wednesday morning.' He pointed at the file. 'Is that really a file full of secret information that you took from a murdered woman's kitchen?'

'It is, bubba.'

'What's that mark on the corner?'

Lance leaned forward to inspect it.

'Butter.'

'Oh.'

'Go ahead. Have a look.'

Jonathon picked up the file and examined it.

'I mean,' said Lance, 'have a look inside. I know it's butter on the front.'

'Right.'

Jonathon opened the file. The first thing he saw was a piece of paper, yellowed by time, with a green crest at its head: a curly-horned creature perched on a crag, beside the words 'Girard Leviticus Ltd'. Below the crest was typed the word 'CONTRACT'. The parties to the contract were Augustus Zazel, signing for Girard Leviticus Ltd, and Andrew Forbes Thompson.

He looked at Lance. 'Thompson?'

'That's right. I saw him today, to get him to sign a contract. Something weird is going on.'

'Weird?'

'What you said yesterday made me think a bit more clearly. What if the murder wasn't personal? Who would have most to gain from the death of a woman about to leak a file full of contracts with Andrew Thompson's name on them?'

'Andrew Thompson?'

'That's what I thought. So when I saw him today I hinted that I knew the murder was professional.'

Jonathon took a big gulp of beer. 'What did he say?'

'He stopped dead. He asked me if I was testing him.'

'You were, weren't you?'

'Yes.'

'And then?'

'He told me not to get carried away by my imagination. And he queried the contract, which I think was a sort of warning. If I lose us this job because I've implied that our client had his secretary murdered then … Well, I'll be investigating insurance claims for the rest of my career. At best. They might even transfer me to the contracts department with Jamyn. God, that would kill me.'

'What if you showed this file to the papers?'

'I don't know what it means – I suppose Sarah Morecambe was going to explain it to me. They're all just contracts. The first one's eleven years old. The last one's two months old. They're all with this company Girard Leviticus: headquarters in the Cayman Islands. I can't find out anything else about it or about this Augustus Zazel.'

Jonathon, who had been flipping through the file as they spoke, began to look more closely at the first contract.

'Have a look. I'll go to the bar,' said Lance.

'So,' he said when he returned, 'what have you found out?'

'Um. Look.' Jonathon put the first and last contracts side by side on the table, among the fragments of beermat. 'The logo changes. It gets more abstract. In the old contracts it's definitely an animal standing on a rock. By the end it looks like an oblong standing on a triangle. And the name changes too, from Girard Leviticus Ltd to GL.'

Lance gave him an even, empty-eyed stare.

'Right. I leave you to find out why these documents might have led to someone's death and you have mostly noticed emerging trends in corporate branding. Thanks.'

Jonathon flushed. 'But don't you think it might mean something?'

'Like what?'

'I don't know. The contracts are quite secretive: they're almost all about confidentiality, with a big bit about one of the parties following instructions.'

'So what's that got to do with the logo?'

'Maybe the name and logo give away a secret. When my dad was writing *The Carousel Code* he used to talk about the book of Leviticus all the time. It's all about laws and rituals with secret meanings.'

'And Girard?'

'Nicholas Emir Brunsengett talks a lot about someone called some-one Girard – André Girard? – in *The Sound of Five Hats Thinking*–'

'You read some idiot-arse books.'

'Um. Yes. I do. But Girard wrote about religion. Maybe there's a link?'

Lance covered his face with his hands. 'Oh God.'

'What?'

'Let's just pretend the last three minutes didn't happen. OK?'

'What do you mean?'

'I mean that I need to work out what to do next. It sounds to me like you're saying the answer is "read the Bible". In my experience, whenever the answer to any question is "read the Bible" then you can be absolutely certain that you're asking the wrong question.'

'But–'

'I also have a new rule of thumb. Whenever the answer to any question is "read the works of Nicholas Emir Brunsengett", you're not only asking the wrong question but speaking entirely the wrong language. You may also be dreaming, blind and insane.'

'Oh. Sorry.' Jonathon took a sip of beer, hiding his shame behind a glass.

'Right.' Lance sighed. 'But you looked at the contracts though. That's good.' He smiled encouragingly and gave Jonathon a playful punch on the arm. 'Confidentiality and instructions. What else did you notice?'

'Um,' Jonathon was afraid to say something stupid again. 'RSG.'

'What?'

'RSG. Thompson is defined in the contract as "the RSG".' He pulled a contract from the pile and pointed to the first mention of RSG.

'Isn't that just a standard legal term?'

'I don't think so. I've never heard of it.'

'Why would you? You work in menswear.'

'I did a Law A-level.'

'What did you get?'

'I got a B.'

'Maybe you'd have got an A if you knew what RSG means.'

Jonathon put the rest of the file on the table and crossed his arms.

'Hey, sorry,' said Lance, seeing his expression. 'I was just goofing about.'

Jonathon continued to say nothing.

Lance said, 'I'm worried, that's all. Tell me about RSG.'

'I'm only trying to help,' said Jonathon.

'I know, I know. Go on: RSG.'

'Well, usually contracts define the parties involved. Like if it's a lease then they talk about "the lessor" and "the lessee". Or it could be a "buyer" and a "seller". But all these contracts say they are between "A" and "the RSG". And it's Thompson who's defined as the RSG.'

'OK.'

'Well, you don't know what the contracts are about, but you know Thompson's the RSG. If you knew what RSG stood for then you might have an idea of what his role is.'

Lance sighed again. 'I might,' he said. 'But how do I find out? If I ask him he'll suspect something.'

Lance drained his drink. He pointed to Jonathon's almost full glass and raised his eyebrows.

'Um, not for me. Thank you.'

Jonathon watched him waft over to the bar. Within a minute a girl had appeared next to Lance. She jogged his elbow accidentally and turned absently to apologise. When Jonathon's eyes returned from their next perambulation of the pub she was saying something and Lance was nodding, and this led on to a full-scale conversation. She was wearing a white vest-top and her black hair was pulled back a little too severely from her forehead into a sleek ponytail.

Lance was grinning as he sat back down with their drinks. 'Guess who scored?' he asked.

'Me?' asked Jonathon, sarcastically.

'Close. It was actually me.'

'Damn.'

A second later the girl came over, having fetched her coat from another table. Lance introduced her to Jonathon.

'This is Jonathon.'

She smiled and did a little wave. 'Helloooo!' she said and laughed. 'I'm Mel.'

'And Jonathon this is…'

'Mel?'

Mel giggled and swished her ponytail about as she watched Lance tidying the papers away into the file and putting it in his briefcase.

Jonathon grasped surprisingly quickly what was required of him. After about five minutes of staying in the background of the conversation he looked at his watch, said, 'Shit! My bus!' then grabbed his jacket and was gone.

CHAPTER TWENTY-NINE

She opened her eyes narrowly, unsure about waking. The brandy-fog was still around her. She felt terrible. In fact, she felt so terrible that it occurred to her that she might actually be dead. Just then she felt a cool hand brush the hair from her forehead.

'Ginia?'

She mumbled in reply.

'Ginia, it's late. I've ordered a taxi for you. Are you all right?'

She sat up, uncertainly, disliking this return to a world in which she had to move about and say things. How pathetic of her to fall asleep – he would know she wasn't used to brandy. He was sitting beside her, clutching her coat, his shirt buttoned but the sleeves rolled up. She felt his hand touch her leg.

'How are you feeling?'

'Hmmmmm?' Her mouth was dry and tacky at the same time. 'How long have I been asleep?'

'Not long, but it's getting late,' he offered her the coat. His voice seemed very paternal now. 'Is there anything you'd like before the taxi arrives?'

She tried to smile, but couldn't. She desperately wanted to be at home now, in her pyjamas. There's innocence in pyjamas.

'Where's the bathroom?'

He stood up with her and motioned her towards the bathroom. Inside she locked the door, took a deep breath and looked at herself in the mirror. She almost screamed. Her mascara was smeared across her face, and her lipstick seemed to have jumped an inch to the right. The thought of the mess she must have made on the sofa bothered her. She stayed there in the bathroom for quite a while, washing her face and mouth, avoiding her own eyes in the mirror, hoping to last out until the taxi came. Sitting on the toilet, she thought she was going to cry. But she didn't. After all, she thought, she had got what she had come for: sex. To protest about it would be like going to a barbecue and saying indignantly, 'Well I had no idea there would be *hot dogs* here'.

There was a knock at the bathroom door. It opened and Thompson came in with a glass of water for her. He whispered gently that the taxi had arrived. When she had drunk the water she followed him out of the bathroom to the door of the flat. He opened it and led her out into the corridor. Ginia still felt woozy, and she knew that Thompson could tell. He held her by the shoulders and looked deep into her eyes.

'Are you all right, Ginia?' he asked.

She looked back at him, not really knowing what to think or say. They were standing there in the corridor, outside his flat, while he looked into her eyes and she looked at the light switch behind his head. He kissed her on the lips.

'Ginia?' His voice came to her from a long way away. 'Oh Ginia.' He sounded tired and a bit sad, but oddly comforting.

He held her close to him, and she was a child again. They stood like that for a while, until the taxi sounded its horn again outside. Then Thompson kissed her on the forehead and stood back from her again.

'Are you steady enough on your feet?' he asked.

She managed to mumble that she was.

'Here's some money for the taxi. Make sure he takes you right to your door and stays until you're inside. All right?'

She nodded.

'You remember where the front door is?' He smiled again, and pointed down the stairs. 'Just one flight of stairs.'

Ginia looked down the stairs. She felt a bit less dizzy now. 'I'll be fine, thank you,' she said. 'You can go in. I don't need to be watched down the stairs.'

He looked at her again, smiled, and then walked inside as she'd asked and gently closed the door behind him. She had wanted him to go inside so that she could cry quickly now, before going outside to the taxi.

WEDNESDAY

CHAPTER THIRTY

That morning Jonathon's body woke at seven and, ignoring his protests that he had the morning off, refused to allow him to go back to sleep. He pulled on some clothes and rattled downstairs to the kitchen to make himself some tea. Then he hauled himself back upstairs to drink it.

He lay on his bed, staring at the sloping ceiling that made him stoop, and thinking about how annoyed he was with Lance. Not only had Lance sat him down and told him a few things about women, but he had then mocked Jonathon's advice about the file. It wasn't as though Jonathon had ever claimed to be good at giving advice on stolen secret documents – in fact, he didn't even claim to be good at the things he was good at. And then, having belittled Jonathon's opinions, Lance had taken off with some cheap Jezebel.

Jonathon was especially annoyed with Lance because he thought they had got on well the other times they had met. He'd been quite proud that the person he suspected might be his first friend in London was so cool. But perhaps Lance had just been pretending to get on with him.

Lance had obviously been born under a lucky star. He had, thought Jonathon, probably been born cool and good-looking. He had probably slipped nonchalantly from the womb, tossing the umbilical cord carelessly over one shoulder like an offal scarf. The midwife had probably been unable to bring herself to give him the traditional slap with which babies are inducted into the world. Jonathon imagined Lance's mother cooing over him for months, surrounded by the friends who had suddenly begun to visit much more regularly, bringing toys and clothes for her dashing baby.

Jonathon, on the other hand, had been born under a collapsed star, a black hole. He had probably taken a long time to get half-way out, and then, just when everyone had lost interest, suddenly plopped out looking embarrassed and apologetic. When the midwife had finally noticed his presence and given him a half-hearted slap he had probably not cried but just shot her a hurt glance.

It suddenly occurred to him that, rather than feeling aggrieved at the manner of Lance's imaginary birth, he should be feeling happy that Rachel had given him her phone number. He got up and checked his suit pocket for the beermat she had written it on. It wasn't there. He wasn't even surprised. Of course it wasn't there. It was something good, and he knew very well that good things either a) don't happen, or b) are immediately cancelled out by bad things. He checked his trouser pocket but it wasn't there either. Nor was it on his table, the floor or the bed. It wasn't in his Folder of Important Things. It wasn't at the bottom of the wardrobe. It wasn't under the bed with the posters and the three magazines (which he might not now make himself throw away). It wasn't on the stairs. He didn't even know whether he'd taken it from the pub, as he couldn't clearly remember leaving, journeying home or arriving in his room.

It was gone. He decided to spend some time lying face down on the floor.

After a few seconds he was startled by a knock at the door. It was probably Avi, wanting to tell him something about the bathroom. He continued to lie face down on the floor. The knock came again. *What if it's Rachel?* said a voice in his head. *It definitely isn't Rachel*, he told the voice in his head. Despite knowing that it definitely wasn't Rachel he got up, looked at himself in the mirror, and wiped some bits of carpet from his face. The knock sounded once more and Jonathon thought he heard footsteps retreating. *Don't let her go!* shouted the voice in his head.

He scrabbled at the handle, pulled it open and charged into the corridor, only to find he had been wrong about the retreating footsteps because he nearly barrelled straight into Lance, who was standing outside.

'Whoa,' said Lance.

'Hup, um, oops, sorry,' said Jonathon, rearing like a frightened horse and looking confusedly around him.

'Hi,' said Lance.

'Um. Hello,' replied Jonathon.

'Sorry, I mean hi-amundo,' corrected Lance.

Jonathon grinned.

'Actually do you mind if I don't come in, I prefer to be less comfortable,' said Lance.

'Oh sorry. Come in.'

Lance breezed past into the room. He moved over to the table and picked up a pencil, tested its strength between his fingers, and put it back down.

'Do you want a cup of tea?' asked Jonathon.

When they had their tea in their hands they began to talk.

'Hey, I'm really sorry about last night,' said Lance.

'What do you mean?'

'I mean being a wanker when you had the Bible idea, and then going off with that girl. I just – I'm sorry.'

'What for? I left first. It's fine.'

'I don't know, I just feel bad about it. I mean, I just shagged someone right in the middle of our conversation. I was enjoying that conversation as well. And I think you're right about this RSG thing.'

'Um.'

'It's just a sort of reflex, I guess. Whenever there's something worrying me, I just pick up some girl and take her home.'

'Wow.'

'Anyway, it was rude, so,' he held out his hand, 'sorry.'

Jonathon shook it.

'You still got this morning off?' asked Lance.

'Yes.'

'How would you like to come along on an assignment?'

'What kind of an assignment?'

'A very cool assignment.'

'A cool assignment?'

'I think I already dealt with that question when I said a *very* cool assignment.'

'Sorry.'

'Hey, it's nothing. Coming?'

'Um. Yes. I – Let me just change my trousers. And go to the bathroom.'

'You do what you have to do with your trousers. I'll be in the car.'

Jonathon gathered up a pair of jeans and disappeared into the communal bathroom he shared with six others. Its emptiness was a miracle, as it was almost constantly occupied by a man called Avi who lived downstairs. Jonathon had often wondered whether the man might not in fact be some sort of land-going fish, able to survive only for short periods outside a bathroom environment.

Having changed into his jeans, emptied his bladder, cleaned his teeth and become briefly distracted by a new kind of toothpaste, Jonathon emerged from the bathroom. He hoped Lance – whose descending footsteps he could hear on the stairs – hadn't seen anything embarrassing while he'd been in the room alone. He changed into a jumper which, though slightly threadbare, was currently one of the few leisure garments he owned that didn't make him feel like a member of staff in a sixth-form science department. As he was trying to make his hair lie down at the back a horn sounded in the street outside. He grabbed his keys and ran downstairs.

CHAPTER THIRTY-ONE

'It's because Suzie and Pierre got divorced when she was so... Oh, look – here we are.'

Lisa grabbed the murderer's sleeve and pointed down the aisle. He brought the trolley to a halt and tried to follow her finger. Gemma, sitting in the little plastic seat mounted at the back of the trolley, waved her cow, trying to distract him.

'What are you looking at now?' he asked Lisa.

'Paints, love.'

'I thought we was going to look at washing machines,' he said, already pushing the trolley over to the paints.

'We are, but we need something to put on the walls, don't we?'

The murderer bent, picked up two large cans of paint and set them in the trolley.

'Done,' he said.

'Hold on, love. You can't just go painting everything white.'

'Why not?'

'Well, it's boring – and cold.'

'No chance of that the way you are with the heating. Paint'll probably melt off of the walls. Probably 'vaporate.'

'Seriously love. White won't go with the units.'

'You're joking aren't you? What doesn't go with white? Anyway, the units are practically white.'

'That's why you can't have the walls white. You need a colour opposite.'

'I need a wife opposite, that's what I need. What's a colour opposite when it's at home?'

'It's ... It's too complicated to explain, specially when you're in this mood.'

He stooped and picked up Gemma's cow from the floor.

'You drop that again and we're leaving it,' he told her. 'You hear?' Then, turning to his wife, 'What mood am I in all of a sudden?'

'Never mind. Let's leave the paints. There's one place – Wickes, I think – where they let you mix your own. Could go there another day.'

He had begun pushing the trolley on but he brought it up sharply.

'What do I want to mix my own paint for?'

'Well, so you can mix exactly what colour you want.'

'I don't want. I want some ponce to do that for me, give it a name like "Orchard Breeze" or something, charge me twenty quid a can.'

'Oh, love.'

'What? Even better, just mix some white and some white, give it a name like – oh, now let me see – "White", charge me a fiver.'

'Let's look at them washing machines.'

They started off again, making for the relatively interesting area of the shop where the machines were.

'What was that about Suzie and Pierre?' he asked.

'You just want to argue today, don't you?'

'How's that arguing? You was saying something about Suzie and Pierre and then stopped to talk about colour opposites...'

'All right, love,' she interrupted. 'Sorry.'

'I was *only*–'

'I know, love. I'm sorry. I was just saying they got divorced when she was fourteen – bad age for it.'

'Bad age for what?'

'Bad age for your mum and dad to get divorced, that's all. Not good for her, you know.'

'Well she's better off without Pierre. Don't know what Suzie ever saw in him. Did them a favour when he pi– when he hopped off back to France.'

'I'm just saying that she don't trust relationships, that's all. That's why she don't have a boyfriend.'

'Why should she have a boyfriend?'

'Don't you think she's pretty?'

'Course I do. Gorgeous. Don't mean she has to have a boyfriend.'

'I'm not saying she *has* to have one–'

'Used to be a boy myself. I can tell you she's best off keeping away from them. Scum we were at that age. Wait till she finds the right one.'

Lisa shook her head the way she did when she thought he was

114

missing the point.

'It'll be the same for Gemma,' he persisted. 'I hope she don't have a boyfriend at nineteen.'

'Well I hope she does.'

Gemma threw the cow over the side of the trolley again, and the murderer stooped to pick it up.

CHAPTER THIRTY-TWO

Lance was sitting in a black BMW in the street outside, playing with its cigarette-lighter, which seemed to be of an unusual design. Jonathon got in and Lance lit a cigarette, then offered the pack to Jonathon, who hesitated only slightly before taking one. Lance pulled smoothly off and they scooted nimbly through the back-streets and got stuck in a traffic jam as soon as they hit the main road.

'Is this car yours?' asked Jonathon.

'No, it's the agency's. They have three black Beamers – all identical, except that one of them's a turbo. No one ever uses them, so I booked this one out.'

'What's the, um, what's the assignment?'

'Remember I told you it was very cool?'

'Yes.'

'Well I was lying. At least, I was lying if you consider very cool to be parachuting into a Russian dacha, taking out the guards, kidnapping the beautiful wife of a mafia boss, then finding she's in love with you whilst you whisk her away in a specially modified light aircraft.'

'That would be very, *very* cool, you just promised very cool.'

'OK. You might not be disappointed then. We're going to the heart of the British political establishment – Whitehall.'

Not knowing what to say, Jonathon contented himself with 'woo'.

'Woo indeed, Mr Fairfax. Actually we just have to pick up a new contract from my office and take it to Andrew Thompson, talk him through it, get it signed and then return it to the office.'

Jonathon hadn't really been expecting anything, but the idea of going both to Lance's office and to Whitehall was quite exciting, particularly for someone who got nervous just asking for a straw in McDonald's.

They drove along by the Thames, its grey waters twinkling silver in the morning sun. Neither had talked now in a good five minutes. Lance seemed preoccupied. He kept tapping his hands rhythmically on the wheel and chewing his lower lip. Occasionally he would shoot a nervous glance down a side street, or turn around to look behind them.

Finally he broke the silence. 'You know what the problem with me is?' he asked.

Jonathon opened his mouth but didn't venture a reply, so Lance answered his own question.

'The problem with me is that I'm a very shallow sort of person. I have a cool job, some nice clothes, good hair, I could do with a shave...' He felt his chin speculatively, and seemed to have lost his thread a bit, before he remembered himself and continued, 'I earn good money, and get laid whenever I like. But I feel like I'm having a ... a...' He hesitated.

'Crisis? Enema? Ice cream?'

'Problem. With these documents. But even then, these are secret government papers that I found in a murder-victim's flat. All I can think about is how cool that is. See? Shallow. People just see me as this cool, dashing guy with no depth at all.'

'Um. But,' said Jonathon. He was feeling awkward. Hearing this from Lance was like hearing the Pope protesting that he was just seen as a religious figure. The only reasonable response was, 'Well yes, but isn't that the point?'

'I envy you,' Lance continued. 'You're a complicated sort of person. You have neuroses – everything's such a *trial* for you. You make everything into a sort of weird little game just so you can get through it. I bet you even do it with stuff like eating food and doing your laundry.'

Jonathon didn't know what to say, except to congratulate Lance on his extraordinary perspicacity. He struggled for a while, but finally found a response.

'But isn't it better to be cool, sexually active and free of weird neuroses than to be...' He trailed off, not wanting to say 'like me'.

'You've got depth. Depth's worth a lot.'

'How much?'

'Easily a tenner. Minimum.'

The traffic was glutting around Cleopatra's Needle and their conversation stopped in sympathy with it. Jonathon had just opened his mouth to say something, when a red Ford Transit tried to pull in front of their car. Lance pressed a button and the window slid open.

'Fuck off,' he remarked to the van driver.

'Quench my grief!' said the driver, a beefy man in a vest made of string.

Both seemed to accept the other's position. They sat quietly, equably.

After a while Lance turned back to Jonathon and said, 'I keep thinking about what RSG means. It can't be Royal Society of Geographers. It just can't.'

'No one would give Thompson a contract to be the Royal Society of Geographers.'

'Exactly.' Lance frowned. 'That fucking *file*. If only I knew what I had, I could do something with it.'

'I ought to get that put on a T-shirt.'

Lance looked at him sidelong. 'Do me a favour and you can have all the T-shirts you want.'

'A favour?'

'Yes. I think I've thought of a way to find out what RSG stands for.'

They eventually arrived in Soho. The BMW trickled through the busy streets, past the vestiges of seediness. The nostalgically preserved sex shops were like scattered remnants of an ancient civilisation destroyed by the hordes of TV production companies, up-market bars and new concepts in design-led marketing consultancy which had swept through the area.

They arrived in Soho Square just as a giant Mercedes pulled out of its parking space outside Lance's office. Lance eased the car into the space and jerked the handbrake on.

'OK. Let's go get us that contract,' he said.

Jonathon undid his seatbelt at only the second try and followed him. Inside, Lance grinned at the skinny security guard in his over-sized blazer and moustache, and sauntered over to the lift.

'The guy in the contracts office is a wanker,' confided Lance as they glided upwards. 'So just try to ignore him if you can. His name's Jamyn.'

'Jay-min,' repeated Jonathon.

'Call him Jason if you want to really annoy him. And believe me, you will want to really annoy him.'

The lift stopped and a synthesised female voice said, '*Third* floor. Doors … *op*ening.'

As Jonathon followed Lance out of the lift, he was startled to hear it say 'Thank you'. He jumped slightly and muttered his thanks in return, grinning with embarrassment and tripping over his feet in his haste to escape from another tricky social situation.

The door to the contracts office was open and through it Jonathon could see a man sitting in a luxurious leather chair at a flimsy desk topped with sticky-backed plastic. He was typing something on a computer that looked like a piece of the future had been cut into an interesting shape and then polished to a high sheen. Grubby filing cabinets, shelves, racks and an old chest of drawers were the room's main furniture, clustered around the walls. On the wall facing the door hung Jamyn's Oxford degree certificate.

'Hey Jamyn,' said Lance in an amiable way.

The man at the computer looked up and spun his chair around to face them. He obviously enjoyed spinning in his chair, and he did it now with the sort of well practised glee that spoke of many long hours with the door closed and no pressing business.

'Lance! Grand to see you,' said Jamyn in a very public-school accent, garnished with a light sprinkling of finely-chopped cockney. He was a thin man, and so tall that even seated he seemed to tower over Jonathon and Lance. He wore pin-striped trousers with red braces and rolled up shirt-sleeves. His tie was pink, and his hair so solidly gelled it looked as though he probably just took it off and left it on the mantelpiece when he got home at night.

Lance made a courtly gesture towards Jonathon.

'This is Jonathon,' he said. 'We're delivering the contract to Thompson.'

Jamyn stood up and stretched across the desk to shake Jonathon's hand.

'Grand to meet you,' he said, giving him a firm handshake. All his gestures and mannerisms seemed somehow foreign to him, as though he had learned them from a manual. Jonathon became briefly confused as he tried to work out how firm he should make his own handshake. By the time he had decided to make it as firm as possible, he should already have given Jamyn his hand back.

Jamyn extricated his hand and turned back to Lance. 'Been working hard?' he asked, flexing his shoulders as though he had just done a couple of sets of imperceptible bicep curls.

Lance nodded.

'Ah-ha! But have you been *playing* hard?' asked Jamyn, miming a tennis volley.

'As hard as I can,' replied Lance.

'Why am I asking this man if he's been playing hard?' asked Jamyn, giving a textbook chuckle, 'Like asking the Pope if he's been … been…'

He was obviously having difficulty with the simile, and Jonathon couldn't help but suggest 'praying hard?' just as Jamyn finished with 'Polish'. Lance flinched a little and Jamyn did the chuckle again, then mimed a golf swing across the carpet. He actually shielded his eyes and looked into the distance, watching the ball recede down the invisible fairway. After a couple of seconds, apparently satisfied with his shot, he returned to his chair and tapped a couple of keys on the computer.

'Now – the contract,' he said.

'Yes,' said Lance, clapping his hands together. 'I think Thompson's playing games with me. He said that the contract was about five percent more expensive than he'd agreed with Bob Plover.'

'Oh, he noticed,' said Jamyn, leaning back ostentatiously, hands behind his head.

'What?'

'We make all the contracts five percent more expensive than the client agreed. No one ever spots it.' He smiled a large white smile.

'How long have we been doing that?'

'Since Plover arrived, so I suppose it's been–' he checked his watch '–over a year now.'

'I've never noticed.'

'People don't.'

'Thompson did,' said Jonathon.

Jamyn shrugged.

'So what do you do when people notice?' asked Lance.

'I don't know. Say sorry?'

'This might actually help us,' said Lance. 'Can we print the contract again, but with a discount that brings it down to the right price?'

'Yah. Discount. Nice idea. That's a 4.7619% reduction to get it back to the right price.'

'Right.' Lance looked momentarily surprised about the maths, but shook his head and continued, 'And can you label it "RSG discount"?'

'No problemo.' Jamyn rattled away at his keyboard. 'Control-P – print. What does RSG stand for?'

'No idea.'

'This guy!' Jamyn pointed at Lance, shaking his head and pulling a face. 'What a guy.'

Jonathon, attempting to mirror Jamyn's expression of admiring disbelief, once again ended up with Princess Anne.

'So, Lance,' said Jamyn. 'You've talked people through these contracts before, haven't you?'

'Yeah.'

'Grand,' said Jamyn, leaping balletically from his seat, checking his lacquer helmet again and moving over to the printer.

'He obviously takes the white copy and you bring the yellow, blue and pink copies back here, if that's OK.'

The contracts were still printing, so Jamyn took another couple of practice swings and checked his hair again. Finally the printer eased out the last copy. Lance shook hands with Jamyn again, said that it was grand doing business with him, and Jonathon, not wanting to seem rude, bagged a brace of grouse with both barrels of an imaginary shotgun.

Then they went to see Thompson.

CHAPTER THIRTY-THREE

'I'm free!' said Plover in a growly falsetto, putting the phone to his ear and leaning back into the most relaxing of his chair's seven ergonomic settings.

'Yeah, I suppose it is a quotation. "Are You Being Served", the programme was called. Surprised you've ever seen it.' He put his feet up and reached for a paperclip with which to pick his teeth.

'Mr Humphries, he was called.'

'I wouldn't go that far. Just a bit theatrical, that's a–'

'Course. Business.'

The smile flopped from his baggy face.

'I've told you,' he said, putting his feet on the ground and bringing his chair to its second most tense position, 'I don't *know* what went wrong.'

'Course I'll tell you. Soon as I know.'

He stood up.

'He's a very difficult man to pin down.'

'Believe me, you don't want to talk to him direct.'

'I'm doing all I can.'

'Yes, I've been round there. He don't go there every day though, he's...'

He stopped. 'How do you know about that anyway? I never told you.'

'Fine.' His sigh flapped his cheeks about. 'Best not tell me on this phone anyway, even if you wanted to.'

He listened, nodding his head impatiently, and trailed the phone over to the window.

'Word of advice. Since you watch so much telly all of a sudden. You seen that insurance ad? "Why not cut out the middleman?" Well, there's a fucking good reason not to cut out the middleman. Don't you ever underestimate how much the middleman does.'

He interrupted again. 'You cut out the middleman and you might save a tenner – you *might* – but the insurance company will come round and burn your house down.'

'What? No, it's a metaphor.'

'You know exactly what I'm saying. You might be the puppet-master controlling everything behind the scenes, but your problem is that your power's secret. Not many people want to do you a favour. And because you're posh you'll never really understand how the muscle end of this business works.'

'Fine. I called him an hour ago but I'll call him again now. Yes.'

'Bye-bye!'

He slammed the phone and receiver together, then took them over to his desk and rapidly tapped out a number.

He waited.

'Finally! I've been trying to get hold of you for ages.'

CHAPTER THIRTY-FOUR

Jonathon was beginning to grow nervous about going to Whitehall. He had prepared a cover story in case he was picked up by the security men on the door, whisked away to an underground interrogation chamber and grilled by a weary, heavy-set man with a vicious temper and a thin, intense agent who smoked incessantly. He would tell them that he was accompanying a friend who was delivering a contract to a minister. The fact that the cover story was identical to the truth only added to its baroque cunning, making it more plausible and easier to remember.

In any event the cover story was unnecessary. They were issued with a permit by a little security guard with an oversized blazer and moustache, and then ushered into a waiting room by a slightly jollier security guard in vaguely nineteenth-century formal wear.

Eventually a man of about Jonathon's age, who introduced himself as Gareth, came to guide them to Thompson's office. They followed him up a flight of stairs and round a few carpeted corridors while he pointed out various priceless treasures being helpfully kept in trust for the people. Finally, disoriented, they arrived at the door to Thompson's kingdom.

The door stood open, revealing a large, stately room badly disfigured by filing cabinets, computers and a secretary.

'These gentlemen are here to see Mr Thompson,' said Gareth smoothly.

The woman looked at them and raised her eyebrows.

'Lance Ferman and Jonathon Fairfax, Lenin & Plover Associates,' explained Lance, slipping her a card.

She took the card disdainfully and pressed a button on her phone. 'A Mr Forman to see you from–' she glanced at the card '–Leonine and Plougher. It's not in the book.'

She paused, listening.

'Well I wish you wouldn't.'

Another pause.

'Right. I will.'

She looked up. 'He says you're to go in now.'

Gareth bounded to the door at the end of the room and opened it, graciously ushering them inside.

Thompson was already on his feet as they entered, his veiny hand outstretched to shake both of theirs. Jonathon thought he could detect a faint look of surprise in the minister's eyes as he took in Jonathon's jeans, jumper and sticking-up hair. It was the first time in his life that Jonathon had seen in real life a man whom he had also seen on television. Thompson was smaller than he had expected, and much more detailed.

After the introductions, the polite smiles, the settling into chairs and the silent wishing that Jonathon wasn't wearing jeans, they got down to business. Jonathon was glad that Lance hadn't tried to explain the presence in this Whitehall meeting of a Harrods sales assistant who had trouble cooking fish. As it was, Thompson would reach his own entirely acceptable conclusion, whereas any explanation they gave would seem invented and bizarre.

'You have the new contract?' asked Thompson.

Lance withdrew it from his briefcase and passed it over the desk. 'I'm very sorry. Our finance department neglected to apply your discount.'

'Ah.' Thompson smiled the smile of a man who is politely pretending to believe a lie. 'Let's see…'

Jonathon had heard the expression 'the blood drained from his face' but had always assumed that it was just a figure of speech, like people's hair standing on end. Now he had seen it with his own eyes. The glow had gone from Thompson's face, leaving it a sort of lightly tanned grey colour, like expensive porridge.

'What … What's this?'

'What's what?' asked Lance.

'This discount.'

Jonathon realised that this was his cue. 'I was wondering that myself,' he said. That, at least, was what he meant to say. The words that reached his ears were, 'I wond wasering that myself.'

He tried again. 'I was wondering that myself. What *does* RSG stand for?'

This time the words 'was wondering' were eclipsed by the sound of the door opening. His question seemed to hang in the air for a moment. There in the doorway stood the second real-life person whom Jonathon had also seen on television. His moustache was gigantic and black, his head perfectly flat. He was smaller than Jonathon had expected and, again, far more detailed, like a baby's hand.

'I'm awfully sorry,' said Mangiafuoco. 'Your secretary told me you didn't have anything in the diary.'

Thompson had by now pushed some blood back into his face. 'I don't have this in the diary,' he said, reclining and attempting a smile, 'and my secretary's punishing me for it.'

Mangiafuoco surveyed the two visitors.

Lance rose. 'I'm Lance Ferman, Lenin & Plover. And you must be the honourable Tristan Mangiafuoco.'

'I have that honour,' replied Mangiafuoco, with what struck Jonathon as being a hideous oily grin.

Mangiafuoco shook Lance's hand, then turned to Jonathon, who was rooted to his chair.

'Ah,' said Lance. 'This is Jonathon Fairfax.'

'Jonathon,' said Mangiafuoco, leaning over and shaking his hand too. He raised his eyebrows, as though expecting Jonathon to be explained in some way.

'Tristan Mangiafuoco,' said Lance to Jonathon.

'Right,' said Mangiafuoco foolishly, as though this was the explanation he had been waiting for. 'Pleased to meet you.'

'Um. M-meat to please you,' said Jonathon.

Mangiafuoco raised his eyebrows again. There was a silence which grew so long and dense you could have wallpapered it. Finally Mangiafuoco collected himself and said, 'Er, forgive me. I believe you were asking a question when I intruded.'

'Oh. Um. I was just asking what RSG stood for, on the contract.'

Mangiafuoco and Thompson exchanged a glance.

'Can. Ah.' Jonathon was terrified, but persisted with the question. 'Can, can you think what it might be, Mr Thompson?'

'Please, call me Andrew. And no, I've no idea. I rather thought that you Lenin & Plover people might understand your own contracts. Who prepared it?'

'Jamyn, in Contracts,' said Jonathon.

'I've just remembered,' said Lance. 'I was told earlier. Slipped my mind. It's Royal Standard Gratuity. That's the highest. One up from Duke Standard.'

'Well, we didn't learn much from that,' said Lance, handing Jonathon his briefcase and buckling his seatbelt.

'Oh,' said Jonathon, surprised. 'Didn't we?'

'Unless Thompson explained what RSG means in a voice only Jonathons can hear. Did he?'

Lance turned the key and the car took a breath.

'No,' said Jonathon, trying to wrestle more seatbelt from the dispenser by his shoulder.

'So what did we learn?'

'How do you get this to give you enough seatbelt?'

'Just pull,' said Lance, nosing the car out of its parking space.

'I am.'

'You're snatching. You need to pull.'

'I thought I was.'

'Let go.'

Lance leaned across and pulled the seatbelt out for Jonathon.

'How come it works for you?'

'Because I treat my seatbelts the way I treat my women.'

'How's that?'

Lance said, 'I pull them without them noticing.' He winked roguishly.

Jonathon looked out of the window at some drunken Australians.

Lance said, 'I guide them gently but firmly across my lap.' He winked roguishly.

Jonathon continued to look out of the window.

Lance said, 'I slacken them off and plug them in.' He winked roguishly.

Jonathon turned. 'That one doesn't even mean anything.'

'Yes it does.'

'What?'

'Get your momma to tell you.'

Jonathon relapsed into silence.

'So what did we learn?' said Lance again.

'Well, I thought we saw the way Thompson went pale and Mr Mangiafuoco looked at us when we said RSG and that made us think that maybe Mangiafuoco has something to do with the whole thing.'

'Like what?'

'I don't know. I thought you knew,' said Jonathon.

'Hm,' said Lance. 'Maybe we did think that.'

'I thought we did.'

They drove on in silence for a while.

'*Royal Standard Gratuity* – pretty good, eh?' said Lance.

'Um.'

'What? Don't you think it's good?'

'It's er, it's not a gratuity though.'

'What do you mean?'

'Well, a gratuity's a tip. This is a discount.'

'Same thing. They won't notice.'

'I think they might.'

'Seriously, it's just a nice tie.'

'I think you pronounce it nicety.'

'What?'

'*Nice-etty.*'

'Whatever. It's just a detail.'

Streets slipped by. They were approaching Jonathon's house, and he thought he wouldn't be too late for work. Tonight he would call Rachel.

Oh. He suddenly remembered. Damn.

'You know that beermat I had in the Barnaby Rudge yesterday?' asked Jonathon.

'The one with the little lady's phone number on it?'

'Don't call her the little lady. But yes.'

'Yes.'

'Did it get mixed up in the file somehow?'

'No. You took it.'

'I didn't.'

'Oh.'

'Are you sure it's not in the file?'

'Yes.'

'Oh.'

Silence fell again.

'Where is the file?' asked Jonathon.

'It's in a very, very safe place.'

CHAPTER THIRTY-FIVE

'Now, why are we standing on your balcony?'

Thompson could immediately see the reason for Mangiafuoco's question. They were, after all, standing on the balcony of Thompson's office. Far down below, beyond the fearsomely sharp Gothic turrets, was London. Horse Guards was lit up, beyond it was St James's Park and all around was a feast of palaces. Mangiafuoco was still panting: his stubby limbs weren't built for clambering up on to window-ledges and then out on to extremely narrow, largely decorative balconies.

When Thompson looked anxiously left and right, he could see that the balconies on either side of his – some distance away – were occupied by flowers and plants in such profusion as to make it difficult even to open a window. They would not be overheard.

These were small, uncomfortable balconies, and what made Mangiafuoco's question even more pertinent was the cold and the slight drizzle.

'It has a magnificent prospect,' said Thompson at length, unwilling to launch into the real reason so soon.

Mangiafuoco looked down at his shoes. This was what he tended to do when trying to curb his impatience. It spurred Thompson to begin his confession.

'Perhaps more importantly, I – I have something to tell you that I want kept from prying ears. In fact, it is vital that it stay strictly and forever *entre nous*.'

'Is that why you're whispering?'

'Yes.'

'Then I shall join you in whispering. Do you think your office is bugged?'

'I have no idea. It may be.'

'Do you think your balcony is bugged?'

Thompson looked around in alarm, then said, 'No.'

'Why not?'

'Where would one put it?'

'I see. What's troubling you, Andrew?'

'You've known me for a long time now, Tris. Fifteen years?'

'Seventeen, I think.'

'Exactly. Seventeen. Do you remember about ten years ago I went through a patch of – well, of *sustained misfortune*.'

'Yes I do. It worried me terribly.'

Thompson looked out over the hissing damp city, suddenly unable to meet Mangiafuoco's eyes.

'I offered to lend you money,' said Mangiafuoco.

'And I gratefully declined.'

'Wisely.'

'Possibly not so wisely,' said Thompson. 'You see, the thing is that I've rather hocked my soul to the devil, as it were.'

'What are you talking about?'

'Well, at the height of my period of sustained misfortune – the roof was caving in, I was dismissed from the two directorships I had, my own little business had collapsed, I had a mountain of debt and I was on the point of being deselected by my constituency ... I even thought Margaret might leave me–'

'Surely not?'

Thompson nodded. 'And then, at the height of it all, just when I thought things couldn't possibly get any worse, they very suddenly stopped getting worse. In fact, they very suddenly became very much better.'

'What happened?'

'I was leafing through my mail one day – I opened my mail with a loaded pistol on the desk in front of me at that time, so that I should be able to blow my head off if something particularly dreadful emerged–'

'I had no idea you were so desperate!'

'One has no idea whether one would have had the strength to go through with it, but the pistol was there all the same. I still have it: a Luger P08 – it once belonged to Heydrich, you know.'

'Andrew, you're straying. The letter.'

'Yes, the letter. I was trying to determine whether each envelope in turn was a bill, so that I could avoid opening it – envelopes were more often plain in those days. Only ten years ago, but envelope-marking technology has come on in leaps and bounds–'

'Andrew…'

'Sorry. There was one doubtful case. It had a serious air about it, and so could have been a bill. But on the other hand there was some slight indication that it might be something else. I was burning my bills in those days – I could so easily have missed it. Who knows where I would have been today if I had?'

'Is the drizzle increasing in its severity?'

'Sorry, I'll get to the point. I opened the envelope with my paper-knife – God knows where it's got to now – and what should I see?'

'What?'

'The most curious thing. A letter with a company crest at the top of the page: a rearing ibex, I believe the creature was, beside the words 'Girard Leviticus', all in green. A most unusual crest. Of course they call them *logos* now – spastic bloody word – and everyone has them. Not everyone did then, just ten short years ago – you had to mean business in those days to have a crest.'

'Was there anything written on this letter?'

'Yes, there was. An offer. Don't judge me for accepting it–'

'How can I judge you?'

'We've known each other for a long time but–'

'I mean, how can I judge you when I don't know what the offer was?'

'It was this. To cut a long story short, the letter was from a Mr Augustus Zazel. He said that he had an agency. He said that, as I had discovered, from time to time the best-laid plans go awry and enterprises of great pith and moment–'

'Ah, this is Hamlet isn't it?'

'I do wish you wouldn't attribute my allusions, Tris.'

'Sorry. Go on.'

'He said that enterprises of great pith and moment run aground.'

'Surely he didn't mix his metaphors?'

'Why do you think not? Shakespeare did. Why not Mr Zazel?'

'From what little you've told me of this Mr Zazel, he sounds like a man who would write with a sort of spare elegance.'

'Yes, I was paraphrasing in my own words. I suppose his writing was rather, as you say, spare. Spare, but not elegant. His prose style was a little flat, I would say. I think I remember the phrase, "Sometimes well planned and managed enterprises fail." That's what he said. "You have discovered this in your own affairs."'

'And you had.'

'I had. "The same is true for governments and corporations. Sound projects fail." It's coming back to me now. The flat spareness, that's the key.'

'Could we move on from the man's prose style?'

'Sorry, Tris. "Sound projects fail. It is no one's fault. But someone must be blamed." He laid it on the line.'

'Do hurry up.'

'Well, he said that there are also people such as myself who currently find ourselves in a difficult financial situation, but who would make plausible appointees to responsible positions. "Why not," he said, "solve two problems at once?"'

Tristan was looking at his shoes again while London fizzed below them in the drizzle.

'How?' he asked.

There was a knock on the window pane.

CHAPTER THIRTY-SIX

Jonathon closed the door of his room and took off his tie. He decided that, on balance, a half day at work was worse than a whole day. The money was halved but all the worst aspects of the day were retained intact. There was still the journey there (rising dread) and back (lingering horror), and the psychological imprint of hours spent traipsing around empty aisles, drifting between racks of trousers and overcoats, occasionally punctuated by ambush as a rich person asked for help buying a suit or a poor person asked for help buying the cheapest thing in the shop that entitled them to a decent-sized carrier bag. Harrods was, in many ways, very much like 'Nam, though with less chance of being iced by gooks.

While he had been meandering around Harrods occasionally measuring someone's neck, his brain had occupied itself with replaying the previous evening, trying to identify the exact second at which he had misplaced the beermat with Rachel's number written on it.

Even now that he was back home his brain was still trying to do the same thing. He decided to distract it by looking at the free local paper. Perhaps there would be a job he could do. What he needed was a job that involved wandering around the local area in the hope of bumping into Rachel, or one that would make him colossally famous, so that she would get in touch with him. At the same time he needed to spend as much time as possible in his room, in case she came round to see him. He needed to see a job advert for an itinerant home-working rockstar.

He looked anyway. There were in fact several jobs that involved 'earning £££s working from home', but even Jonathon knew that these were lies. Otherwise businesses in the area needed only waitresses and accountants. He flipped idly through the rest of the paper, read a story about a slightly misconceived swimming pool, turned the page and stopped.

There before him was the face of the man who had asked him for directions to Acacia Road while wearing a luxurious balaclava. In the advert the man was not wearing his balaclava. He was wearing a vest and an expression of grim triumph as he flexed his biceps and jutted his jaw. 'Goliath Gym: Be fit, not fat' said the writing at the top of the advert. At the bottom it followed this up with 'Come to my gym and learn to be a hunk, not a lunk' in smaller letters that obscured the man's midriff.

Jonathon realised that in the excitement and hope of meeting Lance, Jane and Rachel all on the same day he had entirely forgotten about the large threatening man in the balaclava who had asked directions to Acacia Road on the day the murder had been committed.

Why had he not thought before to tell the police about it?

He got up and left the room, making for the payphone in the hall. Halfway down the stairs he stopped. What if the police wanted to question him? Could he trust himself not to mention that Lance had been in the dead woman's kitchen? What if the man in the advert was not the man he had seen? He had, after all, only caught a glimpse of the man's face without his balaclava.

'Tut. Why you stop on the stair?'

'Oh. Sorry Avi.'

Jonathon squeezed himself against the wall and Avi stumped past shaking his head, a towel around his shoulders. One day Jonathon would tell him that 'tut' wasn't a word, only a conventionalised representation of a sound. That day, however, was not today.

Perhaps, thought Jonathon, he should stop apologising and squeezing himself against walls and get out there. Perhaps he should go to Goliath Gym and find out whether the man in the advert was the man in the balaclava before bothering the police. Yes it was dangerous, but if he were to bust the case wide open by identifying the murderer then he might be on the news, and Rachel might get in touch. And he could become muscular at the same time.

CHAPTER THIRTY-SEVEN

Later, it occurred to Lance that perhaps the boot of the car he had borrowed from work was not, in fact, a very, very safe place. Neither was his kitchen table. He went to a shop.

'Hello,' he said. 'I'd like one of those briefcases that you can handcuff to your wrist.'

When he returned to his flat he realised that being able to handcuff his briefcase to his wrist didn't really solve the problem of where to put the files. Instead it introduced a new problem: he couldn't do anything. Having a briefcase attached to him would, he could now see, make it very difficult to go to the toilet, eat, sit comfortably, sleep, fondle women's breasts, make a cup of tea or safely open a bottle of beer. All he could do was stride about, go to meetings and sit with a briefcase on his lap.

He was sitting with the briefcase on his lap on the chaise longue, drinking a bottle of beer with his free hand. His other hand, freshly gashed from opening the bottle of beer, gripped the handle of the briefcase. He thought about how very much he would like some cocaine.

Very much.

He hadn't had any since August, and he was pleased with himself for having given it up. Although cocaine helped to make being with his awful superficial friends more bearable, it simultaneously helped to make being with himself less bearable.

In his natural state, Lance was rarely at a loss for words and enjoyed talking about how great he was. This, he had discovered, is the state other people are seeking to attain by taking cocaine. So, when Lance took cocaine it turned him into a monster. As soon as it hit the back of his nose he began to talk voraciously, loquaciously and salaciously about the greatness of himself and his life. This would not have been a problem – at such times everyone else was also taking cocaine and therefore not listening, only waiting for a gap so that they could talk again about themselves.

Unfortunately, Lance was afflicted by a curse so terrible and poetic that it could have been used to punish an errant Norse god: he was unable to avoid listening to what he said when he took cocaine. He was horrified at how boring he was – and yet he could not help wanting some more cocaine immediately, even while he was in the middle of putting some of it into his nose.

This circumstance had made him very unhappy indeed for the months that it had lasted. Finally, he had overcome it by working out how many nice clothes his habit would pay for. *A great deal* had been the answer, and this had stopped his cocaine habit overnight. He was pleased with this tactic of using one aspect of his shallowness to overcome another. If he could find some way of extending this strategy to encompass every aspect of his shallowness then he would, he calculated, become one of the most profound men ever to have lived. At the very least he would one day read a book all the way through.

But now he was on the verge of losing that prospect. He was in danger of being driven back to drugs by the contents of the briefcase handcuffed to his wrist. What could he do with the files?

He needed to talk it through with someone. It had to be someone safe, someone who would listen, someone who wouldn't immediately spot that this was an opportunity to sell him some cocaine. Jane fitted the bill, but he suspected that she would disapprove of his stealing from a corpse. The only other possibility was Jonathon.

Lance hauled himself to his feet, put his hand on his car keys and was about to leave the flat when the door-bell sounded. He made his way through the kitchen, catching himself a nasty blow to the shin with the briefcase that was handcuffed to his wrist. Opening the door he saw standing there, in a pink vest-top this time, the Girl From The Pub.

In Lance's life there had been so many girls from so many pubs that they had all blurred and run into each other, becoming a single Girl From The Pub amalgam, to whom Lance was, in his way, remarkably faithful. The allocation of different names to the many emanations of this same creature had always struck him as being a kind of bureau-cratic imposition forced on him by a jealous world.

The Girl From The Pub looked at him with an expectant nervous-ness, a sort of defiant shyness. This was, they both realised, contrary to all one-night-stand etiquette. Lance was even slightly shocked: he felt a bit like Jack The Ripper might on opening the door and finding last night's victim standing there, asking to come in for a chat and perhaps another quick throat-slashing.

'Hey baby,' he said, remembering that this had been a joke last night, and clutching at it as an alternative to a full name-remembering.

She smiled. 'Hey baby.'

'Chaise longue?' he offered, pointing across the scruffy kitchen to the much nicer living room, and catching himself another nasty blow – this time to the hip – with the briefcase that was handcuffed to his wrist.

'Cigarette?' she countered.

'Drink?' he raised.

She nodded enthusiastically, got out cigarettes for them both, and made her way over to the chaise-longue.

'Beer, coffee, or Sambucca with cigarettes in it?'

She pretended to consider it. 'Hmm, I think I'll have the beer.'

Her voice was Essex, with traces of a North London accent-graft which hadn't taken, but her vest was pink and last night's breasts were still bobbing about beneath it. She was poised exactly at the point where ripeness begins to turn soft, which for Lance was the most desirable moment in the lifecycle of the Girl From The Pub.

He was wondering how quickly he could get rid of her, and cursing the reflex which had made him invite her in. There was very little for them to talk about.

He handed her a beer.

'Oh. What are those three cuts from?' she asked.

'Them? They're nothing. I'll just put this briefcase under the bed.'

CHAPTER THIRTY-EIGHT

The sky was very nearly dark and the time was very nearly seven. From across the road, Jonathon looked at the whitewashed three-storey brick building. The gym's doorway was narrow, squashed between the frontages of a betting shop and a drycleaner that shared the ground floor. Above, a sign ran along almost the whole width of the building: the G of both *Goliath and Gym* had been turned into the beard and hair of a cartoon muscleman in a Philistine tunic.

Jonathon pushed open the door and padded over elderly blue carpet tiles till he reached a staircase where another Goliath sign pointed upwards. He stopped, his feet reluctant to climb the worn rubberised steps.

Eventually, Jonathon had to pick up his left foot with his hands and place it on the lowest step. That got him started. At the top of the steps was a door. He took a breath and pushed.

Jonathon emerged blinking into a large room full of lights, men and sweat. Music strained quietly from speakers mounted high on the walls: *work your body good / so I see you pumping / the* something something / something *beat is jumping.* There was a laminated counter to his left, and behind it stood a swarthy, oblong man, almost twice as broad as he was tall. The man was a full head shorter than Jonathon, with a gleaming, unnatural tan and a sweat-band tied around his forehead.

His wiry black hair and his stubble could, together, have been used as makeshift velcro, if you were marooned on a desert island with him and desperately needed to construct an easy-open fastener.

It took a few moments for Jonathon to realise that the man was saying something to him and that he wasn't listening because he was thinking instead of how to turn the man into velcro. There was no way he could explain this, so he stared stupidly.

'Sorry?' he said.

'Listen mate, I'm not here for the good of my health.'

'Oh. Ah. No. Me neither.'

The man looked at Jonathon as though wondering whether to snap him.

'I'm doing you a favour.'

'Sorry,' said Jonathon.

'I *said:* you have to have an induction to come here. But I'll let you in this time, long's you book one now.'

'Right. Thanks.'

He paid some money and booked an induction for the next Tuesday, all the time thinking that this was the time for him to ask whether the man in the advert owned the gym, and all the time wondering why he wasn't asking whether the man in the advert owned the gym. He took his appointment card and his receipt and walked towards the changing room.

Despite the proliferation of lights, the gym wasn't bright. The illumination crept from fluorescent tubes and struggled from one full-length mirror to the next, growing dimmer and dimmer until finally it fell, dark and exhausted, upon the men who hoisted the weights and worked the machines.

The place was heaving with heaving men. Two or three of them looked normal – or, in this setting, almost obscenely delicate. Some were simply muscular, many were huge and a few were such ungainly, tottering piles of muscle and fat that Jonathon doubted if it were possible for them to leave the gym, speak or put on ordinary trousers. He realised he was walking nervously, but when he tried to swagger he stumbled and felt even more foolish. He could feel the hostile stares already.

Thankfully the changing room was empty. He put down his bag, slipped off his jeans and pulled on his shorts, hoping that no one would come in while he was doing it and make fun of his legs. Glancing over his shoulder, he caught sight of something that made his heart leap up and try to exit his body through his mouth.

There, on the wall by the lockers, was a picture of the balaclava-wearing man who had asked him for directions. It was the same picture as he had seen in the newspaper advert, except much larger and much clearer. This time there really was no doubt about it. It was the same man.

Jonathon pulled himself together. The man was not here, he told himself, would not recognise him and in any case had not murdered anyone. Hundreds of people had probably been on Acacia Road on the day of Sarah's murder, and who knew how many of them got a cold face and thus had to wear a balaclava? Besides, it wasn't as though Jonathon had come to this gym to bust the Sarah Morecambe case wide open or anything. He was just trying to take his mind off the fact that he had lost Rachel's phone number, that Rachel had a girlfriend and that his life was pitilessly awful.

With this ingenious pep-talk, Jonathon pushed himself back out into the gym, changed and ready for action. Jonathon realised that he had no idea what to do. Perhaps the velcro man hadn't been doing him such a favour when he'd let him off the induction.

He spotted a device – a seat with a handle above it – that looked simpler than the others, so he stumble-swaggered over to it and sat down. The handle was attached by a steel cable to a stack of weights, with a bolt to select exactly how much of the stack was to be lifted. Beside it was an identical machine, so Jonathon could see exactly what he was supposed to do. Each time the man using the other machine pulled down his handle, his entire stack of weights lifted up. He had even piled a couple of extra weights on top. At each heave he forced his breath through his nose, making his thick moustache flutter while his eyes, fixed on a nearby mirror, watched his shoulder muscles swell.

The bolt in front of Jonathon was inserted midway up his stack. He should be able to lift less than half of what the other man was lifting, shouldn't he? He didn't want to make it lighter: better to look like a weak man trying hard than a weak man lifting easy weights.

Jonathon took a couple of deep breaths, reached up to the handles above him, grasped them securely and pulled with all his strength. The pile of weights remained as entirely unmoved by his efforts as St Paul's Cathedral might have. Jonathon pretended that he hadn't started yet. He tried again. Still nothing.

He was going to have to lighten the load: better to look like a weak man lifting easy weights than a weak man failing to do anything at all.

This time he managed to drag the handles down a couple of inches before having to let them go, causing the small stack of weights he had lifted to crash back down on top of the others. Everyone seemed to turn simultaneously and stare at him in annoyance before looking again at the nearest mirror.

Jonathon could feel his face flush bright red. He stared furiously at the ground. Hoping to buy time, he slowly re-tied his trainers. There was no way he could allow such a simple machine to defeat him, and yet he couldn't possibly make such a supreme effort again. He worried that if he did, the weight would wrench his hands from his wrists, leaving them dangling from the handles above his head, blood dripping down while Jonathon tried desperately to conceal his stumps from the men looking on in annoyance around him.

'Been ill, mate?' asked the man at the next machine. His face was so full of sinew that it was impossible to tell whether he meant this kindly. Jonathon told him that he had indeed been ill, sensibly omitting to mention that it had been a purely spiritual malaise.

Somehow he spent another hour there: waiting quietly for each piece of machinery, selecting the minimum weight, and then almost dying. Whenever his determination began to flag, he would think again of Rachel. It never crossed his mind that she might not want a man who could lift two hundred pounds. Nor did it cross his mind that she might ever accept him as he was. The fact that she had a girlfriend also left him unperturbed. It was the principle. He knew he could never have her, but he thought that at least he could be worthy of her. Or at least he could be nearly as strong as the sort of man he vaguely imagined might be worthy of her.

Afterwards, he had to lie on the long wooden benches in the changing room until he stopped feeling sick and giddy. Then he sat up and changed only his top half, unable to bear the extra time that taking off his trainers and shorts would take, and the risk that his pants would come off with his shorts. Twelve long years of PE lessons had not taught him nothing.

 After the exercise everything seemed unreal and far away, and this allowed him to overcome his fear and ask the velcro man whether the giant pictured in the advert was the owner.

'Yeah,' said the man. 'Why?'

Jonathon couldn't think of an answer but neither could he say nothing.

'Is he in?' he found himself asking.

CHAPTER THIRTY-NINE

Rachel had been afraid that it would turn out this way. During the course of a day at Sam's, supposedly writing essays, the two of them had regressed at the rate of approximately a year per hour. Now, as the time was approaching eight, so were they. Rachel was desperate to smooth things over, but she had no idea how.

'Will we get a takeaway?' she suggested, naughtily, looking up from her pad of paper through her fringe.

'Why?' said Sam.

'I don't know. Because we'll totally die if we don't eat?'

'That's why you can't concentrate, you know – because you don't eat properly.'

'I *do* eat properly. And I *can* concentrate.'

If Sam heard this devastating riposte, she gave no sign of it. Instead, she got up from her desk, ostentatiously stretched her arms above her head so that her taut, tanned midriff tautened even more – *where does she keep her internal organs?* wondered Rachel – and then began collecting a day's worth of tea mugs. Her hair was the colour that spun gold would be if it had any choice in the matter, and it perfectly set off her cropped sky-blue T-shirt, which in turn perfectly set off her stomach, the light brown of which then went on to perfectly set off the pink hipsters that shouldn't have worked but nevertheless totally did work.

'I'll do that,' said Rachel, getting up. As she did so she caught sight of herself in the mirror and almost burst into tears. Her hair was the boringest medium brown that had ever lain on human head (you couldn't even call it brunette, it was so boring), and her clothes tried too hard to be like Sam's, which only accentuated how far she was from having Sam's effortless, almost accidental style. Something in her chest hurt as she remembered how new and stylish her outfit had been when she had put it on that morning to come over to Sam's. *Who wears a green T-shirt?* she thought. *And why didn't anyone tell me that I've got the biggest, spongiest hips ever?*

'Come on,' said Sam. 'I'll show you how to cook.'

They returned from the kitchen to Sam's room with bowls of soup. It was the sort of soup that only Sam could make: thrown together from cheap, nutritious ingredients in absurd combinations, and tasting not only good but virtuous – the way Sting's life would taste if you could somehow turn it into soup.

They sat side by side on the bed. Sam picked up the remote control and turned on the television. A bearded face appeared, smiling and looking down at a man whose face seemed to have been applied with a wrench.

'*So, Shaun, tell me – why Billy Idol?*'

'*Well, I don't really know, Matthew. I've always just looked up to him, like. He's just, you know, a great entertainer...*'

'*So you could say that he's your "idol"?*'

The man with the clumsily constructed face stared uncomprehendingly at the man with the beard and microphone.

'*Like I said, he's a great entertainer.*'

'*Well Shaun, that's...*'

Click.

'*... police are appealing for information about the murder, which took place at around five o'clock on Sunday afternoon in Acacia Road in North London. The killer is believed...*'

'Sa-am!'

'You're not watching it.'

'I was! I totally was watching it!'

'It's rubbish anyway.'

Sam pressed the remote control again. A man who looked almost entirely unlike Billy Idol was standing amid some dry ice, dressed as Billy Idol and writhing awkwardly.

'*For-got to be your lov-er!*' he snarled, baring his upper gums.

'That's a bit careless,' said Rachel.

'I thought you said you liked this.'

'I didn't say I liked it – I just said I wanted to watch it, that's all. It's all about murderers on the other channels anyway.'

'That's because it's *the news*. If a murder happens it's *news*.'

'I know but … Why are we being like this?'

'Being like what? I'm not being like anything. It's you who's being all whiney about the telly.'

'I'm not – I...'

Rachel had stood up. She was horrified to find tears had forced themselves into the corners of her eyes. This was exactly like spending a day indoors with her older sister in a wet half-term week. Sam was looking at her, completely self-possessed, as Rachel stood there awkwardly holding her bowl of delicious healthy thrifty soup. She could feel Sam looking at her stupid green T-shirt, her unbearably brown hair, her ridiculous hips and her hipsters with their silly slightly flared ankles.

'I'm going home,' said Rachel. 'I've got to go home.'

'Fine.'

Rachel continued to stand for a moment, trying to work out why this had happened and what she needed to do next.

'Oh my *God*,' said Sam. 'You're not actually *waiting for a lift,* are you?'

Five minutes later Rachel was on the bus, still breathing hard after running all the way from Sam's. *Serve her right if I get murdered*, she thought.

CHAPTER FORTY

Thompson opened the window with difficulty.

'How long have you been there?' he asked.

'What? About three seconds,' said his new secretary.

'What do you want?'

'Wanted to tell you I'm going home now. Don't want any problems when I bring you my time sheet.'

'Yes, yes. Don't worry about that.'

'What are you doing?' she asked, peering out at him and Mangi-afuoco, jammed together on the tiny balcony.

'We're admiring the prospect.'

'Both of you?'

'Yes.'

'You know it's raining?'

Mangiafuoco glared at her.

'Yes,' said Thompson.

She smiled and left the room.

'And close the door behind–' called Thompson.

When he had closed and locked his office door, he squeezed himself out on to the balcony again. Mangiafuoco stood there looking damp and annoyed.

'You were about to tell me what happened,' said Mangiafuoco.

'In a nutshell, I became an RSG.'

'That rings a bell – didn't those chaps from Lenin & Plover mention RSG?'

'Yes. That's why I'm telling you now. I think someone's on to me, and I can't keep it to myself any longer.'

'Can't keep what to yourself?'

'The fact that I'm an RSG: a Registered Scapegoat.'

'And what is that?' asked Mangiafuoco, wiping the rain from his moustache.

'Well, if a company or government department embarks on a particularly large and risky new venture – a new Tube line, for instance, or an attempt to unseat Marks & Spencer from its dominance of the sensible underwear market – it appoints a Registered Scapegoat as its head, or as the head of that project. The RSG – that's the abbreviation – attends all the meetings, agrees all the decisions, is seen to suggest all the ideas.'

'And this is all secret?'

'Of course: nobody knows he's an RSG except for those who hired him. Then if the venture fails, the RSG's job is to take the bullet, to stand up and say "it was all my fault" – in the most convincing possible way of course, perhaps with a show of making a fight to stay in office. It allows the people who are really in control to get things wrong without paying the price.'

'Very clever.'

'Isn't it? And very well paid. The RSG gets the salary that goes with the position, plus ten percent. If he has to take the bullet then he continues to get the same amount, until his next assignment.'

'And if he isn't needed? If the project goes well?'

'That's the beauty of it. In that case he moves on to another project, and because everyone thinks he's responsible for the success of the first project, he makes an even more plausible scapegoat, and so the position commands a larger salary. Everyone wins, no matter what happens.'

'And what was it called – the company that arranges all of this?'

'Girard Leviticus. *GL*, I mean.'

'What's in it for Girard Leviticus?'

'I presume it is also paid handsomely by the same organisations.

With the size of the projects involved, several millions could easily be scraped out of the budget.'

'So, it appears that everyone is happy,' said Mangiafuoco. 'What is the problem?'

'I'm something of a fluke case. I was one of the very first government RSGs, and I've been put in charge of some pretty big things, as you know.'

Mangiafuoco nodded. 'But you've never resigned.'

'That's because, as I said, I am something of a fluke case. Every single one of my postings has been a success. I've never needed to be scapegoated. After a while I rather forgot that was how I came to power. I began to think it was all down to my own efforts – except that every now and then I would receive a letter on GL-headed paper telling me what to do. And when one project ended, I would receive a contract for the next.'

'I see. And now something has changed this idyllic scenario. What?'

'A file full of my contracts has gone missing. I think my secretary took it – my murdered secretary – and I don't know what to do.'

'I asked you whether she might have anything that could compromise you, and you assured me it was impossible.'

'I'm sorry. I don't know how she got access to these contracts – they were in my own private filing cabinets. But the contracts *are* missing and I can't think who else might have taken them. I'm sure they wouldn't make much sense to the casual criminal, or to a jilted boyfriend. But if someone who knows what they're doing gets hold of them, then I'm finished. Finished.'

'In what sense?'

'Every sense. Perhaps even the ultimate sense.'

'The ultimate sense?'

'Death. I don't know quite know what to believe, but I have three times been anonymously sent newspaper cuttings about the disappearance of prominent men – whatsisname who oversaw the privatisation of BRKKPH, someone senior at ICI, that man who stopped the railways working. In other words, men who might easily be RSGs.'

'That doesn't prove anything.'

'That's what I thought. But then, do you remember when I had responsibility for reforming the Governmental Agency for the Guardianship of the Aged? It seemed the programme was doomed, and I didn't want to have to take the blame, to go down in history as the chap who ripped the cardigans from the backs of a million grandmothers. I started trying to manoeuvre Bagshaw into position to take the blame.'

'What happened?'

'Two things. I found a brochure of Welsh holidays on my desk one morning, with occasional words highlighted.'

'Which words?'

'Anything dark or disturbing. Words such as "death", "murder", "wife", "disappear"–'

'Those don't sound like words one would find in a holiday brochure.'

'It was a *Welsh* holiday brochure. I thought I'd mentioned that.'

'I take the point.'

'One complete phrase was also highlighted.'

'What was it?'

'*Llandudno cellar treatment.*'

'In what context did the phrase occur?'

'I can't recall. Something to do with cheese? You must remember that I was extremely disturbed. No one in the office could explain how the thing had appeared, you see.'

'What did you do?'

'I went straight home to see Gargy. And when I arrived, what should I see?'

'What?'

'On the carpet in the hall, written in bubbles, were the words "Llandudno cellar treatment".'

'Written in bubbles?'

'Yes. You know, soap bubbles. They must have been put there immediately before I walked through the door. But there was nobody in the house except Gargy – all the staff were ill that day. The message in bubbles stayed there for a minute at the most, and then it was gone.'

'And you're sure you didn't imagine it?'

'Quite sure. I've never imagined anything less.'

'Hmm.'

The drizzle had passed now and the day was dimming. Thompson's fists were clenched, his eyes fixed on the balcony's balustrade.

'I am afraid, Tristan. Truly afraid. I have no idea with whom or what I am dealing. I've never met anyone connected with this wretched GL outfit. No one has ever mentioned it in any of my appointments. The only reason I know it's real is the contracts and the money – and now the contracts have been stolen. Perhaps I should just "go public", as they say – tell everyone about it and hang the consequences.'

Tristan shot him a glance. 'Do you think you might?'

'No.' Thompson sighed. 'Not really. I don't know what might happen to Gargy, and I don't want to risk this "Llandudno cellar treatment", whatever it is. I imagine horrible things. You wouldn't believe the nightmares I have.'

Tristan was silent a long time, looking down on the buses and the speckled rash of tourists' anoraks below.

'Would you like my advice?'

'Please, Tris.'

'You know I believe in openness and fair play above everything else?'

Thompson nodded.

'In this case, however, it seems that the dangers are so great and so beyond knowing that the most important thing is to tell no one. Keep *absolute* secrecy.'

'But other people seem to know already – those two from Lenin & Plover.'

'Only them?'

'Yes.'

'Yes, I was coming to them. They mentioned a name, didn't they? What was it?'

'Justin, I think, or Jason.'

'*Jamyn*, I think they said.'

'Yes, that was it.'

'And how much do you think the two we met today know?'

'I have no idea. All I know is that Lance is very, very good at what he does. A professional, I'd say.'

'I was more concerned about the other one.'

'Really?'

'Yes. What do you think he meant by saying "Meat to please you"?'

'Just awkwardness, I thought. Tripping over his words.'

'I think it's more than that. Did you see his eyes? Very clever eyes.'

'I can't say I thought they were clever-looking. He had something of the look of a lightly sedated meerkat.'

'That's just a ploy, I think, to make us underestimate him. A ploy that he took a little too far – who would wear an old green jumper to take a brief from a minister of the Crown?'

'Well, an idiot. Or someone who wasn't expecting to come.'

'Precisely. But to be representing Lenin & Plover at such a young age – well, you'd have to be pretty smart, I think.'

'Perhaps you're right. I hadn't looked at it that way.'

'Let's invite them to a meeting tomorrow: get a better sense of what's going on and how much they know. Perhaps it's just a question of money. In any case we can have them followed and see where they go first – who they know.'

'I have a feeling it will take more than that,' said Thompson.

CHAPTER FORTY-ONE

Rachel stepped down from the bus and zipped up her jacket, though it wasn't cold. She walked with quick steps and her head down. The frightening thing about Holloway Road is not so much the people – even though many of them deliberately make themselves look as evil as possible – as the general air of decay. The road is wide, but almost everything in it, even the street lamps, seems to be crumbling. She rarely saw any police there, but could always hear sirens, as though that was the sound made by the ghostly scavengers that gnawed away at the buildings when no one was looking. Holloway Road often made Rachel feel suffocated and panicky, as though she might be infected by the area's decay and become broken, neglected, and absent-mindedly violated like everything else.

It was after half past eight now, and already quite dark. Ahead of her a man was pulling down the shutters over the front of a wholesaler called 'Nice Fashions', which seemed to specialise in tracksuits for babies. She crossed over the road to avoid him, as he looked like the sort of man who might start talking to her – despite the awful brownness of her hair. Why were men so undiscerning? A bit further up there was a convenience store called Eazy Fruit'n'Vegg, which she often stopped into for chocolate on the way home from Sam's. In the dark she almost tripped over the middle-aged man who spent all his time sitting in the street, leaning against the shop facade. He never asked for money, or at least Rachel had never heard him ask for money, only for cigarettes, which most people either don't have or are more loath to part with than money. This time he was silent, apparently asleep.

She bought some chocolate, and began to feel better as she ate it. The streets started to seem less threatening, their decay less contagious, and she slowed her pace. Just as her heart rate was beginning to slow, she rounded a corner and collided with someone walking in the opposite direction.

Rachel felt the tears well up in her eyes for the second time that day as she leapt backwards, raising the chocolate bar as though ready to plunge it into her assailant's neck. Although there are a lot of people in London, and at any given time you'd have thought that roughly half the walking population must be going in the opposite direction, it is still a rare and shocking thing to walk straight into someone else. It took her a couple of seconds to realise that it was Jonathon.

She hadn't recognised him immediately because he was wearing shorts, and he was so not-a-shorts person that they seemed to turn him into someone else. He also had on a hooded top, cheap trainers and a rucksack. His face, even in the darkness, was flushed, and he somehow contrived to stand so as to hide his legs behind one another. He was plainly terrified, especially after he had realised who she was.

'I'm sorry,' she said and instantly regretted it, because the expression on his face told her he was mortified at not having been the first to apologise.

'Are you all right?' he asked.

'I've had a totally horrible day,' she said.

'Oh. Ah. Oh no.'

'Oh sorry – you meant because of the … walking-into-each-other thing. Yes. I'm totally fine.' She lowered the chocolate bar.

'I'm sorry,' he said anyway.

There was a pause. Both still stood in the same positions, ready to deal with a conversation, should one break out.

'You're wearing shorts,' said Rachel.

Jonathon couldn't deny it, but he had the look of a man who is trying to give the impression of having a pair of trousers on.

'I've just been to the gym,' said Jonathon.

'I didn't know you were a sporty person.'

'It was my first time, I…'

'Which gym?'

'Um, Goliath? It's not very good. I'd be better off going to a gym called David, where they teach you how to be really good with a sling.'

'No way!'

'Yes. What? The sling? I just meant like in David and Goliath…'

'No. I mean: no way, that's totally my uncle's gym. He owns it.'

'Really? Sorry. I didn't mean… about it not being very good. I just meant… I bet if your uncle heard me say that he'd…'

'He'd probably give you free membership.'

'Really?'

'My uncle's *lovely*. He's just the biggest pussy-cat you could ever meet. He'd totally ask you all about what was wrong and how to make it better. He's one of those people that they call… oh, you know…'

'A gentle giant?'

'Yes! That's it! That's totally what he's like. He's really sensitive…'

'Really?'

'Yes. He gets a really cold face, so I got him this big thing like a bobble-hat that goes over your whole head.'

At this Jonathon felt a wave of relief pass over his whole body. His shoulders dropped and he suddenly realised that he'd been holding his breath slightly all day. The whole thing had been a misunderstanding. And he hadn't risked his life to bust the murder case wide open, he'd just been to a gym owned by a really nice man who got a bit of a cold face.

'It's getting a bit cold now,' said Rachel.

'Would you… I mean, you could always have a coffee at my place. It's just up the road… Brickfield Terrace.'

'That's a coincidence – I live on a brick-something road: Brickhouse Road. Number 64.'

'Does it have a bamboo door?'

'Like in the song? No. That would last about forty-five seconds round here.'

'So, um. Do you want to?'

CHAPTER FORTY-TWO

A shadow fell across Bob Plover's plate.

'Bob,' said the murderer, holding out his meaty hand.

'All right mate,' returned Plover, taking the murderer's hand and shaking it casually but firmly.

'Very nice,' commented the murderer, eyeing Plover's plate.

'All-day breakfast mate.'

'All-day breakfast? This time of night?'

'That's right – all day.'

'Blimey,' said the murderer.

'O'Reilly,' finished Plover.

'See what you done now? I'm only going to have to get one of them all-day breakfasts, aren't I? Came in here not even hungry at all. Flipping starving now, thanks to you.'

The murderer shouldered his way through the empty cafe to order his food. When he returned he had a mug of coffee in his paw and he looked much brighter.

'What you looking so happy about?' asked Plover.

'I'm getting an extra piece of bacon,' replied the murderer.

'So did I.'

'*And* an extra sausage.'

Plover thought a while, then conceded, 'No mate, that's where you have the advantage.'

They smiled at each other, then the murderer blew on his coffee and Plover let his eyes roam over the cafe, with its small, neat tables, its chipped salt and pepper pots, its yellow plastic tablecloths, its adverts on the walls for cultural events which none of the customers would ever attend. He returned his eyes to the murderer, who was watching him.

'Just like the old days, eh?' said the murderer.

'What's that?'

'Like the old days – meeting here.'

'They didn't do breakfast all day in the old days.'

'Fair point. But other than that – just like the old days. I remember meeting you and Greg here. Thursdays, four o'clock. Like clockwork.'

'Yes mate. The good old days,' said Plover.

'Course now is also the good old days. Just that the days aren't so old, that's all.'

'I'll eat to that,' said Plover, stuffing another hash brown into his mouth.

'What happened to Greg?' asked the murderer.

'Still on the force.'

'You're joking!'

'No. He's on the corruption squad now.'

'Tell you something: of all you–' the murderer paused, making a quick substitution '–police officers, I thought he would be the first to leave. What happened to that home security company he was setting up?'

'Never happened. He got promoted.'

'Stone me.'

The murderer's all-day breakfast arrived and he instantly bowed his head and set to work. Plover mopped up some stray bits of egg with the last of his toast.

'Been trying to get you on the phone all week,' said Plover.

'Phone's been on the blink. Only fixed this morning – just before you called.'

'Know why I was calling?'

'No.'

'Some people I know are very unhappy with you.'

The murderer put down his knife and fork but said nothing.

'I'll do what I can,' said Plover. 'But there's plenty you'll have to do to work off your mistake.'

'What mistake?'

CHAPTER FORTY-THREE

Jonathon fumbled with his key in the lock, feeling terrified and very pleased. He didn't know whether this was the 'exercise high' that people talked about or a Rachel high. Perhaps it was both. That would explain why he felt like smiling so much. They made their way quietly up the stairs, though it was only quarter to nine. He showed her where the squeaky step was, and she trod on it by mistake, which made them both laugh. Luckily, he had tidied his room that morning, saving him the embarrassment of having her see the fish-plate again, which had assumed more and more terrifying proportions the longer he had left it.

'Sorry there's only one chair,' he said, as she took a seat on the not-too-badly rumpled bed.

'Coffee', traditionally used as a euphemism for sex, in this case meant tea. He went off to make it in the tiny shared kitchen, grabbing a pair of trousers from his cupboard as he passed. Changing into trousers in a shared kitchen is embarrassing, but not nearly so bad as doing it in front of the woman of your dreams. Rachel allowed Jonathon to discover this by walking in and making small talk as he was halfway through the tricky second leg. He had taken off his shorts beforehand but had elected to keep his trainers on to speed things up. By a lucky coincidence he was wearing his most presentable underwear: a pair of blue Marks & Spencer jockey shorts.

'You've got nice legs,' she said.

Jonathon fell over.

'Thank you,' he replied from his supine position, pushing his foot even more forcefully against the stubborn material.

She frowned, as though at a complex logical problem. 'You just need to pull this bit,' she said, pulling the end of the trouser leg. His shoe slid along.

'And now move your foot round to the right … no, the right. And. There!' She looked down at him triumphantly. He looked up at her with a mixture of relief, devotion, discomfort and acute embarrassment.

A few minutes later they were both sitting on the bed, sipping tea. Jonathon was now fully trousered and feeling much more comfortable.

'Where did you learn trouser-operating skills like those?' asked Jonathon, still trying to get over the embarrassment of having Rachel help him on with his trousers.

'My granddad came to stay with us for a year when he started dementing.' She looked up at him, as though she were asking a question, and then broke off, beginning again on a different tack.

'I'm really glad I bumped into you tonight, I totally didn't want to have to go home on my own. Me and Sam had a fight …'

'A fight?'

'An argument,' she explained. 'We weren't … boxing or anything.'

'What was it about?'

'About watching Stars In Their Eyes, kind of.'

150

Jonathon spread his hands and pulled a face to indicate that he, too, often quarrelled with his lovers about Stars In Their Eyes. The face didn't turn out quite the way he wanted it to. Rachel laughed and then immediately looked distraught again.

'It wasn't really about Stars In Their Eyes,' she said. 'It was about something else, but I don't know what. I don't know why it goes like that sometimes. The thing is that Sam's just so amazing – she looks amazing and she does everything totally brilliantly … she made this soup and, well … I think she knows that I really want to be like her, but I never will be. I never will.'

Jonathon looked helplessly at her.

'I don't think she really likes me, sometimes,' Rachel continued, looking at the bedsheets. 'I don't know why she would.'

'But, but … there are hundreds of reasons why she would – why she should. I mean… I'm not a, you know, *lesbian* or anything…'

At this, Rachel suddenly burst out laughing and was unable to stop for a long time. She had to give Jonathon her mug to stop it from spilling. Throughout, Jonathon sat with an awkward smile on his face, his happiness at her laughter almost equally balanced by his annoyance at himself at saying something so stupid.

When she had finished laughing and carefully wiped her eyes with a tissue, Rachel took a couple of deep breaths and then turned to accept the cup of tea that Jonathon was holding out for her. As soon as she saw his face she collapsed again, and this time had to go out of the room and into the corridor to stop herself.

'Sorry,' she said as she came back in. 'It's not you. I get like this when I'm tired. You do have a funny face though – in a good way I mean – even though you aren't a, you know, *lesbian* or anything.'

Jonathon felt his funny face go red, slowly, from the chin to the temples. Rachel started giggling again, but this time kept it under control.

She sat down beside him and put her hand on his shoulder.

'Sorry,' she said. 'Can I have my tea back now?'

He pretended to think about it, then handed it gravely back to her. 'Thanks.'

Jonathon said, 'I only meant, you know, just that men and women have really different ideas about what makes women attractive. That's all. I didn't mean to…'

'Sam says that men look at women as objects.'

He thought for a second. 'Well, men do objectify women,' he said.

'But a lot of people forget that men also objectify other men. That's just how we are. We also objectify children, houses, otters, sponges, trousers, hairstyles, RE teachers and pretty much everything else.'

She laughed. 'Do you objectify sponges? You know, personally,' she asked.

'Constantly. I can't help myself.'

'And women?'

'I don't know. Not in the way most men do, I don't think. For me, women are mainly um …' He paused. For him, women were mainly terrifying, unattainable objects of wonder (at least attractive ones were – he was fine with the other kind, such as dinner ladies and his mother). However, he couldn't face saying that to Rachel, even though she had the good grace to be equally unattainable to all men. He decided to change tack. 'Women don't seem to mind objectifying things either – it's not as though men have a monopoly on it. For every young and beautiful trophy wife there's a rich trophy husband. They're just different kinds of objects.'

'Very clever,' she said.

They sipped more tea, and Rachel suddenly said, out of the blue, 'Maybe Sam's like a trophy wife. Sometimes I think I'm just going out with her because I'm jealous of her. I never think of myself as a lesbian.'

'Me neither,' said Jonathon.

Rachel reached out her hand and laid it on his arm. 'You know, you would be such the perfect brother.'

Jonathon grinned at her, feeling as though he had been elected to some important post but disbarred on a technicality from accepting it.

'Will we watch some TV?' she asked, as though it were related.

'It's not very good,' he said.

'It doesn't matter.'

'OK.' He got up and made his way over to the small, ancient, black-and-white TV standing in the corner of the room. He pulled it nearer the bed.

'ITV doesn't work,' he said, 'And the rest of the buttons are encrypted. BBC 2 is on button five, BBC1 is on button three, and Channel 4 is on – and this is the clever bit – button four.'

'Why don't you retune it?'

'That's how I lost ITV. I'm not making that mistake again.'

Jonathon made some hot chocolate, and they turned the pillows and duvet into an improvised back-rest. The only thing on was an old

French film, which made Rachel fall asleep on Jonathon's shoulder, and made Jonathon cry.

When the film was over, Jonathon turned the TV off with his toe and leant his cheek against Rachel's head. Now he had found her again he didn't really want to be involved with terrifying men, balaclavas and cases that needed to be busted wide open. Unless it somehow impressed Rachel. He put his arm around her, as though unconsciously, and eventually fell asleep.

THURSDAY

CHAPTER FORTY-FOUR

A pen flicked into his hand, poised over a new leaf on his pad.

'Good morning, Lenin & Plover. Lance Ferman speaking.'

His telephone smile appeared.

'Hello, Mr Thompson.'

'Yes: *Andrew*. Call me Lance.'

He leaned back, listening.

'Tristan Mangiafuoco?'

'Yes, the PAPA minister. I know.'

'This morning? Of course.'

'Ah, he might not be available.'

'No, it's just that Jonathon has another assignment which keeps him pretty busy.'

'Exactly.'

'Hold on, my pen's run out. Ah, wait – here's one.'

'The British Riot and Urban Tactics Assessment Laboratory. And where's…'

'Brixton? OK. New Park Avenue.'

'Yes. Eleven AM.'

'Oh, he liked that, did he?'

'To be honest I've never tried to make it into a boat.'

'Cool – by which I mean, as ever, splendid. See you and Mr Mangiafuoco at eleven.'

CHAPTER FORTY-FIVE

Bob Plover ducked back into a shop doorway, badly upsetting an old lady who had just emerged.

'Beg pardon,' he said.

The old lady looked shocked and affronted, but then Plover's air of rumpled rapport reached her and she smiled.

'Not to worry,' she said.

156

'Take care now,' said Plover, and was gone again.

Plover was worried for a few seconds that he had lost his target. But no, he could see a teenager giggling with her friend, and that led his eyes back to the man he sought. He threaded his way through the crowd, deftly dodging between two traffic wardens, avoiding a hot-dog stand, pushing through a crowd of Scandinavians who had inexplicably stopped in unison outside Jigsaw, and then ducked back into another shop doorway just before the man he was following glanced back. His target didn't seem to have seen him. Plover's following skills were as sharp as ever.

He craned his head around the doorway just in time to see his fol-lowee go into Harrods. He hoped he wasn't doing all this following just to see a shopping trip. After walking cautiously past the first entrance, he ran along the road and dashed in through the second set of doors.

He was in a marble lobby housing two sets of escalators. Beyond it, in the shop proper, were large models of perfume bottles, huge pictures of beautiful women who smelled nice, saleswomen in dark suits or shapely white lab coats, and a smattering of customers.

Plover glanced about quickly, making doubly sure the target was not around, and then walked forward with slow steps. He kept rub-bing his eyes and pinching the bridge of his nose to obscure his face, in case the target had reached this part of the shop already.

He stepped gingerly, trying to stay behind the clumps of people at the perfume counters, contemplating a strategic move into men's casuals. Plover moved into the shadow of some South Africans and checked up the corridor, reassuring himself that his target hadn't passed this point. Then, with a quick glance about him, he deftly hurled himself across the intervening space into a cluster of leather jackets in a recessed area.

Frowning and stroking his forehead, as though he had a headache, Plover moved cautiously back towards the aisle and took a long look through the gaps in a rack of suede leisure waistcoats. There he was.

His target was leafing through a rail of Chester Barrie suits in the men's ready-to-wear formal section. Plover continued to watch him. The man approached an elderly assistant with a starched face and asked something casually. The assistant looked around distractedly, then consulted his watch and said something. The target tutted, started to say something, then seemed to think better of it and left.

Plover knew that his man would return to his car. He decided it would be safest not to follow him directly, but to return to his own car by a different route and then continue the follow (as they called it in the trade) from there. He was getting more and more worried that the target would recognise him.

Plover needed something to cover him up. Being new, it would undoubtedly be unrumpled, especially if he bought it in Harrods, and this could only add to its value as a disguise. Plover's own mother wouldn't recognise him if he weren't rumpled. He stepped out of the leather casual-wear grotto and walked straight into an assistant hurrying from the escalators.

'Sorry mate,' said Plover to the assistant, who had been too busy trying to make the hair at the back of his head stay down to notice him. 'Got any coats?' he added.

'Um. Coats. Yes, yes we do sir. They're over in the corner, just by the um ... those other things. I'll show you.'

The assistant guided Plover towards a sort of overcoat oasis. A small area of the store had been set aside exclusively for the display of knee-length men's coats which could be worn over a suit.

'What's this, mate?' asked Plover.

'That's a Loden coat.'

'And this?'

'That's a covert coat. Um, sir.'

'And what's this one?'

'That's a Loden coat again.'

'Just testing. I bet you've got to stay on your toes in this job, eh?'

'Yes. Well – toes or heels. Actually any part of the foot's fine.'

Plover grinned at the assistant, not really listening, his amiability motor just ticking over.

'What sort of coat would you like sir? Have you considered a trench coat? I've been selling a lot of those recently. Or maybe something in turquoise?'

Plover made a face. 'I'd rather have a trench coat than something turquoise.'

'Certainly sir. You'll be a forty-two regular I imagine, won't you, sir?'

'I'm a forty mate.'

'You have to go up a size for overgarments, I think, sir.'

Plover tried on the trench coat. It flapped about agreeably, with enormous lapels, buttons and a big belt. It made him feel like Humphrey Bogart.

'Um. Perhaps sir would like a hat with that?'

Back in the street, Bob Plover's new trench coat billowed behind him as he ran. He had spent longer in Harrods than he had intended – it had taken him a while to choose the right fedora – and now he was afraid he might have missed his target's return to his car. Plover found it easier to think of him as the target, rather than Lance. It kept him professional.

CHAPTER FORTY-SIX

'All right Velcroman?' said the murderer, pushing open the door of his gym. He walked over to the reception desk and put down the small pile of new picture books he had bought for Gemma.

'Don't call me that,' said Shane.

'Well get a haircut then.'

Shane scowled, then smiled, then did both at once.

The murderer ran a hand over his own head, feeling the bristles of fine hair around the patches of smooth skin. 'No, you leave it as it is,' he said. 'Average us out and we both got a good head of hair.' He waited a beat then added, 'But we're only five foot tall.'

'Come on then,' the shorter man said, baring his teeth and putting his fists up. 'I'll punch your kneecaps off.'

The murderer shuffled into a half-hearted fighting stance, then shook himself out and gave Shane a businesslike look, signalling that the messing about was over.

'Who we got in?' he said, picking up the clipboard that members signed when they arrived.

'The usual,' said Shane.

'You know what? That's the problem with this place. We got members but they come in *all the bleeding time*.'

'Shows we're a good gym.'

'Maybe. Shows we'll never be rich. What we need is some *normal* people here.'

'What do you mean?'

'They got gyms now where people sign up just because they feel a bit fat after Christmas. Pay every month and hardly ever go. How many members we got?'

'Don't know. Hundred and fifty?'

'Hundred and forty-three. And the place is always packed out. This lot practically live here, some of them. If I came in here at three in the morning I'd probably find Phil asleep in the shower.'

'You know Phil. He's committed. Gives it hundred and ten percent. That's why he's big.'

'Exactly. How many Phils can you fit in a place like this? Not many, that's how many. You start getting normal people in you can have five, six hundred members and always plenty of space – because they hardly ever come.'

'Yeah, but if no one gets big, what's the point?'

'Point is, I need to get serious about this place. This place is my pension. And what happens when Gemma grows up, needs help buying a flat? What am I going to say? "I can't give you no money, darling, but here's twelve of the biggest fuckers you've ever seen in your life. Use Phil as the back wall. Use Craig–"'

'Thought you had plenty of money from … other things.'

The murderer looked away. 'Well… Maybe not much longer. Point is, we got to get serious about this place. Can't believe I haven't taken the jolly green giant off of the wall out front. Stupid idea, that was.'

Shane looked at the counter for a couple of seconds and then, to show that he too was getting serious, picked up a sheaf of papers and began to count them. The murderer knew that they weren't papers that needed counting, but he appreciated the gesture.

'Anyone been in – because of the ads?' asked the murderer.

Shane pulled his thinking face. 'There was a kid yesterday.'

'Oh yes?'

'Yeah. Asked if you was the one in the advert.' He pointed to the poster on the wall.

'He knew my name?'

'No, just asked if you was the owner in the advert.'

'What did you say?'

'Well, yes. I mean… You are.'

The murderer put his hands on the desk and looked intently at Shane. 'Go on.'

'That's it. Oh, then he asked to see you.'

'What about?'

'Didn't say.'

'Did you ask him?'

'No.'

'What's he look like?'

'Average height. Hair sticking up at the back–' Shane mimed a tuft of hair that wouldn't lie down. 'Skinny. Like a student. Looked a bit like that monkey.' He pointed to the front cover of the picture book on top of the pile.

'This monkey?' said the murderer, holding up the book and raising his eyebrows.

Shane craned his neck and looked at it more closely. 'Yeah.'

'This monkey on the cover of "The Cat in the Hat"?'

Shane looked again. 'Yeah. Only a bit, you know.'

'This monkey wearing a hat? This monkey that's the only animal on the cover of the book?'

'What? Sorry. I was only saying.'

The murderer looked at Shane. Shane stared back.

'Never mind,' said the murderer. 'Did he say anything else? Ask anything else?'

'No, don't think so.'

'Fill in a membership form, did he?'

'Course. Booked him in for an induction Tuesday.'

'Let's have a look.'

Shane sorted through a folder and put the piece of paper on the counter. The murderer picked it up and looked it over.

'Jonathon Fairfax,' he said. 'Brickfield Terrace.'

'Hang about,' said Shane. 'Someone else asked for you, and he phoned and all.' Shane looked down at his pad. 'Bob Pullover.'

'Right. Anything else you forgot to tell me?'

'Another bloke called. Posh fella. Wouldn't give his name.'

CHAPTER FORTY-SEVEN

Plover clacked the door shut and ticked the key round in the ignition. The BMW let out a growling breath, like a waiting wolf relaxing into motion.

Ahead of him, the target's car eased out of its parking space and pulled smoothly away. Plover looked anxiously over his shoulder: he needed to put another vehicle between himself and the target. A red Vauxhall Corsa instantly appeared, as though sent by providence.

Plover yanked on the wheel and put his foot down. In the ancient and adored Jaguar Mk 10 that Plover was used to driving, this would have moved him smoothly out into the Corsa's slipstream as it passed by. The BMW 535i Turbo was a very different beast, however – so keen to obey his order that it seemed to move forward a second or two before his foot hit the accelerator. It sprang out of the parking space and into the road without apparently passing through the intervening space. Plover stamped on the brake, halting the car atoms away from the door of the passing Corsa.

The Corsa also jammed on its brakes. It then did something that no car in London had ever done before – it politely moved back to let Plover out. This was precisely what Plover didn't want. He slid the gear lever into reverse and the BMW leapt backwards, almost hitting a parking meter.

The Corsa waited where it was. Plover waved at it to go on. The man in the Corsa politely waved at Plover to go on. Plover rudely waved at the man in the Corsa to stop waving and just go the fuck on. The man in the Corsa made a complex series of waves, possibly intended to signal his disappointment at Plover's lack of grace, and then finally drew forward, no doubt resolving never again to drive considerately in London.

At last Plover was moving, the Corsa acting as a shield between him and the target's BMW, which was – surprisingly – still only just ahead. They drove in convoy along Brompton Road, on to Knightsbridge and then Piccadilly, past the Ritz. Plover had a knack for picking shields who were going exactly the same way as his target. He was pleased that the knack was still there: he hadn't followed a car for over a year.

Suddenly, the Corsa was gone. Plover had no idea where. His attention must have slipped, lulled by the soft breathing of the engine, the blue-etched dials of the instrument panel. He was directly behind the black BMW. The target need only check his rear-view mirror to see him. Plover pulled his hat down over his eyes and looked desperately around.

Then he saw it: a blue Cadillac. This was the ideal shield, something that would grab the target's attention and make him even less likely to notice that he was being tailed. Like the perfectly timed Vauxhall

Corsa, the Cadillac seemed to have been sent by providence: Plover had no idea what other power could compel someone to drive one of the widest cars in the world around central London. He slowed and slotted himself neatly behind it. The target pulled off into Soho. The Cadillac followed him, with Plover behind.

On Great Windmill Street the traffic lights changed just as the target arrived at them. Plover pulled to a halt, uncomfortably aware that there was only an open-topped Fifties impracticality between himself and the rear-view mirror of the man he was following. Now the Cadillac which he had welcomed moments earlier seemed a terrible liability. Plover ducked and pretended to be searching for something in the footwell.

And then, for a third time, providence smiled on him. With a shiny tinkle of finger-cymbals, a great loose stumble of Hare Krishnas rounded the corner and began to cross the road in single file between Plover's car and the Cadillac. He smiled broadly at the leading member of the troupe, a surprisingly fat man with a T-shirt under his robe and the ghost of a recently departed beard showing pale against tanned cheeks. The man waved cheerily at him and smiled, as did the next Hare Krishna, and the next. After barely a dozen of them had crossed, the lights changed and both the target's car and the Cadillac pulled away.

Still the Hare Krishnas came, each with a smile, a wave, a bow or a minute clash of cymbals. Plover dared not edge forward: he didn't think the BMW was capable of it. It would flatten three brace of them with the slightest pressure to the accelerator. The lights changed again. Providence clearly favoured the Hari Krishnas over Plover.

When the lights showed green a second time, the last of the Hare Krishnas had just reached the safety of the kerb. The car leapt forward and was round the corner before Plover had even thought the words 'better pull off now'. The target's car was gone. The road ahead was clear all the way up to Oxford Street, where the traffic piled up black and motionless as always.

Plover moved on, nosing ahead, following his instinct. He thought he knew where the target would go: Soho Square. And that, after an altercation with a scooter, was where Plover went. Sure enough, there was a black BMW lodged beside the big concrete toilet at the north end of the square. But where was its driver?

Plover loitered in one of the roads leading off Soho Square, watching the car. It suddenly struck him that he couldn't see the BMW's registration plate, and so couldn't be absolutely sure it was the target's. What if the target had already left? What if he had gone somewhere else? What if he was behind him? Plover twisted nervously in his seat. Lance was not there, but a silver Mercedes was pulling off, leaving a single parking space in the otherwise jammed street. Providence had returned. He pulled into the space, noticed that there was still time on the meter, and then set off at a run to check the black BMW's registration plate.

There were scooters parked like clustering ducklings all around it, so Plover had to walk right up to the car and even crouch down before he could see its registration.

N835 2LX

Correct.

Now all Plover had to do was stroll back to his car, sit and watch. He rose, turned and was horrified to see the target emerging from Number 12. Plover instinctively ran into the concrete lavatory, turned right, into a cubicle, and closed and locked the door behind him.

He stood on the toilet seat and looked over the top of the cubicle, into the road beyond the doorway, hoping to see the black BMW pull off. The second it left, he would be after it. They had wanted to know where Lance would go before the meeting in Brixton. Well now they had the answer: Harrods and the office. Plover couldn't decide whether that told them anything at all.

That was when he noticed the little girl. She was standing by the door, watching him, wearing a large pink coat and a rainbow sweatshirt. Her eyes moved slowly from his face to the symbol on the door. The triangle that the symbol wore on the lower half of its body indicated that this was the women's branch of the toilet. The little girl looked at him again and took a step backwards. Beyond her, he could see the back end of the black BMW.

It pulled away.

Plover gave a sigh of relief, unlocked the cubicle and stepped smoothly from the toilet seat.

'Sodium chloride,' he said, 'is the chemical name for which common household product?'

'Er, salt,' said the girl.

'Correct,' he replied, stepping around her and out of the toilet.

As Plover walked away he heard the girl calling her dad, who was presumably in the men's part of the toilet. Luckily he had bought himself some time. He had always rated trivia highly as a means of distraction.

Back in the car he checked the clock: 10.40. Lance must now be on his way to the appointment. With a little fast driving, Plover believed he could beat him to it. Then he could watch him arrive, wait in the car, and follow him to see where he went afterwards. Plover put his foot down hard on the accelerator, regretted it, eased off and sped on towards Brixton.

'Your name's not on the list, sir,' said the man in the booth after a long look at the list and then another long look at Plover's business card. Plover had made good time; Lance was almost certainly behind him. He glanced anxiously over his shoulder, dreading the approach of a black BMW.

'I know, mate. Could you call inside? They know who I am. They'll buzz me in.'

'Right you are, sir.'

The man slowly unhooked the telephone from its cradle, put it to his ear and, on hearing the dial tone, laid the receiver on his desk. He looked at something on the wall of his booth and pressed a key on the telephone's dialler. Then he picked up the receiver again.

'Hello. I've got a … a Robert Polver here for Mr Thompson.'

He listened, slowly. 'Right you are,' he said.

The barrier clanked up and Plover sped in. He was round the first corner in a flash, and – in another flash – crashed directly into the side of a parked car.

Shit.

Once again Plover cursed his decision to take the turbo. The back door of the parked car, a brand-new Rolls-Royce, was crumpled in the middle and its window was shattered.

He looked around, back at the booth. The man inside was bent over a crossword. If he could just park, he might get away with it: there was no one around.

At that moment the other black BMW arrived at the barrier. Plover could see no parking spaces anywhere around. All he could do was leave the car park. He had to get out. His car jerked two feet backwards, almost hitting a parked Rover. Why did this thing have to be so sensitive? *Just get me out of here without crashing again.*

CHAPTER FORTY-EIGHT

Lance coasted to a stop in front of the red-and-white striped barrier. He enjoyed the soft *weem* of his window disappearing neatly inside the body of the door at the slightest pressure from his thumb.

'Good morning, sir. Do you have an appointment?'

For a second Lance was surprised that the man in the booth was a standard-issue security guard, complete with drooping grey moustache, baggy eyes and crossword. He had expected a kevlar-clad paramilitary.

'I'm Lance Ferman, here to see Andrew Thompson and Tristan Mangiafuoco.'

'Right you are.'

On second thought, it made sense. This man approached the task of finding Lance's name on his list with the same leisurely brio he would apply to a wordsearch, sucking the corner of his moustache all the while. He had the air of a man who has never, ever administered a savage beating: another boon to his employers, who might otherwise have found their visitors kettled and teargassed in a corner of the car park.

'Stick this to your window please, Mr Felman.'

'Sure thing.'

The barrier clanked up and the BMW scooshed into the car park. Lance voomed it around a corner and chunked it neatly into the only space he could see. Then he prunked open his seatbelt buckle, sat for a second as the belt slithed back inside its receptacle, gave the slightest tug on the door trigger and gloried in the soft *mick* as the seal opened and his leg registered the inrushing of the cold air. He tocked the door closed and walked towards the entrance of the building that squatted beside the car park.

The building was big and grubby, panelled and layered, a beached Lego boat. And yet, in its way, on this damp March morning, it was *right*. He took in a deep breath through his nose. Nothing, he thought, is better than parking a really expensive car.

He found himself walking slowly, swinging his briefcase loosely in his hand, running his eye over the rumps and noses of the cars around him like a racehorse trainer: Sierra, Scirocco, Seat, Saab. Smashed.

The car at the end of the row was smashed. Its rear door was caved in and the window shattered. Lance looked around. He could see no one but the security guard in his booth, bent over his crossword, sucking the answers out of the end of his pen. Lance glanced through the car's broken window.

There on the back seat lay a Manila file, just like the one he had found at Sarah's house. 'HM GOVERNMENT' was stamped on one corner.

He looked around again, then reached through the smashed window and took the file.

He opened it.

The first thing to catch his eye, on the first page, was the number of times 'RSG' appeared.

He slipped the folder inside his jacket, tucking the edge of it into the waistband of his trousers, and then began to walk back towards his car.

Roaring the BMW out of the car park, he narrowly avoided hitting a man wearing a hat and a long raincoat.

He couldn't wait to find out what Jonathon would think of the new file.

CHAPTER FORTY-NINE

At half past seven that morning Jonathon's eyes had sprung open and he had leapt out of bed while his alarm clock was still halfway through its first beep. He couldn't remember ever having done this before. He felt fantastic, even though he had only slept for three hours the previous night. He had spent the rest of the time lying there with his eyes closed, remembering how Rachel laughed or frowned or sneezed. He had replayed every word she had said, and re-said all the things that he had said, only better.

They had talked, watched a film, and then she had woken up and he'd walked her home. And it had all happened because he had been brave: because he had gone to track a murderer down in his own den, or his own gym, or at least a gym belonging to someone who… Who what?

Too much thinking, he thought, *let's get back to being happy.*

There weren't many colours in his little room, but those there were seemed unusually vibrant as he pottered about, putting on trousers and humming dreamy airs. It was almost as though someone had come along during the night and sorted out his settings – as though a skilled Jonathon engineer had let the air out of his pipes and reset his thermostat. It wasn't just colours that seemed deeper and more real, it was everything. There was a delicious nip in the air. And when he was dressed, the nip was replaced by a wonderful cosy glow. Clothes, he reflected, really do make you warmer. His tea tasted hot and friendly. He had inadvertently woken into a different world, and he couldn't wait to put up some posters.

There was a kind of warm, comforting tang in the back of his throat as he walked to the Tube station, and when he breathed in deeply, the fantasticness of the air and the cleanness of the day made him shudder happily. At the station all the people were so human – so bumbling, funny and basically well-meaning – that he felt a great wave of affection for them all surge over him. As the Tube doors closed and he leaned back against the carriage wall he realised that everything he'd ever worried about had been pointless.

How could he have worried about making friends in London, one of the most populous cities on Earth? Of course it had never been even remotely possible that he would fail to find friends. He had three more friends this week than last week – an increase of, well, of an infinite percentage, since he'd had zero friends last week. If the trend continued then next week he would have more friends than there were people in the world. Or, if he did the maths in a different way, he would have six friends. Actually, he would be happy just to hold on to those same three friends next week.

He would be especially happy to hold on to Rachel next week, or any time. She had talked about him being like a brother, but that didn't necessarily rule out a sexual relationship. After all, she liked lesbianism, so why not incest as well? Everything was going to be just fine.

That morning, rather than hiding among the endless rows of long coats, hoping that customers wouldn't stumble upon him accidentally while browsing the racks, he actively sought people out and tried to be as friendly and helpful as possible. A round, rich man with a thick, gargling accent asked Jonathon what he thought of a terrible, ill-fitting suit he tried on, and Jonathon advised him honestly and tactfully not to take it – rather than lying and getting him to buy a big turquoise hat as well, as he might have done on any other day.

Mr Reiss's eyebrows signalled that he was doing a good job, and hinted that he might soon be made a full-time, permanent member of staff, probably with managerial responsibilities. It was suddenly obvious that Mr Reiss was the best boss anyone could ever hope for.

He had never realised before, but people were all just brilliant. Each he came across seemed more loveable, honest and good-natured than the last. Even measuring their necks was a pleasure.

And then, around a rack of duffle coats, came Lance. He was carrying a black briefcase that was handcuffed to his wrist, and he looked as though he was thinking of North By Northwest, as he was stooping slightly and wearing that poised, sardonic, hunted look pioneered by Cary Grant.

Jonathon smiled at him. 'Um. Hello.'

'Jonathon. No time for smiling. I need your advice. Come with me.'

'My lunch break doesn't start till two today.'

Jonathon suddenly realised that they were by the escalators. Lance had hold of his arm and was walking him subtly out of the building.

'No time to wait. Call them later and tell them you got sick.'

'I can't do that. Mr Reiss–'

'He won't mind. Everyone does it these days. I went to see Jamyn this morning and he had just left his jacket on the back of his chair and swanned off somewhere. Been gone ages. If he can do it so can you.'

By this time there was no point in arguing. They were out on the pavement beside a large black BMW.

'You've still got the car,' said Jonathon.

'You bet your ass.'

'But I don't want to. At best I'd just win another ass.'

'Shut up and get in the car.'

They buckled their seat-belts in silence. Lance unlocked the briefcase's handcuff, took two Manila files from inside and handed them to Jonathon. As Jonathon opened them, Lance started the car and pulled off.

'What do you think?' asked Lance, putting on his shades.

'Have you read them?' asked Jonathon.

'I've read the one we read in the Barnaby Rudge.'

'Ah. What about the other one?'

'I always said that if we only knew what we had then we could do something with it. Well, I've got a feeling that the second file explains the first one. Found it about an hour ago. The first thing I saw in it was "RSG".

They turned off Brompton Road into Knightsbridge.

'Hey,' said Jonathon, flipping through the file, 'the first one has my beermat in it! With Rachel's number on.'

'Keep it. I want you to have it.'

'You told me it wasn't in there. You said you'd checked.'

'What can I tell you? I'm lax, baby.'

'Don't call me baby.'

'Sure thing. At least it's turned up.'

'I risked my life getting her number again, and–'

Jonathon stopped dead.

In the second file, among a sheaf of contracts with the green GL logo on them, was a flyer for the gym that Jonathon had attended the night before.

He gulped, shook his head, blinked several times and then looked at it again.

It was a flyer for the gym that Jonathon had attended the night before, complete with its picture of the terrifying man/lovely pussycat jutting out his jaw and sucking in his belly.

What did this mean? He didn't know much about Andrew Thompson, but Jonathon was certain that Thompson wasn't the sort of person who would go to Goliath Gym. In fact, it was very unlikely he had even heard of the Holloway Road. So what was a flyer for the gym doing in this file? He remembered the relief he had felt last night when he had found out that the terrifying man was Rachel's uncle. That had seemed to guarantee that, despite looking terrifying, he had nothing to do with Sarah Morecambe's murder. But finding the flyer in this file threw all that into doubt.

Jonathon replaced the flyer – there would be time to be astonished about that later on – and began to look through each of the contracts and letters in turn, absorbing the contents. It was like last-minute exam revision on the bus, except that they were in a BMW and Jonathon had a feeling that he would remember the contents of this file for the rest of his life.

'I think my boss suspects there's something weird going on with this assignment,' said Lance.

'Suspects?'

'Yeah. You know, no one really trusts each other in the business I'm in, and – to be fair – it's usually with good reason. Most people in it are lying, cheating, two-faced motherfuckers, and pretty much all of them are up to no good.'

'Mother-fuckers?' echoed Jonathon.

Lance laughed. Jonathon had noticed that people tended to laugh when he swore, which was why he didn't do it very often. He suspected that he and swearing didn't go together – mismatched concepts, like NATO and special fried rice.

Suddenly Lance stopped laughing.

'Shit,' he said.

'Shit?' replied Jonathon.

Lance looked worried, but again couldn't help but laugh.

'Can you see the car behind the one behind us?' he asked Jonathon.

'The black BMW?'

'Yes. Notice anything about it?'

'Um. It's the same as this one?'

'Exactly. Anything else?'

'No.'

'It's been two cars behind us ever since we left Harrods.'

'Are you sure?'

'Trust me, kid,' said Lance, unconsciously slipping into a Han Solo impression.

'Does that mean it's following us?'

'We'll soon find out,' said Lance, suddenly slewing the car to the left and accelerating.

Of course, in London it's only possible for two cars per day to suddenly slew to the left and accelerate. Lance got half way through the manoeuvre before the lights changed to red and he had to stamp on the brake. This left them embarrassingly straddling two lanes, one of which was the left filter. All around them, Jonathon could feel the drivers projecting silent disapproval.

'Shee-it,' said Lance.

'Um, did we shake him?' asked Jonathon.

Lance shook his head.

'No, my little friend, we did not shake him.'

The lights changed and Lance managed to pull fully into the left-turn lane. Then, just as the lights changed back, he switched lanes again and went straight ahead. This manoeuvre only brought him to the other side of the box junction, where the traffic tailed back from the next set of lights. The silent disapproval intensified, then spilled over into a single horn blast. Jonathon settled back in his seat and took a surreptitious look in the rear-view mirror: the other BMW was now also in the left-turn lane.

'Perhaps he knows what we have,' suggested Jonathon.

'Perhaps he does.'

'If he goes straight ahead now, you'll know he's following you.'

'No shit, Sherlock.'

'Or he might take the left turn and run parallel to you – I've seen cars do that in films.'

'Have you ever seen a car chase set in London?'

'No.'

'That's because there's absolutely no fucking way you can do that sort of shit in London. If he turns left now he'll be in Stoke Newington before he gets a chance to take a right and head me off at the pass. Jonathon, you're about to be involved in your first low-speed car chase.'

'Wow.'

Jonathon dived back into the file, skimming through more letters and contracts. The lights behind them changed, and the black BMW did suddenly pull into the centre lane, badly upsetting a man and his dog who were driving a yellow Vauxhall Astra. The black BMW was again two cars behind them. Lights changed somewhere way up in front. The traffic moved forwards twenty yards and stopped again. Luckily, the driver to Lance's right was doing his hair in his rearview mirror and so Lance was able to pull in front of him.

'So, *do* you think he's following you?'

'I think so. Partly because that BMW also belongs to my agency.'

'Are you sure? Have you seen the registration?'

'Oddly enough, I never memorised the number plates – something else always came up whenever I set aside the time.'

'So why do you think it's the same one?'

'Just a hunch,' said Lance.

'Do you recognise the driver?'

'He's wearing a hat and dark glasses.'

Jonathon didn't know what to say next. 'You're insane!' seemed too harsh, whereas the situation seemed to demand more than just the vague head-nodding he found himself doing.

But once again the traffic had lurched forward.

'Hang on to your hat!' warned Lance, and stalled the car.

'What…' said Jonathon.

'He's going to have to overtake us,' said Lance, flipping on their hazard lights as the cars scudded past, including the black BMW. Lance allowed a few more cars to trickle past and then rejoined the flow, ignoring the blaring of horns.

'He's four cars ahead of us now,' observed Jonathon.

'And that's where he's going to stay,' said Lance, his teeth gritted and a look of fire in his eyes which bespoke a fierce determination to drive more slowly than the car in front could conceivably manage.

'Are you going to turn left here?'

'That's just what he wants me to do. I'm going–' he broke off. 'Shit! He's just managed to change into the middle lane. He's dropped back. He's only two cars ahead now.'

'What are you going to do?' asked Jonathon. He didn't know whether this whole thing was a joke, a disturbing case of paranoia, or a serious situation. Whichever it was, it seemed imperative to him too that Lance should drive as slowly as possible and put as large a number of cars in between him and the other black BMW as could feasibly be done.

'I'm going to park.'

'In London?' asked Jonathon, incredulously.

'You think I'm crazy, don't you? Well I'm not. I'm going to park this baby, and I'm going to park it good. Here we go.'

And then Lance executed the most beautiful manoeuvre Jonathon had ever seen or even heard of. They had been sitting still again. Then, as the traffic surged forward once more, Lance moved the car through the right-hand lane, pouring it through a gap not more than a millimetre longer than the car itself, precisely matching the speed of the other vehicles, so that the mother of two in the car behind didn't even have to think about braking. Then – in the same smooth action – he peeled off into a dark space between two buses that no one could have guessed would be capable of holding a large BMW. The delicate sine curve Lance had just described with his manoeuvre was a thing of rare and precious beauty, a work of art which quite took Jonathon's breath away.

'That was incredible,' he said.

'No. Getting out again will be incredible,' replied Lance, with much the same expression on his face as John Wayne might have worn in a similar parking situation.

CHAPTER FIFTY

Thompson sat in his office, doodling on a large sheet of paper on his leather-topped desk. It was five o'clock. The office was quiet and his new secretary had gone home. He was very glad to be alone. Things had been moving quickly and he felt that he needed time to take stock. The way he did this was to find historical parallels for everything that bothered him.

What bothered him most was Ginia. When he had embarked on the seduction it had seemed like a small footnote in history, something that agreeably rounded out an important political personage (himself) without at all affecting the substance of his achievement: something like Lord Melbourne's philandering with Queen Victoria's Maids of Honour. Now, he suspected that his conquest of Ginia was an act of self-deluding recklessness comparable with Operation Barbarossa, Hitler's invasion of Russia. *Ginia*, he wrote, *Melbourne or Barbarossa?*

There must be a better parallel. After all, his seduction of Ginia could hardly draw him into a disastrous war on two fronts resulting in his going mad and shooting himself in the head with a Luger P08, could it? The fact that he was a Registered Scapegoat, and a damned successful one at that, paradoxically meant that it was in some very powerful people's best interests that any minor indiscretions of his were swept under the carpet – no one wanted him to resign unless it helped them. If this one got out, Mangiafuoco was more likely to lose his job over it than Thompson.

And besides, it never would come out. He circled the word Melbourne, added 'Lord' before it and then wrote 'STD' beside it. STD stood for 'save till dotage'. He used it for episodes that were so embarrassing and discreditable that he would have to be well into his eighties before he told anyone, but which he would then – being beyond the reach of any conceivable retribution – relate constantly and with huge delight.

His first STD incident had been at Oxford: the theft of an ashtray from the Dean's rooms during a dinner given there. He had only just taken up smoking, and had absolutely no idea where one might go to buy an ashtray. So, seeing a nice one on the Dean's sideboard, he had pocketed it, assuming it wouldn't be missed.

It turned out that the ashtray had been given to the Dean's father by Edward VII, and was a treasured family heirloom. The whole college had been threatened with expulsion, but Thompson had been unable to return it, even anonymously, for fear of being found out as the original culprit. Instead he had hidden it beneath some liquorice and given generously to a whip-round for a replacement. The fuss had eventually blown over, but Thompson had never admitted his guilty secret. Even now there were people who might physically hurt him if he admitted the truth about the ashtray.

He needed to be sure that Ginia also saw their night together as an STD, so he picked up the telephone, took it out on to the balcony and dialled. Far below, two troopers of the Life Guards sat perfectly still on huge black horses while the tourists milled about.

'Ah Claudine. How are you?' For some reason he had expected Ginia, not her mother, to answer.

'Glad to hear it,' he chuckled. 'All alone in the house are you?'

'Ginia's gone sneaking?' He tried to keep the horror from his voice, but he could feel his chest tightening. 'What do you mean?'

'Oh, *skiing*.' A wave of joy and relief broke over him. 'Where?'

'Wonderful. Spur of the moment thing?'

'Well of course I do. That's because I *am* very happy. That's why I called: simple high spirits.'

'Yes, it would be wonderful to get together again.'

'Sunday? That sounds wonderful. It's only a two-seater though. Where would we put Tris?'

'Oh, won't he? But...'

'Well I'd like to get to know you better, but...'

'Yes.'

'No, Claudine, I'm not saying I don't find you very...'

'Yes, of course...'

'But...'

He stared down at the telephone in his hand, listening to the hum of a broken call. Damn. Why did he have to be so irresistible to the Mangiafuoco womenfolk? If there was one thing that he was absolutely sure of, it was that he was not going to have an affair with Mangiafuoco's wife, Claudine. There was, of course, a certain appeal in the symmetry of it – the wife and the daughter – but it was stupidly dangerous. If Ginia was Barbarossa then Claudine was Pearl Harbour.

And besides, he had told Mangiafuoco about being an RSG: he couldn't afford to lose his friendship now. What's more, he liked Mangiafuoco – apart from his irritating habit of attributing everyone's literary allusions – and he didn't *want* to lose the friendship. There was no question of his attending the assignation with Claudine on Sunday. In fact, he would call Mangiafuoco this second. He would tell him that he had just been on the phone to Claudine, and that she had suggested the two of them meet on Sunday. Then he would ask Mangiafuoco to apologise to her as he had just remembered that he had a prior engagement. This would make him appear honest and trustworthy, so that his seduction of Ginia would seem less plausible. He needed to establish his innocence beyond all doubt: no more skulking about, no more secrets. He climbed back into the room from the balcony, sat down and dialled.

'Tris? Andrew. How the Devil are…'

'Oh. *Stolen*? When?'

'Do you think it has anything to do with the Lenin & Plover chap not turning up to the meeting?'

'Well what sort of documents were they?

'I did tell you about leaving things in your car. It was bound to…'

'Yes. Sorry.'

'I know. *After the event even a fool is wise.*'

He frowned. 'Yes, it is Homer. I do wish…'

'But you still haven't said what the documents were.'

'And how will you do that?'

'But…' He tutted.

'It's just that you're not telling me anything, Tris. What were the documents and how will you get them back?'

'*Thomas* Grey, actually: *Where ignorance is bliss, 'tis folly to be wise.*'

'Why was I calling?' Thompson stared down at the paper in front of him: *Melbourne or Barbarossa?*

'Oh, just to chat.'

'This and that. You know.'

'Well, I heard that Preece opened the door of a certain stationery cupboard last week and who should he see there having a *tête-a-tête*?'

'No, guess again.'

'Fatty Anderson, with Claire Newman.'

'The researcher.'

'No, the other one. The one with eyebrows like larks' wings.'

'Yes, and his trousers around his ankles.'

'Yes, I…'

'Is it? Oh well, better answer it I suppose. No, nothing else. Ciao.'

Thompson sat back in his chair. *Why didn't I tell him I'd talked to Claudine?* he wondered.

CHAPTER FIFTY-ONE

Tonight's Girl From The Pub was Scottish, and Lance was again having a tricky time remembering what he was supposed to call her. He kept wanting to call her Morag for no reason but that he'd always found the name funny. Her real name might have been Maria, but he had no way of knowing. For the last half hour he had responded to almost everything she'd said by saying 'Aye hen,' which made her laugh and pretend to try and hit him, which in turn made him catch her hand, pretend to wrestle with her and then kiss her. It was almost the perfect relationship.

They pretended to live near enough to each other for it to be worth sharing a taxi, and when they arrived at Lance's building he asked her if she wanted to come inside for a good hard shag – by which, he went on to explain, he really meant coffee.

'Aye hen,' she replied, and got out of the taxi.

He held her hand as they went upstairs and he insisted on carrying her over the threshold of his flat, which was made even more difficult by the fact that he had a briefcase chained to his wrist. Remarkably, he managed to keep both Morag and the briefcase in his arms as he turned on the light. It blinked twice then hummed into life.

Looking around, he couldn't help noticing that the place had been destroyed. He dropped Morag on the floor.

'Shit,' he said.

The mess was incredible. The cutlery drawer had been pulled out and its contents dumped on the floor. The door of every kitchen cabinet stood open. Particular attention had been paid to the sink unit: the shelf had been smashed, the base levered up, and the lacquer of the doors deeply scratched with broad, straight strokes, as though he could have been hiding something beneath their deeply unpleasant blue plastic veneer. Even the pipes leading to the sink had been partially dismantled. His cooker-hood looked as though it would never extract unwanted odours again. The place smelled terrible: his old yoghurt had become significantly older since being emptied out of the fridge.

'This place really needs a woman's touch,' remarked Morag.

Lance wandered through into the living room. The pattern had been repeated, but here some things were actually missing: the TV, the video and a bottle of whisky.

His bedroom was the same. In the bathroom the lino had been put in the bath and a couple of floorboards taken up.

Lance was suddenly very, very glad that he had kept the file with him. If he had not become paranoid and bought the briefcase that was handcuffed to his wrist then all the files would have been in the flat and he would now have been completely fucked.

Maybe it was the drink, but he suddenly felt immensely relieved. All his suspicions had been proved correct. His opponents, whoever they were, had revealed their hand, but Lance was holding all the cards. He really hoped that this was one of those games where the object is to collect as many cards as possible, rather than one of those other games where the object is to be the first to play all of your cards. His cards were chained painfully to his wrist.

He laughed and Morag looked at him.

'Fancy a drink?' he asked.

'Too fucking right,' she said.

FRIDAY

Lance was a night person rather than a morning person. He had seen four-thirty in the morning before, but he more usually approached it from the opposite direction. He had never *got up* then.

His clock's large face stared blankly at him like an idiot child as he rolled back the reluctant blankets and reached for his trusty kimono. Despite Morag, he had slept fitfully, waking often, with the vague feeling that there was something he should be doing. Finally, he had given in and got up. Morag still slumbered peacefully.

The shower gave him only a slightly chilly pummelling – he had obviously caught it unawares – and his clothes received him stiffly. He waded through half a bowl of dry cereal and drank a cold cup of instant coffee as he sat hunched in his smashed kitchen.

At five he pulled his briefcase from under his bed and left a note for this incarnation of the Girl From The Pub. He tried to make it as nice as possible to compensate for the fact that he still couldn't remember what he was meant to call her this time.

Hey Hen,
Great to see you. Have to go to work early. Bread & coffee etc in kitchen. But toaster and kettle are missing. Sorry. Shower fucking freezing – best not stand under it. Make yourself at home.

Lance

As he left the flat (by the back door today, then over the wall into the alleyway) he was already regretting the words 'make yourself at home'. He was worried that he might get back that evening and find her wearing one of his shirts, flipping through furniture and babywear catalogues, with a meatloaf in the oven. Well, he comforted himself, he could always get a new flat.

Out on the street, there were pensioners, postmen and dustmen. One man said 'good morning,' mistaking Lance for a member of the morning club – the people who habitually get up very early. For them the world is an entirely different place: it is much less heavily populated than the world everyone else lives in, as well as being chillier, slightly more polite and almost infinitely less fun. As a result, the morning club is full of coldly jolly people with no feelings.

At ten past six the newsagent had already put out his battered yellow bin and his old metal ice-cream sign. A photocopied note in the window said 'Photocopies – 5p'. Lance entered.

The shop was rectangular and divided into two sections. One of them contained newspapers, magazines and sweets, along with a couple of books, a few videos and some gold-plated cigarette lighters in a display case. The other section housed bizarrely expensive flimsy toys, cards with pictures of motorbikes or boats on them, bits of stationery, dusty artists' equipment and a photocopier.

'Good morning Mr Ferman,' said Mr Patel. 'Come to pay your newspaper bill?'

Mr Patel looked up from the pile of newspapers he was marking and smiled unnervingly. He wore a knitted tank top and a moustache, and he nestled a cup of tea beneath his right breast as though it were a small baby owl that he was taking care of.

'Better than that Mr Patel, I've come to use your photocopier.'

'Wonderful. Do you want to pay your bill while you're here?'

'I'll have a *Financial Times*, a photocopy card and this Double Decker please.'

'And settle up the bill?'

'Mr Patel – I'll tell you about my bill.'

'And pay it too?' The man's dogged, polite optimism was impressive. 'How much?'

'Three hundred and twelve pounds forty-seven.'

'And these things?'

'That's six forty-five.'

Lance quickly flicked a ten-pound note into Mr Patel's hand.

'Fifty-five's seven and three's ten,' said Mr Patel automatically, handing the change over without blinking an eye.

'Thanks,' said Lance, triumphantly.

Mr Patel hung his head, realising that Lance had exploited his shopkeeping reflexes yet again, and Lance moved over to the photocopier. He worked quickly, making three copies of all the documents in both files. As he fed the documents into the machine he found himself worrying again. Usually he never worried, not even when he spilled something on his trousers. Now he seemed to be worrying all the time.

Duplicating the files was a good first step. It should make him safe from any large men in dark glasses who might otherwise be tempted to break into his house and kill him. There was the worry that they might do this anyway, before he could tell them that he had duplicated the files. There was also the related worry that he might be bundled into the back of a black BMW when he emerged from the newsagent's carrying the originals and all three copies.

Should that fail to happen, he had decided to give two of the copies to people he could trust not to do anything stupid with them – dependable civilians who were not part of the incestuous, paranoid world of Lenin & Plover. He would distribute them before work and keep one copy. He didn't yet know what he was going to do with the originals. Or rather, he suspected that he did know what he was going to do with them, but wasn't yet letting himself in on the secret. He would find out when the time came, in due course.

Distributing the files would insure him against crime and disaster, but still leave the worry of what he should actually do next. Well, tomorrow was Saturday: he would have time to read his copy of both files. Then perhaps he would know what to do with them. Or would he? Lance was becoming dimly aware that, even if he navigated his way through this minefield, on the other side might lie all the things that everyone else worried about. Things like the environment, traffic, the price of tomatoes, and how to get his clothes really clean even at low temperatures, or ideally without washing them at all.

He decided to lighten the load a little. Before he left he gave Mr Patel a cheque for his paper bill.

The doors of the Tube train opened and Lance waited until all the postmen had got in before taking a seat himself.

Lance was up so early because he wanted to foil whoever was following him. Whoever it was knew that he had the BMW, so they would not expect him to get up early and use public transport. Even better, the small number of people around at this time in the morning made it easy to tell whether you were being followed, especially on the Tube.

He had never before seen the first Tube of the day, and thus he had never before seen so many postmen in one place. This prevalence of postmen pleased Lance, as it made the non-postmen much easier to spot. It wasn't just the uniforms: there was something in the set of their faces and the line of their shoulders. Everything about a postman says 'postman'.

Lance shook out his copy of the *Financial Times* and sat back. Plover had taught him that the *Financial Times* is the best surveillance paper. Its pinkness camouflages the flesh tones in Caucasian faces and hands, and it never carries any interesting – or even comprehensible – news on its front page. Anyone looking in Lance's direction would have seen the words 'Big chill puts orange juice on two-year high', closely followed by 'LBMA paints rosy gold picture'. The paper projected an aura of there being nothing in the immediate area for anyone to attend to.

The journey from Ladbroke Grove, London's coldest Tube station, to Holloway Road, its third most desolate, is one of the world's longest, taking few minutes but many lifetimes. What's more, the Hammersmith and City line – narrowly ahead of the District line – is London's most dispiriting means of conveyance. Lance somehow kept up both his spirits and his *Financial Times*, putting in an utterly convincing reading performance while constantly surveilling all carriages and platforms in range. He managed this despite still being handcuffed to a briefcase and having three carrier bags of secret documents lodged behind his back.

At King's Cross he changed trains, walking through the miles of corridors and turnstiles between the Victoria, Piccadilly, Northern, Metropolitan, Circle, and Hammersmith and City lines, pretending to be lost. At every corner he stopped and looked back. Lance was still getting used to the number of people in trench coats – a fashion he hadn't seen coming and couldn't understand. Some people wore them with ripped jeans, some with pinstriped trousers, one with shades and a fedora. None of them seemed to be following him.

Lance did another tour of the platforms and escalators before boarding a Piccadilly line train running deep underground. Again he deployed his *Financial Times* to repel interest while inspecting everyone around him – more numerous now and entirely composed of non-postmen. Then he was out, along the long platform and into the lift, still apparently immersed in his newspaper.

When he emerged from the station the feeling of being deep underground persisted. The sky was still dark, the street lamps shone orange, Holloway Road stretched out before him like a great river, banked by squat buildings. To his left was a railway bridge on which someone had written 'fist yourself' in two-foot high letters. Opposite was a van-hire place, which Lance made straight for. He walked purposefully through the entrance, inspected a van with apparent interest, and kept an eye on the entrance to the station. There were quite a large number of people hanging around aimlessly, at least one of whom was wearing a trench coat, but no sign of anything unusual. He left the van-hire place and walked briskly up the road, past an obscure department store and a hundred chicken shops, and on towards Brickfield Terrace.

CHAPTER FIFTY-THREE

Bang, bang, bang.

'Mr Jonathon!'

Bang, bang, bang.

It took Jonathon several seconds to realise that the banging noise was not a result of the nail he was hammering into the coffin in which he was sealing Mr Reiss, that he was not hammering anything into anything, but only dreaming that he was, and that Avi was pounding on the door and calling his name. He opened his eyes and looked at the red digits of the clock face, taking a moment to bring them into focus. It was 632 AD, so somewhere around the middle of the Dark Ages. Who would be banging on his door at this point in history? Mr Reiss, obviously. That was why he needed sealing up in the coffin. Where was that hammer?

Bang, bang, bang.

'Mr Jonathon!'

He opened his eyes again, realising with a start that despite his best intentions he had been tricked into dreaming again. He focused his eyes on the red digits of the clock face. It was 6.32 AM. Why was his clock going off? It wasn't. Why not? Mr Reiss's evil influence was clearly at work. If only he could be sealed up in some way…

Wait.

He wasn't going to fall for that a second time. He sat up. His whole body hurt. After a day's grace, every muscle he had used in the gym on Wednesday evening now clamoured to tell him how upset it was with him.

'Mr Jonathon!'

Jonathon fell out of bed, put on a jumper and wrenched open the door. Avi was standing there, wearing a white dressing-gown, a towel around his neck.

'Umph,' said Jonathon.

'There is someone at the door.'

Jonathon looked around, surprised that Avi should feel he had to tell him this elementary fact.

'It's you. Isn't it?' he asked, confused.

'The door downstairs.'

'Oh.' Jonathon stood there, staring blankly at Avi.

'Go downstairs and answer the door please.'

Jonathon pulled on some trousers and went downstairs. At the door he found Lance, who had a briefcase handcuffed to one wrist and was carrying three plastic bags in the other hand.

'Morning Jonathon,' said Lance.

'Jonathon,' said Jonathon.

'Sorry to get you up so early.'

'Mumph.'

'Are you even awake?' asked Lance, peering at Jonathon's face.

'Awake. Yes.' Jonathon could feel his eyes closing even as he said the words. He had never been less ready to get up.

There was a pause which Lance broke by saying 'Come on in' in a welcoming voice, stepping into the house and ushering Jonathon before him.

'Thanks,' said Jonathon, failing to notice that he was being invited into his own house.

'Fancy a cup of tea?' asked Lance, leading Jonathon into the kitchen.

Jonathon sat down on a stool and stared at the table while Lance made him a cup of tea.

'How many sugars?' asked Lance.

'None. Please. I mean none sugars, thanks.'

When it was ready Lance pushed it into his hands, then picked up his own mug.

'Come on up,' said Lance.

'Thanks,' said Jonathon.

He followed Lance upstairs and slumped down onto the chair.

'Drink your tea,' said Lance. 'I've got a favour to ask you.'

'There's sugar in this.'

'You need it. I can't ask you a favour if you're still half asleep.'

Jonathon took a large slurp. 'This is coffee,' he said.

'You need it. I can't ask you a favour if you're still half asleep. Drink some more.'

The hot, sweet, milky coffee traced a path down Jonathon's throat into his stomach and then, magically, back up to his brain. He opened his eyes properly.

'Um,' he said. 'Hello Lance. What are you doing here?'

'That's better.'

'Did you say something about a favour?'

'Yes. Are you awake?'

'I think so.'

'Right. You know those documents I have?'

'Yes.'

'I need you to look after a set of photocopies–'

'Photocopies?'

'Yes.'

'Where will you put the originals?'

'In a very safe place.'

'Right.'

'Anyway, I need you to look after a set of copies. And if you don't hear from me, or if you find out something has happened to me, I need you to post them to the address written on the large envelope I've put them in. Will you do it?'

'Yes.'

'Don't answer yet. Have this other coffee and think it over, then let me know.' Lance handed him his own untouched mug.

'I don't think I can face any more coffee,' said Jonathon, drinking it anyway.

'What were you doing last night?'

'Worrying.'

'And the night before?'

'I went to the gym.'

Lance raised his eyebrows.

'And then Rachel came here.'

'Go Jonathon! You old sex dog.'

'We watched a film and she fell asleep.'

'Is that code for something filthy?'

'No.'

'Oh. Well. Go Jonathon! You old platonic friendship dog.'

'Thanks.'

'No problem.'

'Where shall I put the photocopies?' asked Jonathon, looking into his coffee.

'Under the bed?'

Jonathon looked worried.

'What have you got there?' asked Lance.

'Posters.'

'What else?'

'Nothi…' Jonathon stopped and considered. 'Three copies of *Naked Ladies*.'

'Are they under something?'

'A rolled-up bit of carpet.'

'Sounds perfect.'

'OK.'

'Listen, don't rush into it. Think about it while you have your shower. I'll wait here.'

'OK. Don't look under the bed though.'

'You got it, hotshot.'

'Don't call me hotshot.'

'No problem, hombre.'

CHAPTER FIFTY-FOUR

Just as she picked up the tray, the phone rang. Jane jumped, spilling tea on the toast that was waiting quietly in its rack.

'Blast it,' she said. She had wanted to surprise Geoffrey by waking him up with breakfast in bed – something she had never done before. Now he would be awake, and perhaps grumpy from the phone call. It was bound to be for him.

'Darling!' he called.

She walked into the hall. 'Yes?' she called back.

'It's for you!'

She picked up the phone in the hall.

'Oh. Hello lambkin,' she said.

'Well I shan't say a word if you're calling from your portable telephone – I know how temperamental it can be.'

'You're with Jonathon? How is he?'

'Sorry, I know I promised not to say a word. It is rude not to ask though.'

'Is that good or bad?'

'Oh good. I am glad. So on balance, Jonathon is in good health.'

'Yes I know, but you did tell me anyway ducky.'

'All right my precious, from now on my lips are sealed.'

'Apart from to answer questions, as you say.'

'I am sorry, it's just that you...'

'No. I am sorry. I shall try to be serious. And quiet as a mouse.'
She laughed.

'Oh *files*. I thought you said...'

'Well, there we go.'

'Of course, if you need my help. Anything.'

'So you just need me to hang on to a copy of these piles – I'm sorry files – do I need to hide them?'

'I'm not being flippant. No, it's just that Ilse from church is coming over for our regular Scrabble morning later on. I have to use up all my larkiness by then or...'

'Königsberg.'

'No, not since the war.'

'Listen ducky, I'll look after just as many files or piles as you want me to, just...'

'Well, I shall see you later then. Yes. Goodbye Lance.'

CHAPTER FIFTY-FIVE

At ten o'clock, Bob Plover arrived in Soho Square. He was still wearing an unrumpled trench coat, a pair of dark glasses and a fedora, which had turned out to be a remarkably effective disguise. No wonder the outfit had been standard issue for all spies between 1920 and 1970. Sometimes the old ways are the best.

He was extremely tired. The evening before, he had been drawn into a long argument about curtains with his wife, Debbie. She wanted ochre and he hated ochre. After that he had gone out to work, which had consisted of dozing in Hammersmith in a rented multi-purpose van until a light flicked on in an upstairs window and he had instinctively woken. Then he had followed Lance on an exhausting tour of the Tube, after which he had hidden in a bush near a large, unhappy-looking building on Brickfield Terrace, watching to see which bedsit Lance entered. He had then followed Lance to a nice townhouse in Notting Hill.

Now, as he climbed the three steps to Lenin & Plover's offices, he was footsore. He pushed open the door, unconsciously made amiable small-talk with the skinny security guard in the oversized blazer and moustache, and rode the lift up to his office on the fourth floor.

'*Fourth* floor. Doors … *op*ening,' said the lift.

'Cheers mate,' muttered Plover and ambled over to his office.

Once he had made himself a coffee and sat down at his desk, he checked his answering machine.

'*You have … FOUR … messages. Message … ONE … received at … SEVEN … OH … FIVE … AM.*'

'Ochre.'

'*Message … TWO … received at … SEVEN … FIFTY-THREE … AM.*'

'Bob man! Come and have a look at this! It's Dave, Crimson Indian.'

'*Message … THREE … received at … EIGHT … THIRTY-ONE … AM.*'

'Bob. Visited the place you said. Turned it inside out. Nothing found.'

'*Message … FOUR … received at … EIGHT … THIRTY-FOUR … AM.*'

'Fucking hell Bob man, get your laughing gear round this lot. Dave. Obviously. Seriously Bobby, you need to see this. Dave. Crimson Indian.'

Plover hauled himself to his feet, put on his rumpled jacket and wandered off, still very tired. He picked up a latte and a Danish on the way, and while he walked over to Dean Street he bestrewed his tie with flakes of pastry.

Dave worked for a TV editing company called Crimson Indian. He worked the night shift, which mostly meant transferring things from film to tape and eating pizza. He always had plenty of time to skim through the security tapes which Plover received every day from buildings all over London. Usually there was nothing to report, but while Dave was waiting for his big break, he watched them anyway. He knew the sorts of things to look out for, and could watch a three-hour tape on fast forward in seconds.

'What have you got for me, Dave mate?' asked Plover as he entered the viewing suite.

Dave sat in a large padded chair with his legs curled under him.

The only light came from five large monitors arranged at eye level. On the desk beneath them were several black machines with glowing blue time displays and banks of controls. Some of the popcorn Dave was eating had got caught in his bushy sideburns. From the darkness, hair and snack emerged wild and eerie, lit by the ghostly light of the monitors.

'Just look at this Plovey me old beauty,' said Dave, rewinding the tape.

He pressed play. On one of the monitors a white door appeared. Plover could see immediately that this was very high-class CCTV. It was black-and-white, but smooth and very clear. A girl approached the door, checked her appearance in a little mirror from her bag, took several deep breaths, turned around twice and then rang the bell. The door was opened by Andrew Thompson, who grinned wolfishly and kissed her before ushering her in and closing the door behind her.

'Looks like Tommo's consorting with the ladies of the night eh?' said Dave. 'World's oldest profession, eh squire? Nudge nudge. Know what I mean? Watch what happens now.'

He turned a dial and the high-pitched racing of the tape could be heard as the numbers on one of the displays began to flicker. The image of the door remained perfectly still. Dave released the dial.

Thompson opened the door and gently led the girl out. She was obviously unsteady on her feet. He moved away from her, still holding her by both shoulders. He looked at her, apparently making sure she was balancing properly. Then he kissed her on the lips. She just stood there, dazed, looking at him. He took her gently back into his arms and they remained in that position for a while. She was as stiff as a shop dummy. Then Thompson kissed her on the forehead and stepped back. He said something to her. She nodded. He said something else and she nodded again. Then he pointed back down the stairs and disappeared into his flat, closing the door behind him.

'Watch this, matey,' said Dave.

The girl burst into tears. She stood sobbing for a while, shoulders hunched. Then she took something from her pocket, dabbed her eyes, straightened her back, glanced up and down the stairs, and was gone.

'Errrrr … remarkable! Let's see that again shall we Bob?' burbled Dave happily, rewinding the tape. 'Tommo in Prozzo Shocko, eh?'

Plover still hadn't said anything. Suddenly he pulled up a chair and sat in it, leaning forward. 'Go back to that bit where she looks round again.'

'No sooner said than done, mio maestro.' He shuttled the tape forward again.

'Can you play it slowly?'

'Frame by frame, me old beauty!'

They watched, accompanied by the tape's muffled ticking noise as the images edged along.

'Stop,' said Plover.

On the screen, the girl's face was clearly recognisable – if you knew who she was.

CHAPTER FIFTY-SIX

'Hello?'

'No I'm afraid he's not here presently now. May I take a message?'

'Oh, hello Bob. Didn't recognise your voice at all. You been doing them ventriloquist classes again?'

'Well whatever it's called. Now, what can I do you for?'

'Tomorrow afternoon? Not much. He's meant to be mowing the grass, but that won't bother him. You need him for something?'

'That's a bit of a mouthful for this time in the afternoon, isn't it? Yes, no problem dearest. Hang on, me pen's run out. Just a minute. All right. Jane Archer-what? No, you'll need to spell that one for me. A – R – C – H – E – R. What? Like a dash? Oh, I know what you mean. Sorry, I'm miles away today – clearing the kitchen out. H – O – L – L – I – S. Jane Archer-Hollis. Eighty-one Powis Square, Notting Hill. So what you want him to do?'

'Oh there's another one as well? Sorry love. What's that? Sounds like a washing powder. F – A – I – R – F – A – X, John. Got it. Room F, 60 Brickfield Terrace. OK.'

'No problem. Ooh Bob, I just remembered. Barbecue on Sunday. Fancy coming over?'

'Well, we have to, cos of the kitchen, so…'

'I know it's March. Meant to be sunny though. That's what they said on the telly anyway.'

'No, they usually get the weekend weather right.'

'Well they've got all week to work it out, don't they?'

'All right darling, see you soon. Ta-ta.'

Lisa put the phone down and the kettle on, and then got straight on with making up the sheet for this latest assignment.

CHAPTER FIFTY-SEVEN

'Mr Thompson?' asked a young man, putting his floppy blond head around Thompson's door.

'Yes?'

'Hi, I'm Oliver,' said the man, bounding into the room, 'working for Tristan Mangiafuoco. Researcher.'

'Oh yes.'

'He'd like to see you in his office.'

The young man delivered the message with the air of a pleased labrador, as though he wouldn't be surprised if he were given a biscuit and tummy-rub for doing it so well.

'When?'

'About now?'

Thompson felt his face turn pale. Why send a researcher? He had been in his office all day. Mangiafuoco could easily have phoned him.

He pretended to consult his diary. 'I should just about be able to manage that.'

'Thanks. I'll say that you're on your way.' The young man rushed off, wagging his tail and carrying Thompson's acceptance like a beloved tennis ball.

Thompson rose, straightened his trousers and jacket, smoothed his hair and set out along the corridor. The wood panelling, the subdued light and the old carpets reminded him of school. Ridiculous to think of it. He wasn't on his way to a caning. Of all the men Thompson knew, Mangiafuoco was one of the most level-headed (literally as well as figuratively).

The sweat was beginning to collect in the underarm seams of Thompson's shirt. The more he thought about it, the more he became convinced it was all about Ginia, and the more afraid he became. If

Mangiafuoco had found out about Ginia, then their friendship would take a lot of repairing. Why had he done it?

Mangiafuoco had always indulged Thompson. He had always shown patience. But Thompson knew that his friend's forbearance did not stretch to allowing his daughter to be used for casual sex by men of dubious character who were now well into their fifties. If it did he would be more in demand for dinner-parties.

As with the trip to the Headmaster's office, Thompson both hated the journey and wished it would go on for all time. He could see the door now, glossy and white, with Mangiafuoco's name on it. He walked those last few feet slowly, but still the door drew nearer. When he was just inches from it he halted and straightened his tie. Men are known to react better to having their young daughters seduced if the cad has a straight, decently-knotted tie.

After smoothing his hair again and checking his shoes, Thompson rapped smartly on the door. It was opened by Rose, Mangiafuoco's secretary. Thompson smiled sweetly at her, and she replied with the sort of tight-lipped grimace you might use if you opened your door and found Idi Amin standing there wearing an ingratiating smile and holding a suitcase.

'Hello Rose,' he said.

'Good afternoon Andrew. Please do come in.'

'Thank you.'

He moved into the room, noticed the uncharacteristic shutness of the door leading in to Mangiafuoco's office, and stood helplessly in the middle of the great Persian carpet which covered the floor.

'Won't you sit down, Andrew.'

'Yes. Thank you.'

He sat in a large green armchair and wiped his clammy palms on its arms.

'Tea?' asked Rose.

'No, thank you.'

She sat down at her desk and picked up some index cards which she began to examine with a concentration and concern that Thompson found uncomfortable to watch.

'Will he be finished soon?' he asked.

'He'll buzz me as soon as he's ready to see you.'

As soon as he's ready to see you. The words didn't actually cut Thompson – that would have been ridiculous and impossible – but they certainly hurt him. *He'll buzz* me *as soon as he's ready to see* you. Mangiafuoco was communicating more freely with his secretary than with Thompson. Meanwhile Thompson's own secretary was dead, and she had hated him and tried to ruin his political career. She had probably had herself mysteriously murdered just to inconvenience him.

He felt bitterly sorry for himself at that moment, seated in a huge green chair in Mangiafuoco's office, waiting for his only real friend to unleash his anger on him. He had been left sitting there with the secretary and the vast Persian carpet, in a room which in happier times he'd only ever passed through.

'Do you know what this is about, Rose?' He couldn't keep the trepidation from his voice.

Rose shook her head sadly. There was a hint of sympathy in her eyes now. The exchange suddenly brought to mind Rommel's final interview with the Gestapo in 1944. No doubt there had been a sympathetic secretary at Gestapo headquarters: 'I'm sure it's nothing, Herr Generalfeldmarschall. They certainly won't drive you to a deserted spot in the countryside and force you to take cyanide.'

Thompson's palms were sweating madly now, and the chair arms could probably not absorb much more moisture. He smoothed his hair and straightened his tie. He should have told the researcher that he had an important meeting and wouldn't be able to come.

Even now, there was still time to leave. He could look at his watch, tut, and say that he had an urgent appointment. But that would only delay things, give his palms time to sweat out all the water in his body, leaving him a dried, wrinkled old husk with bloated palms. Perhaps he should leap up, take the paper knife from the desk and drive it into his breast, cursing the gods for their inconstancy.

Just as he had made up his mind to leave, the buzzer on Rose's desk did what buzzers do. She stood up and walked over to Mangiafuoco's office door, motioning to Thompson as she twisted the handle. He dried his palms one last time and then tottered across the carpet on suddenly feeble legs.

Thompson smiled at Mangiafuoco as the door closed behind him. Mangiafuoco looked at him over his glasses and indicated the chair in front of his desk.

'Andrew.'

'Hello Tristan.'

The chair was wooden, affording no opportunity for wiping away the sweat that poured from his palms. Mangiafuoco sat for a long time, not saying anything, staring at a point on the ground just to the right of Thompson. Thompson waited respectfully.

Finally, Mangiafuoco looked up. Running a hand across his flat, bald head, and then down through his lank, shoulder-length hair, he sighed and said, 'Ginia told me.'

Up until that time, Thompson had been terrified. Suddenly, with the danger upon him, he became himself once more. The terror dropped from him like a cat from a wardrobe, and he was able to think rationally.

Thompson rapidly calculated what Mangiafuoco knew. Had Ginia really told him? After all, she was away skiing. And if she hadn't told him, where did his information come from? He decided to play for time, to draw Mangiafuoco into telling him more, and then to strike at the source rather than the information. All the way down the corridor he had been sure he would admit the truth to Mangiafuoco. Now he knew he was going to deny it for all he was worth.

'Told you what?' he asked.

'She told me what happened. I went home at lunch-time. We had tea and she told me.'

Unless Ginia had unexpectedly flown home that morning, this was a lie. Thompson could see that he had a hope. All he had to do was avoid making Mangiafuoco angry. He decided to use some elementary diversionary tactics.

'If it's about those cigars of yours, I don't blame you for being angry, but I can explain all that.'

Mangiafuoco hesitated for a fraction of a second, then took the bait.

'What cigars?'

'The Havanas I said I'd be able to get for you? I gave them to Eddy. I'm sorry.'

'I'm not talking about cigars,' said Mangiafuoco. The diversion had not been well-enough thought out. He needed a diversion that was close enough to the bone to kindle a spark in Mangiafuoco, something big enough to make him very slightly angry. But what? He just needed time. That was all.

Mangiafuoco gave him none.

'Ginia told me what you did, and her story has been confirmed. I didn't expect you to lie about it. Here.'

In true film-noir style, Mangiafuoco pushed an envelope across the table to Thompson, who picked it up – and then realised that he shouldn't have. Inside the plain brown Manila envelope was another envelope, this one marked 'Happy Snaps'. On the cover a tanned, avuncular man was carrying a laughing young girl from the sea while a beach ball lurked merrily in the background.

Inside there were black-and-white photographs of Thompson letting Ginia in, and others of him standing in the corridor with her, looking in her eyes, kissing her. The last photograph was of her standing alone, crying.

The first thing that went through his mind was what an extraordinarily good-quality CCTV camera they had in his building. The second thing that went through his mind was that, with the exorbitant service charge he paid, the CCTV ought to be good quality. Also they should have no need to sell the footage. The third thing that went through his mind was that, if these were the only pictures Mangiafuoco had – and if Mangiafuoco *was* lying about Ginia having admitted what had happened – then he had a good chance of talking his way out of it.

'But this is ludicrous, Tris.' He caught the severe look in his friend's eye and quickly added, '-tan.'

'Ludicrous?'

'Yes, ludicrous. Ginia came over for a tête-à-tête – she was worried about…'

Thompson stopped, noticing that Mangiafuoco's face was beginning to mottle and swell, and that his hands were clenched into clammy fists. He remembered a columnist's description of Mangiafuoco: 'a fat, flat-headed matador.' The image of Mangiafuoco dressed as a matador made Thompson grin.

This grin, it turned out, was Thompson's second mistake. He realised immediately and with a horrible jolt what his first had been: he had used the expression *tête-à-tête* the day before as a euphemism for sex.

'How dare you!' shouted Mangiafuoco, his voice breaking with rage during the 'dare', so that he finished the sentence a good two octaves higher than he had begun it. His face was bright red.

'How dare you come here and grin and swank and lie and then, and then *eupheme* as though I were a common … As though…' He was almost choking with fury and his voice was modulating all over the place. 'How dare you *eupheme* at me!'

'…' said Thompson. It was an opening of the mouth, a movement of the vocal cords, but no recognisable word. He had no idea what to say.

'Get out!' yelled Mangiafuoco.

Thompson had heard Mangiafuoco shout perhaps twice in his whole life. He now realised why Mangiafuoco took such care to keep his temper in check: anger robbed him of all control of tempo, pitch and even the basics of pronunciation.

Thompson tried again to reply.

'...' he said.

'Git oUt!' Mangiafuoco squealed in falsetto, pointing imperiously at the door.

'...' parried Thompson.

'Ite!' barked Mangiafuoco.

'...'

'GEAT OWT!' bellowed Mangiafuoco.

Thompson tried another '...', but Mangiafuoco bore down on him with a 'Get out!!' which was half whisper, half broken squawk. The violence of his shouting had knocked his finger off target. It was pointing now at the mantel-piece, and this seemed to enrage him even more than Thompson's subdued '...' as he fled.

What might a man like Mangiafuoco do when driven to anger?

CHAPTER FIFTY-EIGHT

Driving along the Holloway Road on the way back from Homebase, the murderer decided to pay a visit. His instinct told him that a quick frightening now might save trouble in the long run. It was almost six, and almost the very worst time to be making impulsive stop-offs in an area infested with one-way streets and unadvertised dead-ends. But if a man can't trust his instinct, what can he trust? Besides, this was a good time: if Jonathon Fairfax had a job he might be home by now, and if he was a student then he would probably be up but not yet out.

The murderer found a parking space miraculously close to the house. He turned to Gemma, in her chair in the back.

'You OK to wait here for two minutes, babe?'

She glanced up at him, and then returned to a minute examination of her left shoe.

'All right. Here's your new book, case you get bored of your shoe.' He passed her 'The Cat in the Hat', prunked open the door, heaved himself out and slammed it behind him.

Bing-ding.

He waited. He wanted to be quite close to the door when it was opened, because that was most frightening, but he also wanted to pace about impatiently. After a minute or so he pounded loudly on the noisiest part of the door and also clacked the knocker for good measure.

He waited for another minute. He walked back to the front gate and looked up and down the street. No one. How could a street in London be deserted at five past six on a Friday? What did everyone do?

He walked back to the door and pounded again. There was clearly no one in. What could he do?

There was a small sheaf of leaflets sticking out of the letter box. He pulled them out and flipped through them. Then he pulled a flyer for his gym out of his jacket pocket. That was what he would do.

The leather bench sighed as he let himself fall into the back seat, beside Gemma. She was putting some crumbs of biscuit in the little patchwork pocket on the front of her denim dress.

'Lend us that book, will you?'

He picked up the big glossy book leaning against her car seat and set it on his knee.

'Monkey?' she said, pointing to the picture on the cover.

'Not you as well. It's a cat, isn't it?'

'Yes?'

He used the book as a desk, resting one of the leaflets from the letter box on it as he set to work.

'Bot dat?' asked Gemma.

'That's a fried chicken shop leaflet, isn't it?'

'Yes?'

'Fried chicken. Can you say that?'

She looked at him expectantly with her clear blue eyes and rosy face.

'Fried chicken,' he said again.

'Fie tit?'

'Fried chic-*ken.*'

'Fie ticky?'

'Close enough. Let me just cross out some of the letters on this leaflet and we can go home. Maybe we'll have some fie ticky for tea, eh? Is that what you want?'

'Car?'

'Yes,' he said absently, blocking out letters in the leaflet with a heavy black marker pen.

'House?'

'Yes. That's right.'

'Fie ticky?'

'Oh, you like that, don't you? Is that your new word?'

She laughed, delighted. 'Fie ticky!'

'You say that again, do you know what's going to happen?'

She shook her head, suddenly grave.

He didn't smile. 'Someone's going to get tickled.'

'Ticky?'

'Yes. And I'll tell you something else: it's not going to be me.'

He extended his tickling finger, ready, and slipped into his *Dirty Harry* impression. He only did impressions for Gemma.

'This is a Magnum finger, the most powerful finger in the world. And it would tickle your head clean off. So you gotta ask yourself one question: "Do I feel lucky?" Well, do ya, punk?'

She smiled and clapped.

'Go ahead,' he breathed, 'say fie ticky.'

'Fie ticky!' she shouted.

'Ah-wigglewigglewigglewiggle...'

'Ello lover,' said Lisa, turning as the murderer pushed his way in through the kitchen door. 'What you got for me?'

'Hello, love. I've got some presents that you are going to just love. We've got: one box of paint samples–' he plonked a box on the chair '–and one punk.' He handed her Gemma, who had been tucked under his left arm. 'She got out of line, so I had to tickle her head off.'

'When will she ever learn?' smiled Lisa, hugging Gemma and kissing her on the top of her head. 'Lucky she grow a new one.'

'Best present of all: we got a new word.'

'What is it?'

'Take her dummy out, find out.'

Lisa took Gemma's dummy from her mouth with a quiet *flup*.

'What's your new word?' she asked.

Gemma looked at her with open eyes and made a grab for her dummy.

'Go on, Gemma,' said the murderer, 'tell your old mum your new word.'

'Car?' hazarded Gemma.

'No, you been saying that for ages. What did you say to me in the car, when I had that leaflet?'

'Car?'

'*In* the car. Leaflet.'

Gemma busied herself with the top button of Lisa's blouse.

'Did you say leaflet?' Lisa asked. 'That's a funny thing to say.'

'No. She didn't say leaflet. She said–'

'Ee,' said Gemma, very softly.

'There see,' said Lisa. 'She said leaflet.'

'No she didn't!'

'What did she say then?'

'I don't know, do I? It weren't even a word.'

'Don't get cross, love.'

'I'm not cross. I got plenty to be cross about but believe me, this ain't cross!'

'All right! Since when did you say "ain't" anyway?'

'What? I've always said it!'

'No you haven't!'

Their voices were raised, their cheeks were red. And then something inside Gemma, like an old engine, puttered twice and ignited: *A-ka. A-ka. Aaaaaaah!* She let out the throttle and switched up a gear: *Aaaaah! Eeeeeeeeeeh!*

'Now look!'

Lisa wrapped her arms more tightly around Gemma, bouncing her gently and rocking from side to side. She kissed her cheek. 'It's all right, Gemma. We wasn't arguing. It's all right.'

The murderer could see that tears had started in Lisa's eyes too, but he still said it.

'We had ever such a nice afternoon, just me and her, in the car. And the second she gets home…'

Lisa put her head down and ran past him, Gemma still held in her arms. He heard her steps moving rapidly upstairs, into the bedroom.

The murderer stood alone in the kitchen, listening to the crying from upstairs. He looked at the cardboard tray full of tiny pots of paint, at the boxes full of pans and utensils, packed up ready for when the redecoration started. He thought of his conversation with Plover on Wednesday and with Shane on Thursday, and he put out his arms and asked the ceiling, 'Why? Why me?'

He opened the fridge, took out a beer and put it on the draining board, next to the phone and the message pad. On the paper were two names and addresses – one of them unfamiliar, the other belonging to the kid he had just tried to visit. Funny. What did that mean?

He pulled open the drawer for the bottle-opener, but the drawer was empty.

'Lord help me.'

He sighed and trudged upstairs.

When he sat next to her, Lisa shifted away, rocking Gemma gently from side to side. The little girl was quieter now, though still crying, and Lisa's eyes were red. He moved up next to her again and this time she stayed where she was. He put his arms around both of them.

Later, when they had kissed and made up and they were all back in the kitchen, he said, 'Saw them two addresses by the phone. What are they?'

'Scarings – Bob called.'

'Funny.'

'Why?'

'Tried to see one of them today – Fairfax. He come into the gym. Told Velcroman he wanted to see me.'

'Anything to worry about?'

'Probably not. If I have to worry about him, he has to worry about me more, whoever he is. When they for, these scarings?'

'Tomorrow.'

'Spose I won't be doing the grass.'

'Spose not.'

He tore the page from the pad and put it in his wallet. On the page beneath, there was a name and phone number.

'What's this?'

'Sorry, love. I forgot. Very posh bloke called. Said did you fancy working for him direct, not through Bob.'

'Better tell Bob about that. He won't like that.'

He tore that page off too and slipped it into his wallet with the other, ready to show Bob.

'We can't eat here now, can we?' said the murderer. 'Not with the kitchen in this state. How about we go out?'

'Or we could just get a takeaway. Eat it off our knees.'

'I'll stick with plates, if you don't mind,' he said and she flashed up a smile. 'What do you fancy?' he asked.

'Apart from you? Don't know. Bit of fried chicken?'

SATURDAY

CHAPTER FIFTY-NINE

The March sun shone like summer that afternoon. It was the sort of clear, fresh day on which it's good to be alive, and probably not too bad to be dead either. The yellow sunlight splashed about, dripping from lamp-posts and running in rivulets down the bonnets of the cars stuck on Brompton Road. Beside the pools of sunlight, thick black shadows had been painted in and finished with a delicate fine-edged brush, so that they lingered in baroque detail around doorways and behind post boxes.

Jonathon appreciated these things more than anyone else in the whole of London. The fact that he had hardly slept at all the night before didn't seem to matter. He had the afternoon off work and was walking jauntily from Harrods to his first deliberate meeting with Rachel. This fact made him supremely, divinely and stupidly happy. It made him astonishingly happy.

We're going on a date, said an excited voice in his head.

We're not *going on a date*, he told the voice categorically.

How come we feel like this then? the voice asked. *Massive quantity of endorphins:* check. *Raised pulse rate:* check. *Churning, fluttering feeling in stomach:* check. *Spring in step:* check. *We're going on a date with a woman we're in love with.*

No we aren't, Jonathon replied. *We're going to tell a lesbian that we suspect her uncle is a murderer. And stop saying 'check'.*

Feels like a date to me. How come we're so happy?

We're not happy. We're scared. Remember the threatening note, the car chases, the politicians, the secret files, the dead body? What's there to be happy about?

We're going on a date!

Shut up, he grimly told the voice.

Seconds later he realised that he was whistling *Good Day, Sunshine*.

The night before, he had rushed home from work and immediately – without even stopping to take off his tie – spent an hour working up the nerve to call Rachel. He had let the phone ring for two minutes. Then he had called back straight away, in case she'd been in the bath or something (all naked and wet and lathered) and this time he had let it ring for five minutes. There had been no answer.

Fifteen minutes later he had received a new shipment of courage and called again. This time she answered. He thought she sounded pleased to hear his voice, but then he'd never called her before – maybe that was just the way she sounded on the phone. He said that there was something important he needed to tell her about, and asked if they could meet the next day. 'Yes,' she had replied. This had floored him, ruining all his carefully worked-out responses to the various objections she was going to raise. And so they had arranged to meet at Pun In The Oven, a new shop in Covent Garden.

He swung happily around a sun-spangled lamp-post to turn the corner, as though he were in a musical. Ahead of him the huge glass roofs of the market gleamed, and even the dirty uneven brick paving managed to shine where the crowd had left a neat rectangle around a street-performer who was trying to co-ordinate a dog, a drinks tray, a stepladder and a sheet of flame. He smiled.

We're not going on a date, he told himself again. *This is serious.*

Pun In The Oven was smaller than he had expected, tucked between a shop that made soap out of chocolate and another that sold jewellery designed by Vikings. Like its neighbours it seemed to have been allowed to balloon unchecked from a mildly diverting notion into a serious commercial concern. In fact, Covent Garden was thick with mildly diverting notions which now had their own branded carrier bags.

Unlike the idiocies which surrounded it, Pun In The Oven was slightly famous. A new celebrity chef, appealingly young, thick-tongued and chaotic, had agreed to attend the opening after the shop had given him a Filo-fax – a confection made of filo pastry in the shape of a fashionable diary. And the opening had made it onto the TV news as the item at the end intended to make people feel better about all the preceding murders and wars and football. Thus the shop had become one of the relatively small number of places that Jonathon had heard of.

He had imagined that there would be plenty of things to look at while he waited, and had planned to do plenty of waiting by turning up as early as possible. In the event, he was probably only between seven and fourteen minutes early, but this was still an awkwardly long time to spend in such a small shop, even before it had become clear that Rachel was going to be late – or worse.

Presumably, after the initial idea, the owners had found it very difficult to come up with a shop's worth of pun goods. They had tried to compensate for this by getting expensive designers in to do the interior.

It was all rose-tinted wood and lilac-coloured counters surmounted by appealingly curved glass bubbles under which the goods were displayed.

'Can I help you?' asked the middle-aged woman behind the counter.

'I'm um just waiting for someone,' said Jonathon.

'That's fine,' said the woman brightly, with a sudden sharp smile that said, *You definitely have to buy something.*

Jonathon browsed the tiny range of products even more intently after that. He had almost lapsed into a sort of tense trance over a display of car-shaped hors-d'oeuvres when he felt a hand touch his elbow.

'Sorry,' said Rachel. 'I didn't mean to make you jump.'

'Oh. That's all right. I didn't mean to jump.'

'Am I late?' she asked. 'It's the watch. I tried to set it forwards so that I'd always be early, but it didn't really work.'

She pointed to her watch, to illustrate her statement. He looked at it, but of course it just looked like a watch, on the most distractingly beautiful wrist he'd ever seen.

Rachel was looking adorable again, this time in a pair of faded Levi's and a baggy old jumper. It was just the sort of outfit that Jonathon favoured, though he knew that the same clothes on him would have made him look like a callow Belgian fisherman. Rachel, on the other hand, looked almost unbearably wholesome and pleasing, like a really sexy loaf of bread.

It had been too long since he'd said anything.

'Herm,' he tried. It wasn't a word, but at least it was a sound.

'Show me some puns,' she said, simply and naturally, as though it was just what one said after 'herm'. And with that the spell of awkwardness broke.

They browsed around the shop together, Jonathon showing Rachel the things he had noticed while waiting for her.

'This is the Filo-fax,' he said. 'It's stuffed with dates.'

She giggled, and he could tell it wasn't at the pun.

'What?' he asked.

'Nothing. Just that you really like the fact that it's stuffed with dates. It's so sweet.'

'But real diaries are stuffed with dates. That's why–'

'You don't need to *explain* it to me.'

'It's the double meaning of the word "date".'

'I know.'

'It's a kind of fruit and an appointment,' he persisted, still pretending that she didn't understand.

She hit him lightly, still laughing, and then Jonathon made his obligatory purchase and they left.

They walked to Leicester Square, on along Piccadilly, past the shops and hotels for very rich people, down through Green Park, past Buckingham Palace and into St James's Park. When they arrived, Jonathon realised that he couldn't remember who had suggested going there, or whether they had both just known that it was clearly the thing to do.

They walked over the bridge and found, on the south side, a patch of grass that seemed to have been reserved for them. Jonathon tried to put his jacket down for Rachel to sit on, but she told him not to be silly. They sat and opened their bag of puns – two Volvovents and a pair of choux.

'It's like the kind you wear when you go bowling,' she said as he bit into one of the choux. 'What's inside?'

'Marzipan.'

'Marzipan?'

He nodded.

'What sort of pun's that? They should have plates of meat inside.'

He grinned.

'You know,' she said. 'Plates of meat – feet. It's rhyming slang.'

'You don't have to *explain* it to me.'

'Because feet go in shoes,' she persisted, as though he still hadn't understood.

They sat and talked about Cockney rhyming slang and had ideas for shops as the ducks passed. Every now and then a small party of ducks would stop by to enquire about crumbs, and Jonathon or Rachel would shake some more out of their paper wrappers. They were just discussing the prospects for a shop selling outfits to the street performers who somehow coax money from tourists by standing perfectly still when Rachel broke off.

'Oh my God,' she said, staring at a bush a few feet away from them, by the lake.

Jonathon followed her eyes.

'What?' he said.

There was a rustle of leaves and then Jonathon saw what she had been staring at. A white creature stepped with comic dignity from behind the bush. It was two feet tall, tubby and feathered, with a question-mark neck and an immensely long lemon-yellow bill. The handy built-in bag beneath the bill flapped in the breeze as it fixed them with a disapproving orange eye. There was something about the bird's dangerous stare and impossible physique which reminded Jonathon of someone.

He clutched his head, remembering all at once the reason he had needed to see Rachel today.

'What is it?' she said, looking at him.

'A pelican.'

'I mean what's wrong with you?'

'Oh God.'

The pelican had turned the full force of its orange stare on Jonathon, clearly irked by his behaviour. It did not move on though. It seemed curious to discover what the wingless cretin before it might have to say.

'It's about your uncle,' said Jonathon, pulling some pieces of paper from his pocket. 'Look at this…'

He handed one over.

'It's a menu from a fried chicken place.'

'I know. But read it.'

She took the piece of paper from him and read. The pelican watched her scornfully.

'*Ken's Plucky Fried Chicken. Kaptain Ken prepare special blend farm herb & spice's on every piece chicken. Our chicken has the great taste having recipe of dixie farm kentucky herb & spices flavour!! We only use HMC certified meat and poultry.* And then there's a load of food and prices. You don't want me to read the whole list out do you? I'm sure my uncle hasn't got anything to do with this place.'

'Sorry, I gave you the wrong one.'

He passed her another flyer.

'It's all been crossed out,' she said.

'Not all of it.'

He pointed to some of the letters in the blurb at the top of the menu:

'~~Ken's Plucky~~ Fri~~ed Chicken. Kapt~~ai~~n Ken prepare special blend~~ fa~~rm herb & spice's~~ ~~on every~~ piec~~e chicken. O~~ur ~~chicken has the great taste having recipe of~~ dixie ~~farm~~ k~~entucky herb & spices flavour!!~~ We ~~only use HMC certified meat and poultry.~~'

'What does it say?'

'It says "Fairfacs you die keep away."'

Apparently satisfied, the pelican lurched carefully off, eyeing a plump pigeon a few yards away.

'But … how do you know where the spaces between words are?'

'Where else could they go?'

She peered at the flyer. 'And that last 'y' – that's a bit crossed out.'

'Do you think he meant to say "Fairfacs you die keep awa"?'

She looked at the flyer again, as though she could change the message by examining it closely enough.

'It came wrapped in this,' he said, and handed her another piece of paper.

She opened out the Goliath Gym flyer.

'That's your uncle, isn't it?' he said.

CHAPTER SIXTY

'Just them two, mate.'

'Seven ninety-eight please, squire.'

'There you go. Twenty.'

'Lovely.'

The till opened with a ring, the assistant – shiny and solid as though carved from a bar of soap – took what he needed with a card sharp's practised hand, and the drawer clacked shut again.

'I'll take the ten,' said the murderer, 'and you put the rest in the charity box.'

'Cheers mate,' said the assistant, dropping the change into the hole in the head of a small model dog.

'No problem.'

The assistant pushed the plastic bag containing two kitchen knives across the counter.

'You get through them quick, don't you mate?' he said, grinning.

The murderer frowned. 'Been here before, have I?'

'Don't you remember? Just a couple of weeks ago. What you using them for?'

'I, er, I do a lot of chopping, as it goes.'

'What you chop then?'

'Just vegetables and that. I'm a chef.'

'Must be some tough old vegetables you're chopping up there, mate.

Don't fancy eating at your place!'

The assistant laughed good-naturedly and slapped the counter. The murderer hauled the corners of his mouth into a sort of smile and turned to leave.

The assistant smiled too, obviously seeing that the murderer was a bit put out and trying to make amends.

'Seriously though, what's the place called? Maybe I'll stop by some time. Have a bit of a nosh.'

'It's called er–' the murderer looked down '–er, Hand and Bag.'

'Oh,' said the assistant. His face fell and he hoisted up a less convincing smile to replace the genuine one that had just departed. 'Unusual name.'

'Yes. Unusual. I'm er Alan Hand, and the other chef's called Jimmy Bag. So we put our names together.'

'Right. Good, er, good. Good.'

The assistant's smile was starting to creak. He looked into the murderer's eyes, and something made him add, 'Where is it?'

'Mile End.'

'Oh, nice. I got family there. Whereabouts?'

There was a terrible moment of silence in which neither of them moved. Then the assistant's face twitched. He began to talk, like a man who has come to hate silence.

'Whereabouts in er…? No, I'll … I'll look it up in the phonebook. Getting late. Only forget anyway. Only forget. Brain like a wossname. You know. Like a…'

He sprang backwards, his head hitting a display of hammers behind him, and then he sank to the floor.

'… like a punch in the face,' finished the murderer, thinking it was the sort of thing Bruce Willis might say.

As he left he added to himself, '*Jimmy Bag*. Jesus Christ.'

Staring vacantly out of the window, Thompson gradually became aware that he could see, reflected, his name on the front page of a newspaper being read by a man on the opposite side of the carriage. Unfortunately, because of the way the man's paper was folded, his own name was the only word Thompson could make out.

The paper was the *Guardian*. He desperately wanted to see it, and wished he hadn't refused to look at the papers that morning. Perhaps this was one of those stories that only interest the *Guardian*: perhaps he'd been spotted drinking full-fat milk or being unkind to a poor person. Maybe it was only the woman he'd offered a coffee last week. Perhaps she was a *Guardian* journalist: 'Today Libby Hesketh-Myers presents a searching exploration of how it feels to be offered coffee by a minister'. He needed to see the *Mail*. If they had a story about Princess Diana on their front page he knew he would be all right.

Irritatingly, none of the other people he could see in first class were reading papers. They were mostly people somewhat like himself – high-flyers returning to their country pads after a week of work and a night of fun. They seemed mostly to be in business, and consequently they were looking at management books with titles like 'Inside The Eight-Fold Portfolio: A New Guide To Corporate Zen' or 'Riding The Capital Bronco'. He climbed unsteadily to his feet and ran to the buffet car, where he found that they had sold out of papers. There was some comfort in the fact that the people behind the counter weren't sniggering at him.

On his way back he happened to notice a copy of the *Sun* lying on the floor of a lavatory. Without hesitation he stooped and picked it up. Then, looking around to make sure he wasn't being watched, he locked himself in the cubicle.

The paper was slightly damp and rather trodden on, and open at a page which was almost entirely taken up by an enormous-breasted woman wearing a beret and a string of onions. The caption read 'French student Michelle is a real Eiffel, to be perfectly Franc. Her favourite food is s-baguette-i!!!!' On and on the inane drivel ran. He couldn't help but read it to the end before turning to the front page.

There it was. There *he* was. 'Fancy a Mangiafuoco?' was the headline. Beneath it was one of the pictures Mangiafuoco had shown him on

Friday: him kissing Ginia outside the door to his flat. Inset on one side was a photograph of Ginia looking young and holding her father's hand. On the other side was one of the media's favourite photographs of Thompson, shaking hands with General Galtieri and contriving to look as though he were winking lewdly at the old man. The story began: 'Love-rat minister BONKS colleague's daughter and leaves her crying all night. She is the THIRD beauty he has bedded in a year. See page 6 for sensational photos.'

Page six had two more photos: one of him looking into Ginia's eyes and one of her alone, crying. There was more text: 'Andrew Thompson scored a hat-trick last week when he SEDUCED sexy Gina Mangi-afuoco (18). Gina's dad, Tristan Mangiafuoco, is FURIOUS...'

There was also a double-page spread of women he had allegedly slept with and a feature by someone he had never met, describing how she had fellated him while he was doing a telephone interview for the Today programme.

He tried to flush the paper down the toilet, but it seemed to swell and stop the water leaving the bowl. His face on the front page floated gummily to the surface and lay there like a leering layer of filmy scum. He delicately laid toilet paper on it until his face disappeared, then washed his hands.

He was seething with rage by the time he arrived at Wantage, the local station. A driver was waiting for him, along with about a hundred journalists who all surged towards him as soon as he got off the train. The jackals, running forward to feast off his carcass. It didn't matter what he said to them: they would spindle and fold his words to their own ends. It all suddenly seemed so unfair.

They surrounded him in a seething hubbub as the driver led him towards his car. Voices and questions merged into one long string. 'Mr Thompson is it true ... can you confirm ... constituents? ... resigning issue ... how old? ... wife taking it ... aren't you?'

'Oh, do shut up!' he snapped.

He heard someone ask whether he had slept with Ginia. He answered, 'Would you be here otherwise?'

And then a clear voice emerged. 'Do you feel any regret about what you've done?'

'Yes,' he replied. 'I've lost my best friend.' Then he accidentally jabbed the questioner in the genitals with his briefcase and marched briskly on.

As he reached the safety of the waiting car, another clear voice

– this time female – asked, 'Are women just sex objects to you, Mr Thompson?'

He stopped and fixed her with his eyes. 'Not at all,' he said. 'Many of them can cook.'

And he climbed into the back seat and was gone.

At Blythesides there was no trace of Gargy. He went straight up to his study, locked the door and disconnected the phone.

It was just his luck that the story of him shagging his best friend's daughter had come out on a quiet news day. And when everything had been going so well too. Who had sent the pictures to the *Sun*? The news programmes on the radio had mostly finished, so he braved the world outside his study just long enough to ask the gardener to pop out for the papers. Gargy must have taken the ones that had been delivered. He wondered where she had gone, and when she would return.

He re-read the *Sun* and was rather cheered to find that someone he actually had slept with was quoted as saying that he was a 'magical lover', although he suspected it wasn't quite verbatim. The *Mirror* had the same exclusive photographs as the *Sun*, but it had printed more of them, and its front page featured a big close-up of him kissing Ginia. It was obvious that these pictures had come as a godsend for both papers. Nothing even remotely interesting had happened since Sarah Morecambe's murder, and all the tabloids had been looking restlessly around for something to follow it up with.

None of the other papers had the pictures, which must have been sold only to the *Sun* and *Mirror*. The *Guardian* tried to make up for its lack of pictures with a front-page comment piece condemning the *Sun* for printing the photos and him for making them possible. Judging by the number of journalists at the station, all the papers were going to pick this up for their Sunday editions. His only hope was that some enormous story would fortuitously happen along and knock it off the front pages. A French invasion ought to do it.

So far as he knew, Mangiafuoco was the only person who had the pictures of him and Ginia. But he must have got them from somewhere, and surely he wouldn't have sold them to the papers himself. If he had the pictures he would have paid for them, and presumably paid enough to prevent them being sent to anyone else. In fact, if there was one person in the world who ought to want those pictures to be published less than Thompson, it was Mangiafuoco.

It suddenly struck him that he, Andrew Thompson, was the innocent victim of someone's attempt to hurt Tristan Mangiafuoco. At that moment Thompson stopped feeling guilty about Ginia and began to feel wronged. Well, all he could do for now was put on a brave face and wait to see how the game played itself out. Perhaps when this cooled down a bit there would be a chance for reconciliation. He hoped so, since Mangiafuoco knew a lot of damaging things about him – including the fact that he was an RSG.

If that came out, he would be on his way to Llandudno before you could say 'knife'.

CHAPTER SIXTY-TWO

The door opened.

'Hello?' said a wide triangular man in a dressing-gown.

'Hello. You Jonathon?'

'No. I am Avi.'

'Pleased to meet you,' said the murderer. 'Is Jonathon Fairfax in?'

'No. Only me.'

'I think he's in. Check for us will you? Room F.'

'I will check. But he is not in.'

'Just check.'

Avi stumped upstairs. A second later the murderer heard him knocking on a door.

'Mr Jonathon? Hello?'

He knocked again, then came back down.

'Not in.'

'Fudge. When's he back?'

Avi shrugged.

'Roughly?'

Avi shrugged again.

The murderer thought about using his 'like a punch in the face' line again, but it didn't really fit the conversation. He sighed.

'All right. Cheers mate.'

He walked back to his car. There was going to be some violence tonight. He could feel it.

CHAPTER SIXTY-THREE

By the time he rounded the corner into Brickfield Terrace, Jonathon was immensely tired. His lack of sleep the previous night – born in equal parts of his excitement at the prospect of seeing Rachel and his fear at the prospect of death – was telling on him. After the bliss of the first part of the afternoon with Rachel, the second part had tailed off somewhat, as afternoons often will if you tell the person you're with that you think their relatives mean to kill you.

She had been inclined to dismiss his evidence, while also being very obviously upset by it – as though she believed it enough to suddenly have doubts about her uncle, but not enough to believe that Jonathon could be in any danger at all. This left him feeling that he was making a fuss over nothing and that he was deliberately ruining his friendship with her.

After all, what proof was there? Her uncle was known to get a cold face, and he could have any number of reasons for wanting to go to Acacia Road. It was reasonable for his gym to post flyers through the doors in his street. And anyone could amuse themselves by defacing chicken-shop menus in terrifying ways. Perhaps Avi had done it, in a fit of pique at the unwarranted interruptions to his aquatic life caused by Jonathon's occasional visits to the toilet.

But then again, why had there been a flyer for the gym in the second file Lance had shown him? Had Lance put it there to scare him? Had he, Jonathon – disoriented by suddenly knowing people, failing to sleep and going to gyms – accidentally dropped it in there himself?

All these questions tumbled about in his head, wearing his brain away and making him more and more tired. He could feel himself slumping even as he began the short walk up the path to the front door. Then he remembered that he had to work all the next day. There was nothing he wanted more than to go to bed and fall out of existence for a few hours. But there was nothing he wanted less than to go upstairs, close his eyes and then open them again and find that it was morning and that he had to get up and go to work.

He turned the key in the front door and eased it open. There was another pile of leaflets, menus, flyers and cards there. He carefully closed the door, sat down on the bottom step and sorted through them. To his immense relief there were no death threats and no flyers for Goliath Gym. As he stood up he was thrown forward into the hallway by someone behind him. His hands flew up to prevent his face hitting the wall. He whirled around.

'Tut,' said Avi, regaining his balance and obviously alarmed at having just walked into Jonathon's back. 'Why you sit on stair?'

'Wah-ha,' said Jonathon. 'Ag ag wag wah!'

His hands were clenched and his legs were shaking. What's more, he seemed to have forgotten how to speak.

'Simmer down,' said Avi, with a slight air of pride at having used the phrase. 'What are you a crazy person?'

'No. Just... Sorry. I'm a bit on edge.'

Avi squeezed past him, leaving small white fibres from his dressing gown on the front of Jonathon's black suit. At the kitchen door he halted and turned.

'By the way,' he said. 'A man comes here ask for you.'

'What... what was his name?'

'No say. He is very big – a colossus.'

'Was he, er ...' Jonathon mimed a tall, slim person, someone a bit like Lance.

'Very tall and very very big across here, his body.'

'What was he wearing?'

'This brown coat, quite short like to here. Some blue jean. White shoe. And hat which go all over his head. Red hat. He say he might come more later on.'

'When did he come?'

'Thirty minutes ago. I am in the bath. Typical, isn't it?'

Jonathon was already peering through the letter box, checking the street outside. When he saw it was clear he opened the door and fled.

CHAPTER SIXTY-FOUR

Twenty, twenty-two, twenty-four. Here he was. The murderer knocked on the door and waited. A couple of minutes later he heard footsteps tapping smartly down the hallway. Sounded like tiles. He didn't know why rich people could never be bothered with carpets. Who wanted cold, hard, noisy floors? Give him an Axminster any day.

The door started to open and he could see within a split second that there was a chain on it. Quick as a flash he pulled the stiff bolt cutters from inside his coat, reached them up and closed them on the metal. There was a sharp intake of breath as the person on the other side of the door saw the cutters and tried to push the door closed on them. It was too late: the flimsy chain had flopped in half. The murderer pushed his way inside, pulling on his balaclava.

'All right, love?' he asked, pushing the door closed behind him.

The woman stood straight and her face seemed composed.

'What can I do for you?' she asked in a steady but brittle voice.

'Well, love,' he said, smiling pleasantly and scratching his head as though trying to think. Then he roared at the top of his voice, pushing his face within an inch of hers, mouth open wide.

It produced the effect he was after, an instinctive reaction: she screamed and threw up her hands in front of her face.

'That'll do for starters,' he said.

It was a trick he had learned a long time ago: swamp their system with adrenaline. If they're frightened already it will make them terrified. He noted with approval that there was no puddle on the floor, but the woman was now shaking uncontrollably and wouldn't look him in the eye.

A cat put its head round the door from one of the rooms adjoining the hall and stared at the murderer with huge eyes before turning tail and running off again.

'Puss puss!' called the murderer. 'That your cat?'

'No, I've never seen it before,' said the woman.

'You know something, love? You're a very poor liar. Not to worry, it's not the cat I'm after. Thing is, I can't stand around here chit-chatting all day, much as I'd love to, so I'll get down to business. Tell Lance that you're not safe till he hands over the files, would you?'

Jane didn't say anything.

'Got that, love?'

Jane nodded, with dignity.

'OK. Repeat it back to me.'

'I have the files you know,' she said.

'Photocopies?' he asked.

She hesitated, then nodded.

'No good to me. Lance needs to get himself down to the Ritz in Piccadilly, with the originals and any copies he's made. He puts them in a bag and hands them in at the reception desk. Says it's a package for Mr G. Formby. He's got till midnight. You got that?'

'Yes, of course I have.'

'There's a good girl. I'll let myself out – don't you worry yourself. Ta-ta. I might be seeing you soon – but you better hope not.'

He winked at her, walked back to the door, opened it, and was gone, whistling 'When I'm Cleaning Windows' to himself.

CHAPTER SIXTY-FIVE

Lance was hanging about listlessly in his flat. The whole day was almost gone and he still hadn't been able to make himself sit down and really study both files. Whenever he tried he found something else that was smashed: the table, say, or all the chairs. He tried to fix them but it's difficult when your only tool is an old, smashed hammer. Why had they smashed the hammer? And what with?

He'd had a beer but it didn't seem to help. At seven o'clock he finally decided to really make a proper start. He would have a cup of tea and then get down to it. Half an hour later, just as he had found the power cord for the kettle, the phone rang. He ambled over, pressed the record button on his dictaphone and then switched on the telephone's speaker.

'Hello,' he said, carefully casual, his mouth close to where he hoped the telephone's microphone was.

'Lance?' It was Jane's voice.

'Are you all right?' he asked, catching the note of panic in her voice.

'No, Lance, I am not.' Her voice caught in her throat. 'Lance,' she said, and burst into tears.

'Jane, Jane, Jane. What's the matter?' He picked up the receiver but the sound continued to play from the phone's speaker.

'I'm so sorry. I'm …' She broke off. When she continued, her composure seemed to have returned. 'Lance, I've just had a visit from … from a man. He said … He said that I wouldn't be safe until you gave the files back. He broke in. He screamed at me. He just *screamed* at me. I am so frightened, Lance.'

'Jane, I'm sorry. I'm sorry. Poor Jane. I'm sorry. I'll give them back. Don't worry. Listen, I'm coming round now. I'm sorry. Oh God. Are … will you be OK till I get there? Ten minutes. I'll be there in ten minutes. Why … ? Fuck. Shit. I'm sorry.'

'Yes. I shall be fine. I'm just a bit shaken, that's all. It's nice of you to come round.'

'Don't be silly. Ten minutes. Drink some hot tea with sugar. Are you sitting down?'

'No I'm not, but really…'

'Sit down. Where's Geoffrey?'

'Golf.'

'Don't worry. I'll see you soon. OK?'

'OK.'

He put the phone down. Well, there was no need to think about what he should do any more. He would have to give the files back. He'd been stupid. As though he'd ever really cared about any of the stuff in them. It had just seemed cool to have files full of secret documents. He'd been stupid.

He ought to collect the files from Jonathon's. He should really pick them up on the way round to see Jane, or at least warn Jonathon that there were people out looking for them. Shit. Jonathon. He picked up the phone and noted with annoyance that it seemed stuck on playing through its speaker rather than the receiver. Odd, he thought, that a thing like that could still annoy him at a time like this.

It rang for a long time. He counted the rings, waving the useless receiver in time with them. Twelve, thirteen, or fourteen if you counted that other one. Fifteen. Sixteen.

'Hello?'

Lance felt a rush of relief. An answer.

'Is Jonathon there?'

'What?'

'Er, Fairfax, Jonathon Fairfax. Skinny guy, hair sticks up at the back. Looks a bit like…' Shit, Jonathon didn't look a bit like anyone. 'He lives on the first floor.'

'What?'

The man on the other end of the phone sounded Turkish. Not that it was possible to tell over the phone. He certainly didn't speak English as a first language. Not even as one of his top ten by the sound of it.

'For fuck's sake. Upstairs. He lives upstairs. Up the stairs. Room F, I think. F. Skinny guy. Hair. Wears jumper.'

'Mr Jonathon?'

'Yes!'

'I see for you,' said the man.

There was the sound of footsteps walking very slowly, agonisingly slowly, upstairs. They creaked across the first-floor landing, creaked over somewhere else, creaked back to where they had originally been. There was a sound of knocking.

'Hello Mr Jonathon!' The knocks continued. 'Mr Jonathon?' More knocks. The steps could be heard creaking back to the staircase and slowly plodding down it. Lance suddenly knew that he couldn't bear to hear the man tell him that Jonathon wasn't in. He slammed down the receiver, yanked the phone from its socket and threw it with all his force at the battered wreck of the cooker hood.

'Fuck!' he shouted, as loudly as he could.

He felt better afterwards, but wished he hadn't destroyed his phone, virtually the only intact object in his flat. Shit. He hoped Jonathon was all right. He'd have to go round there. He'd go to Jane's and calm her down, calm his guilt down, then he'd drive round to Jonathon's and get the files from where he'd hidden them. And he would never put anyone in danger again. He would never mess about with anything big again. He would confine himself to girls in pubs and having good hair. He realised suddenly how much he loved Jane. The idea of anything happening to her made the insides of his bones hurt.

He grabbed his car keys and his coat and rushed out of the door, where he bumped into a large number of policemen who immediately arrested him.

CHAPTER SIXTY-SIX

The sky was a dark, inky blue. Everything else was yellow and red, gigantic writing, clowns' faces, ghostly locomotives – all lit by neon or, for the older rides, rows of lightbulbs. A klaxon sounded, the harnesses were released, and thirty nauseated tourists rose from the roller-coaster at once and wobbled to the exit, passing from the attraction's violence to the melee of the crowd.

Hyde Park Fun Fair, thought Plover: not fun, not fair but definitely in Hyde Park. Convenient for the night's work.

The man counting the next passengers from the queue caught Plover's eye, gave the fastest wink Plover had ever seen – a mere flicker of skin over the pupil – and then put his arm down decisively after Plover had passed through, preventing anyone else getting on the roller-coaster. The woman in the ticket kiosk mouthed 'What the fuck?' but the man who counted passengers simply held up one finger in reply. The woman shrugged and lit a cigarette.

The car at the back of the roller-coaster was empty but for a bald man with a drooping moustache, a flat head and a shiny double-breasted raincoat. Plover shambled over and sat down beside him.

'Mind if I sit here?' asked Plover, sitting down.

'One of the epaulettes is coming off your trenchcoat.'

'So it is.'

The thick rubberised harnesses came down and locked in place in front of their chests. The klaxon sounded again, and the roller-coaster was tugged, juddering, up the first hill.

'You're a bit security-conscious, aren't you mate?'

'The one time I leave a file of extremely sensitive material in my car, I find that the car has been rammed and the material removed. And you were not present to witness the act. Either we are dealing with clever people or you are no longer to be trusted.'

Plover picked at his epaulette, but was spared a reply by the arrival of the roller-coaster at the top of its first hill. There was a clank and then they dropped vertically a hundred and twenty feet. Just as Plover was adjusting to being much closer to the ground, the roller-coaster darted to the right, moving so fast and slowing so suddenly that his stomach, which had been hurrying to catch up with him, hit his ribs with considerable force.

'Oof,' he said.

They were flung leftwards and he gritted his teeth. Then suddenly they were upside-down.

'Oof,' he said.

He had come to this meeting with a very particular aim, and he realised that he wasn't going to achieve it if he continued to alternate between staying silent and saying 'oof'.

'Listen,' he managed as they righted themselves. 'Talking of trust, I heard you ignored my warning about cutting out the middleman and went straight to old–'

'Well, what was I supposed to do?' interrupted Mangiafuoco. 'When you've become so unreliable.'

'Unreliable?' Plover gripped his harness as his body was rattled about. 'You try anything and you'll see how unreliable I can be. Sending those photos of Ginia to the papers – that was just a warning.'

He saw Mangiafuoco's jaw clench, but the politician said nothing – either through self-control or nausea.

'There's worse than that if you don't keep your promises,' continued Plover. 'You promised me the rough stuff was over. You said I could go straight.'

The roller-coaster, as though to illustrate his point, stopped ducking around and went straight.

'Don't talk to me about promises. What about Sarah Morecambe?'

They plummeted again, Plover's cheeks wobbling around his ears.

'If,' Plover said, as they were being cranked up another hill, 'it hadn't been for my CCTV racket you wouldn't even have known she'd taken Thompson's contracts.'

Mangiafuoco was silent a moment. He let out a breath. 'True,' he conceded. 'Nonetheless–'

'Look. It was a failure of communication. I said I was sorry and I'll fix it. Even disappeared that Jason bloke to Llandudno. But after tonight, that has to be it.'

'I am just as anxious, Robert, to end our dependence on violence as you are. That way of doing things is over.'

Plover stifled a scream as his organs upended themselves and his spleen smashed into his heart.

All at once they were the right way up again. Plover and Mangiafuoco gasped in unison.

'You mean no more Llandudno cellar treatment?'

'Prehistoric. I promise, you can wind down our facility in Llandudno.'

'That's what you said a year ago, when I first said I wanted to go straight – started the partnership with Barry Lenin.'

Wang, wang, wang, wang went the roller-coaster as it shuttled them through a set of chicanes.

'It was true then and it's even more true now,' said Mangiafuoco. 'I have given you contacts with politicians and businessmen, just as I said I would.'

'Blugablugablugablug,' conceded Plover indistinctly – his tongue had dropped down the back of his throat and needed retrieving before he could continue. 'But one of them was Thompson, who got us into this mess.'

The roller-coaster dashed through the centre of the loop they had traversed not long before, heading for another dive.

'Once we've retrieved the files and have safely destroyed them, there will be one final job for your muscular contact: Andrew Thompson has accomplished his last seduction. From there on out the violence will be behind us.'

This – or possibly g-force 3.2 suddenly pressing down on his bowels – made Plover so deeply uncomfortable that he lapsed into silence.

'Listen,' said Tristan as the pressure eased. 'There's nothing for you to worry about. Nothing at all.' He laughed a jolly reassuring laugh that, if his life had turned out differently, would have made professional Santa work a real possibility. Plover was still silent.

The ride drew to a halt.

'In many ways,' Tristan continued, 'this is my fault.'

Plover gave a signal to the man holding the queue back. The queue continued to be held back, the harnesses were not released and the people in the other cars looked around in confusion. A man wearing an 'I Heart London' baseball cap covered his face and began to moan.

Tristan said, 'I shouldn't have made those early contracts and letters so explicit. They were a time-bomb. But I've learned, over the years. They're so much more circumspect now. They don't even say Girard Leviticus now, simply GL – no cryptic clue any more. I've even made the logo more abstract.'

The klaxon sounded and they began the slow up-hill pull.

'It looks daft now, the logo – like a hurdle standing on a triangle.'

'It doesn't matter a whit. It's making money now: the logo could look like Andrew Lloyd-Webber's face and no one would care. And I've collected together all those early, explicit letters and contracts.

True, they've been taken from me. But tonight, you shall recover them. We'll destroy them. And then that's it: the violence stops and you're straight and clean, the co-proprietor of Lenin & Plover, the respected and legitimate investigative solutions consultancy.'

'Just so you know, if anything happens to me tonight there's a variety of material that will automatically be released over a few days – drip, drip, drip, drip. Till I'm back safe and sound.'

Click, click, click, click went the mechanism pulling them up the hill.

'What could possibly go wrong tonight?' asked Mangiafuoco.

'Nothing. But I got thinking. It might be convenient for you if I disappeared, and I've noticed that what's convenient for you is generally what happens.'

Whirr, tick. Silence.

'That's ridiculous.'

Clank. They plunged once again into the terrifying abyss.

CHAPTER SIXTY-SEVEN

Tim took the cigarette from his mouth and looked at it as he exhaled. He held it crossways, so that the smoke billowed over it. It wasn't obvious what he expected to see on that cigarette, or even whether he expected to see anything. Perhaps he was used to ones with jokes printed on them, like lollipop sticks. He pulled at a loose thread on one of his socks, sucked at one of his fillings, and swirled the coffee around the bottom of his cup. Then he checked his bald spot and his moustache, as though to make sure both were still there. Having satisfied himself on that score, he took another drag from his cigarette. Again he held it crossways as he blew the smoke over it. It looked as though he was going to go through whole the routine again, but instead he looked up at Lance.

'So it wasn't you then?' he asked.

'No,' said Lance.

'Who do you think it might have been?'

'The murderer.'

'And who's that?'

'I don't know.'

'But you were in her house?'

'Yes.'

'After she died.'

'Yes.'

'We know you were. Your DNA matches.'

'I've just said I was.'

'I'm just saying.'

'How do you have my DNA anyway?'

'Police Library of Occupational DNA. You're an insurance investigator. You gave a blood sample last year.'

'Oh, that.'

'So?'

'OK.'

'So you were in her house.'

'Yes.'

'And why did you not alert the police force?'

'I did. I told you I called from a phone box at about eight.'

'Anonymously.'

'Yes.'

'Why?'

'Because I didn't want to have to go through all this.'

'All this questioning?'

'All this everything.'

'All what everything?'

'All *this* everything.'

'Ah.'

'Listen. I was telling Richard who I talked to before that I'd like to have my phone call. He told me I could have it when you took over.'

'You haven't had a phone call?'

'No.'

'Well you'd better have your phone call. It's your right.'

'I know.'

'Better hurry up though before Richard gets back.'

Tim opened his desk drawer and took out a phone which he handed across to Lance. Lance suddenly felt very tired as he dialled the numbers. The phone on the other end rang. It rang again. Lance looked up at Tim and smiled awkwardly. The phone was still ringing.

'Come on,' pleaded Lance into the phone.

'Oh, hi,' said Lance, 'Is Jonathon there please? I called earlier but got cut off. You know, skinny guy, hair, F, up the stairs.'

'I know he wasn't in an hour and a half ago, but he must be back by now. I'm meant to be meeting him.'

'You couldn't just check for me could you? Please? It's really important.'

'Thanks. Just check.'

'Thanks.'

Lance waited, listening. A long wait, then he winced.

'Shit. Can I leave a message?'

'No, a mess*age*.'

'It's all right.' Lance put the phone down.

Tim looked at him with raised eyebrows.

'He wasn't in,' explained Lance.

'Bad luck.'

'That didn't count as my phone call did it?'

'What, you want another one?'

'Can I?'

'Of course. Knock yourself out.' It sounded like this was one of the first times that Tim had used the phrase 'knock yourself out' – it still had that tang of newness to it. Tim was obviously pleased with it because he leaned back in his chair and puffed contentedly up through his mouth, making his moustache shake.

Lance dialled again.

'Ah, hello. Could I speak to Jane please?'

'I know – she told me. Listen Geoffrey, I really need to talk to her. I've got some news that might make her feel better.'

Lance waited again, biting his lip.

'Jane? Jane I'm so sorry. I've been arrested.'

'The police. They've arrested me.'

'Yes, me.'

'For a crime I didn't commit. Listen, I want you to be safe and I don't know how much longer I'm going to be here. I think a while. I might not be able to talk to you again. Do you know Jonathon's address?'

'Damn. I hate to do this to you, but you need to go to my flat and get the address out of my Filofax.'

'I can't tell you.'

'Exactly. That's exactly the reason.'

'There's a key buried in the geranium bush by the front door.'

'The Filofax is in the flat.'

'I can't tell you.'

'No, I just can't remember.'

'Yes.'

'Then go to Jonathon's place. Look behind the wardrobe.'

'Yes. The originals. I hid them there.'

'Well, it's like that children's programme – Doctor Octopus's Luncheon Factory. The one Jonathon told us about.'

'You know, *the best hiding place is with someone who thinks he's already hiding some other thing*. Or something.'

'No, I have no idea where he's put the copies.'

'Is that really where they told you to take them?'

'By midnight?'

There were footfalls in the corridor outside. Tim looked over to Lance and made an urgent cutting gesture at his throat.

'Yes, do that then. Listen. I've got to go now. I really am sorry. This is the only way to keep you safe.'

Lance put the phone down just as the door opened.

CHAPTER SIXTY-EIGHT

Jane had made a list, in pencil, on some Amnesty notepaper while Lance had been talking to her. It said, 'Jonathon's house. Address – Lance geranium bush key Filofax forget flat.' There was a break where she'd started to write it out in full, but had crossed it out, then it continued, 'Wardrobe files balaclava Formby Ritz.'

'Darling?' she called.

'Yes?'

'I'm just popping out for a while.'

Geoffrey appeared in the doorway, looking perplexed.

'I'm a bit perplexed darling. Have they found the intruder? Do you need me to drive you?'

'No darling, I'm fine. Thank you.'

'But where are you going?'

'I'm going to look at a geranium,' she said, thinking it was just the sort of thing that Emma Peel might have said in *The Avengers*.

Jane made her way over to her ancient but immaculate powder-blue Mercedes. She thought about checking it for booby-traps, but then realised how ridiculous she was being: she didn't even know what booby-traps looked like. She quickly wiped the condensation from the windscreen, pulled on her driving gloves and started the car. No booby traps went off, so she put it in gear and pulled smoothly away.

The night was sharp and she was shivering half with cold and half with excitement as she moved through London's streets. It was half-past nine and the traffic was quiet, except on some of the larger roads. By the time she pulled up in front of Lance's house the car had warmed up and it was definitely excitement she was shivering with.

It hadn't until that moment occurred to her that the police might be at Lance's flat. Luckily they weren't, but it hadn't occurred to her that they might be. She would have to be a little bit more alert than that if she were to succeed in this mission. There was no one in the street as she slipped out of the car and clunked the door softly behind her. Two steps forward. Wait, she thought, what if the police had the building 'staked out'? She should walk to the door as though she lived there, so as not to arouse suspicion.

Halfway up the steps to the front door she remembered that Lance had said the keys were buried in the geranium bush, and that she had a trowel in the boot of her car. She went back for it. After all, that was what she would have done if she had lived there.

The geranium bush held out for longer than she had expected. She had to gouge out a good portion of its soil before she eventually found a small jar marked 'nutmeg' with a large bunch of keys inside. There must be one for each of the flats. She looked behind her suspiciously, checking to see if anyone was watching, again justifying it with the thought that it was exactly what she would have done if she lived there. Then she began to try each of the keys in the front door.

She had barely got to number three before she heard steps slowly coming down the stairs. Had someone heard her? What should she do?

She tried to think what Emma Peel might have done, but reflected that it would almost certainly have involved agility, youth, a leather catsuit and possibly a gun, of which she possessed none. Thinking quickly, she put the keys in her pocket, threw the trowel behind a nearby wall and tipped the geranium over. Then she began to knock feebly on the knocker, trying to make it sound as much as possible like the noise she had made with the keys. It didn't sound anything like it of course. The stratagem seemed painfully transparent to her, but who could accuse a woman who was nearing sixty and wearing driving gloves of having knocked over a geranium and attempted to break into an apartment building?

In fact no one accused her of anything: no one appeared. The footsteps stopped on the first-floor landing and a door slammed noisily. Jane thought it would actually have been much easier if someone had opened the front door. They could have let her in.

She resumed her pitiful scrabbling with the lock, and was patiently inserting key four for the third time, trying it anticlockwise this time, when someone above her shouted, 'Oy, what do you think you're doing?'

Jane's heart stopped. She froze, feeling as though she were a schoolgirl again, as though in all the time since she'd left school people had just been pretending to treat her like an adult, and now reality had finally caught up with her.

'Did you do that to the geranium?' the voice asked.

Jane looked up into the face of a bearded young man in his thirties and caught his expression change from annoyance to blankness as he saw that Jane was a respectable lady approaching sixty.

'Sorry, love,' he said.

'That's quite all right, ducky. You frightened me half to death though.'

There was a silence.

'Can I help you?' he asked.

'Well you could let me in, ducky. Lance gave me his keys, but I can't seem to make them work.'

'Wait there, love,' the man told her.

A minute later the door was unlocked by the bearded young man, wearing a huge pair of striped shorts.

'Don't mind me, love,' he said when he saw her looking at them, and he beckoned her into the building. He had a pleasant voice and what sounded to Jane like a Yorkshire accent, but Jane had no ear for that sort of thing.

'I've picked your geranium up for you,' she said sweetly. 'It doesn't seem to be too badly hurt.'

As he led the way upstairs, he asked, 'It were Lance you said, wasn't it, love? I don't know why he give you them keys, cos he never locks his door. This is it.' He pushed open Lance's door.

As the young man stumped upstairs Jane entered Lance's apartment, thinking as she did so how nice it was that she didn't look like a little old lady when viewed from above.

The first thing she noticed was the washing-up. She had been to Lance's flat more than once, and had always been appalled by the washing-up. She noticed it again when she turned the lights on. She also noticed that the place had been smashed up. Finding Lance's Filofax might be more difficult than she had thought.

The first place to try was by the phone, but even locating the phone was no easy feat. Eventually she found most of it in a pan on top of the cooker, with a couple of fragments embedded in the cooker hood. Whoever had done this to Lance's flat had obviously been an animal. What sort of monster would destroy a cooker hood?

She now had all the pieces of the phone, but was no nearer to finding the Filofax. What she really needed to find was the place where the phone was usually kept, rather than where the phone was now. No one keeps their diary and address book on their cooker. It suddenly occurred to her that the vandals might have taken the Filofax – or destroyed it as comprehensively as they had everything else.

Thinking laterally, Jane decided first to locate the phone socket, and then to work from there. She found the socket in the first corner she checked, along with the phone table. She could tell it was the phone table because it had a couple of shelves underneath stacked with directories and old copies of Time Out. There was, of course, no Filofax there.

Then she remembered that Lance had a desk, and set off to find that. The desk was in the living room. It had been dismantled and its top had been left leaning against the door of a drinks cabinet, which was empty except for a full bottle of limoncello. This was impossible: she was going to have to search every inch of Lance's flat to find the Filofax. She suspected briefly that Lance might have engineered this whole thing just to get her to tidy his flat for him.

She decided to check each room in turn, establishing zones in each one for the various objects and fragments she found, depending on their use or origin. After spending twenty minutes on the desk zone of the living room, she realised that this approach would take her at least the rest of the night. What she needed to do was just turn the whole flat upside-down again.

Feeling like a change of scenery, she wandered into the bedroom and found the Filofax lying on the bed. This simultaneously pleased and annoyed her.

But there was no time for feeling anything; she had a job to do. She flipped through the Filofax, looking first under 'F', then under 'J', where she found Jonathon's address. She decided to try ringing first, in case he had come back. Remarkably, when she had reassembled the phone and plugged it in, the remains of the thing worked – though it seemed to be stuck in speaker mode.

Jonathon's number rang for a long time.

'Hello?'

'Oh hello. Is Jonathon Fairfax there please?'

'No. He is not there.'

'You couldn't possibly just check for me could you? He's in Room F.'

'He is not there.'

'Please?'

There was a sigh down the phone. The man shouted 'Mr Jonathon!' at the top of his voice and waited a few seconds.

'He is not there,' said the voice, and put the phone down.

Jane sat in her car, drumming her gloved fingers on the dashboard. The traffic was much the same as it had been forty-five minutes earlier, which was oddly reassuring. This was going to be the real test, as she didn't even have keys for Jonathon's house or room. She steeled herself for a difficult time. Lance's place had been a pushover compared with what was to come.

The nearer she came to Jonathon's house, the more uneasy she grew. She hadn't driven this way in a very long time. In fact, she had quite possibly never driven this way before. Since passing Finsbury Park, she had already seen two armoured police vans, both with enormous black cages covering the windows, both parked and both full of sleeping policemen, as though they had been getting naughty and over-tired in the police station and the inspector had taken them out for a drive, as Jane had done with her cross toddlers, knowing it would lull them to sleep.

The street was easy to find on the map, but surprisingly difficult to get on to, being hedged in by one-way roads and junctions designed by MC Escher. However, on only her fourth lap of the area she found herself suddenly and unexpectedly driving past a sign saying 'Brickfield Terrace'. She uttered a tiny scream of triumph. There was nowhere to park, but that was by no means a problem for a woman of her new-found resources. She turned the corner at the end of the road and parked there instead.

Jane sat in the car for a few moments afterwards, basking in her success and thinking about the task to come. Getting into Jonathon's room would be more difficult than getting into Lance's flat. But once in, all she had to do at Jonathon's was find a wardrobe. The difficulties probably balanced each other out. She did, however, need some sort of rudimentary plan for gaining access.

A minute later Jane knocked on the door of Number 60, Brickfield Terrace. A lot of the other houses round about were Victorian and, she thought, quite charming. Number 60 was one of a different type, plain and dumpy, built at some indeterminate time when no architectural style was in vogue, or perhaps even available. She waited, but there was no answer. She knocked again, then rang the bell. By this time it was nearly quarter to eleven, and she knew that she shouldn't really be disturbing the occupants. Still, Lance was depending on her. In fact – according to the man in the burgundy balaclava – her continued health was depending on her. She was on the verge of ringing one last time when she heard a door slam inside the house and the hallway light came on. A figure trudged downstairs. Even through the narrow pane of frosted glass in the front door, Jane could tell the man was wearing a dressing-gown.

The door opened. The man stood before her, bandy legs planted far apart, dressing gown drawn tightly round a big balloon of a belly and a towel draped around his meaty neck. His head – which rose from a broad, flat jaw and tapered up to a tiny crown surmounted by little wisps of brown hair – was thrust forward suspiciously. He looked like a big samosa made of terylene, and he dried the back of his neck as he spoke.

'Hello,' he said.

'Hello, is Jonathon in please?'

'He is not there.'

'Are you sure? I say, I don't suppose you'd mind if I just went up and checked would you?'

'He is not there.'

'...'

'He is not there.' And with that the man closed the door in Jane's face.

CHAPTER SIXTY-NINE

He checked his inside pocket again: the knives were still there. He checked his face: no balaclava. He checked his side pocket: balaclava. He checked his jeans pockets: wallet and keys. He looked at a little sliver of paper: the word 'glockenspiel' was written on it, along with a phone-box number.

He was ready.

He didn't know why he was nervous. There was no reason to be. The afternoon's work had been fine. Now he was prepared for the evening's.

He put his head around the door of the front room, where Lisa was curled up on the sofa with Gemma, reading 'The Cat in the Hat' to her in a tired voice.

'She still not asleep?'

'No,' said Lisa.

He padded over and felt Gemma's forehead with the back of his hand.

'Blimey. You could fry an egg on that.'

'I know.'

'Still, she looks nearly asleep now.'

'Every time I stop reading she gets all upset.'

'Try her on a video again.'

'It don't work. Not even "Beauty and the Beast".'

'You can't read to her all night though. No point you getting sick as well.'

'I know. What time will you be back?'

'Dunno. Near to half twelve as I can make it.'

'All right, love. There's pizza in the fridge.'

'Cheers. Might get myself something hot on the way back home. Need to build my system up if I'm going to live with two invalids.'

'I told you I'm not poorly.'

'Well keep it that way. If she's not out by half ten, give her a bucket of Night Nurse and put your earplugs in.'

'You're full of good advice, you are.'

'Seriously, love, don't wear yourself out.'

He kissed her, felt her forehead, then kissed the top of Gemma's head. Gemma watched him with shining, vacant eyes, her cheeks a ketchup red, as he walked out of the room.

Just as he'd opened the front door he heard a shout of 'Love!' behind him.

'What's that?' he asked, putting his head around the door again.

'Forgot to tell you. Rachel called while you was out earlier.'

'Oh yeah?'

'Sounded really serious. Said she wanted to talk to you, face to face.'

'What about?'

'She didn't say.'

'Clues?'

'None, really.'

'Why am I surrounded by bloody mysterious women?' he asked Gemma's unresponding eyes.

'She just sounded upset, and like it was serious. Asked if you could go round today.'

He looked at his watch. 'It's a bit late now.'

'Sorry. Should have told you earlier, only you was out and then I forgot.' She pointed to Gemma with her eyes.

'I'll see what the traffic's like,' he sighed. 'But Bob likes to know I'm around a bit early.'

'All right, love.'

CHAPTER SEVENTY

Jonathon stood outside Rachel's door for a long time. He needed to see her, but he was afraid she would not want to see him. It was an odd thing to do, turning up in this state, in the dark. As he knocked, he half hoped that she wouldn't be in.

His hands were shaking and so were his legs. In fact, he was shaking all over. Was it just fear? Was he just scared for his own skin? Yes. That was definitely part of it – most of it even. But there was more than that. He simply couldn't cope with the uncertainty. Was his life in danger, or was it all just a misunderstanding? Was he really mixed up in a murder with political connections, or was Lance just a paranoid fantasist with some forged documents? In no sphere of Jonathon's life did he have the first idea what was going on, let alone any means of controlling it. And here he was coming to see Rachel, who was the source of even more confusion. He wished he had slept the night before.

He just couldn't take it any more.

He knocked again, looking through the pane of frosted glass into the lighted hallway, straining his eyes for a sign of her presence. Just as he had decided that she wasn't in, a dark smear appeared on the glass and began to enlarge. It was her. He hoped she wouldn't be angry with him for coming.

The door opened and there she was, framed by the warm light of the hallway, standing out against the dark and grey that loomed on all sides. She was still wearing her sexy bread costume and her eyes looked pouchy and heavy-lidded, as though she had been asleep or crying.

'Sorry,' she said, stealing the line he had planned to use.

'I ... Can I come in?' he asked.

She opened the door a little wider and stood aside, then closed it behind him. They stood together in the hallway.

'Your ... your uncle came to see me this afternoon, while I was out,' he said.

She looked at him. 'Look, I know something's going on. I ... want to talk to my uncle. But I can't think about it all now. I can't.'

He nodded.

'You look terrible,' she said.

'I didn't sleep last night. I'm ... worried about it all. Scared. And then this afternoon. I hoped we would ... be friends, and then I thought you probably wouldn't want to be, after...'

'Don't be silly,' she said. 'Of course I want to be friends.'

'Sorry for coming round. I'm not very good company at the moment.'

'Don't be silly,' she said again.

They stood for a few more moments in the hallway. Someone skipped across the landing above and into the bathroom. Rachel rolled her eyes.

'Jess,' she said. 'She's in there *all* the time.'

They did a bit more saying nothing and then Rachel said, 'Will we watch some TV?'

Jonathon nodded.

'Let's pretend,' she said, 'that everything's just normal. Let's pretend there's totally nothing going on.'

Jonathon nodded again.

'Will I make you some cocoa?' she asked.

He nodded yet again, and managed a small smile.

Rachel showed Jonathon to her room, switched on the small, neat colour television in the corner and disappeared downstairs to make the cocoa.

'...Lindsey, your first question please, chuck.'

'Thanks Cilla. I've always really loved takeaways – the steamier the better! So what I'd like to know is, if you were a takeaway, what kind of takeaway would you be? And that question's for contestant number two...'

'Well, Lindsey, I'm a bit of a fitness nut, I like to keep in shape by running and swimming, so if you ordered a takeaway from me, it'd get to you really quick because I'd run really fast with it.'

When Rachel returned, Jonathon had not moved. He sat with his head in his hands, palms pressed to his eyeballs. Rachel set the two cups of cocoa on her desk beside an incongruously placed toast rack, and sat down next to him. She switched the television off.

'It's all right,' she said.

He still didn't move. She wrapped the quilt around him and then put her arm across his shoulders. She began to stroke his hair and make soothing noises, like a child comforting a distressed pet on Bonfire Night.

'It's all right,' she whispered.

Eventually he found he could speak again.

'Sorry,' he said.

She said nothing.

He looked in her eyes. 'Thank you.'

She began to cry, he didn't know why.

They sat like that for what seemed a long time. He was still very upset, but now simultaneously very happy to be in Rachel's arms. He was wrapped in her quilt, which smelled of her, even more than she did, and she was holding him like a quilt-wrapped parcel. He felt happy, upset and foolish, all at once. How far from the manly ideal was he? How far from being the strong silent man protecting the fragile damsel? He had been plunged into despair by some documents, a missed night's sleep and an ambiguous uncle, and now he was being wrapped in a blanket by his womanly ideal to help him over it.

Rachel was gently rocking him, humming in a comforting but very off-key sort of way, as though she were lulling him to sleep.

'Lie down,' she said.

They both lay down on the bed. Jonathon was wrapped less tightly in the quilt now. Her arm was across him, and she was still holding him as though she needed to take care of him just as much as he needed to be taken care of. Occasionally, she would make the humming sound, like a little girl playing mother. She stroked his hair, soothing him. He didn't feel so bad now: the overwhelmingness of his distress was passing. Instead he felt stupid and fraudulent, as though he had gained admission to her bedroom by pretences. He began to stroke her hand, awkwardly, tentatively. After a while he realised that he had missed her hand and was stroking an area of quilt.

She didn't seem to have noticed. She was leaning on her elbow now, still stroking his hair, still humming comfortingly sometimes. This time he precisely triangulated the position of her hand before moving his own over to it, stroking it. Rachel brushed the hair out of his eyes. None would have been there if she hadn't brushed it into his eyes earlier on. Although the exhaustion and anxiety of earlier still made him feel remote from the situation, he couldn't help his heart beating faster at the nearness and affection of Rachel.

Just at that moment she leant in towards him and cradled his head in her arms. He put both his arms around her middle and held her just as tightly. Then he felt a kiss on his forehead. Even in this state it astonished him. That anyone would want to kiss his forehead seemed hardly believable. Of all the parts of his head, the one just above his eyes seemed particularly unworthy of affection.

His face was level with her throat. When he'd seen her before, she had worn a silver disc that nestled in the hollow where her collarbones met, but tonight her neck was completely nude. He kissed the warm skin of that hollow. She turned more fully on her side and kissed his forehead again. He filled the vacant hollow with another kiss. She moved down. Before, he had been expressing his devotion to her in a private way. Now she was right there, looking in his eyes, kissing him on the lips.

Jonathon hadn't often kissed women on the lips. Most of his experience was confined to school discos in the out-of-the-way places his dad tried to live. He had always worried about how he should kiss. Was he meant to chase the girl's tongue around? Should he check her teeth for any scraps of food she might have missed while flossing? He'd had no idea. This time it didn't seem to matter. Kissing actually seemed natural: just a way of communicating – as easy as a conversation about puncakes.

They kissed more. He found her hand and clasped it as they kissed. When she pulled her hand away, Jonathon was suddenly afraid that she'd realised who he was and that it was all over. Instead she shifted her weight, moved her hands, and pulled her jumper off over her head, getting her hair in her eyes. Jonathon thought this was adorable, even in this muddled state, suspended between lust and despair.

It shocked him that she had taken off her jumper. Firstly, because he had assumed that all this was an accident, rather than something she was deliberately doing. Secondly, he felt that by rights he should be taking off her jumper. There again, by rights he shouldn't be half-wrapped in a quilt with tear-stained eyes and a mug of cocoa cooling nearby. He carried on kissing her. Maybe he could wait until she was asleep, and then quickly put the jumper back on and take it off – fulfilling his masculine role without her noticing.

She started to fiddle about with the front of his trousers, but seemed not to be able to find the zip. Finally, he unzipped them himself.

CHAPTER SEVENTY-ONE

Jane had always approved of wheelie bins. They looked so much better than the traditional battered corrugated metal ones, and they could be wheeled about, removing the need for bin men to carry them on their backs, which had always made her worry. It had always seemed wrong to her that the only segment of the population at serious risk of slipping on banana skins is also the only segment of the population who carry on their backs large pieces of battered metal full of filth. The whole thing seemed a public scandal to Jane, but she could never make anyone else see the problem. Hers had seemed a voice in the wilderness, until the invention of the wheelie bin.

But in all the time she had spent thinking about wheelie bins, she had never imagined that she would one day be standing on top of one at the back of a house in north London, trying precariously to haul herself onto the roof of a kitchen extension. She was very glad that she was wearing a trouser suit, and almost equally glad that all the hours she had spent walking the dog had kept her relatively trim.

The roof of the kitchen extension was covered with a coarse, black material of a sort with which she had never previously come into contact. Usually she had no truck with roofs – or kitchen extensions, or bedsits or secret documents or threats from burly men in balaclavas. In fact, the range of things with which she had a truck had swelled dramatically over the past few hours. The coarse material – it was like felt covered in tar and asphalt, but of course it couldn't be – scratched the palms of her hands as she heaved herself painfully up, using the window frame as a foothold.

At last she had her whole body on the roof. Her whole body seemed much heavier than she remembered it being the last time she'd had to heave it anywhere. A one-eared cat looked at her, miaowed very quietly, and then jumped from the roof into the darkness, disappearing from sight. Looking around, Jane noticed for the first time how tightly the houses were packed together, as though for ease of storage. There were lights on in many of the windows, music drifted down from a house further up, and from somewhere she could hear a shouted argument about Wings. Above it all, faint against the dense orange glow of the London sky, hung the Plough's luminous question-mark. Having put it in context, the kitchen extension she now crouched awkwardly upon suddenly seemed rather less threatening. All she had to do was walk along this bit of roof to the main body of the house and step up to the first-floor window ledge, which was at about chest height.

It was at this point that she realised she had nothing to step on to reach that window ledge. Back down there, in the concreted garden, it had seemed insanely ambitious even to think of getting on to the roof of the kitchen extension. The window ledge beyond had seemed a mere nothing by comparison. Now she could see how upsettingly high up it really was. What she needed was the stool she kept in the kitchen at home, the one she used for getting to really high things, like the storage space above the cooker hood.

If only she could actually get on to the window ledge she was certain she could get in. The window had two panes – a smaller one at the top, which was open, and a larger one below, which was closed. She knew that the smaller of the two panes had a special name, but couldn't for the life of her remember what it was. Whatever it was called, she was sure she could reach in through it to open the handle of the larger one, which she didn't believe had a name of its own.

Perhaps there was something in the garden that would help her reach the window, something like a concealed stepladder, or ideally an escalator. She edged nervously toward the garden end of the roof to have a look, trying to ignore the appalling pain in her knees, and also trying to ignore how high up she was.

Jane had always denied she had any fear of heights. She confirmed that denial now. There was no fear, they just made her feel sick and dizzy and prone to thinking about falling. Naturally she was afraid of actually being sick or fainting or really falling, but all that was separate from the height issue. Heights, in themselves, left her entirely unafraid.

This vital point clear in her mind, she moved forward again. Slowly, slowly. She looked down. She felt sick. She looked down again. There was nothing to feel sick about, she told herself. It wasn't the distance. If someone just said 'ten feet' that wouldn't make her feel like this. It wasn't even that it was ten feet *below* her. Much of the world was probably ten feet below her much of the time, but she didn't shudder with horror if she happened to read about Holland, say, or East Anglia. At least, not always. The problem here was just that most of the bits of the world she could currently see were ten feet below the small bit of the world she was on at this second.

She forced herself to look down into the hard garden. There was no stepladder. There was, however, a very sturdy-looking bucket. The bucket was on the ground. She was going to have to get it and bring it back up here. The thought made her almost want to cry.

Gritting her teeth, she inched slowly back towards the wheelie-bin. Getting down looked even harder than getting up. She was afraid of what might happen if she fell. She would almost certainly break a bone. That was one of the few things everyone had been consistent about, right through her life. Over the years scientists and bores had changed their minds about everything from the nutritional value of fat to the basic composition of the universe, but had always been quite certain that old people have brittle bones.

She set her jaw. Brittle bones or not, because she had been stupid enough to get up, at some point she would have to get down. And it would be more stupid of her to get up and down from a roof once and have nothing to show for it, than to do it twice and have some important documents that could get Lance out of prison and save her from the man in the burgundy balaclava that had such fine stitching around the mouth and eye-holes.

She gingerly explored the side of the kitchen wall with her right foot, trying to find the window frame below. It seemed much further down than it had been earlier. She gritted her teeth again, glanced down very quickly at the wheelie bin, shut her eyes to the roaring vortex of nausea that swam through her head, and stepped back.

CHAPTER SEVENTY-TWO

Jonathon jolted from his doze with a start. He wasn't sure how long, or even whether, he had been asleep, but he was wide awake now. The cause of his sudden wakefulness was Rachel giving an abrupt, loud snort and saying 'Decorate the bumblebees?' in an odd, high-pitched voice. Despite her words she was sound asleep and breathing heavily, with one of her hands resting on her hair where it spilled onto the pillow, as though she had been stroking it when she fell asleep.

Jonathon hoped she wouldn't wake suddenly and see him watching her sleep. It would almost certainly scare her. He wanted to smooth her hair, stroke her cheek, play with her breasts, but of course he knew that all these things were out of the question. It must have been a mistake: she must have had sex with him by accident. After all anyone who can, while still asleep, request that the bumblebees be decorated is clearly capable of anything. Maybe she had got him mixed up with someone else, someone handsome or female.

He checked his watch. How many other people, he wondered, could sell a houndstooth-check coat in the morning, meet someone in a pun-shop at lunch, have the best hour of their life followed by the worst hour of their life in the afternoon, be pushed in the early evening into a crisis by a visit from a man who is either a murderer or the biggest pussy-cat you could ever meet, and then have sex with the woman of their dreams – and still be able to fit in a bout of insomnia and another quick crisis *before midnight*?

None. That was the answer. None other people could do that.

After a while it became obvious that he was never going to go back to sleep. He was too excited by Rachel's nearness. He kept having to look over to check that she was really there, and each time he did he worried that she would wake at that second and scream at the sight of him. The whole thing reminded him of childhood Christmases – being able to see presents that you knew it was too early to open, while at the same time being almost blinded by fear.

As a child, Jonathon had been terrified of Santa Claus – a fear that had taken hold when a beery, incoherent Santa had visited his nursery school and given everyone identical presents. The idea of being given another Snoopy pencil in the middle of the night by a fat old derelict straight from the chimney had scared the absolute shit out of Jonathon and ruined at least two Christmases. In the end his mother had been compelled to tell him that Santa Claus didn't exist, taking the opportunity at the same time to nullify two of Jonathon's other obsessive childhood terrors – the Tooth Fairy and God.

He had to admit that he was terrified now by the thought of the next morning. What would he do about his hair? What would they talk about? What if he slept later than her? What if she was still burbling on about bumblebees? He pictured her drumming her fingers on the kitchen table, eating muesli and regretting her mistake as he sat forlornly with his geek mohican standing vertically above his head. The talk was bound to be awkward, even if he spent the rest of his insomnia preparing conversational flash cards for them.

It suddenly struck him that he had to go to work in the morning too. He had another nine-thirty to one-thirty shift, and he needed to rearrange the trenchcoats. Everything was pointing in the same direction: he was going to have to go home. He was going to have to leave Rachel here in bed and slink off to his sloping ceiling, nauseating sink and cold sheets. And if he was going to leave, he was going to have to write Rachel a note. He eased himself slowly out of bed.

CHAPTER SEVENTY-THREE

Jane couldn't help doing her victory scream again when she realised she was standing on the wheelie bin with all her brittle bones intact. Descending from the wheelie bin was a breeze compared with getting down from the roof – she just lay on her stomach and gradually slipped down one side. Back on solid ground, she collected the bucket and steeled herself for her return to the roof.

As she stood on the bucket and pulled herself back onto the wheelie-bin, she wondered how she had got onto it the first time. She couldn't for the life of her remember. It was quite a mystery, it really was. Once on the wheelie bin she did her sprawling thing again and plucked the bucket from the ground. Then she stood up, feeling her knees click and crunch and howl as she did so, and tucked the bucket up onto the roof. Again she heaved herself up, feeling the rough material beneath her hands, almost losing her foothold on the window frame, but catching herself just in time.

On the roof again, she found that it didn't feel nearly so high up as it had the last time. In fact, she felt positively relaxed about using the bucket to climb onto the windowsill. Once up there, she snaked her arm through the top bit of the window – the name of which she still couldn't remember, though she must have used the word a million times – and calmly turned the latch to the larger window pane which she knew didn't have a name.

Jane climbed inside. The room was small, with a sloping ceiling that made her stoop and a rudimentary sink that made her sick. She wondered why there was a sloping ceiling in a first-floor room. Beside the sink, on the longest wall, stood a large, prefabricated wardrobe. *Behind the wardrobe*, Lance had said. The wardrobe was pressed close to the wall and it was difficult for Jane to see behind it, especially since she hadn't put the light on. She tried to move the wardrobe, but her arms were already hurting from pulling herself up on to the kitchen roof twice, and she didn't have the strength. She looked around the room for something with which to reach into the gap behind the wardrobe. Only a cheese sandwich and a pair of shorts were visible in the gloom. She was going to have to switch the light on.

First she peered through the window, checking that there was no one in the garden, then she moved over to the light switch and – very gently, so that it didn't make a click – eased it into the 'on' position. In the yellow light, Jonathon's room took on a new aspect. The sink loomed more menacingly, upsetting the room with its chilling leg and its great grey mouth, and the orange nylon carpet was displayed to full effect.

There was a pair of tweezers on the sink shelf, which Jane picked up before heading back to the wardrobe. She had no idea what Jonathon could possibly be doing with tweezers – perhaps he plucked his chin rather than shaving.

Peering into the narrow gloom behind the wardrobe, she could make out the brown outlines of a cardboard folder, wedged near the sink end. She was going to have to lie under the sink and pull the file from behind the wardrobe with the tweezers. Jane caught sight of herself in the small mirror above the sink, and noticed that the piece of egg from the bin had edged on to her lapel, like a buttonhole.

The odd, jaunty grubbiness of her new nosegay pleased her, and she realised that she actually wasn't a little old lady, that she was barely even old. Her mother, she reflected, had probably been old in her late fifties, perhaps even in her late thirties, but *everyone* had been so much older then, except children. All this time she had been worrying quite unnecessarily about being a little old lady. How could she be old when she had scaled a roof and broken into a bedsit?

The reflection made her feel pleased and slightly heroic, and she bent herself to the task of retrieving the folder with a new zest. It took her a few minutes of patient pulling and tweezering to dislodge, but finally it was in her hands. She opened it. The first thing she saw was a piece of paper, yellowed by time, with a green crest at its head: a curly-horned creature perched on a crag, beside the words 'Girard Leviticus Ltd'. Below the crest was typed 'CONTRACT'. This was what she had come for: the original documents.

Now she just had to find Jonathon's copy. And get to the Ritz in precisely – she checked her watch – zero minutes.

CHAPTER SEVENTY-FOUR

Jonathon was not a writer. He saw that now, after staring for ten minutes at the only blank sheet of paper he could find on Rachel's desk. He was not, of course, anything else either, not even really a men's ready-to-wear sales assistant, but it was the writing thing that troubled him at that moment.

The problem was that he couldn't bring himself to apologise for leaving because he couldn't help thinking that she'd be relieved to find that he had gone. Nor could he tell her that he would ring her to sort everything out, because he knew it would be at least fifty-seven times as difficult to make himself call her as it was to make himself write this note. Also, he didn't want to strike terror into her heart at the thought that he was going to keep pestering her after her shocking lapse of judgement. He thought of her having dinner with Sam somewhere nice, constantly looking over her shoulder, worrying that he was going to follow her in and ruin everything.

But then again, neither could he quite bring himself to commiserate with her for that shocking lapse, assure her that he would never darken her doors again, and promise to leave the country quietly. For one thing, he desperately wanted to see her again, and for another there was a glimmer of hope that tonight hadn't been a mistake, and that she would want to see him again.

If only he could be cool and laconic in the note. If only he could simultaneously just be himself and treat her mean, as Lance (among many others) had advised him. He tried to imagine what Lance would write, but then gave up, realising that Lance had almost certainly never had to flee the flat of his ideal woman because the situation reminded him too much of childhood Christmases and he had to be at work in the morning. Lance was more the sort of man who has to make beautiful women flee his own flat so that he can bring other beautiful women there.

After another ten minutes of crouching in the dark, alternately wracking his brains for things to write and plunging off down overgrown, tangential avenues of thought, he hit upon a solution. He arrived at this solution by a process of elimination. He couldn't just leave: Rachel might think something had happened to him and call the fire brigade, assuming that he had got wedged under the sink or sucked down the drain or something. He couldn't write her a fond, affectionate note for fear of misjudging the way she felt about him. He couldn't write her an insouciant, cavalier note, because he desperately wanted to see her again, and he didn't know how. There was only one solution, and though it was a simple thing to write and contained very few words, he still took five minutes over it and got it a bit wrong.

He cast around for somewhere to leave the note that would be easy to find, but not so obtrusive that she'd have to encounter it before she'd had a cup of tea and come to terms with the new day. Finally he settled on the incongruous toast rack on the desk, just a few feet from where Rachel lay softly snoring.

SUNDAY

Bob Plover was lounging invisibly behind a medium-sized indoor palm tree and a large circular table covered in linen an inch thick. The baroque yellow and white chair on which he sat was designed to make lounging prohibitively uncomfortable, but Bob lounged nevertheless.

The lounging was part of his paper-reading technique, developed over several years to perfectly fulfil all requirements: it looked natural, it obscured his face and it gave him a clear view of whatever he wanted to surveil. Tonight, the object of his surveillance was the Ritz's high circular lobby, a cathedral consecrated to expensive bad taste. More specifically, he was watching the highly polished wooden altar of its reception desk.

Plover sometimes ran courses in surveillance, and paper-reading was one of his specialisms. The trick is to sincerely believe that you are reading the paper while secretly not reading the paper. This becomes difficult when you've been doing it for an hour – it was now half-past midnight – but that's what marks out the professional.

Earlier on, he had used his finely nuanced paper-reading technique to order a coffee while remaining inconspicuous, and he was just considering repeating the feat when Jane Archer-Hollis marched in and approached the reception desk. She ignored the three men with white gloves on their shoulders, instead singling out the oldest desk clerk, a nice little old lady with half-moon glasses, rosy cheeks, and grey hair in a neat bun. As she talked, Jane put down the large John Lewis carrier bag she had been holding and looked nervously around the lobby, completely missing Plover.

Plover couldn't catch her words, but neither could the desk clerk. She looked up at Jane and said loudly, 'I'm sorry madam, I didn't quite catch that.'

Jane hesitated and then said, 'Could I have a coffee, please?'

'Certainly madam,' replied the desk clerk, and hobbled obligingly off.

As Jane walked across the lobby to a vacant table, Plover thought she looked a bit like Lauren Bacall might have done had she aged differently and worn egg on her clothing. She carefully placed the bag on the table, and looked around nervously before sitting down. Even when seated, she kept a gentle hand on the bag, as though it were a wilful and inquisitive puppy that might wander off somewhere at any moment.

He doubted for a second whether she really was Jane Archer-Hollis. After all, he had seen her yesterday for the first time, and that was mostly from behind a wall. She might even genuinely be Lauren Bacall, having had some expensive Californian treatment to make her look English.

But no, there was no mistaking that kindly imperiousness. Either this was an incredible coincidence, a trick, or Lance had sent her with a bag of files to leave for a Mr Formby. Plover could see that the bulge in the bag was pretty much exactly the size of four copies of some secret documents, so why hadn't she handed them over? Could this be a diversion? He dismissed the idea: Lance couldn't know Plover was here, and – more importantly – there was nothing to divert him from. The deal was simply 'hand over the documents or we start hurting kindly ladies in their late fifties'. There was no room for diversionary tactics, particularly not ones that involved those ladies.

The desk clerk – a proper story-book little old lady who probably made jam on Sundays and left out milk for hedgehogs – hobbled back with the coffee and placed it solicitously before Jane. Plover watched as Jane drank the coffee in rapid, small sips, frowning as she did so. She seemed impatient to get the coffee drinking over with as quickly as possible. Plover carefully checked the rest of the lobby to make sure he hadn't missed anything. There were a few people around, but they all looked unnatural enough for him to be satisfied that they were genuine customers.

Jane was finishing her coffee. She kept putting it down with an air of finality, and then having one last sip, like an artist who can't bear to admit his masterpiece is complete. When the coffee was unequivocally finished, Jane got up quickly, picked up the John Lewis bag, and strode over to the reception desk.

At the counter she paid for the coffee. The desk clerk was much too polite to tell her she was making all her coffee transactions in the wrong place. She nodded her wrinkled head wisely, smiled, and hobbled off. Jane called her back and asked her something that Plover couldn't quite catch. The desk clerk pointed to a bank of shiny brass-plated rococo telephone booths in one corner.

Jane disappeared into one of the booths and, a couple of seconds later, Plover folded up his *Financial Times* and slouched briskly over to a neighbouring booth.

CHAPTER SEVENTY-SIX

Jonathon eased open the front door of his building. Had he done the wrong thing? Perhaps he should have stayed. Wasn't it the mark of a cad to sneak off in the middle of the night, post-ravishment? Maybe he should just turn around and go back. No: he wouldn't be able to get in. Shit.

Well, he had made his bed (or at least unmade the only other bed he might have used) and now he would have to lie in it. He began the slow trudge upstairs, wondering if Avi would be in the bathroom.

The phone in the hallway rang. He knew it was Rachel. He ran downstairs and paused a while, collecting himself, before answering.

'Hello.'

'Oh. Hello Jane.'

'No, I was just passing the phone.'

'Well, I went to work and then a place called Pu–'

'Oh. OK.'

'Are you all right? You sound a bit–'

'Did you?'

'Oh. He hid it behind my wardrobe? Why didn't he tell me?'

'With some tweezers?'

'Sorry. I'll try not to.'

'You didn't um look at anything else under my bed, did you?'

'Of course it isn't.'

'Arrested? Where are you?'

'Formby, right. Have you–'

'Are you sure you're all right?'

'Yes, I've read both sets. On Thursday. Haven't you?'

'He hadn't read them when I saw him yesterday. He showed me them on Thursday and I read them, but then he thought we were being followed and he forgot to ask me about them.'

'Um, well there's a lot more in the second file. They're all letters and contracts signed by Augustus Zazel, the owner of Girard Leviticus.'

'In the second file there are letters as well as contracts. The early ones are quite detailed: RSG stands for Registered Scapegoat. Politicians – especially the new ones who've come from business – were taken on as RSGs when they were in trouble. Then the RSG is given a job and has to look like he's in charge, but really he's just a front, so if something big fails–'

'Yes, or like the Privately-Operated Orphanage Programme. So when something big fails the RSG resigns and takes all the blame, so that none of the people who are really in charge have to do anything differently.'

'Well Lance wasn't going to give them to the papers because he only read Thompson's file – which doesn't make much sense on its own. You…'

'You're not in danger, are you? Because–'

'You're running out of what? Oh.'

'Spent it on a coffee? I've got loads of change … Hello? Jane? Hello?'

CHAPTER SEVENTY-SEVEN

The murderer unpacked himself from the car, stumbled the few feet to the telephone box and crammed himself inside. Being big wasn't all laughs: in a world designed for much smaller people, he practically had to dislocate his shoulders every time he wanted to call someone – or, as now, answer a ringing public phone. He ought to get one of those new portables.

He opened the door of the phone box as far as it would go in order to give himself enough elbow room to pick up the receiver.

'Glockenspiel,' he said.

'No, we said the password was "glockenspiel".' He was tired and irritable.

'Don't know why we need one anyway.'

'All right, keep your hair on.'

'Yes, of course I am. Otherwise I wouldn't be talking to you, would I?' He leaned his head out of the phone box to give himself room to rub his eyes.

'Right. I'll come down right away. Where will you be?'

'The *Financial Times*? The old eye-hole trick?'

'I don't know what's the matter with you. You're all wound up.'

'No, course I won't.

'Right. See you in five.'

'Minutes, obviously.'

He replaced the receiver, shook the phone box from his shoulders and prepared to encase himself again in the car.

CHAPTER SEVENTY-EIGHT

She replaced the ornate white telephone on its hook, checked to see if it had returned any change, and then took the John Lewis bag firmly in hand and left the booth. There was no question in her mind now of handing the documents in at reception. She was going to tell the world about the whole rotten scheme.

A man with a pair of white gloves on one shoulder held open the door for her. Beyond was Piccadilly and, round the corner, her car. She was on the point of stepping out when she felt a tap on her shoulder. Turning around, she saw a man wearing a slightly rumpled trench coat and holding a copy of the *Financial Times*.

'Jane Archer-Hollis, isn't it?' he said.

She was shocked to hear him say her name. How did he know?

'Yes,' she replied.

'Listen, it's all right, love. I know what's going on.'

'What do you mean?'

'I mean – do you mind if we sit down?'

Jane hesitated, looking around. There were still a few people sitting about, which was reassuring, and there was something in the man's manner that inspired not trust exactly, but comfortableness. He had a friendly face, albeit one much too large for the head on which it was mounted. There would, after all, be no harm in hearing him out. Jane raised her eyebrows in the direction of the coffee-table area and they walked slowly over to it.

Jane sat down, the John Lewis carrier-bag clutched tightly in her arms, and waited for Plover to say something. He smiled at her, wrinkled his eyes, looked down at the table, ruffled his matted hair, slapped his cheeks rhythmically and pinched the bridge of his nose.

She was the one who broke the silence. 'What do you mean, you know what's going on?'

He looked tired, like Peter Falk just after he's finished his face-stretching exercises, but he smiled.

'What do *you* think I mean?' he asked.

'Are you a policeman?'

He shook his head.

She looked towards the lobby and its door. 'I'm very sorry, but I rather think I shall be going now, if...'

'All right. Fair play,' he said reasonably, as though it was all one to him whether she stayed or went.

She stood and picked up the John Lewis carrier bag.

'I know what's in that bag,' said Plover.

She paused, arrested by his unusual strategy. She imagined him behaving like this on University Challenge, constantly pressing the buzzer, saying 'Yes. I know the answer,' and then relapsing into friendly silence.

'You know, ducky,' she told him, 'I really think that you're going to have to start saying what some of the things you know are.'

'That bag you've got there has got four sets in it of some documents you shouldn't have.'

'I see,' she said, remaining standing.

'Lance Ferman asked you to hand them in to the reception desk in the name of a Mr G. Formby.'

She smiled thinly at him, but remained standing.

'Lance might wonder why you haven't handed them in,' he suggested.

That was true. But who was this man to tell her so? Was he an enigmatic ally or an amiable enemy? She looked at him, trying to puzzle him out.

'*I* wonder why you haven't handed them in,' he said.

'And who are you?'

'My name's Bob.'

Bob. That was a friendly name. Had anyone ever suffered from the actions of a Bob? She didn't think so: Bob Hitler, Bob Sauron, Bob Pot, Bob Gein. It just didn't fit. But then, what basis was that for making one of the most important decisions of her life? She sat down again, ready to give him one more chance.

'Who are you, Bob?'

'I'm a friend.'

'Yes, but whose friend?'

'Lance's.'

Was that true? Maybe Lance had called this man and asked him to check that she handed the files in.

'I could be your friend too,' he said.

'That's lovely, but why are you here, ducky?'

'I'm here to help Lance. And you.'

'Help us in what way?'

'By getting you to hand those documents in, like he asked.'

'Did Lance send you?'

'Yes.'

'And where is Lance now?'

She saw him hesitate. 'He's in a safe place.'

'That's one way of describing it. What is that safe place?'

'Listen, let's just say it's a *very* safe place. We both know where we're talking about.' He looked her directly in the eye. His shoulders were a little tense and he was no longer slouching.

'I don't think you do know where you're talking about,' she said.

'Fine. The point is, is that if you don't hand the documents in you're in big danger. Lance told me you was threatened. And Lance is in big danger too.'

'Even though he's in a *very* safe place.'

'Nowhere's safe.'

'It's lovely to talk to someone who isn't bound by dreary old consistency, but it's a long way past my bedtime and I'd really like to get back home. Good bye, Bob.'

It was just what Emma Peel would have said. She stood up.

Bob stood up too. He suddenly looked tired – not in a friendly, rumpled way, but simply in a tired way. He also looked deeply annoyed and not at all amiable.

'Look, just give us the bag and we can all get home,' he said.

'That is just what I was thinking,' said a deep voice, behind her and a long way up.

She turned and saw a suede bomber jacket, a Tottenham top and, worn around a huge neck, a gold chain and an MCC tie. She decided not to look up at the man's face. After all, she had just wet herself.

CHAPTER SEVENTY-NINE

Jonathon had never really thought of himself as a decisive man of action. He sometimes wondered how differently the great events of the world might have turned out if he had somehow been in charge of them, with his unique repertoire of vacillation, prevarication and inaction. The Storming of the Bastille would have been known to history as The Alternate Storming and Not-Storming of the Bastille. The Charge of the Light Brigade would have been The Several Cups of Tea of the Light Brigade. And the Great War would have been dubbed instead The Great Uninterrupted Continuation of Peace. Given a choice between Option A and Option B, Jonathon generally pursued a course composed of all the distilled worry and inactivity of both courses, divested of their substance, labour and potential for success: Option 0. In multiple-choice exams, he frequently ticked outside the boxes.

So, it was something of a surprise to him that immediately after Jane's call was cut off, he found himself ringing a minicab company and asking to be taken to the Ritz. Going there was understandable: Lance had been arrested, Jane had been threatened and she was now on her own in the Ritz with some secret documents, no change for the phone and a sort of tense catch in her voice. What was not understandable was why he hadn't dithered and putzed around before taking action. However, there was no time for thinking about that. He looked down at himself, noticing that he was still wearing his suit, which would make it much easier to get into the Ritz. He took his tie from his pocket, then ran up to his room and counted out a finely calculated amount of money for the cab and the night bus home. He could afford this as long as he didn't think about how he was going to buy his lunch on Wednesday.

A horn sounded in the street, and he ran out to the waiting minicab.

There in the middle of the road was an ageing Sierra with its front bumper missing and its registration plate secured by gaffer tape. The driver, a youngish man with a baseball cap on backwards, flashed the lights and Jonathon ran over and opened the door.

'Is this my cab?' he asked.

'You Fairfah?' asked the driver. Jonathon could see that he had one of those beards made up of exactly twelve strands of hair.

'Fairfax, yes. I'm Jonathon Fairfax.'

'Yeah, get in Fairfah. Cold.' The driver made a busy mime with his hand of each individual stream of chilly air entering the car. His ethnicity was a puzzle: darkish skin, a struggling beard, a baseball cap, a basketball vest bearing writing in an unusual alphabet, a thick padded coat and, wound around the rearview mirror, a string of what looked like rosary beads.

Jonathon got inside.

'Where you go, boss?'

'The Ritz, please.'

'Ritz. That's right.'

The car jerked and then rumbled forward. The mission was a foolish and unnecessary over-reaction. Jane would be in no trouble at all. She would have sorted everything out and gone home by the time he arrived at the Ritz. Then he would have to get a bus home. The night would leave him tired and poor, and no one would know how heroic and decisive he had been. Still, at least he would know his own heroism. And if he didn't go he would feel bad. At least he was taking action: that was progress. And Jane really might be in danger. Surely he wouldn't feel this tense and keyed up if she weren't.

After a couple of minutes the driver turned casually to Jonathon and remarked in a conversational tone, 'Where is Ritz?'

'Don't you know?'

'I been thinking, boss. Not quite sure now. You know where is?'

'It's ... it's...' Jonathon had no idea. He had never been there. It was just one of those places everyone's heard about, like the Eiffel Tower or the Hoover Dam. They didn't really need addresses.

'Haven't you been there before?' Jonathon asked.

'Not quite sure. Maybe,' said the driver. He seemed as friendly and unconcerned as if they were discussing whether he'd seen Three Men and a Baby.

'So where are we going?' asked Jonathon.

'Ritz,' said the driver, with a puzzled frown.

'But how do you know whether you're going the right way?'

'Right way?'

'To the Ritz.'

'You know where is, boss?'

'Haven't you...'

Jonathon took a deep breath. He needed to break what could easily become an infinite loop of conversation.

'Listen,' he said, 'I'm in a massive hurry. My friend she might be in danger. Big danger. Want to reach her quick. She's at Ritz. Need to get there fast.' Why was he talking like that? Was he being racist?

'Who is in danger?' asked the driver, looking at Jonathon with deep concern.

'My friend. A woman. Um, Jane.'

'She is your wife?' They were heading down a clear section of Holloway Road, and the driver had, unnervingly, turned fully to face Jonathon while doing sixty.

'No.'

The driver gave Jonathon a look that seemed to mix bafflement, scepticism and disappointment, and Jonathon decided to modify his answer.

'Yes. Yes, she's my wife,' he said.

'OK. Let's go,' said the driver. He sailed through a red light, ducking his head down to the level of the steering wheel as though hoping it would improve the car's aerodynamic profile. He did the same trick at the next light, and then at the bottom of the road he swung around the Highbury Corner roundabout, somehow harnessing the centrifugal force and the slipstream of a lorry to fire the Sierra off down Upper Street with enough momentum to once again sail through the next set of traffic lights, outside the Hope and Anchor.

Jonathon's fingernails were deeply embedded in the plastic sides of the Sierra's seat as he clung on.

'Do you have to go this fast?'

The driver looked at Jonathon with incredulity, his mouth hanging slightly open.

'Wife danger. Yes!'

Well, at least we'll get there quickly, thought Jonathon, *or die*. Meanwhile he needed to remember where the Ritz was. There were thousands of places he knew the locations of just because they sounded right together. He'd never been to Chelmsford, for instance, but he knew it's in Essex because 'Chelmsford, Essex' sounds so right. That was also how he knew Boston is in Massachusetts, Foyles is in Charing Cross Road and the heart is in the thoracic cavity.

The Ritz, Chelmsford. No. That was a relief. At least he knew when it didn't sound right.

The Ritz, St Martin's Lane. No.

Ahead of them a delivery lorry was parked outside a convenience shop and two men were unloading crisps. Without slowing, the driver simply slung the Sierra around the lorry. *The Ritz, Oxford Street.* No.

An Audi was heading straight for them. There was no possible way to avoid a crash. *The Ritz, Trafalgar Square*. No. There was a fierce gleam in the minicab driver's eyes, that look of holy courage that people adopt as they die for their beliefs. *The Ritz, Regent Street*. No. Jonathon suddenly realised that he had not put his seatbelt on. *The Ritz, Savile Row*. No. They were both definitely going to be killed.

The moment stretched into an endless river of time.

They had been hurtling towards the Audi for years. Jonathon had been looking at the determined holy courage in the minicab driver's eyes for so long that he was bored of it, frankly. Why had he never realised there was so much time in a single second? He could have done all his A-level revision in a couple of minutes, if only he'd known. He could have devised a complete and self-consistent theory of quantum gravity. *The Ritz, Pall Mall*. No. His mind slipped away. He remembered a day in the rain at Skegness when he was five and how pleased he had been to be given a new bucket in the shape of a castle, red with a green handle. Catching a bus on his own for the first time. The taste of sausage from a fish and chip shop. Socks with snowmen on them. The Tube journey to work. Rachel. *The Ritz, Tottenham Court Road*. No. He remembered that you should let your body go limp in a car crash. Tensing up is what does the damage. Drunk people always come out of accidents best. The long second continued. They were still hurtling towards the Audi.

He let his body go limp. Very slowly he slipped from the seat into the passenger footwell. It smelled of Fanta. *The Ritz, Piccadilly*. Yes. Too late.

CHAPTER EIGHTY

Police cells were not Lance's ideal environment. It was impossible to get a drink, they were incredibly uncomfortable, no one seemed to care what they looked like and there were almost no women. On the plus side, the shower was much better than his. He got himself through the first few minutes by pretending he was in one of those uncomfortably fashionable bars where the seats are hard and the decor minimalist.

The cell was about six feet square, with a wooden bench jammed against one wall. It was superficially clean, but there was a kind of lingering, ingrained grubbiness in everything, like a cubicle in a municipal swimming baths. The cell was tiled – floor, ceiling and walls – with nobbled beige slabs of porcelain, held together with scummy grouting. It had all been designed to give the inmate nothing to do but ponder the enormity of his crime, whatever it happened to be.

He had been given dinner after the first bout of questioning had ended. It was all-purpose institutional food that could equally well have been found in a school or hospital. The carrots were a pale yellow colour, the sprouts were white, and the peas and meat were a uniform grey. Lance decided fairly quickly not to eat any of it, and instead used it to try to take his mind off how little remained of his cool. He flicked the peas at the closed cell window, eventually achieving an impressive accuracy. Then he hid the carrots in the most inaccessible corners of the cell, hoping to really confuse the cleaners. He made the meat and sprouts into a face. Then he got bored of the whole thing and was instantly engulfed by worry.

Would Jane have been able to find the documents? Would she get them to the Ritz on time? Would whoever had threatened her keep their side of the bargain? He didn't want to imagine anything terrible happening to Jane, and yet that was all his brain seemed able to do at the moment: there was Jane being bundled into the back of a van, there she was being garrotted, there she was being dumped in concrete and becoming part of a new flyover. All in incredible photorealistic detail. And all because of him.

Him.

Oh shit. He had himself to worry about as well.

What if he was charged? What if justice was, as many well informed people had told him over the years, a sham? What if he was sent to prison? What if he ended up being used as a surrogate wife by a gigantically violent psychopath? That was almost certain to happen if they put a man as good-looking as Lance in prison. Damn it, he was so good-looking that it would probably happen in the van on the way to prison.

CHAPTER EIGHTY-ONE

'What you do, boss?'

'What?'

'What you do on floor?'

'Are we dead?'

The driver changed down a gear and gave a huge exultant laugh.

'No, we are not dead, my friend. We are alive!'

Jonathon dragged himself back up onto the seat and buckled on his seat belt. The driver accelerated through in the last millisecond of an amber light, dodged a car slowing to turn right, beeped his horn and accelerated again down St John Street.

'What happened to the Audi?'

The driver looked blankly at him.

'Back there. We swerved around a lorry and there was an Audi heading straight for us.'

The driver waved his hand dismissively over one shoulder. 'Gone. He stop.'

'Jesus.'

'I am very good driver. You see.' The driver again made high-speed direct eye-contact, gesturing back and forth between Jonathon's eyes and his own. 'You see?'

'Yes, I see. You are very good driver.'

The driver laughed.

'Now, we go Ritz, my friend.'

'It's in Piccadilly.'

'Piccadilly. I know this. I remember.'

They pulled up at a light. Jonathon looked around, wondering what could possibly have caused this, and then saw a police car pass in front of them.

The driver pulled out his wallet and flipped it open.

'Boss,' he said, passing it to Jonathon. 'This is my wife.'

The picture deepened Jonathon's confusion about the driver's ethnicity: she looked Chinese, with perfectly straight black hair and a disciplined smile. The driver couldn't be Chinese though, could he? Did Chinese people wear baseball caps? Was *that* racist?

'What you think?'

'She's very ... nice,' said Jonathon, settling on 'nice' at the last minute as being almost certainly true without being too gushing. She was only a small photograph after all. The only other thing he could guess about her, based on his very slight acquaintance with her husband, was that she was insane and had no sense of danger.

'Yes. I am in love with her,' said the driver. He took the wallet, replaced it in his pocket, and sprang through another red light with a laugh.

By now they were on Shaftesbury Avenue, and all that remained was for the driver to make a perfectly timed or horribly reckless dash the wrong way across the complex junction in Piccadilly Circus. And then they were in Piccadilly itself. Just as he was getting used to this, Jonathon had to get used to the fact that the driver had pulled up outside the Ritz. Getting used to this fact was tricky, coming as it did so quickly on the heels of having to get used to not being dead in a car crash.

Jonathon looked at his watch. 'That took fourteen minutes,' he said.

'Only five miles, boss. Easy.'

He waved away the money Jonathon offered him.

'Give your wife,' he said.

As soon as Jonathon got out, the scarred Sierra roared away, the driver giving a long blast on his horn.

If Jonathon had seen the doorman in white gloves, he would probably have hesitated. This would have been a big mistake.

As it was, distracted by the memory of his recent near death, he strode blindly towards the entrance. The doorman, possibly taking unconsciousness of doormen as a sign that Jonathon was the right sort to be let in, swung the door open sleekly and smoothly, with a murmured 'Good evening, sir.' Little did he suspect that he had just let in someone who had counted out exact change for the bus home and did not know where his Wednesday sandwich was coming from.

Stepping inside, Jonathon found himself in an awful person's over-decorated idea of paradise. In the centre of the lobby stood a colossal bunch of pink roses on a golden altar. Beside his elbow a statue of a golden weeping woman held aloft a dozen electric candles. To his left, a golden handrail swept down a dramatic flight of crimson stairs, ending next to the reception desk – a crescent of glossy marble-topped wood. On the wall behind it, among a scrambled mass of intricate gold, Jonathon dimly made out a clock face. It was ten to one.

Beyond the lobby, screened here and there by smallish palm trees, lay an area of linen-encrusted tables and funny yellow-and-white chairs. This palm and linen oasis looked like the sort of place in which rich people might buy coffee at night. It was about a quarter full and was clearly where he should look for Jane.

First, however, he had to negotiate the Ritz's next line of defence.

'Good evening, sir,' said another, rather older, doorman, his hands clasped in front of him. 'How may we be of assistance?' He managed, while being perfectly polite, to project an air of scepticism about the whole business of Jonathon.

Jonathon was temporarily struck dumb by the man's magnificence. He had the face of a civilised horse, a shirt whiter than the centre of the sun and a jacket that seemed to have been designed for a Grand Admiral of the Austro-Hungarian Empire. A mechanised smile slipped into action, remained in display mode for a second, and was faded smoothly down.

'Sir?' prompted the man.

'Um, I'm here to see Jane Archer-Hollis,' said Jonathon.

At the mention of the double-barrelled name the doorman's scepticism diminished a little. How he conveyed this was a mystery, since neither his posture nor his expression changed.

Jonathon felt he needed to follow this up with something. 'She's my aunt,' he said. There was something about a rich aunt that made his presence more plausible. He was sure that Jane wouldn't mind – after all, she'd already been his wife that evening.

The magnificent doorman smiled a little smile.

One more push, thought Jonathon.

'She's taking coffee here,' he told the doorman.

At this the doorman, who had never been overtly blocking Jonathon's entrance, nonetheless somehow, and without moving, stood aside. He clearly felt that, whatever the state of a young man's hair, if he wears a suit and tie, has an aunt with a double-barrelled name and says 'taking' instead of 'having' coffee, then he may be admitted to the palaces of the mighty.

'Please do let me know if you encounter any difficulty in finding her,' said the doorman.

'Thank you.'

Jonathon paced quickly through the lobby, heading for the shelter of one of the larger palm trees, amazed that so many rich people chose to have coffee, liqueurs and expensive snacks so late at night. He looked back to check that the doorman wasn't following him and walked straight into a wall. It hurt.

'You again!' said the wall.

On closer inspection Jonathon could see that it was not a wall that he had walked into but a gigantic torso. Above it was the face of the terrifying man who had asked him for directions. The man had Jane's arm in one hand and a straining John Lewis carrier bag in the other. Jane's face was white and she was shivering. She kept her eyes on the floor, not seeing Jonathon.

Jonathon felt a response was needed. 'Hup, um. Oop,' he said.

'What do you mean "Oop"?'

'Um,' said Jonathon.

'I'll give you "um",' said the terrifying man.

There was another man on the other side of Jane, standing very close to her, his arm behind her back. He was wearing a trench coat, a fedora and a rumpled face.

'All right, calm down,' said the rumpled man to the terrifying one. Then he looked again at Jonathon and said, 'You again!'

That was when Jonathon remembered him. The man seemed to have lost a great deal of his easy amiability since he'd bought the coat, but then Harrods clothes can do that to you.

'Ah,' said Jonathon.

'"Ah"? What the ... "Ah"?' said the terrifying man. He seemed enraged by everything Jonathon said.

'Forget him,' said the rumpled man. 'Let's just get out of here.'

'How can I forget him?' said the terrifying man. 'He's standing on my flipping foot.'

'Keep your voice down,' said the rumpled man. Turning to Jonathon he said, 'Get off his foot, and get out of here.'

He gave Jonathon a shove.

Jonathon stumbled back a single pace and then stood rooted to the spot. Once again, time slowed to a crawl and his life began to pass in front of his eyes.

He was reliving the trifle incident at his fifth birthday party, watching helplessly as pudding was ladled into his fire-engine shorts by the evil Wayne Titley. Meanwhile, in the present, Jonathon was watching helplessly as the terrifying man's hand reached out, infinitely slowly, and planted itself in the centre of his chest. The shove, when it finally came, shot him backwards into the palm tree behind him with such force that he rebounded into approximately the same place as he had been before.

His head was now hurting but at least time was once again running at normal speed. Looking down at the John Lewis carrier bag, he saw that it was full of documents. He also saw that he was standing on the terrifying man's foot again.

'Sorry,' he said. And then, he did not know why, added, 'Give me the bag.'

'You what?' said the terrifying man. His face muscles clambered over each other to express beefy disbelief.

'Give me the bag.'

'I'll give you a bloody punch in the face,' said the terrifying man. He let go of Jane's arm and drew back his fist.

Jonathon, fully in the moment, limber from his recent shove and with reflexes tuned to concert pitch by the almost-lethal taxi ride, instantly went limp and slipped to the floor. The terrifying man's fist sailed over him and connected with the crown of the palm tree just behind where his head had been, sending it crashing to the floor.

At this point people began to take notice. Some of the nearer ones got to their feet.

Jonathon opened his eyes and saw the John Lewis carrier bag right in front of him, its handle still grasped in the terrifying man's prodigious hand. He grabbed for it and pulled. The plastic handles, already stretched by the weight of the documents and the size of the hand, tore away easily. Jonathon scrambled to his feet, holding the bag like an oversized rugby ball, and ran.

When he had tried to do this in actual games of rugby he had instantly and invariably been smeared over the turf like a meat-based spread. His technique worked much better in the Ritz. He dodged around a Louis Quatorze chair, narrowly avoided a golden urn, and squeezed through the gap between a pottery lamp and an overworked candelabrum, making for the doors. Behind him, the terrifying man let out a great bellow of rage and charged after him, but fell over a chair toppled by a fleeing diner.

'Stop him!' shouted the rumpled man.

A bearded man put down his coffee and rushed to intercept Jonathon. A nearby doorman turned at that moment, saw two running men, and made a split-second decision about who should be stopped. The bearded man went down like a kipper.

There was another cry of 'stop him!' and the doorman, on the point of getting the bearded man in a headlock, was himself poleaxed to the floor. Jonathon ran past.

'Stop him!' shouted the terrifying man, pointing at Jonathon.

Someone else took up the cry. 'Stop him!'

Here, Jonathon's failure to make much of an impression on people at last came to his aid. He could feel everyone mentally editing him out of the picture. *Stop who?* said the expressions on people's faces, *the person behind that inoffensive jogging blur?*

There was an increasing number of people who could be stopped. A diner brought a hurrying waiter to the ground. A man rushing in for a late supper was punched in the face by the maitre d'. The terrifying man dodged a tackle and fell over an urn depicting the god Pan and some grapes.

'Stop him!' shouted the rumpled man again.

Diners rushed waiters, doormen charged diners, porters set upon doormen, people having liqueurs legged up coffee-drinkers, and the terrifying man threw a relative of the Duke of Portland over an occasional table. 'Stop him!' 'Stop him!' echoed the shouts all around. Amid the melee, Jonathon was unscathed, the doors in sight.

Ahead of Jonathon, the magnificent doorman watched the chaos erupting in the palm tree oasis and now spreading into his lobby.

'Lock the doors!' shouted the magnificent doorman. Another doorman sprang forward with a key and the escape was sealed.

The magnificent doorman brushed off his Grand Admiral's uniform, put on his gloves and picked up a filigreed candlestick. He came at Jonathon, obviously meaning to guard the doors with his life. Jonathon caromed out of the way, knocking over a chrysanthemum.

Shit. He'd have to go back and try to hide among the palm trees.

He turned around and began the run back. As long as he could keep clear of the terrifying man, everything would be fine – another plan would come to him, he was sure. He was almost out of the lobby when he saw the terrifying man. The man hit someone with a vase and looked around. His eyes met Jonathon's. There was, incredibly, a clear stretch of carpet between them. The terrifying man moved with surprising speed, like a panther or possibly a puma – he was so fast there was no time to say which. There he was, right in front of Jonathon. He made a grab, but Jonathon managed to duck through his grasp.

Jonathon looked up just in time to avoid running headfirst into a palm tree. He skipped nimbly around it, feeling suddenly – and for the first time in his life – that his body knew exactly what to do. All he had to do was let it. Adrenaline surged through him. There was no thinking now, only movement, and each movement was perfect. Unfortunately, he only had two seconds in which to enjoy this new sensation, because after that he was struck from behind by what felt like a falling palm tree and everything went dark. He sensed the bag slip from his grasp and he tumbled gracefully beneath a table.

'Armed police!' someone shouted through a megaphone. 'Everyone...'

But what followed that 'everyone' he never knew. Sound followed vision into the darkness.

CHAPTER EIGHTY-TWO

'Armed police! Everyone assume a stationary position and place your hands upon your heads.'

There was a sudden and total silence as everyone simultaneously stopped beating their neighbours and froze in place.

Blimming heck, thought the murderer. This, now, just when he'd finally knocked that flipping kid down. With a palm tree as well. Beautiful shot.

The kid was lying motionless under a table. The bag lay a couple of feet away from the kid's feet, where he'd dropped it. The old lady stood nearby, looking at the bag at her feet. She stooped and placed a hand on it. Plover was a couple of yards away from her.

In this kind of situation it can be difficult to know when the game's up. The police, with their guns, were still over by the lobby door. The bag was close by. The murderer was a little more than the height of a decorative indoor palm tree away from it. On the other hand, there was a flight of stairs in the opposite direction. Should he grab the bag or run for the stairs? He had at most a second to make the call.

Run for it, he decided.

He picked up a pineapple from the floor and threw it at a chandelier on the other side of the room, hoping to create a big enough noise to distract the police. He missed, but it didn't matter. At that second Plover provided all the distraction anyone could need by leaping on the old lady. This was immediately followed by another huge helping of distraction when Plover howled like a fox as the old lady rammed her knee into his genitals.

The murderer grabbed a large silver tray by its walnut handles. Using it as a shield, he ran for the border between the palm oasis and the lobby, where the grand staircase swept down in a cascade of red and gold.

Police were still pushing into the lobby, disturbing those who were already there. The murderer saw one of them level a gun.

'Halt or you will be fired upon!'

You won't shoot that thing in here. Too many people.

The cop obviously thought the same. The murderer threw the tray at him and tore up the stairs, almost tripping near the top. In front of him was a long corridor, flanked on each side by doors. At the end, a hundred feet away, a left turn would give him a bit of safety. He hurled himself along towards that turning. Behind him he could hear the pounding steps of police coming up the stairs.

'Place yourself upon the ground now!'

'Armed police!'

They must have a clear line of fire, and if they fired at him he was dead. But he didn't think they would fire in a corridor of the Ritz: the chances of accidentally hitting the American ambassador's wife were too high. Doesn't help anyone's career to do that.

He hoped he was right.

His legs were moving frustratingly slowly, like in one of those dreams. This run down the corridor was taking hours, easily longer than Gemma's birth. His feet sank into the luxurious deep pile of the carpet as though he were running through quicksand. His legs were hurting with the effort. It's difficult to propel that quantity of muscle down a corridor at top speed, especially when you've been propelling it about the lobby and tea area of the Ritz for the last God knows how long. *Is this corridor ever going to end?*

Finally he was round the corner and still running. The cops were up the stairs now, and he could hear them pounding down the corridor. They would be quicker than him, he knew that. These weren't the fat ones in luminous coats. These were the ones who mean business, the ones who wear black, shave their heads and go to the gym. If he just kept running they would catch him. He needed to do something now, in the few seconds before they came round the corner.

Bung! An artificial luxury gong sounded from somewhere in the corridor ahead. A little man appeared wearing a uniform with a pair of white gloves on one shoulder.

The little man gestured politely to someone in the lift. *A frigging lift!* The little man turned his head and saw the murderer rushing towards him. His eyes widened to the size of fried eggs. Then the murderer barrelled straight into him, sending him rolling through the deep pile of the carpet. The murderer jumped into the lift, pressed the topmost button, and then pressed the 'close doors' symbol.

In the lift was a tubby man in a checked suit. He opened his mouth, then closed it. It fell open again.

'*First* floor. Doors *closing*,' said the lift.

'Stop!' shouted one of the police from the end of the corridor.

That voice and the others with it faded away as the doors closed and the lift was hauled upwards.

'Don't know why they have to put someone in the lift. Easier to do it yourself,' remarked the murderer to the tubby man.

'Yes. No,' said the tubby man in an American accent. Then, collecting himself a little, he added, 'You in town for long?'

'Not if I can help it, mate. Not if I can help it.'

Bung!

'*Fifth* floor. Doors *opening*.'

'This is me,' said the murderer.

'Have a great visit!' The tubby man's tone was exactly what it would have been if he'd been talking to a holidaying lawyer from Cleveland Ohio, but his eyes were glassy with terror and one leg of his trousers was now noticeably darker than the other.

The murderer took him by the shoulder and stood him in the doorway of the lift, so that the doors wouldn't close.

'You stand just here and do not let that lift door close. Yes?'

The man looked blank, and the murderer added in the voice he used for foreigners, 'THE ELEVATOR DOOR, HE STAY OPEN. Yes?'

'Ah, sure.'

The murderer towered over the man, his face so close that their noses almost touched in an Eskimo kiss. 'If not,' he said quietly, 'I will find you and I will make you eat your own feet. I will also kill you. Do you understand?'

The man nodded dumbly.

The murderer turned and ran down the corridor. He knew that he had bought himself a little time – as many minutes as it took the police to find the nearest stairs and run up four flights of them.

He knocked on the door at the end of the corridor, where it turned the corner.

'Room service!' he shouted.

He jogged from leg to leg, waiting for the door to open.

Finally, a bouffant man in a silk dressing-gown appeared.

'You took your time, didn't you?' said the murderer. 'This punch in the face is getting cold.'

The murderer delivered the punch in the face, dragged the man inside and closed the door. He vaulted over the bed to the other side of the room and looked out of the window.

'Bloody Ada,' he said.

Below was Piccadilly. The wide street was lit up by blue flashing lights, the hooing of sirens bouncing from building to building. 'They don't like trouble at the Ritz, do they?'

He must have got disoriented in the chase: he needed to be on the other side of the building to have any chance of getting out. He vaulted back over the bed, wrenched open the door and ran full pelt down the corridor, slowing halfway to bestow an unsettling grin on the tubby man in the checked suit, standing just where he had left him. He could hear voices from below, the sound of running feet on thick carpets.

At the other end of the corridor, he knocked on the nearest door and shouted, 'Police! Open up!'

He jogged from leg to leg again. Do people open quicker for the police than for room service? There was no sound from inside.

'Room service!' he shouted, banging on the door again. Leg to leg. Jogging.

Running out of patience, he banged again. 'Open the bloody door!'

To his left another door opened.

'Do you mind?'

A stern grey-haired lady in a fuchsia-pink dressing-gown stood with her arms folded. 'Some of us,' she said, 'are trying to sleep.'

'Sorry love,' said the murderer.

He ran into her room, pulled her in after him, shut the door and locked it. In a second he was out on her balcony.

This was more like it. Two storeys below was a wide terrace, almost empty of tables and chairs. He couldn't see anyone on it. At the end of it, a flight of stairs led down to an atmospherically half-lit garden. And over the garden wall was the darkness of Green Park and his only real chance of escape.

He threw the balcony doors open wide.

'Right love. Get in the cupboard and be as quiet as a mouse.'

'That's a wardrobe, not a cupboard.'

'Get in it anyway.'

The grey-haired lady sternly stepped into the wardrobe, imperiously sweeping aside the clothes that hung there.

'You shall hear about this,' she said as he locked the wardrobe door.

He stripped the sheets and blankets from the bed, knotting them around his middle. Then he rummaged through the chest of drawers until he found some tights.

'You should have a job, a man of your age,' said the lady in the wardrobe.

'I've got a job,' he said, using the tights to tie pillows over his knee-caps. 'That's the problem.'

He tied another pillow around his neck. Then he manhandled the mattress on to the balcony, heaved it on to the ledge, stepped up, looked down and jumped.

CHAPTER EIGHTY-THREE

It's unsettling to wake up and find that a scene has unfolded around you while you've been standing there. The last thing Jane remembered, she had been in the lobby of the Ritz, holding a John Lewis carrier bag and about to step out through the doors. Then the man had appeared, huge as a minotaur and with the same air of having been sent as a curse by a slighted god. She had simply shut down, as though some part of her brain had decided that she would be better off for a while without the higher functions of thought and awareness. She must have been stumbling around in a daze.

What had brought her out of it was the shout of 'armed police'. As a reasonably wealthy lady of a certain age and class, Jane knew deep in her soul that the police were especially there to help her. At the phrase 'assume a stationary position and place your hands upon your heads', she had fully returned to consciousness. She had always loved the police's odd turn of phrase. It was deeply reassuring – the product, as she saw it, of not-very-bright working-class people trying to ape the way educated people like her talked – and as endearing as a little girl wearing mummy's shoes and lipstick.

She tried to comprehend what must have happened while she'd been lost in her terror fugue. The Ritz's Palm Court looked as though it had been vigorously shaken. Tables were overturned, chairs were toppled, many of the palm trees were lying down. People had frozen in place. A man in a Prince of Wales check was draped over a Grecian urn. Another, in opera clothes, held up his hands to ward off a blow that never came. A waiter was paused in the act of raining blows upon the midriff of a portly man in a velvet coat. And everywhere on the floor were trays, cups, sugar lumps, silver teaspoons and liqueur glasses, bound together by a mortar of parma ham, melon balls and pâté.

In front of her was a table that had miraculously come through it all unscathed, though she could see a pair of shoes protruding from beneath it, and she wondered if they were attached to a person. She hoped that Jonathon had not come to the Ritz. She could distinctly remember the note of – well, almost of *manly concern* – in his voice when he'd asked on the phone if she was in danger.

Then she noticed the John Lewis carrier bag close to the table, almost at her feet. The handles were broken, but she could clearly see that it still contained the files she had decided, after talking to Jonathon, to make public. She picked it up.

There was a movement to her left. Instantly, she felt the fog of terror begin to return. There, a little further away than the length of an ornamental indoor palm tree, was the minotaur man. In his hand he hefted a pineapple. Was she dreaming? He was not looking at her, but at the ceiling, and as she watched he calmly and deliberately threw the pineapple with great force across the room and then turned and ran for the staircase that swept magnificently down from the first floor in a cascade of gold and crimson, between the Palm Court and the lobby. He ran fast for such a big man, his huge shoulders pumping beneath his suede jacket. As he receded her head cleared again.

A rumpled mass slammed into her from behind, wrapping itself around her. A hand grabbed for the John Lewis bag. She half-turned and her knee rose of its own accord, shuttling all her strength into what she distinctly felt to be the most sensitive area of her assailant's trousers. A high, unearthly shriek sounded in her ears, but the man kept hold of the John Lewis bag. She felt herself overbalancing, falling.

CHAPTER EIGHTY-FOUR

A two-storey drop onto a tiled terrace – even when you're wearing a bed and landing on a hand-made king-size mattress – is painful. The murderer lay there for a full minute, accustoming himself to being much lower down, working out how badly he was hurt. The fall had knocked all the air out of his gigantic lungs. He thought he might have cracked a rib and he knew that his neck would hurt unbelievably the next day.

He stood up and took a few slow steps over to the staircase leading down to the garden. He could walk, that was the main thing. Above him he could hear the noise of many voices shouting and many doors being pounded on. He broke into a gentle jog down the stairs. His chest ached. So did his knees, despite the pillows strapped to them. He was getting too old for this sort of caper.

At the bottom of the steps there was a paved area from which led two parallel footpaths. He took the right-hand one, moving as quickly as he could. Flower beds lined the paths, illuminated by tall old-fashioned fake gas lamps. Here and there was scattered a birdbath, a fountain or a sleeping stone lion. Halfway down the garden the formal flower beds began to give out and trees and bushes appeared, though with all the wildness pruned out of them. He broke into a run, his hand clasped to his ribcage. The wall at the end of the garden was high and bare, surmounted by razor wire. The trees stopped ten feet away from it, denying him help, and an armoured security camera was mounted prominently in the corner. At any moment, he knew, someone would see him. He was surprised it had taken them this long. The mattress was just lying there on the terrace, after all. But perhaps the police had been distracted by the door he had left open on the Piccadilly side. Perhaps the stern grey-haired lady was still standing quietly in her wardrobe, and maybe even the tubby American hadn't yet moved away from the lift door.

He unwound the sheets and blankets from his torso, gasping when he touched his rib. Then he knotted them together, tied one end of this improvised rope around the paunch of a conveniently small stone cherub, walked a few paces back and tossed the cherub up into the razor-wire entanglement at the top of the wall. He tested it with his weight. The metal stanchions mounted on top of the wall didn't move and the razor wire remained taut. *Thank God some security firms still take a bit of pride in their work*, he thought. He braced one leg against the wall, wound the blanket rope around his arm and began the climb.

Half-way up, he heard the noise he'd been waiting for: running feet on the terrace.

'Armed police! Assume a stationary position or you will be fired upon!'

He continued to climb. He didn't know if they could see him or if they were just shouting blindly, hoping he'd think they knew where he was. There was no light on him.

At that moment, three-quarters of the way up the wall, a security light mounted on one of the trees clicked on, illuminating him. He continued to climb, covering the final five feet in seconds. As he grasped the metal stanchion nearest to the cherub that had saved him, a shot rang out. He didn't feel anything, but you don't – not at first. Had he been hit?

'You, climbing the wall! Stop or I will fire again!'

In one movement he pulled himself up, rolled over the wire at the top – he could feel it tugging at the back of his jacket, but he had momentum – and fell down the other side.

A burst of gunfire sounded.

His right arm was nearly yanked out of its socket, and he realised that he was still hanging on to the improvised rope. He was suspended three feet below the top of the wall, on the Green Park side. Lamp posts ran along the two main paths – one running westwards alongside Piccadilly towards Hyde Park, one running down southwards beside the wall, in the direction of Buckingham Palace. Beyond the lamp posts was blackness: grass and trees made invisible by the dark. He let go.

He toppled through the air, rolling as he landed, his knees saved by the pillows that were still strapped to them. He could hear the police shouting to each other from over the wall. *Not a very polite way to refer to me*, he thought. He struggled to his feet and raced off into the heart of the darkness.

A few seconds later he collapsed into some tall grass in the shelter of a clump of trees, some way from the two lit paths. He knew that Piccadilly was full of police, and it ran along the whole of the north side of the park. The park tapered to a point as it ran west, meaning that the further he went in that direction, the more likely he was to be seen by police in Piccadilly. The only way he could go was south – towards Buckingham Palace. There wouldn't exactly be a shortage of police around there either, but at least they might not be expecting him. He had to move fast. He quickly divested himself of the pillows around his neck and knees, and checked himself all over. His hand came away bloody wherever he touched himself, and it was a couple of seconds before he realised that he had not been riddled with bullets but had only cut his right hand. There were deep gashes from the razor wire running down the centre of his palm, along his forefinger, and all across the heel of his hand. Blood poured out of them. He shook the case off one of the pillows and wrapped it around his hand to stem the bleeding. Then he set off again at a jog. From the Piccadilly side of the park, beside the Ritz, he could hear the sound of running feet and dogs barking.

As he approached the south edge of the park he forced himself to slow to a walk. He tried to calm himself down, see the situation rationally, from the police's point of view. It would have taken a lot of men to search every floor of the Ritz and deal with the mess in the lobby. And getting a load more police cars and vans into the heart of London on a Saturday night wasn't a job that he would have wanted. Some police knew that he had got over the wall, but by the time they had told a controller, they couldn't be sure whether he was still in Green Park. They might even worry that he had somehow slipped northwards across Piccadilly. The larger the area they had to deal with, and the more people there were looking for him, the more difficult it would be for them to manage the search. That was all he had going for him: the fact that organising a load of men with guns is a nightmare, especially when they're not allowed to shoot innocent people. He knew that from his army days. Of course, the situation wasn't exactly a walk in the park for him either – except in the literal sense, obviously – but it was important to remember that hunting for him would worry the shit out of whoever was in charge, and there was no end of things that could go wrong for them. That was comforting.

On the other hand, the dogs and the men with machine-guns would probably love it, and if he slipped up he was dead. That was less comforting.

In front of him was the huge roundabout that someone had decided should be right outside the Queen's house. From the centre of the roundabout, a statue of an old woman peered grumpily at the traffic. On top of her pranced a dirty gold girl with wings. Immediately to the west, beside the railings of Buckingham Palace, were several policemen in black coats and peaked caps, holding machine-guns and watching over the motionless guards in their red jackets and giant fur hats. It had always seemed pointless to have guards who aren't allowed to move or react to anything. It just means that you need another load of guards to guard them, as well as some more guards to guard whatever it was you wanted guarding in the first place. That was why he didn't pay tax – they just wasted it.

He zipped up his jacket, put his head down and his hands in his pockets, and stepped from the darkness into the light of a street-lamp. The traffic wasn't too bad at this time of night. He glanced right and left, and stepped out into the Mall. If he could just get across this brightly lit road, south, he could get into the darkness of St James Park. Then he would have more options.

He could hear the crackle of the police radios over by the railings, two hundred yards away. He could hear the dogs barking in Green Park, behind him. He could smell the sweat and blood on him. He was still breathing hard but trying not to show it. He kept his head down and tried to walk slowly.

Half-way across the road. Doing well.

Keep calm.

'Sir!'

It was a police voice, off to his right, just far enough away for him to pretend not to have heard it.

'A word with you, sir!'

He didn't react, didn't change his pace, kept his head down.

'Stop!'

He was over the road now, on the pavement. Not far to go.

'Oy! You!' shouted the voice. 'You in the bomber jacket! I said stop!'

He heard one of them say something into his radio. He heard the ominous rattle of guns being swung into position, magazines being checked, safety catches being flicked. He heard running feet. *Here we go again.*

His ribs were hurting more than ever but he forced himself to run along the pavement, through the gates and into St James Park. Four shots sounded behind him. Was it just him, or were the cops more trigger-happy than they used to be? He didn't know what had got into them these days.

Again, the main path was lit. He vaulted over the low fence beside the path, into the grass and trees, away from the lights. He could hear the police running, but their footsteps stopped at the gate. That probably meant they were going to try to seal the exits and call for backup.

He needed to get across to the more open south side of the park, and away.

There were a lot of problems with that. The main one was that he would have to cross the lake that cut the park in two. There was only one bridge, and that was well lit. If there were any other armed police around, it was an obvious place for them to go. And as he was within quarter of a mile of every major government department in the country, as well as Buckingham Palace and Downing Street, it was extremely likely that there would be plenty of other armed police around. If he didn't cross at the bridge, he would have to go round the east or west sides of the lake – one of them a stone's throw from Downing Street, the other from Buckingham Palace. He realised that despite thinking all this, he was still running in the direction of the bridge. The darkness was purple and golden. His breath came in thick clumps of steam. Every step felt as though someone was stabbing him in the knee.

The only possible way out was to swim. The water would be dark, and in the middle of the east side of the lake he knew there was a small island covered in trees. He was glad they'd taken Gemma to see the Trooping of the Colour now, and glad they'd come to the park after and paid three quid for a bloody ice cream. He could swim to the island, see where the police were, and – if the coast was clear – swim the rest of the way across. It was a stupid plan, but much less stupid than all the other plans he could think of at that moment.

He ran as fast as he could, staying off the path, slipping on the grass. He could see that on the bridge there was a man in a tit-shaped helmet and a luminous coat. He didn't think the ones with helmets ever had guns but he didn't know who else was nearby. He ran on, keeping to the grass. To the north, along the Mall, he could hear the crackle of radios. There was still the comforting swoosh of traffic along the Mall. If they hadn't stopped the cars then they didn't yet have enough police on the ground.

The island was approaching. He was mid-way between the bridge and the east end of the park. He ran south, hurdling the low fence, crossing the lit path, vaulting another fence, dropping to the grass, rolling and entering the lake as quietly as he could. The cold water hit his scalp, came through his clothes in a second and shocked the air out of him, but he bunched himself up, pushed off and swam beneath the surface, reaching out into the cold and dark, kicking himself along. His body told him that this was not so much swimming as gradual drowning in a horizontal direction, but he wouldn't let himself come up until his hands touched rushes. When he broke the surface for air, he was just feet away from the island. Then there was mud beneath his feet and he was hauling himself up the short bank. He dropped down beneath a tree and lay there, scanning the park for movement. The pains in his ribs, knees and neck had been joined by others in his lungs and the muscles of his shoulders. He was dog tired. He could hear sirens everywhere. The cop on the bridge was still alone but there were torches shining along the north edge of the park. The east edge was open and brightly lit, brightly dangerous. The big parade ground of Horse Guards shone. To the south, it was dark. Even the path beside the lake was dark on that side, deeply shadowed by overhanging trees.

He was tempted just to stay there on the island, sleep through it, but sooner or later the whole park would be rotten with police. He crawled across the small bump of earth, between the trees, checked that the man in the helmet was looking the wrong way, and slipped again through the mud and into the rushes and cold water. Half way between the island and the south shore of the lake was an outcrop of rock. Swimming is hard work when you weigh a lot, especially if you're also wearing trainers, jeans and a suede jacket. If he could reach the rocky outcrop he could have a breather and look out for the police before swimming those last few yards.

One stroke. Two strokes. Three strokes. His breast stroke was turning into a doggy paddle. Four strokes. He reached out a hand and grabbed the rock. He was panting and shivering, only his head and one hand out of the water. On the bridge, the policeman was looking south, waving. There must be more of them coming from that direction too, but at least it was darker. If the policeman looked to his left, he might easily see him, despite the blackness of the water.

The murderer looked up and into a dark, glittering eye. 'Bloody hell,' he whispered.

The bird was white with a black back end, as though someone had used its bottom to paint a really big fence. Its beak was long, with a huge floppy bag built into it. It continued to look at him with haughty disdain. *I hope it isn't going to make a racket.*

After a few seconds the pelican broke eye-contact and gazed off into the distance, magnificently ignoring him. Police were crossing the bridge, making for the north side, joining the ones already there. He hoped they thought he hadn't crossed the lake.

As gently as he could, he felt his way around to the side of the rocky outcrop furthest from the bridge. Then he took a deep breath and slipped beneath the surface.

Four lifetimes later, his fingers again touched reeds and he came cautiously to the surface. His lungs were on fire, but he couldn't let himself take a big noisy breath. He peered around, water streaming down his face. To the north it was all torches and voices, but here on the south side of the park it was quiet and dark.

He heaved himself out of the water, climbed heavily over the low fence and rushed gratefully into the blackness. He waited in the unlit shelter of the trees until he had got his breath back and his lungs had stopped hurting so badly. He thought he might be sick and he was freezing cold, so he hugged the worst of the wet out of his clothes. He would have liked to get rid of his heavy, cold coat, but it would only help the dogs, when they came. To the north more sirens screamed: reinforcements. He was going to have to keep going. At least now he was in the dark and away from the main concentration of police. He wished he was smaller and less conspicuous. A kid like the one in the Ritz could probably have escaped a nationwide manhunt unrecognised at a televised gathering of his own closest relatives, but the murderer was a conspicuous man, especially in the centre of London, soaking wet, in torn clothes and with a bloody Ritz pillowcase wrapped around one hand.

Come on. Keep going! He forced himself into a jog, through the trees. When he had almost reached the south edge of the park, there was a roar of engines and two shiny black Land Rovers rocked to a halt. The doors flew open and eight men got out and set off at a run. The men looked almost like copies of the same person. They were young, broad and slim, with square jaws, dark suits and very short hair, like a public-school rugby team at a funeral. They pelted off across the grass towards the bridge with an air of clean-limbed efficiency, as though they were showing off on a sports day. None of them saw him.

He ran over to the Land Rovers at a crouch. All the doors had been left open and the engine of one of them was still running.

'Hey!' someone shouted.

Even at the time the murderer thought it was a stupid thing to shout. He didn't turn to see whoever it was, he just jumped into the driver's seat of the purring Land Rover, notched it into gear and put his foot down, roaring off with three of the doors still open.

Sirens sounded all around. He was driving a large stolen vehicle in the most heavily policed part of one of the world's most heavily policed cities. He sped along Birdcage Walk, scattering cars. He could see flashing lights ahead and behind. He turned off the headlamps and pulled left, down a flight of pedestrian steps. It was narrow enough that the walls scraped the Land Rover's doors closed for him. At the end of the steps he turned right, the wrong way down a one-way street. He accelerated, turned right again, then immediately left, then left again into Tothill Street. There were no police cars now. He needed to get a grip on himself. If he drove crazily along with the lights off, he'd be easy to catch. He slowed and turned right into a narrow gully marked 'Dean Farrar Street', reaching for the headlamp switch. A car was reversing towards him fast. He wrenched the wheel to the left and the Land Rover smashed straight into the wrought iron and glass of an old red phone box, then on into the window of the building behind.

There was a bang and the world went white.

CHAPTER EIGHTY-FIVE

Despite the decline in public morals that everyone talks about, it is still not possible for a man to wrestle a lady to the ground in the Ritz with impunity, especially not in a room full of armed policemen. Jane kept her arms wrapped tightly around the John Lewis carrier bag and, within seconds, the rumpled man was lifted from her. She felt a reassuring hand on her shoulder.

'All right, ma'am?'

'Yes, thank you,' she said, sitting up. A few feet away the rumpled man was being held down by three officers. A fourth was trying to fasten handcuffs to his wrists, a job which was severely hampered by the fact that another five policemen were kicking the man as hard as they could and shouting at him that he was a 'toe rag'. *What was one of those?* she wondered. Perhaps some sort of primitive sock.

Meanwhile, other officers were charging up the gold and crimson stairway. At what she presumed were strategic points, more officers 'covered' the Palm Court and lobby, holding their guns in an uncomfortable-looking stiff-armed sort of way. Others talked aggressively into their radios. No doubt it was a consequence of all that time they spent sleeping in their vans. When they got a chance to do something they got a bit carried away and overexcited.

After a while they carried the rumpled man away – now significantly more rumpled. Two policemen began to walk around taking photographs of the wreckage. A thickset waiter renounced his seat on the chest of a man with a disarrayed moustache and instead offered him a chair. An old fellow in a mustard-coloured waistcoat tried to right a table, and a man in a black open-necked shirt sprang to his aid. Voices were heard again, wafting in disconnected strings across the blasted tea-room.

'Sorry about the, er … Do you think they've stopped serving drinks? … Oh, is that your shoe? … We've lost a contact lens! Contact lens! … I'm over here, Chester … Whatever it was, darling, I'm sure they didn't mean it … Blueberries and pomegranates, *I* heard…'

Soon an older policeman arrived and started talking calmly to people. He had yellow hair and a face like a big sober baby potato and Jane instantly felt better about the whole situation. He set himself up at a table by the stairs and began taking statements. Jane queued obediently for a while.

'I saw the whole thing,' a man in a striped blazer was saying. 'It was a waiter – black fellow. Pulled out a gun and started blazing away. Me and Eddie – Eddie and I, should I say – got up and…'

'It wasn't a waiter,' said another, 'it was a man. He was running. "Stop him!" someone shouted, so we got up – OTC training and all that – and that's when the bomb went off.'

'Can we get compensation?' asked someone else. 'For trauma?'

'I've been stabbed,' said another voice. 'Fork right through the back of the hand.'

'What does one do for whiplash? Legs above the head is it?'

Jane went over to a policewoman.

'Excuse me,' she said. 'May I go home?'

'One second,' said the policewoman. 'Matt, we letting them out yet?' she called.

Another policeman came over. He listened to something on his radio and then said, 'Check them for first aid, take a name and address, then start letting them out the side way. Don't let anyone go without a name and address. Six at a time out the side – you need to escort them.'

'You're in luck,' said the policewoman. 'Now, what's the name?'

'Jane Archer-Hollis.'

'And how are you spelling that?'

When the murderer opened his eyes again the world was still white. Was he blind? Was he dead? He was sure his knee and ribs wouldn't hurt this much if he was dead. And he wouldn't be able to see all this white if he was blind. He tried sitting back and found that his peripheral vision returned. Then he moved his head, and realised that the problem was that a huge white balloon had grown out of the centre of his steering wheel, almost filling the windscreen and most of the driver's side of the cockpit. He punched at it, trying to burst it, but his fists bounced harmlessly off the white material. What was the point of making Land Rovers indestructible if they stopped you seeing out of the windscreen when you crashed them?

He needed to stop wasting time. He opened the door and climbed down. There was no trace of the car which he had swerved to avoid. Bloody joy-riders.

The sound of sirens still wafted along on the breeze. The street was empty and not too bright. He limped along it as fast as he could go, noticing that a discreet sign in the building to the left identified it as the headquarters of the Metropolitan Police Authority. It seemed to be closed. As he limped along, he took out his wallet, wondering if he could get a cab. The notes inside were mulched into a thin white paste sandwiched between two layers of leather. He had only ten pence in change.

At the end of the street was a main road, Victoria Street. A bus pulled to a halt on the opposite side of the road, waiting at traffic lights. He dashed across four lanes of traffic, grabbing hold of the pole at the back of the old Routemaster bus and leaping on board just as it pulled off.

'Where to?' asked the conductor, tiredly, swaying his way down the aisle towards him, fiddling with his ticket machine.

'Where can I go for ten pee?'

'Nowhere.'

'Really?'

'Don't get the bus much, do you?'

'Course not. What do think I am?'

The conductor wiped a hand over his moustache and stared at the murderer with hard, pink eyes, taking in his torn, wet clothes, the bloody rag knotted around his right hand, the cuts and bruises all over him.

'When the bus stops, you need to get off,' said the conductor.

The bus slowed to turn a corner. The murderer grabbed the man by his tie, hauled him off his feet and dropped him neatly on the pavement, where he fell over.

'Wish I could think of something to say about that, but I'm too tired,' he remarked to a man slumped drunkenly against the stairwell. He sat down on the bench seat. 'Don't know how Bruce Willis keeps the clever chat going.'

After a few stops he got off the bus. He no longer knew where he was. The sirens were faint now – just the background howling that's part of London's ambience. He trudged on, always choosing the darkest, narrowest and poorest streets. Eventually he climbed into the garden of a boarded-up house, pegged his money on an old plastic clothesline to dry, crawled into a wheelie bin, lowered the cover, pulled on his comfortable but damp balaclava, and fell into a deep and painful sleep.

CHAPTER EIGHTY-SEVEN

At between seven and fourteen minutes before or after seven o'clock, Jonathon woke from a deep and painful sleep. He had no idea where he was or why. All he knew was that the back of his head hurt more than anything had ever hurt before. He was going to have to figure everything out from scratch.

He was lying in semi-darkness on highly polished stonework in a small wooden house with fabric walls. He sat up and banged his head on the ceiling. This made the world go much darker for a few minutes. He thought he was going to be sick. Eventually, the sick feeling went away and so he pushed aside one of the fabric walls and crawled out of the house.

All around, men in burgundy waistcoats were carrying things from one place to another, putting things on top of other things and using long things to move lots of very tiny things along the floor. The men in burgundy waistcoats ignored him as he stumbled loosely across the highly polished stonework, weaved his way around a tall thing with fronds, lambled through a very high circular room and almost fell over a man applying wet stuff to the thing between the floor and the street.

Outside a massive amount of light flew in through his eyes and got lodged there behind them, inside his head-bone cave. He put down a foot then lifted up a foot then put down a foot then lifted up a foot. This made the picture in front of his eyes change in a going-along way, but it was all very big and confusing, and probably best not to think too hard about how it worked.

For a while he was a sitting-down person. Then he was a bit of a going-along person. Then someone was lying down and he found that this too was him. It was what he was doing. He got up and went along again for a bit, then that stopped happening.

There was a big, very loud and rough thing inside his head with him, and after a while he came to realise that this thing was a headache. It was a huge, brown, highly polished headache. He had to budge his brain over a bit to accommodate it.

Outside his head there was also a very loud thing, and he came to realise that this was a road. There was a bus. He was sitting at a bus stop. Why was he sitting at a bus stop? He must be catching a bus. But which bus? Here was a bus.

He got on the bus, which had a convenient hole at the back to let you get onto it and a convenient pole to pull yourself up with. There were seats, and he thought he could sit on top of one. He could. A bit later he saw that the bus was passing Harrods. *That's where I'm working*, he said to himself. He looked down. There was the proof, undeniably. He was wearing a suit and a tie and a shirt. They seemed a bit more crumpled up than suits and ties and shirts are, but he thought they must really be a suit and a tie and a shirt anyway. They were his work clothes. He was going to work. That could happen on a bus, couldn't it?

'Tickets please,' said a man with a beard and a machine that gave out tickets.

'You've got some,' said Jonathon.

The man smiled indulgently. 'Where you going, squire?'

'To Harrods.'

'You've passed it. Back that way.'

Jonathon looked at the man, trying to see what he meant.

'Heavy night?' asked the man.

Jonathon thought about this for a bit. 'Not heavy,' he said. 'Really hard. Really brown and polished.'

'You all right?'

This didn't really seem to mean anything, so Jonathon left it.

'Want my advice? Don't go into work. You'll have a terrible come-down. Milk. That's what you need.'

'I'd better get off.'

Harrods had gone away a bit by now, but the bus stopped and that meant he could get down off the bus and then by walking he could make Harrods come closer to him.

He definitely worked at Harrods. When he was inside he knew where to go. A man with a tape-measure around his shoulders, Mr Reiss, looked at him as he passed, glanced at his watch and raised his eyebrows.

'You're early, Mr Fairfax,' said Mr Reiss.

'Everything is,' said Jonathon.

He went down to the luxurious granite toilet on the lower ground floor and was sick. This made him feel better and worse at the same time. His headache was by far the worst thing that had ever existed, worse than Stalin and the Krankees. Every loud noise jabbed him directly in the brain. He sat down on the toilet and held his head carefully in his hands. What had he been doing last night?

Rachel.

He had gone to Rachel's.

He had gone to Rachel's and slept with her in the most accidental and inept way ever.

And after that?

There was no after that. They must have been drinking. Drinking or quarterstaff fighting. He couldn't remember either, but that didn't prove anything: he couldn't even remember the journey to work this morning. Was he still drunk?

His head was just a big piece of hurt surrounded by a flimsy coating of skin. He looked up. There was a perceptible lag between the movement of the muscles in his neck and the changing of the picture in front of his eyes. He was still drunk.

How could he have let this happen? And how was he going to make it through the whole day without getting found out and fired? And when could he call Rachel to make sure he hadn't done something stupid?

CHAPTER EIGHTY-EIGHT

Rachel woke late the next day after a long, deep sleep. Sunlight was rushing through the window, tumbling the sparks of dust in the air, lighting up the white bedsheets and chiming from the old kettle on her desk. She got up, shielding her eyes, switched on her little bedroom kettle and began to make some tea. There was a shining white note propped in the toast rack that she kept on top of a pile of Tupperware on her desk. Oh. Jonathon.

The note, written in a careful but spidery hand, read:

Dear Rachel,

This is just a quick note to apologise for not leaving you a proper note. Thank you. Sorry.

Ł,

Jonathon

An hour later, she got off the bus and walked four streets, hurrying but not wanting to arrive. What would he say? Should she have called first? Well, it needed to be sorted out. Sometimes it's best not to use the phone.

There she was. She stood for a few seconds in front of the immaculate white uPVC door, between the two neat pot plants that stood on either side of it, feeling scruffy and out of place in yesterday's clothes. Her finger pressed down on the textured plastic buzzer, and somewhere inside the house a shrill Big Ben sounded: *bing-bong bing-bong, bing-bong bing-bong. BONG!*

The door opened and there was her aunt Lisa, face red and swollen, holding a tired and bewildered-looking Gemma.

'Oh, Rachel love! Oh thank God you're here! Come on in.'

'What's the matter?'

'It's your uncle, love. Hasn't come back. What am I going to do?'

'Where did he go?'

'Come on in. Give us a hug. Cup of tea?'

CHAPTER EIGHTY-NINE

'Are you, like, staring at my *ear*?' asked the customer.

'Am I?' asked Jonathon. He was finding it very hard to do everything right: address the correct part of a customer's head, say 'sir' or 'madam' appropriately, not fall over or vomit. How had he ever been able to cope with all this? He must be some kind of genius usually.

'Yes you are. You're doing it again. What *is* it with you?'

This floored Jonathon. He'd never been asked what it was with him before.

'What's what with me?'

'What are you looking at now?'

'What?'

'You're staring at, like, my chin or something.'

'I don't know what it is.'

'And what is it with these pants? Are they, like, made for giants or something?'

'What?'

'These pants are totally huge. Are they like made for, like, giants or ogres or something?'

'What? No. For fat people, I think.'

'Hey, could I get some help over here?' the customer called over to Mr Reiss, Jonathon's manager, who was passing by.

'Sir?'

'Could I get served by someone who isn't like *totally* retarded? If you've got like just a partial retard, I'll see that guy.'

Mr Reiss sent him home after that: 'Go home, Mr Fairfax.' The manager's stiff upper lip made it impossible to tell whether this was an act of sympathy or punishment. Jonathon wasn't even quite sure that he still had a job.

He stayed awake on the journey home by jiggling his leg up and down and jabbing himself with his keys. An instinct told him that it was very important for him not to fall asleep, even if it meant everyone looking at him in a worried way.

Surfacing from the Tube took a long time, and the walk home took even longer. He kept finding himself going the wrong way, and several times he had to sit down until his vision cleared and he stopped feeling like he was going to vomit shit out of his eyes.

Finally, he almost fell through the front door of 60 Brickfield Terrace. There, in the hallway was the telephone. He checked his pockets and found he had change.

First, he would call Rachel and see if he had done something stupid. He was sure he hadn't had sex with her, because that was impossible. That must just have been the drink talking, or the huge bump on the back of his head. How had he got himself into such a state? Maybe he had tried to get drunk by smashing alcohol into the back of his brain. He gingerly put his hand to the swelling and was surprised to find lodged there – in addition to a massive quantity of pain – a very small quantity of tree bark. Another mystery. He suddenly remembered very clearly that he had left a note for Rachel. He had left it on a toast rack. The other thing he remembered was Rachel saying, 'Of course I want to be friends.' Oh God, and hadn't her uncle threatened to kill him? Or had he just watched that on TV, perhaps after listening to the man on Blind Date who was too stupid to say what sort of takeaway he would be. Jonathon would be a Chinese. He was ricey.

This was not getting any telephoning done. One of the very few things he was sure of was the fact that he had to phone Rachel. He took out the piece of paper he carried around with her number on it, and dialled. It rang for a very long time. They had cried and had sex. He remembered. That definitely hadn't been on TV after Blind Date. Sex on TV never involves jumpers or cocoa. He had left her a massively stupid note.

'Of course I want to be friends,' she had said.

He let it ring for even longer. Then he went and sat on the stairs for a bit. Why was it so important to call Rachel? The note. He had to explain the note. He had to tell her something. He would remember what when she picked up the phone.

Back on his feet, he reeled over to the phone, overshot, and had to turn around and find it again. He picked up the receiver and held it to his ear. What was next? Numbers. He needed to push the buttons with the same numbers on them as the numbers written down on his piece of paper. He did it and there was a faint ringing noise coming from the part of the telephone in his hand, next to his ear. The phone rang and rang. Why wouldn't she answer?

'Of course I want to be friends,' she had said.

That's what she had said. Perhaps there was a footnote: 'Unless we end up somehow crying and having sex tonight and then you skulk out at midnight while I'm asleep, leaving the world's stupidest and least articulate note on my toast rack.'

Thinking about it more, it seemed to him that most statements people make are subject to that condition: 'the job is yours', 'your car will be ready for collection on Tuesday', 'I intend to be a reforming Pope'.

He sat down again, to wait a few minutes. The world went a bit black and far away.

CHAPTER NINETY

'Right. Where is he?' said the murderer into the black receiver that smelled of lamb fat and bore traces of sauce on it.

'Him and me both, darling,' he said. 'Him and me both.'

He tried to look over his shoulder, but found his neck was hurting unbelievably.

'I think he'll want to talk to me when you tell him my name.'

He told her his name.

'Tell him he's got ten minutes to bell me back. I'm on a phone box here and I ain't hanging about.'

'Good girl.' He told her the number and replaced the receiver.

The murderer was powerfully uncomfortable in the phone box, but he didn't want to have the bother of getting out and then having to fit himself in again when it started ringing. He hoped it would start ringing. There was no way he was waiting longer than twenty minutes though. Call it half an hour. Longer than that and the police would be on their way, even out here in Acton, where he had eventually found himself.

He waited. Some kids cycled past and laughed at him, squashed into the stupid red box. A man in a tracksuit carrying a can of cider came and waited outside the box until the murderer looked at him and pointed in the direction of away from the phone box. A black cat came and sat outside, looking impatiently about as though it were waiting for its dealer. Someone pushed a shopping trolley past with a baby and a large television in it.

What was he going to do now? Could he risk going home? Just a matter of time till the police turned up there. What was he going to do?

The phone rang and he picked it up, cracking one of the panes of glass with his elbow.

'Hello.'

'That's right.'

'I had to, didn't I?'

'Just wanted to say, I've thought it over and I might just be willing to do that job you mentioned.'

'Good. Few details to sort out.'

'The money's fine. Might be good for both of us if I disappeared afterwards…'

MONDAY

Jonathon woke. He opened his eyes. The ceiling was light around the edges. What time was it? He slid his eyes sideways until the glowing red numbers on his clock face became visible: 12.07. How come it was light? Ah. It must be the middle of the day, not the middle of the night. Luckily it was Saturday, so it didn't matter too much. He closed his eyes again.

His eyes opened. Didn't he have to work on Saturday? No, he would have set his alarm. He closed his eyes again.

His eyes flicked open again. Hadn't he already done Saturday? What was going on? He raised himself on his elbow and every single part of his mind and body bellowed with pain. Gently, gently, he lowered his head onto his pillow. It had never struck him before how unbelievably sharp and vicious his pillow was. How had he managed to sleep all night on the thing?

Very, very slowly, through a process of trial and intensely painful error, he found the only position that did not make him feel as though he was being beaten by an enormously heavy cheese-grater. This was on his elbows and knees, with his forehead resting on the pillow. It was excruciatingly uncomfortable, but by far the best he could do. After a few minutes in this position, he realised that his tie was tickling his nose. Why was he wearing a tie in bed?

A further examination revealed that one of the reasons that his feet were so clumsy was that they were still inside shoes. In fact, he was fully dressed.

Could I get served by someone who isn't like totally *retarded?*
Who had said that?
Go home, Mr Fairfax.
What? Oh, that was Mr Reiss's voice.
Fairfacs you die keep away.
Oh God.
Of course I want to be friends.
That got him out of bed and over to the door, where he was brought to his knees by the horrific agony in his head. If felt as though it was being dynamited in preparation for use as an open-cast vomit mine. And to make matters worse his knees also hurt. It was in this position that he remembered trying to phone Rachel the previous day:

Saturday. So today must be Sunday. That was odd. He had met Rachel in Pun In The Oven on Saturday after having an unprecedentedly fun morning at work. But then he had also been in work and been told to go home. He had had two Saturdays on top of one another. Perhaps this was how you feel when time malfunctions.

He pulled himself to his feet and crept out of his room and down the stairs. There was no one around and the bathroom was empty. Where was everyone? Why would everyone in the entire house, including Avi, go out at midday on a Sunday? Perhaps there had been a nuclear attack and he was the only one who had survived. That would explain almost everything, except for the two Saturdays. Maybe one of them was a hallucination brought about by incipient radiation sickness.

On the mat was the free newspaper which was usually delivered on Mondays. He went and looked at the pad by the telephone, to see if he'd been left a message. There was nothing. Why was he looking for one?

Rachel.

Oh no. He remembered the uncle, the threat, the park, her being upset, him going to see her, Blind Date, taking off her jumper, the note. And then he had tried to phone her, he remembered that. Maybe it was Monday. He was meant to be in work on Monday. But he found that he didn't care.

He went to the kitchen to make himself some coffee, hoping that it would wake him up and make him understand everything. *She almost certainly never wants to see me again*, he reflected as he waited for the kettle to boil. There was a great deal he didn't know about women, but he imagined that they probably didn't like being told that their relatives are murderers, being cried on, being taken advantage of, and being left uncommunicative notes in their toast racks before midnight.

She was gone, he was sure of it. It seemed to him that the only appropriate way to express how lost and pointless he felt would be to lie face-down in some mud and just stay there until he died, until the flesh fell from him, leaving only his useless bones. That was how he felt, though he could see it was an impractical thing to do.

At that moment the phone rang in the hallway. He knew instantly that it was her. He knocked a cup over, toppled the coffee jar, fumbled with the door and rushed over to the urgently peeping payphone. He picked up the receiver and Rachel was on the other end. He could tell it was her before she had even begun to speak. His heart leapt pounding to his throat, his head instantly cleared of its melancholic fog and his eyes grew moist.

She asked him whether he ran a Salsa class on Thursdays, using a man's voice.

'Um. Hum,' he said, caught out by this unexpected ploy.

She repeated her question in a slightly more irritated voice.

It wasn't her, he suddenly realised. It wasn't even anyone who knew her. It was someone from the world of cold weather, damp socks, tripping up, choosing lino, filling in forms at the post office. His vision dissolved into tiny fragments, leaving him boggling awkwardly in the limitless void.

The voice angrily asked if there was anyone there and whether this really was Pineapple Dance Studios.

'No. No. No. There isn't. It. Not. No.' Jonathon replaced the phone on its hook and lay face down on the floor.

After a while it occurred to him that not only did his face hurt too much for him to carry on doing this for much longer, but that he was overlooking something. He stood up and tried to remember what that something was.

Oh yes. Rachel's uncle was almost certainly a murderer.

He had told her that. She had said she was going to talk to him. Then yesterday – or whenever it was that he had last been able to do anything – there had been no answer when Jonathon had phoned her.

Perhaps she was dead.

He had to go and see her. Even if she never wanted to see him again, he had to know that she was all right. He patted his pocket, said 'ow' because his thigh also hurt, and left the house.

CHAPTER NINETY-TWO

'Oh my days!'

Lisa dropped the cup she was washing and wrenched open the kitchen door.

'Oh my days!' she said again, more quietly.

The murderer looked terrible. He had dark bags under his eyes, as though he had let a kid colour them in with charcoal. He was still wearing Saturday's clothes, but one of the seams of his bomber jacket had burst, showing the white woolly lining, already dirty at one edge. Something had been spilled down his Tottenham top, which was sweat-stained and rumpled. His white trainers were filthy. He had a bloody rag tied around one hand.

'All right, love?' he said tiredly.

There was something in his eyes that told her not to do what she wanted most – to rush into his arms. She opened the door wider and put out a hesitant hand to welcome him in.

He stepped inside and looked at the bucket of frothy water in which she'd been washing the cup.

'They've started on the kitchen then,' he said. 'Didn't take long.'

She said nothing. The room was stripped. The units and surfaces were all gone, along with the sink. The washing machine had been moved out. Only the fridge remained, standing beside a stack of flat-pack boxes high enough to use as a table. Two cups of tea stood on it.

'How much is this costing us?' he asked.

'Five grand?' she said.

'Eight, including the floor and ceiling. Remember them recessed bulbs. Don't come cheap.'

She said nothing.

'Eight fucking grand, which we do not happen to have no more.'

She could see that he was ready to blow.

'Why not?' she asked quietly.

'Why not! Why not! WHY FUCKING NOT!'

He had moved closer to her. His face was red and spit came off his lips as he shouted.

'I'll tell you why not! I was going to keep it quiet! But I'm not in that kind of mood no more!'

'Do you want a cup of tea?'

He picked up one of the cups from the flat-pack pile and threw it at the floor, where it exploded.

'Mmm. Lovely cup of tea, love. Can I have another?'

He picked up the other cup, and threw it with such force that it seemed to dissolve into powder when it made contact with the wall.

'Oh no. What have I done, love?' she asked. 'What have I done?'

'You can't bloody read. That's what you've done. Bob says to me Wednesday, "Why did you kill that bird at 42 Acacia? I only said to bloody scare her." So, why did I fucking kill her?'

Lisa said, 'I don't know.'

'You don't know! You don't know! You bloody should know. Hm, let me see, was it because I was *just in a bit of a funny mood* that day? Or was it because that was what your fancy fucking printout told me to do?'

'But I thought that's what Bob's fax said. You know what his writing's like. I thought it said to go round and slay her.'

'And you decided not to give him a fucking ring and check. Too much bloody effort. No, better go off and get your nails done instead – spend my bloody money.'

Lisa said nothing. She was trying not to move or breathe, not to do anything that would stoke his anger.

He looked wildly around the kitchen, breathing heavily, looking for something to smash. There was nothing. He kicked over the washing-up bucket, soaking one trainer and roared, 'FUCK!'

Her breath squeaked. He whirled around, hand up, clenched. 'You STUPID–'

She gasped and put up a hand to protect her face.

He stopped, as though suddenly seeing himself. All the energy seemed to drain out of him in an instant. That was it for Lisa. Though she was trying not to, she began to cry.

'I'm sorry,' she said, sinking to the floor.

He was beside her, his arm around her.

'I'm sorry, love,' he said. 'I'm sorry, I didn't mean that. I didn't mean none of that. I'm sorry.'

His comforting made her cry more loudly.

'I know I shouldn't have lost my rag like that. I'm sorry. I was just upset, that's all. The business was going sweet, that's all. It's only money, love. I know that. I'm sorry.'

They crouched on the kitchen floor for a long time, holding each other.

'I'm sorry, Colin,' Lisa managed at last.

'That's all right, love. "Scare" don't look nothing like "slay" though. You're blind you are.' He kissed her. 'And a nutter,' he added.

She giggled through her tears and he kissed her again.

'What happened?' she asked him.

'Well, what with the phone being on its back I never heard there was a problem till Bob tells me on Wednesday. I weren't going to tell you. Then I been running around all the arse end of last week at Bob's beak and caw, doing jobs for him.'

'What jobs?'

'Just little things. Then on Saturday he needed someone scaring, some old bird who'd stolen some documents – course you know, you took the address. I did my bit of scaring and then I had to go to the Ritz, keep an eye on things. When the old bird sees me she goes to pieces–'

'Good bit of scaring you done…'

'Exactly. But then this kid turns up, grabs the bag and suddenly everyone's rushing about like blue-arsed flies, giving each other rugby tackles and that. I cracked the kid over the head with a palm tree but then the old bill turns up, about fifty thousand of them–'

'How many?'

'Well, a few. They don't like trouble at the Ritz.'

'I bet they don't. Why did Bob choose the Ritz?'

'Says it puts people on edge. They don't like to try nothing.'

'Shows you what Bob knows, at the end of the day.'

'So I had to scarper. Been on the run since.'

'Where'd you go?'

'Went to see a friend of mine. Listen.'

'What?'

'I've got a big job to do for an extremely rich man – the posh bloke you took the message from. If I do it right, we'll be able to get away from here, go somewhere nice.'

'I don't know if I want to go away, love. I'd miss Cath and Rach, and mum.'

'I'm bloody certain I don't want to go away. But if I don't go away I'll be sent away – to the farm. Is that what you want? Visiting half hour a week?'

'You know I don't.'

'Right, well. Sit tight and don't tell nobody you saw me. I'll be back Tuesday.'

Jonathon had never before needed to use so many different emotions in such a short period of time. As he walked away from Rachel's house, his body was flooded with relief.

Rachel wasn't dead.

She wasn't in her house either, but at least she wasn't dead. He had discovered this from a girl in a towel who also lived in the house. Rachel had been back last night, and left again this morning. Apparently, her aunt was upset because her uncle had disappeared.

Since Saturday, Jonathon had done excitement, elation, trepidation, confusion, fear, emotional collapse, love, worry, determination, heroism, despair, concern and now relief. Usually it was a stretch to do, say, irritation and mild satisfaction in the same week.

He suddenly realised that the only realistic response to this emotional rollercoaster ride was to go to the Brown Cafe. After being sickened by terror and joy on the rollercoaster, the Brown Cafe's grim coconut shy was just what he needed.

Once he had arrived and safely ensconced himself beside the khaki plants and the hazel brickwork, Jonathon felt a tiny bit better. All the familiar sights were there: the small piles of skin scooped from the top of innumerable cups of brown coffee, the waitress straightforwardly ignoring him, the old couple sitting silently watching their fascinating table, and the man in the tan suit reading a paper as he stroked his flap of hair. The hair was the one thing that had changed. It had put on an astonishing spurt of growth and now stretched almost two-thirds of the way over his head. His comb-over now worked not only when seen from the right but also from very slightly above.

Jonathon's covert gaze slipped from the man's hair to his newspaper. On the front page was a picture of Jane. Jonathon was so surprised that he walked over and asked to have a look.

'Yes yes. Of course my friend,' said the man, handing him the paper.

There she was, on the front page of the *Sun*, brandishing an enormous pair of latex testicles. There was a column beside her picture, headed 'Glamour Grannie Grabs Government's Gonads'. Above her ran the main headline: SCAPEGATE.

'The Prime Minister RESIGNED last night after admitting to running a SECRET company...' began the article. Jonathon was too excited to read. He turned to the next page. There, opposite a picture of Debbie, 19, was Lance Ferman, 28. And above his picture was the heading, 'Banged Up – For A Crime He DIDN'T Commit'.

'What … what…?' said Jonathon.

'All the politicians they are scapegoats,' said the man.

'I know her,' said Jonathon, pointing to the picture of Jane. 'That's my friend.'

'She tell everyone about GL.'

'GL?'

'Secret company.'

Jonathon sat down and the man politely cleared out of his way a brown hat that was sitting on a plate.

'This is amazing,' said Jonathon, who had got his eyes in some sort of order and was managing to make them read.

'Rene Girard … the Book of Leviticus … Augustus Zazel. Ah! A Zazel, *azazel* – it's Hebrew for scapegoat! I never quite got that.'

'What?'

Jonathon read on. 'Jesus H Shit! It's all here. It's out: every minister is a Registered Scapegoat, except for Tristan Mangiafuoco.' He looked up at the man. 'I've met him.'

The man nodded politely in a way that said, 'You definitely haven't, but I don't mind.'

'*All being controlled from behind the scenes like puppets on a string, this SCAPEGOAT FARM was run by a man who called himself Augustus Zazel,*' read Jonathon. 'And now the Prime Minister has admitted to being the real Augustus Zazel. They've all resigned! Bollocks H Chimney! Mangiafuoco's the acting prime minister! Has he really got nothing to do with the whole thing?'

'You would like a cup of tea?'

TUESDAY

Thompson flopped out onto the balcony again but somehow dropped the whisky bottle and had to decant himself back inside his office to retrieve it. It was nearly empty – yesterday's bottle – so not much had spilled onto the carpet. He picked it up and dragged it back onto the balcony. After drinking all night in his office he felt perfectly sober and his thoughts were clear, but he noticed that he was speaking all his thoughts in a slurred voice and that he kept falling over and dropping things.

'Look at London down there. Shtill going on – on and on and on and on – 's though nothing's happened. Well, you're wrong, London. Hey, you! You London over there! You're wrong! Everything's happened. Everything. Giniagate, fucking Scapegate – disgracegate, resignationgate, endofmymarriagegate, lovelyGargygate, nocareergate, criminalproceedingsgate, bottlegate, mumblegate, mumblegate, finishgate, fuckgate, gategate, happengate, whiskygate, goingtoshootmyselfgate.'

He looked down again at the tiny black beetling taxis that buzzed and tumbled along Whitehall, at the fuzz of tourist anoraks already crowding around the motionless cavalrymen outside Horse Guards, and at the fluorescent green coats of the policemen who guarded the guards. Up here it was peaceful, but soon he would lose this too. The office behind him was a mess of boxes and papers. He was supposed to be clearing his desk. But really he didn't want any of this. He didn't want anything at all. They'd be sorry when he was gone, he thought.

His Luger P08 was heavy in his pocket. It wasn't quite time yet. Perhaps he would jump. Or maybe there was something creative he could do with his tie – attach one end to the window latch and then lean off the balcony, using the tie as a noose. He took it off, looked at it, wondered why he was holding his tie in his hand, then let it flutter downwards in the breeze. It stuck on the sharp bronze of one of the Victorian Gothic embellishments below, and flapped like a flag. Oh yes, that was why he had been holding his tie. Still, no need to be creative when you have a Luger P08 in your pocket.

'Morning, Mr Thompson,' said a voice beside him.

A man had climbed out through the window and was standing next to him on the balcony. He looked as though two muscular men had been pressed together to form a single lump of gigantic strength.

'Go away,' said Thompson. 'Whoever you are.' He decided that he should have sworn at the man, but he had finished speaking now. 'Fucking,' he added, allowing the man to insert it in the sentence wherever he wanted.

He might have known they wouldn't leave him alone at a time like this. Bloody do-gooders. Well, it was a bit late to start caring now. He'd already resigned and lost everything.

'Not a very charitable attitude, old son,' said the man.

Thompson wondered how the man had got through the locked door to his office. Probably they had keys, the security people here.

'Bit rude even,' continued the man. 'Specially when I've been sent to look after you by a friend of yours.'

'Fuck off. I don't need looking fucking after.'

The man wasn't even wearing a uniform. No wonder the country was going to the dogs.

"Fraid you do, sunshine.'

'I can assure you that I don't. Fucking.'

'Well, no point arguing about it.'

The man moved from his sitting position and leaned over Thompson.

'I was sent here by Tristan Mangiafuoco. He wants you to know that.'

'Why should he help me now?'

'You're still not getting this, are you? Well, never mind.'

With that, the man grasped Thompson by the lapels of his jacket and lifted him to his feet.

'What?'

'Is that your last word? "What?"'

'You're not helping. Jacketgate. Musclegate. You're hurting me.'

'Quench my grief.'

Thompson looked into the man's face and totted up the signs of concern and pity in his expression. Zero. He counted again. Still zero. With such huge face muscles the man should be able to make very powerful expressions. It should be possible to read his emotions by candlelight from a dozen miles away.

The man took a firmer grip on Thompson's lapels and lifted him from his feet. Finally a messenger arrived from another, less drunk, part of Thompson's brain. *He's going to kill you!* said the messenger. *Ah*, thought Thompson, *bit rum. Wasn't I going to do that to myself?*

He's going to kill me.

Suddenly he found that he was absolutely and completely sober. A very, very large man was on the point of throwing him from a very, very small balcony. His sober, in-control personality returned like a stern father walking in on the tail-end of his son's first disastrous house party. *I go away for one night and this is what happens!* Well, first things first, let's get this mess cleared up.

He reached into his pocket, pulled out the Luger P08, pressed it to the man's sternum and squeezed the trigger. There was an ear-shattering crash.

It took Thompson a few moments to work out that the noise had been caused by the man forcing Thompson's hand through a window-pane, making him drop the gun.

'Well, I was not expecting that,' said the man. 'Luckily, neither was you, or you'd have taken the safety off. Gave me quite a turn.'

He hauled Thompson onto the balustrade of the tiny balcony. It barely touched the murderer's knees.

'Off you go now,' said the man, dropping him out into space.

Thompson grabbed for the nearest hand-hold. The thick gold chain felt cold and reassuringly solid. In fact, it was so solid that it yanked the murderer off the balcony, the balustrade flipping him neatly at the knees so that they fell together. Thompson closed his eyes.

When he opened them, the first thing he saw was his tie. The second thing he saw was a finely detailed bronze Victorian Gothic finial. Allowing his eyes to move upwards, the next object they lit upon was the body of his would-be murderer impaled on that same finely detailed bronze Victorian Gothic finial.

The gold chain was still firmly grasped in Thompson's hands. There was a huge and excruciating pain in his shoulders and arms. The pain was caused by the fact that he was dangling from the neck of a man impaled on the finial of a turret three-quarters of the way up the Palace of Whitehall. The soldiers sitting astride their horses in their sentry boxes at Horse Guards should be able to see him, if they looked up. But then, of course, they were not allowed to look up. And even if they saw him they were not allowed to move or speak. He wondered how long he could hold on.

His watch showed seven minutes past nine.

CHAPTER NINETY-FIVE

Being dead and unable to leave the scene of your murder is boring. Sarah had counted all the tiles in the kitchen seventeen times. She rationed herself to doing it twice a day: once at nine, once at six. It gave her something to look forward to, and it lent the day some structure. She only wished she had chosen smaller tiles.

The clock on the front of the cooker was also a good source of entertainment. Each number was made up of seven segments, which could be lit or unlit. She watched carefully for the exact moment when the digits changed, to see if she could catch that instant when the segments for both the old and the new number were lit up. At 8.59 that day she thought she had done it, but she wasn't sure whether she had just imagined it. Then again, if she could imagine that, surely she could imagine something more interesting.

Then there was the garden. It wasn't very big: a concrete box full of junk. There was an axle, the corpse of a sofa, eighteen empty wooden crates, nine stacked plastic flowerpots. She knew the inventory off by heart. At 7.53 a bird had visited. She enjoyed the moments when the bird was hopping around, but the excitement spoiled her, making it difficult to cope with the emptiness after it departed.

Yesterday an estate agent had come and measured the kitchen, whistling *Ode to Joy*, which she hadn't expected an estate agent to know. He had only been in the kitchen for five minutes, but it seemed to fill the morning. She hoped a family would move in, so that there would be plenty of activity.

But at 9.07 her worries and boredom very suddenly ceased. She finally left the kitchen.

CHAPTER NINETY-SIX

When Jonathon arrived that Tuesday morning, the Brown Cafe was almost unrecognisable. The windows had been cleaned, the door had been cleaned, even the sign saying 'Caffe Acropolis' sparkled in the sun. Inside the transformation was total. Or rather, the transformation wasn't total – the place hadn't, for example, become a steam-engine made of swans. But the nature of its partial transformation was almost more shocking: it was busy and it looked nice.

The two brown metal columns that held the ceiling up, or the floor down, had been draped in linen and garlanded with flowering vines. Fabric had been artfully strung across the ceiling, giving it an elevated, unworldly feel and hiding the nicotine stains. The walls had been cleaned, revealing that what had seemed merely to be a freak ridge of dirt encircling the room was actually a dado rail. The cash register had gone, as had the horrible tables, to be replaced by nice tables and a counter filled with glasses, silver buckets and bottles of champagne. The mahogany waitress had also gone, and in her place were three polite elderly men in white shirts, black waistcoats and well proportioned ties.

On the wall opposite the entrance hung a large photograph of Lance, and above it a banner saying 'WELCOME HOME'. Nearby, in the corner, was a table covered in cards. Jonathon wondered briefly about the feasibility of producing greetings cards for people celebrating milestones in their dealings with the criminal justice system. Perhaps this was what he was born to do. A verse spontaneously appeared in his head:

We didn't know
If you had stabbed
Someone in the ribs
We thought so
As you were nabbed
And banged up by the pigs
– Congratulations on having the murder charges dropped!

But before he could write it down and put together a business plan, he spotted Jane and pushed through the crowd to her side.

'Hello,' he said. 'Sorry I'm between seven and fourteen minutes late. It's the watch.'

'Hello ducky. Lovely to see you.'

She hugged him and he hugged back, surprised how pleased he was to see his fifty-eight-year-old friend.

'Don't worry about being late. Lance isn't here yet. Have you met Geoffrey?'

'Pleased to meet you, Jonathon,' said Geoffrey, holding out his hand. 'Jane has told me so much about you.' He turned to her. 'You said his hair stuck up at the back.'

'It isn't today,' said Jonathon. 'I don't know why. It does usually. I hope it stays this way.'

Geoffrey smiled and, after shaking hands, passed Jonathon a glass of champagne.

The three of them clinked glasses. 'Cheers!'

'I haven't thanked you yet, ducky,' said Jane, 'for your help on the telephone on Saturday night.'

'Did you call me on Saturday night?'

'Yes. Don't you remember?'

'No. The whole weekend's a bit of a blur. I had Saturday twice.'

'Well, to be quite honest it's all a haze to me as well – especially after that *terrifying* man appeared. All I know is that it was your advice that made me decide not to hand the documents over.'

'Oh.' He frowned.

'So,' she continued, 'Saturday night is a haze from the time I spoke to you until the time the police arrived. I looked down and saw the documents, quite by chance, lying at my feet. So I took them with me and spent all of Sunday talking to newspaper editors and being interviewed and making phone calls about Lance and … and all sorts of things.'

'Oh,' he said again, not knowing how else to vent his surprise.

'And forgive me, darling-heart, I forgot to apologise for breaking into your bedsit.'

Jonathon suddenly found that he knew no acceptable way to express surprise that a fifty-eight-year-old woman has broken into your bedsit.

'Fucking hell,' he said. 'Sorry. I mean, what?'

'Lance hid the original documents behind your wardrobe, as well as giving you a copy of them to look after.'

'But why?'

'Something to do with Doctor Platypus's Dinner Party: *the best hiding place is a friend's wardrobe.'*

'Do you mean Professor Albino's Circus Factory?'

'That's the one.'

'The best place to hide something is in the home of a man who thinks he is hiding something else.'

'Yes. That's it.'

'You, er, you didn't look under my bed, did you?'

But Jane was looking past him and out of the window. There was a shout from outside.

'Oy, Lance! Over here!'

Then another: 'Lance mate! Look this way! Great.'

These were joined by others. Outside, a small crowd of photographers had surrounded a black cab. They stepped back as Lance got out and the sound of flashing cameras could be heard. Lance walked three times from the cab to the front door of the cafe, so that they could all get their pictures. Then he said a few words to a journalist with a microphone and pushed his way into the Brown Cafe.

People held the door closed behind him so that the photographers wouldn't follow, but Lance was now being mobbed by the crowd inside the cafe. He was shaking hands, having his head ruffled, being patted on the cheek and clapped on the shoulder. And then he was there in front of Jane and Jonathon, taking delivery of a glass of champagne.

'Hello Glamour Grannie!' he said to Jane, hugging her.

'Please don't call me that,' she said, smiling through her attempt at sternness.

He took a swig of his champagne. He was wearing a pressed suit and crisp shirt and he looked smart, tired and excited.

'Sorry. I just can't forget that headline and the picture of you holding a big pair of latex testicles.'

Jane laughed. 'I had no idea what they were! Someone just handed them to me, so I politely held them.'

'Someone ought to give you your own TV show – *Don't Let the Balls Drop!* – where you have to catch foam genitals before they touch the ground!'

Jane patted him on the shoulder and smiled in an indulgent way that said, 'I love you, but I'd like you to shut up soon.' Lance grinned hugely, then turned and put his arm around Jonathon. He seemed giddy, like a child.

'Jonathon! My main man-amundo! How's it hanging?'

'Oh, is it hanging again? Sorry, I hadn't realised.'

'This guy!' said Lance to Jane, playfully punching Jonathon on the arm. 'Someone ought to give him his own TV show called *Where's My Jumper?*'

He grinned again and looked pointedly at Jonathon's non-work outfit, which, for perhaps the first time ever, did not include a jumper. Instead, he had on a jacket and a kind of hybrid rugby-shirt and jersey, which, while it defied precise classification, was definitely not a jumper.

'Lance, lambkin, why are you trying to invent TV programmes for everyone?' asked Jane.

'High spirits! Yahey! I'm so *happy* not to be in a very small room talking to policemen or making faces out of meat!' He laughed in a merry but slightly manic and worrying way. 'Also MTV want to talk to me about presenting a programme called *MTV Undercover*.'

'Would you?'

He looked serious for a moment, then grinned again. 'Yes! Definitely! But don't worry–' he smiled confidingly and lowered his voice '–if I do I'll get you your own TV programme too.'

'Actually, Geoffrey and I are going to set up a recruitment agency for people aged over 55.'

'That's great!' shouted Lance, looking around at everyone. 'Everything's great!'

'This,' said Jane, 'is probably as good a time as any for the speech.'

She climbed on top of an upended bucket and gave her glass a single resonant tap with her fork. The hubbub ceased at once and every head turned towards her.

'Thank you all for coming,' she said. 'As you all know, we're gathered here to celebrate Lance's release from custody without charge.'

There was a huge cheer. Jane tapped her glass again.

'I'm still not entirely sure how and why all this has happened. Perhaps, if we trace everything back, we'll find it all has a single cause. More likely, it's just a sequence of accidents. In any case, as far as I can tell, everyone is all right and justice has prevailed.'

There was a smaller cheer.

'One thing is certain. Whether rightly or wrongly, Lance took those documents. Democracy will owe him a debt of gratitude for many years to come, even if he chooses to become a musical television presenter.'

There was a larger cheer. Someone shouted, 'Em-Tee-Vee! Em-Tee-Vee!'

'I never would have expected Tristan Mangiafuoco to be the only untainted politician in the government, but there we are. It just goes to show how wrong you can be. Now, before we toast Lance and celebrate his release, I'd like to thank one other person whose contribution – though less obvious – has made all of this possible. A round of applause please for Geoffrey, my wonderful husband.'

Polite applause broke out. Lance shouted, 'Geoffrey!'

'And now, a toast. To Lance!'

'To Lance!' everyone shouted, and then applauded and whooped or – like Loud Phil – howled like a wolf.

Jane stepped down from the bucket and Lance took her place.

'This is a blast!' he told them. 'Thank you all for coming. Being locked up is almost worth it for the buzz you get afterwards! I feel like Nelson Mandela! Except I've only been locked up for three days! It took him thirty years! Loser! Everything is brilliant!'

There was a huge cheer.

'I can walk about! I can take taxis! I can drink champagne! It's the best thing! Thank you all and may you all be given your own TV shows!'

He seemed about to step down from the bucket, but didn't. Instead he reined in his giddiness and frowned.

'One more thing,' he said. 'I'd like to say thank you to Jane Archer-Hollis.'

Another huge cheer.

'And I'd also like to thank Jonathon Fairfax, who has done more than he will ever know. To Jonathon!'

The Brown Cafe filled with cheering, whoops and claps, and then everyone took a big swallow of champagne at exactly the same time. Jonathon grinned bashfully and backed off to a quiet corner to recover from the barrage of glass chinking, hair ruffling and cheek pinching that followed.

Lance was still standing on the bucket beneath the large photograph of himself and the 'WELCOME HOME' sign, unable to get down because of the press of people straining to shake his hand or touch the hem of his garment. Despite his slight headache and the chasm of hurt inside him, Jonathon felt pleased to have been thanked.

And then he felt a hand on his arm.

'Hello Jonathon. Sorry I'm between fourteen and twenty-one minutes late. It's my watch.'

There she was. Rachel. Standing next to him as though it weren't even remotely unlikely, her hair falling in her eyes. Smiling.

'What... It...' he began.

'Are you all right?' she asked.

'Yes. I mean, how? How come you're here?'

'Your friend Jane Archer-Hollis called and told me about it.'

'How did she know your number?'

'She said that she knows a lot of people all of a sudden.'

He started to say something, but she stopped him. This was lucky because he had no idea what he'd been about to say.

'Listen,' she said. 'This has been a funny time – university and … everything. And then my uncle disappearing–'

'He disappeared?'

'Yes. He must have come back though, I think, because my aunt's suddenly not upset anymore – but she won't tell me what's going on. I don't know what to think. I'm so confused, and then with you…'

'I know,' he said. 'It's all right. I know whatever happened was a mistake and you're with Sam and–'

'But that's it – I'm not with Sam.'

'Not? What happened?'

'Nothing. This whole thing has taught me I need to stop hiding behind lies. I just … I'm a bit scared of relationships, so I tell men that I'm a lesbian to put them off – or so I can see if they like me or I like them or something. I picked Sam because I just, you know, totally wanted to be like her, that's all. She's so confident.'

'Does it work?'

'What?'

'Um. Telling men you're a … a lesbian. Does it put them off?'

She smiled and looked down, then shook her head. 'I hope not. Does it?'

'Ah. Um. No,' he said. 'It's probably a bit counter-productive, if anything.'

They both smiled large stupid smiles at each other.

'Do you, um, want to go to the park on Saturday?' he asked.

She nodded. 'Will we watch TV after?'

Later, when the crowd had thinned out and Rachel had gone to use the phone, Lance and Jonathon found themselves sitting together at a table.

'Jonathon,' said Lance. He was still high, eyes shining and gestures large, but at least he was sitting down now.

'Yes?'

'Give me some advice about women.'

'Why ask me? I'm just a men's-ready-to-wear sales assistant at Harrods.'

'Why wouldn't I ask you? You're a men's-ready-to-wear sales assistant at Harrods who's brought down a government and–'

'No I didn't.'

'It was you who realised RSG was significant. You almost worked out the scapegoat bit – Girard Leviticus and *Azazel*. You're the only one who's read both files. And I've been told that if you hadn't caused an enormous fight at the Ritz then our enemies would have got the documents back and I would probably have gone to prison – for which, I need hardly tell you, I am far too good-looking.'

'I've got no idea what you're talking about with the Ritz thing, but releasing the documents hasn't really done any good. Mangiafuoco's the prime minister now. And he's definitely mixed up in the whole thing.'

'Haven't you heard? He's disappeared. I don't think we'll be hearing from him again.'

'Why not?'

'Just a hunch. Call it detective's intuition.'

'Jane says you're more a loss-adjustor than a detective.'

'Call it loss-adjustor's intuition then. Or, actually, call it being told by a former colleague of mine. Same one who told me about you and the Ritz fight. He said you vaulted an eighteenth-century writing desk.'

'I definitely didn't.'

'You know your problem? You're too modest. Just accept that you've brought down a government, will you?'

'I've done a bit. It was Jane mainly. And you. We all did it.'

'Fine, let's not quibble about who brought down the government. The main thing is that Rachel seems pretty keen on you, and she's the sort of woman I need – except that her hair's a bit *brown*. And she's a bit short. And … Well, anyway. She's perfect for you. The point is, I need a woman like that: a woman you see more than twice and whose name you remember. So, what's your secret?'

Jonathon shrugged and Lance punched him on the shoulder in a 'go on' sort of way.

'Well,' said Jonathon, 'first you need leaflets.' He took another sip of champagne, then picked up some paper napkins to stand in for leaflets. 'Take some leaflets from a launderette–' he somehow mimed a launderette '–to a brown cafe–' his gesture took in the transformed Brown Cafe '– then go home, cook a fish–' he put something dead in an imaginary pan '–and bang! a woman will appear whose random non-evolutionary predilection exactly matches you.'

'Is that the truth?'

'It worked for me.'

CHAPTER NINETY-SEVEN

'Have you ever had one of those mornings?' Plover asked over this shoulder as he clanked down into third gear and revved hard to get around the sharp uphill bend.

The late-afternoon sun was shining over towards the west through a rip in the grey sky. The mountains rucked and bundled in the middle distance, clouds perching on top of them like balloons that might at any moment bounce down and smother the villages that had formed in the valleys. There was no reply from the back of the van, but Plover continued anyway.

'You know, one of those mornings where you're charged with assault for wrestling with a lady in the Ritz, get released on bail, realise that your dream of going straight is never going to happen while a certain person is acting prime minister, rent a light multi-purpose van, kidnap the acting prime minister, and head off to north Wales to wreak vengeance upon him?'

'Mmmm-mmmmm,' said a voice from the back of the van.

'Well I've had one of those mornings today, I can tell you. I can't wait to get to Llandudno and have a cup of tea.'

'Mmmp.'

'I'd keep that to yourself if I was you. People being transported in rolls of carpet in the back of light multi-purpose vans should watch what they say.'

'Mm mmmm mmm.'

'Isn't it though? And not raining either. It might even be sunny when we get there.'

THE END